RISE OF THE TAISHAKU

W. LEE RADCLIFFE

ISBN-13: 9781983491238
ISBN-10: 1983491233

To my wife, Alison,

for her support and patience

PRELUDE

Ayako beamed with excitement as she watched her father prepare the squidding gear for the evening. She sat at the edge of the deck of the large boat, comfortable with the gentle rocking from the undulating waves of the sea as her father checked the jigs on the last of his many squidding lines. From her first memories she longed to go with her father to catch squid each night in the Sea of Japan, and this evening, on his last trip of the season, he finally invited her to join him.

They had arrived less than an hour ago at her father's usual night squidding spot a few kilometers at sea. Ayako looked back to the dimly lit shore, and she saw the same spot where every night she would wave to her father as he left the pier in their small village. She would watch as he took his position among the long gauntlet of other family squidding boats in the area, and then turn on his boat's bright lights to attract squid to his specially configured lines.

Tonight, she was at last allowed to join her father to help out where she could. Ayako did not know that her father had to delay their departure to ensure she was safe by helping her put on a life jacket, instructing her where she could and could not stand, and double-checking that the hooked jigs were safely stored out of reach of her inquisitive and delicate six-year-old hands. They thus arrived later than usual to his normal squidding area. While others around them had turned on their lights and set to their evening routines, his position remained dark as he made his final preparations for tonight's squidding. The delay would prove deadly.

Large metal halide lamps hung along wires across the deck of each boat. The bright lights from the lamps attracted the staple product of many Japanese households and sushi restaurants in the region, the Japanese flying squid, from deeper depths at night to multiple squidding lines hanging from the boats. Special six- and ten-centimeter jigs or lures with non-barbed hooks on one end were attached every 100 centimeters on the lines. The special lures would bob slowly in the current and as the fishermen gently tugged on the lines to make them appear vibrant and alive. Squid, first attracted by the lights from the water's surface and then by the movement of the jigs, became easy prey to the small hooks on the jigs. Because the hooks did not have barbs, fishermen could easily pull the squid off the hooks as they reeled in the lines. While not as efficient as dragging nets at lower depths, this more traditional method caught squid and nothing else. The technique was therefore the preferred method of small-village fishermen like Ayako's father, Michiharu Toda, as well as the Japanese Government, to prevent indiscriminate oversquidding.

It was early fall and squid season was almost over in this part of the Sea of Japan. This was likely the last week any of the fishermen would catch enough squid of the right size to be economically viable. Some fishermen would then head to Japan's northern island, Hokkaido, and then to the Pacific Ocean to continue squidding and fishing late in the year. But Ayako's father Michiharu planned to remain in the village to prepare his small rice paddy for the winter months.

The fishermen were arrayed in a long line at sea, floating parallel to the northern coast of Noto peninsula. On a map, the peninsula resembled a thumb jutting out into the Sea of Japan midway along the main Japanese island of Honshu. The peninsula was almost due east of the Korean Peninsula, and many fishermen and other locals complained that Korea was so close that trash Korean fishermen threw out at sea often washed up along this part of the Japanese coastline. Perhaps assuming their own trash would drift back to the Korean coast, but more likely out of sheer laziness, some of these same Japanese fishermen too could be seen throwing trash out of their own boats while fishing for squid.

Six-year-old Ayako had yearned to accompany her father ever since she could remember, and she had constantly badgered her parents to let her go. "Please, pa, please let me go!" she would plead, pulling at his pant leg as he prepared to leave the house. Her father would tell her only to "ask your mother" when Ayako asked him if she could go, implying that the decision was out of his hands. In reality, Michiharu could not say no to the child, and he knew that if she badgered him enough he would give in long before she was old enough to be at sea safely at night. Her mother would always say no, and the small, gravel parking lot at the pier was as far as she could go with him. But tonight, knowing that the squidding season was almost over in the area, he nodded briefly to her mother when Ayako again begged to go, a subtle sign that on this last squidding expedition he would let her go with him. He admired Ayako's unyielding desire to experience life at sea, a life that was both his passion and vocation, however modest, and finally he could no longer resist her pleading.

Ayako clapped her hands excitedly and jumped up and down when he agreed to take her. "Yea yea yea!" she squealed as she rushed to get her rubber galoshes.

On the boat that night Ayako watched her father finish his nightly routine, the usual cigarette dangling from his bottom lip. He checked the spools of line and jigs to ensure they were not tangled and checked the generator to make sure it was fueled and oiled. Ayako had already finished putting out the buckets for the evening's catch near each spool of squidding line. When the squidding line was to be reeled in, she would be there to help her father unhook the squid and throw them in the containers. Her duties complete, now all she could do is wait for her father to turn on the lights and drop the jigs into the water. She turned her gaze to the sea on either side and noticed the other fishing boats had already turned on their lamps. The accompanying hum of their onboard generators was audible in the distance. The lights were much brighter from her vantage point out at sea than from shore, she thought. And they were louder. She looked back to shore and saw the small, twinkling lights of her fishing village, and she smiled again excitedly.

In the darkness beyond their boat, toward the open sea, the low and barely audible sound of an outboard engine startled her. Ayako sensed it was an engine of some kind but could not be sure; she could not see anything in the darkness. At first she thought she was imagining the noise over the undulating waves and loud sounds of generators around them, but then she felt bigger waves hit the boat, which began to rock up and down. She almost lost her balance from the sudden rocking. *Wouldn't all the boats have their lights on now?* she wondered, not considering that her father had yet to turn on his lights. It couldn't be the Japan Coast Guard, she thought. Even at her young age she knew that they wouldn't interrupt fishermen like her father at a time like this and scare all the squid away. Besides, what boat would be out at sea without any lights on?

The sound grew louder, and Michiharu too had felt the waves and turned to look. He had been aware of the noise in the distance for a few minutes, but he avoided looking more closely to keep from alarming Ayako. He had hoped that whoever the *baka* idiot boaters were would move along before scaring the squid away for the night or colliding with any of the fishing vessels in this area. He knew based on the waves hitting the side of the boat that the mysterious vessel came in fast and then slowed suddenly. It was awfully quiet though, which was strange. He took a long draw from his cigarette as he sat on the deck to peer into the dark open sea. The other fishermen in the area were seemingly unaware of the vessel's approach, engrossed as they were in their own work and numbed from the sounds of the sea by the deep rumblings of their onboard diesel generators.

Kids from the local village sometimes went on joyrides at night with the lights off this time of year, often to drink with friends. It was a very dangerous practice, since someone could fall in the water and drown, or they could collide with a buoy. He cared less about stupid drunk kids hurting themselves than about stupid drunk kids scaring away the squid, especially now during his last catch of the season.

But he did not hear the loud and drunken voices that usually accompany those teenage nighttime boating trips. He then noticed that the larger waves had died down almost as quickly as they began. He could tell that instead of passing by, the larger boat had stopped in the near distance.

The mysterious boat seemed to power down its engine and linger in the darkness. "Ayako," said her father in a brusque voice, "put these broken jigs in their boxes below deck…" He gave her an assortment of jigs and lures while gesturing to the small hatch and ladder immediately behind him. Ayako had helped him with his various jigs at home and knew how particular he was in sorting and storing them. Michiharu knew she would take special care in putting them away properly, which would take some time. Or so he hoped.

"Ok *otosan*," Ayako replied, her attention switching to the important job her father had just entrusted in her, as her father had intended. She rushed below to perform her duties, excited to help. Michiharu watched her stumble down the hatch and then heard a muffled bang. "I'm alright!" she shouted from below, having bumped into something or other. He then heard the clank of the metal chest opening, and then the usual clangs and clomps his daughter made when helping with the jigs at home. Satisfied that she was occupied for the moment, he turned to the darkness beyond and took another long drag from his cigarette. "What the hell is out there?" he whispered, audible to no one but himself. The sea breeze blew into his face, carrying the exhaled smoke from his nostrils along the stubble on his cheeks and then back toward the shore.

Michiharu was so preoccupied with the large vessel and the hypnotic sound of the gentle waves washing up alongside the boat that he had not noticed the muffled sound of the dual outboard engines on another boat approaching from the open sea to the northwest. Despite the presence of the myriad spotlights in a long row of fishing boats at sea, it had slipped past unnoticed and navigated parallel to the formation just out of eyesight. The boat's two occupants remained silent, intent on reaching the pre-designated rendezvous point on time. Their boat's location this close to other fishing vessels meant that radar from the Japan Coast Guard would not pick it out as it would in open water. Or so the occupants hoped.

Ikeda Hatano and his younger brother Taro had been slowly approaching the rendezvous point, piloting their souped-up five-meter speedboat almost on idle to avoid making too much noise or creating too many waves. So intent were they on reaching the designated spot, they failed to notice the glowing embers of Michiharu's cigarette in the near distance. Taro sat in the open space forward of Ikeda, who piloted the boat. Taro looked at his hand-held GPS and whispered, "hey, *nii-san*, big brother, we're here." They killed the engine and each leaned a little forward in different directions, looking intently for their target. Older brother Ikeda knew they were at the rendezvous point since he had conducted this same mission many times in the past two years. Ikeda brought Taro along tonight because he needed an extra hand to load tonight's bigger shipment, and because he thought it was about time to introduce him to the family business. Ikeda grunted in a low guttural tone to acknowledge Taro, and continued to watch for the other boat.

Ikeda's heart pounded hard in his chest from a combination of piloting his boat slowly among the other fishing boats for over an hour and from the adrenaline of this evening's clandestine meeting. The few puffs of crystal meth he smoked a few hours earlier added a sense of euphoria he continued to experience at the moment.

"Hey, *nii-san,* I think I see them, over there," the younger brother whispered toward Ikeda almost breathlessly, pointing at the 2 o'clock position ahead of them. Taro's voice broke from time to time from a combination of trepidation and excitement, and his energetic motion this time shook the boat slightly.

"Careful!" his older brother half-whispered, half-yelled.

Ikeda looked at his GPS receiver and saw that they had arrived on time at the exact coordinates. He looked up and noticed the whitecap of a wave lap up against the bow of another, larger boat just a few meters in front of them. The smaller boat drifted into the larger one.

A rope immediately landed at Taro's feet, and he looked at it and then back at Ikeda.

"Don't just stand there like a dumb fool," Ikeda whispered forcefully, "secure the rope and let's get to work!" Ikeda quickly moved around the helm of the boat and looked up at the deck, waiting.

The two heard the shuffling of feet and muffled voices, but they could not see anything but the side of the vessel. This crew and Ikeda had long ago done away with call signs and secret passwords, so routine had this exercise become. Two individuals took down a section of railing and immediately lifted a large cooler over the side to the boys below. "Here, take this!" one of the men said abruptly. Taro wondered at the man's voice. He spoke in heavily accented Japanese that was further muffled by the cigarette in his mouth as he worked. He then began to wonder what was in the blue cooler he and Ikeda placed on the deck of their own boat, when Ikeda barked at him again. "Snap to it Taro! We have a lot of these to load and then we gotta get outa here." He smacked Taro across his head for good measure and then reached for the next cooler.

Taro hurriedly reached for the other handle, and he saw the red embers drop down on him from a cigarette hanging from the otherwise faceless man above him. This cooler was heavier, and Taro grunted slightly at the added weight.

"Hey, what's that noise?" shouted one of the foreigners on the boat in a low voice, breaking the hurried, hushed tones of the group. He lifted an Uzi 9-mm into the air in the direction of noise, as if to point it out to the others. Younger brother Taro, not knowing what was happening, stood up straight and looked over the deck in the direction the man pointed toward the other side of the fishing vessel. Just as he could make out a large object approaching from above, Taro was suddenly blinded by the glare of a powerful spotlight shinning down at them from the other side of the larger boat. Disoriented, he stumbled backwards and fell into the cold sea, screaming "agghhh!" as he hit the water. Although he could swim, he flailed in the water in a panic, now half-blind. "Brother, help me help me! Throw me an oar! Throw me something!" he yelled as he thrashed in the water.

Older brother Ikeda did not respond. He ducked down into his smaller boat that remained hidden in the shadow cast by the spotlight on the larger fishing vessel. He heard scrambling on the deck above and hurried words in a language he could not understand, and then the larger fishing vessel's engines roared to life. Ikeda Hatano knew these foreigners were about to run, and Ikeda had only a small window of opportunity to escape before he lost his concealment. Ikeda untied the rope between the two boats, jumped over the cargo to the wheel and gunned the outboard engines to life, oblivious to his younger brother still flailing in the water.

As the spotlight scanned the unidentified fishing vessel, a voice boomed from a loudspeaker behind it, in Japanese and then in Korean, "Stop and surrender! This is the Japan Coast Guard! Prepare to be boarded!"

Ikeda heard the firing of the Uzi from the deck immediately above him as an answer: *Take care of business and keep them away from me!* he thought as he piloted his smaller boat away from the larger one and began to pick up speed as he turned toward the coast.

The larger boat lurched forward suddenly as the crew began to attempt their get-away. "*Ike zouu!*" Ikeda heard the rough voice yell in the boat in Japanese—"let's get the fuck out of here!" Ikeda didn't look back. Even though he too was partially blinded by the spotlight, he figured he knew the way back to shore well enough. Blinking away the harsh, white glare that had burned into the retinas of his eyes and squinting into the distance, he glanced to either side at the fishing boats with their bright lamps strung across their decks, and he saw what he thought was a large open space between the two fishing boats closest to him on either side. He turned to head in that direction, oblivious of the shouts from the water behind him: "*Nii-san! Niiii-san! Matte yo!* Wait, brother, come back…!" Ikeda rubbed his eyes with one hand, first one eye then the other, while he steered with the other, aiming as best as he could toward the empty space between the lights. He urged his engines to their top speed by leaning forward into the side throttle control and into the darkness ahead.

He heard more gunfire behind him. If he had turned to look, he would have seen the captain of the mystery boat navigate suddenly in front of the encroaching Coast Guard cutter as he continued to fire, making the large Coast Guard vessel slow and start to turn to follow it, losing precious time. Another member of the crew on the camouflaged fishing vessel undraped an anti-aircraft gun secured to the deck, aimed it at the Coast Guard cutter, and started firing. A second spotlight from a hovering helicopter followed the larger suspect boat. Neither the spotlight from the large

Coast Guard cutter nor the helicopter followed Ikeda's smaller and more nimble boat as it sped toward shore. The mystery boat showed remarkable agility and speed for being a simple fishing vessel as it fled toward the open sea. Still the shots ricocheted over the passive dark water from one direction only: The cutter had yet to fire at the escaping vessel, but kept ordering it to halt.

Cowardly fools, thought older brother Ikeda, *those Coast Guard weenies should blast them out of the water and be done with it!* He smiled at the thought of being at the helm of the cutter, blowing away fishing boats right and left with impunity…*Maybe I could make a career of the Coast Guard myself some day, eh?* He chortled at the half-serious thought.

Just then he heard the whirl of blades overhead and noticed the water begin to swirl rapidly around him as a helicopter descended, and he heard: "Cut off your engine and surrender!" Still dark, he thought he was safe despite the proximity of the helicopter overhead—*they're just guessing where I am…*he thought hopefully, and continued his run to the coast. As if on cue, the helicopter turned its own spotlight on the speeding vessel and repeated its warnings: "Stop and surrender!"

Six-year-old Ayako by now heard the commotion beyond their boat from where she was below deck, and she hurried to complete her task. She knew how important it was for fishermen—and women—to take care of and stow their equipment properly, and not wanting to disappoint her father, she finished her duty before returning to the deck to see what was happening. She rushed up the ladder after what seemed an interminable time below, and just as she peeked over the edge of the boat in the direction of the commotion, she saw a spotlight suddenly focus onto what seemed like a speedboat. It was running very fast, she thought, sort of like those Kawasaki jet skis her older brother was saving to buy, but bigger. And it was coming very fast this way, she saw, and she stood to watch in a combination of wonder and fright. Michiharu, who had been on the deck peering into the distance, ran past her to get to the wheelhouse. He jumped to the controls and started the old boat's engines. He urged his fishing boat forward even as the propellers struggled to pick up revolutions below the waterline. He looked forward, then at the quickly approaching boat, and his cigarette fell out of his mouth. He couldn't avert his gaze, for he knew that nothing could change their fate now…

In his meth- and adrenaline-induced frenzy, older brother Ikeda concentrated on one thing only as he piloted his five-meter speedboat: *Get to shore and get outta here.* Partially blinded from looking at the first spotlight and now under a powerful spotlight from above, he did not see the large and unlit fishing boat directly in front of him. Just as he heard the first word from above, a now-pleading admonition, "Stop!!" he plowed bow-first into the fishing boat. The metal tip of his modified speeding boat pierced the main line connected to the full fuel tank ahead of it. The sparks caused by the metal scraping against metal caused the fuel to ignite. The ensuing explosion lifted the two vessels into the air, while the fireball almost hit the Coast Guard helicopter pursuing it directly overhead. The helicopter lifted quickly out of the way of the fireball, but debris blew into its undercarriage and narrowly missed its propellers above. A few shards of burning metal hit its tail, causing it to spin slightly as the pilot struggled to keep control of his bird. He looked down and to his horror, he saw flames engulfing the wrecked vessels. No one could have survived.

"Maru-One to Echigo," he said listlessly into his headset.

"Echigo here, go ahead Maru-One."

"Maru-One reporting accident. Looks like one of the bandits collided with a fishing vessel. Request permission to commence search and rescue immediately. Over."

"Roger, Maru-One. Will send units to your area. Keep us apprised. Over and out."

The pilot maneuvered for a closer look at the site of the accident. He didn't need his 12-plus years of experience as a Coast Guard pilot to tell him the obvious. There would be no survivors. He looked back to shore and saw his compatriots and the flashing lights of local police vehicles at a spot along the coast. They were searching for the gang members who were waiting to pick up the drugs on shore. *Hopefully something will come out of this drug bust,* he lamented grimly.

CHAPTER 1 – INSERTION

Two V-22 Ospreys flew at 220 knots through the crisp autumn air, their 38-foot prop-rotors whisking mere meters over the treetops below. The two tiltrotor aircraft were nearly invisible in this moonless, pre-dawn hour. They flew in black-out mode, their navigation and other lights switched off to avoid attracting attention from possible hostile forces below and to retain the element of surprise as they approached their objective.

Warrant Officer Hisao Taguchi piloted the lead V-22, callsign Razor One. Taguchi urged his V-22 methodically forward, up to but never beyond its limits, and tonight, during what was certainly the most high-profile mission of his career, was no exception. Taguchi was already a master aviator for the UH-60 Black Hawk and the CH-47 Chinook, and now he was a fully qualified pilot for Japan's newest V-22 Osprey. He was among the best pilots Japan's Air Self-Defense Force had to offer, and it was now his responsibility to deliver his men to the objective and back again with minimal casualties—and with all the hostages safe.

Warrant Officer Isamu Sato piloted Razor Two. Sato was also a master aviator who was every bit a match for Taguchi in piloting skills and tactics, and he graduated V-22 training at the top of their small class, the first for this new platform. The only reason Sato was not in the lead Osprey was because he was one year behind Taguchi in age and in service, so he was thus Taguchi's *kohai*, his junior. Sato only grudgingly yielded to the importance of the *sempai-kohai* relationship in Japanese society, and particularly in the Japanese military. While he followed mere meters behind Taguchi, he knew he had proven himself to be the better pilot and should by merits fly in the lead.

The Ospreys rose and fell along the undulating terrain below, flying along low-lying ravines and river beds. The Ospreys' rotors never strayed more than a few meters from the vegetation below. They had mapped out their route and developed their checklists to avoid power-lines, microwave towers, and other manmade structures that might pose a deadly barrier to their flight path. They also avoided populated areas, which was easy to do in this relatively barren region.

The pilots watched their multi-function displays from behind their night-vision goggles, two in front of the pilots and another two in front of their copilots. The digimap centered on their position, and indicators identified predetermined landmarks by which they would navigate stealthily to their objective. Both pilots had their left hands on the Thrust Control Levers and their right hands on the flight sticks. Sato tightened his grip on his TCL from time to time, fighting the urge to push it and his V-22 further forward into the flight lead.

"Hold steady at ten meters as we approach the final landmark," lead pilot Taguchi ordered as they approached a hill rising from the ravine along which the two aircraft navigated. Both pilots instinctively recognized it without looking at their multi-function displays as the last landmark prior to the final approach to their objective based on almost a dozen practice runs in simulators. Taguchi called to his crew chief in the rear: "*ippun*"—"one minute." The crew chief then semi-shouted in Japanese at the men waiting in the rear, "*ippun!*" and turned to those behind and said again, "*ippun!*" He gestured with his index finger as a further visual indicator, though it was barely visible in the low red glow of the cabin. The men stirred to life, having heard both the pilot and the crew chief call out time to arrival at the objective. They readied their weapons and shook blood back into their numb limbs. Sergeant Shimada elbowed

Sergeant Suzuki, who had fallen asleep next to him, his head bobbing centimeters from Shimada's shoulder.

A similar scene unfolded in the cargo compartment of Razor Two, as soldiers readied their equipment for the insertion.

The lead Osprey rose from the ravine and banked left toward the crest of the hillock. The mission planners chose this route not only because the hillock would hide the aircrafts' final approach, but also so that the pilots could begin to tilt the proprotors of their Osprey aircraft from vertical position during flight to horizontal position for helicopter-like hover operations over the target. The repositioning would take precious seconds to complete, an eternity when the element of surprise was at stake. The planners wanted this operation nearly completed as the Osprey crested the hill.

Before reaching the crest, Taguchi slowed his aircraft's speed by pulling back on the Thrust Control Lever. At the same time, he toggled the thumbwheel on the TCL to begin rotating the nacelles and proprotors upwards into hover mode.

"Clearing the hill at three meters," he announced. Sato similarly updated his crew as he cleared the opposite side of the hillock.

The mechanical tilt-rotor operation proceeded smoothly, and each pilot carefully monitored the change in angle of the nacelles in the upper corner of their primary flight display. They could look out their side windows to watch the tilt take place, but this would distract them from the more important objective just ahead. As they increased altitude to clear either side of the hillock, their noses would be angled upward for valuable seconds, and their angle of attack would be severely limited once they cleared the hillock until they were almost over their objective. They were particularly vulnerable to attack from below, from the objective, at this moment. They needed to focus their entire attention on their controls to ensure they navigated directly to their designated insertion points during this phase of the operation.

Both birds cleared the hillock simultaneously, with Razor One at a higher elevation. They leveled out, both pilots looking through their cockpit window to acquire the objective. Their nacelles had almost completed the conversion to helicopter mode.

"Now at twenty meters, fifteen..." Taguchi continued. Sato issued similar updates upon Razor Two's final approach to the objective.

The pilots each made visual acquisition of the objective some 200 meters ahead. A three-story concrete building was positioned in the middle of a walled complex, surrounded by several smaller buildings. The undulating and forested terrain gave way to a field of wild grass below, which surrounded the complex. The pilots detected no activity in the clearing on the approach to the target or in the courtyard inside the ten-foot-high walls. The scene appeared deathly still.

"Open ramp door," each pilot ordered to their crew chiefs almost simultaneously.

"Ramp door open!" their crew chiefs declared.

"Descending to ten meters in altitude..." Taguchi said over the intercom. The occupants all felt their stomachs tightening at the continued, quick drop in altitude.

"Five meters over objective, deploy rappelling device," Taguchi ordered as Razor One came to a hover over the three-story building. It rose slightly as it came into position, and then settled lower over the roof. The crew chief immediately threw a nylon rope anchored to the top of the fuselage onto the rooftop. "Rappelling device deployed," announced the crew chief. The M240 gunner stood to the side, his weapon pulled aside to allow for rapid rope insertion of the troops from the cargo bay. He held a Type-89 rifle at the ready to provide limited cover if necessary.

"Green light!" Taguchi ordered as the rope hit the roof.

"Green light!" the crew chief repeated and turned to the first troops of Chalk One standing behind him. "*Ikke! Ikke! Ikke!*" Go! Go! Go! he shouted in a gruff voice as the first troops began their fast-rope maneuver from the cargo ramp. The crew chief slapped each one on his back as they reached for the rope, almost pushing them out of the helicopter with his massive arm.

His adrenaline flowing, a now-awake Sergeant Makoto "Mac" Suzuki landed on the roof first, took a few steps forward as he secured his MP5, and then took a kneeling position facing forward. Sergeant Shimada quickly took position facing away from Mac as Lieutenant Watanabe landed between them. Sergeant Keiichi Inamoto followed, landing hard after almost losing his grip because of the moisture and small traces of mud left on the rope from the others' boots. He staggered but quickly collected himself, secured his weapon, and looked at Watanabe. Watanabe gestured toward what appeared to be a door to a stairwell heading to the floor below. It was the only structure that was visible on the roof, and Inamoto ran to it, followed closely by the others.

The four took up position on either side of the door, Inamoto on one side and the others lined up against the outside wall of the stairwell facing toward the door. Inamoto took out strips of flex linear charge, placing it on the hinges and to the side of the door handle itself. The other three around the corner less than a meter away from the door, ready to enter.

Two others had fast-roped down from the V-22 above and now stood on the edge of the roof on the opposite side from Watanabe's team. They looked back at Lt. Watanabe across the roof from their position and saw him make the signal. They both attached hooks to a small guardrail along the edge of the roof, and with the rope draped over their forearms, they pulled a flash-bang grenade from hooks attached to their protective vests. They each pulled the ring and then let the safety spoon drop as they held the grenade in their hand. They silently counted "*ich...*" then dropped the grenades to the small balcony below. One grenade exploded seemingly before it hit the balcony, and the other exploded immediately afterward. The grenade fuses were set for two seconds, they knew, but they didn't want to take any chances of someone below throwing the grenades off the balcony or back at them on the roof, so they timed their release of the grenades to burn a second off the two-second fuze. They then grabbed their ropes with both hands, thrust themselves over the edge of the roof and rappelled a short distance down to the balcony below, turning to face the interior of the building as they did so.

As they dropped their flash-bang grenades over the edge of the roof on the other side of the building, Watanabe, next to the stairwell, nodded to Inamoto once. Watanabe looked away from the door and caught a glimpse of Razor Two lifting off from just outside the gate of the compound. Inamoto then engaged the small charge in his hands, blasting the metal door off its hinges. The door fell to the roof with a deep "thud" sound, dust and dirt rising from around its lifeless carcass. The team heard Chalk Two blow the main gate almost simultaneously on the grounds below, and Chalk Two entered the compound just as Suzuki, Lt. Watanabe's team lead for Chalk One on the roof, entered the stairwell going down.

Razor-One's Taguchi had already lifted into the air after the last man of Chalk One fast-roped to the roof. He watched the scene unfold from his perch in the sky, ready to return to collect his men and return to base. He looked across the sky to his *kohai*, Razor Two's Sato, who had just landed Chalk Two minutes ago. He had taken position opposite of Taguchi in the air on either side of the compound. Sato's Osprey pointed toward Taguchi's as they both slowly circled. Looking back at Sato, Taguchi could sense the animosity lingering just beneath the surface as he looked back at Sato's Osprey. Taguchi knew that Sato thought he should be the lead in this operation, but Taguchi did not care. Sato may be technically more proficient than Taguchi, if just barely, but Taguchi was still the older *sempai*. What Sato would perhaps never understand, Taguchi thought as he watched Razor Two circle in the distance, was that as the *sempai* he was more experienced than Sato, and experience always mattered most.

Now oblivious to the circling V-22s above, Chalk One's Inamoto secured his MINIMI just outside the stairwell on the roof. He covered as the team led by Suzuki began to descend into the stairwell. Shimada followed Suzuki with his MP5 A2 submachine gun angled over Suzuki's shoulder. Watanabe began his descent, and Inamoto took up the rear. The stairwell would have been pitch black if not for their night vision goggles, although they only saw the stairs, the walls on either side of them, and the dancing red dots projected from the laser designators on their weapons. The interior of the building appeared barren.

The door at the base of the stairwell was open to the left. Suzuki hit the wall at the base of the stairwell next to the door, crouched, and peered down the hallway to his left, while Shimada stood on the other side of the door on the bottom step and peered down the hall to their right. Suzuki suddenly fired three rounds, *phut phut phut*, his MP5 silencer muffling the rounds as they exited the barrel. A figure slumped down against the hallway wall just as he approached the staircase, apparently dead.

They heard more flash-bang grenades and then the discharge of weapons in other areas of the building, but they continued their sweep of this section unhesitatingly. "Clear," Suzuki whispered into his microphone after checking the hall again, and then Shimada responded with "clear." Suzuki immediately began down the hall, with Shimada in tow, while Watanabe and Inamoto now followed in the rear.

The team encountered another doorway less than three meters down the hall. This one was not in their intel report on the layout of the building, and the team was moving so quickly that Suzuki stumbled alongside the open doorway before he could stop himself. Suddenly he heard shots fired in his direction, and he flailed backwards to avoid the shots before recovering his balance and crouching beside the door. "*Daijobu ka?*" Shimada asked behind him, "are ya alright?" After collecting himself for a split second, Suzuki answered with a grunt in the affirmative. "Good, cover me," Shimada said, having just tossed a flash-bang grenade he had secured from his protective vest into the room over Suzuki's head.

The grenade exploded, and Suzuki covered Shimada as he crossed to the other side of the door. Without missing a beat, Shimada pointed his weapon into the room and said "go!" immediately crossing through the door. Shimada crossed through the door at an angle toward the far corner of the room and began to fire at two targets that Suzuki had yet to see. One appeared to be a man sitting in a chair pointing a weapon at the door, while another was firing from what appeared to be a closet.

Shimada easily hit the figure in the chair and then fired a burst of rounds at the man firing from the closet, *phut phut phut.* Suzuki, who crossed into the room at an angle just after Shimada, also began firing as he crossed the room with his back against the far wall, and the figure slumped to the floor.

"Secure them!" Li. Watanabe ordered from behind. Suzuki immediately approached the fallen man with his weapon trained on him, finger on the trigger. Shimada pulled the figure from the chair and quickly tied the man's hands behind his back with a plastic zip tie, but then he heard a "pop!" from a small package under the man. "*Kuso!* Shit!" Shimada said, as the package appeared to be an improvised explosive device detonating.

Another figure jumped out of the closet with his hands thrust outward, and Suzuki immediately trained his MP5 on him and pulled the trigger as he turned toward the individual. The figure dropped to the ground. Suzuki saw that this man was unarmed and was dressed in civilian attire, unlike the two guarding him. He kneeled over the man and pulled a photo from his side pocket to ID the four hostages being held in the building. "Damn!" he said as he crouched over the figure, looking closely at the man's face. This was one of the hostages they came to rescue.

Through their earpieces, they heard the other teams report that the building was now secure and that they had located the remaining three hostages. "Ok, pick him up and let's get out of here," Watanabe ordered after glancing down at the casualty. "Razor One and Razor Two are returning for exfiltration."

Suzuki picked up the man with Inamoto's help, placed him on his shoulders and carried him in a fireman's carry. Inamoto then picked up Shimada in a similar manner. The team exited the room and headed to the stairwell. Both Suzuki and Inamoto were fuming now, because the intelligence had been incomplete and they were unprepared for what they found in the room. They now had a dead or dying hostage along with a dead team member.

Once on the roof, they saw that Razor One now hovered with its rear cargo ramp almost touching the roof. They jumped onto the ramp and entered into the bowels of the cargo hold, placing their casualties onto the seats on either side. The crew chief began to raise the ramp and reported to the pilot that the cargo and team were secure. Razor One lifted off.

The hostage casualty opened his eyes and peered straight at Suzuki. He sat up and patted him on the shoulder. "Mac, what did I tell you about that trigger finger of yours?" the hostage asked Suzuki pointedly. "You've got to extend your trigger finger straight, *above* the trigger and not rest it *on* the trigger, otherwise any jerky move you make will cause you to fire your weapon."

"I understand," Mac replied, bowing his head half in deference to his trainer, and half in shame. "I had just fired my weapon, so I had forgotten to pull my finger away from the trigger this time," he explained in heavily accented English.

As Mac explained his situation to the now-revived Caucasian "hostage," Mac and the others saw lights go on around the compound through the side window of their Osprey. Instead of racing away from the area with the freed hostages, Razor One landed alongside Razor Two just outside the compound walls. With the compound lights on, the team could see a crowd sitting on bleachers across a short field from the main building. Mac and his team disembarked from the V-22 Osprey through the back cargo bay ramp with the "hostage" walking at their side. Chief Warrant Officers Kirby and Mills, the U.S. trainers who served as copilots on this mission, assisted Taguchi and Sato in powering down the birds.

After mildly scolding "Mac" Suzuki, U.S. Army Staff Sergeant Solberg then looked at Shimada. "Always remember to check terrorists when you've killed them," he reminded Shimada. "They might be booby-trapped with an improvised explosive device or suicide vest." Solberg referred to the improvised device under the chair of one of the terrorists.

Mac then interjected, saying in broken English, "the bad intelligence report confused us, we did not know the room was there or that a hostage would be held there."

"I know, that's why we gave you an incomplete intelligence report, to see how you would respond. There will be many times when intelligence reports will be incomplete or just plain wrong, we just have to roll with the punches when that happens..." The demonstration exercise over, Solberg led his students to an adjacent building to review the exercise with them, what they did correctly and what they screwed up.

Solberg heard his training team behind him joke with each other as they transitioned to the conference room. "You are dead!" Inamoto teased Shimada about the unnoticed explosive device detonating, pushing him to the side and laughing boisterously. "Be sure not to get us *all* killed next time, will ya?" Inamoto continued, laughing again.

"Cut it out!" Lieutenant Watanabe barked in Japanese at Inamoto. "We have a senior delegation here observing everything, do not make me lose face further by your disrespectful behavior in front of them!"

Solberg did not understand much of what Watanabe was shouting at his men, but he knew it was not good. It was a great honor for Watanabe to have been chosen to lead this team in front of the visiting delegation comprised of multiple admirals and generals, and for Watanabe, Solberg knew that anything short of perfect was unacceptable. Preparation for this and other recent high-level exercises over the past few weeks had really stressed this Japanese team out, and they needed some time to decompress, Solberg thought. He would wait until later to bring this up with his own commanding officer to address with Lieutenant Watanabe. Solberg had learned intimately during his time in Japan that face was everything, and any suggestion to allow time to decompress would have to come from a higher-ranking trainer than himself.

• • •

The emerging dawn light exposed a set of three buildings surrounded by makeshift plywood panels set up to resemble a perimeter wall. The smaller Building One was two stories and several hundred square meters of space, while the larger Building Two had three floors and a total space of almost a thousand square meters. Building Three was the smallest, at just 100 square meters. Each of the buildings was essentially hollow on the inside, with plywood panels configured for the demonstration exercise. They could be moved and removed inside to change the layout for any of dozens of different scenarios. Mannequins were positioned throughout the buildings, some representing "the bad guys" complete with weapons, many others representing children, women, and other innocents. Many of the mannequins were attached to rails and could be controlled remotely from the control room. Cameras were positioned throughout the facility, recording trainees' every move for future review. For this exercise, however, senior leadership wanted live terrorists, which Solberg and others played.

This training complex was located near the small Japanese town of Ya'usubetsu, on the eastern side of Japan's northernmost island, Hokkaido. While Japan's Self-Defense Forces had established several similar Urban Combat Training Centers throughout Japan—such as at the So'ne Training Grounds on the southeastern island of Kyushu, or the Fuji School just outside of Tokyo—those other training centers were located in densely populated centers. Training of this sort could not be conducted discreetly in those locations. Locals sometimes complained about noise, and low-altitude overhead flights to practice insertions were all but impossible. Moreover, neighboring powers were known to have networks of spies who monitored and reported on activities in and around these bases. They easily blended in with the local populace, and they could report when training took place, what units participated, and what aircraft arrived and departed and when.

This was not the case at Ya'usubetsu. Because of its remote location in the north, the complex could host some of Japan's most sensitive exercises and demonstrations, such as this most recent one. Hokkaido featured some of the most-expansive, sparsely populated land in Japan. During the Cold War, it hosted Japan's only training ground for combined-arms maneuvers where commanders could conduct large-scale exercises with tanks, armored vehicles, and artillery. Its generally flat topography was one reason military strategists planned for a possible Soviet ground invasion starting with Hokkaido, a Japanese analog to the Fulda Gap in Germany. By the end of the Cold War, Japan had built over 1,000 tanks and a similar number of howitzers to fight a concentrated battle in northern Japan, on the plains of Hokkaido.

Now, however, the major threat to Japan was no longer a conventional ground force attack from the north. Japan faced the increasingly real threat of ballistic missiles tipped with nuclear warheads from its communist neighbors to the west, the snatching of one or more of its thousands of small islands in the southwest, and the threat of an army of ideologically inspired, fanatical special operations troops trained to blow up civilian nuclear power plants, sabotage dams and bridges, and otherwise wreck havoc during any future outbreak of hostilities. Each of these threats had been leveled against Tokyo in word and, at times, in deed at the end of the Cold War and into the 21st century.

This morning's demonstration exercise attracted highest-level interest from Japanese military brass, senior civilian defense bureaucrats, and hawkish politicians as a proof of concept of new strategies to deal with these threats to the Japanese homeland. They were intensely interested in two aspects of this demonstration exercise this morning. They were of course interested in seeing how this new, indigenous special ops unit performed. But more critically, they wanted to see how the V-22 Osprey could support special operations missions such as these.

Among the senior officers present at the demonstration was Admiral Tetsuya Okada, the new Joint Force Commander of the Kaga task force. While the Kaga was technically designated a "helicopter-carrying destroyer," even the casual observer could see by its expansive flight deck that it was an amphibious assault ship similar to the Wasp-class ships used by U.S. Marine Expeditionary Units. The Kaga commanded a self-contained naval task force in the northwestern Pacific second only to those operated by the U.S. Navy, with China following closely behind. And Japan's new V-22 Ospreys operating from the decks of the Kaga and its sister ship, the Izumo, would have an integral role in ferrying Japanese soldiers and materiel to Japan's most distant islands to defend them from any armed incursions. They could launch together with Japan's F-35s for close air and ground support, under the protection of Japanese jet fighters flying extended missions with the help of Japan's aerial refuelers and advanced airborne warning and control systems, and armed with stand-off and precision strike capabilities. And Okada's advanced AEGIS destroyers provided extended air-defense capabilities for the entire task force as well as regional missile defense for the Japanese homeland. With the new units, his would the most powerful Japanese flotilla to sail the seas of the Pacific since the Imperial Japanese Navy set sail for Pearl Harbor in 1941.

Okada had witnessed the quiet evolution of Japan's naval capabilities in his 35-plus-year career in Japan's Maritime Self-Defense Force. He had attended the National Defense Academy in the bubble era of the 1980s because he somehow did not see himself as a *sarari-man* working 20-hour days for Japan, Inc. He had hoped to become a fighter pilot, but his eyesight deteriorated at the academy to such an extent that he no longer qualified. The five-foot-five Okada remembered thinking that he would rather sail to Japan's defense than march to it, when he was presented with a choice between the re-emerging Japanese navy and army. And at least he'd get a chance to travel to other parts of the Pacific in what was quietly becoming one of the largest navies in the world.

He worked his way up through the ranks on destroyers and served on Japan's first Aegis destroyer in the 1990s, the Kongo. It was at this point that Okada had the first taste of defending the Japanese homeland from a rogue and seemingly mad regime attempting to blackmail Japan and other countries with its artillery and missile forces. The same month the Kongo was commissioned, the North Koreans were threatening to turn Seoul into a "sea of fire" over international demands to open its nuclear facilities to inspectors. The country then fired a series of missiles into the Sea of Japan, making obvious the threat towards Japan. The Kongo was Japan's only line of defense at the time.

Okada took great personal pride while commanding the Kongo a decade later when the first advanced SM-3 missile was tested from her deck to shoot down a medium-range ballistic missile—but one of many medium- and long-range missiles under development in North Korea. The anti-ballistic missile system was not perfect, to be sure, but it was more than what Japan had before, which was nothing. And it could protect a naval fleet, perhaps a city, but it could not protect the entire Japanese archipelago. Japan would one day soon need a reliable missile defense system to protect all its large cities and thousands of islands at once. And that day was fast approaching.

After serving as the naval attaché at the Japanese embassy in Washington, Okada had returned to command a Japanese naval task force with a flat-top at its core. He had seen the V-22 Osprey in action before—one of his primary missions in Washington was to study the viability of the Osprey for use by Japan—and he had even participated in joint U.S.-Japan exercises where U.S. Marines had landed Ospreys on his future ship. But Americans piloted those aircraft, with American Marines inside. Today's demonstration had Japanese pilots flying Japanese special forces to seize and secure an objective. This was truly historic, Okada knew: Japan at long last had an operational military capability that could rapidly deploy to defend any of the Japanese archipelago's thousands of remote islands.

Okada knew that the V-22 Osprey could ferry as many as two-dozen soldiers at a time or transport up to 20,000 pounds of cargo, several times more than a traditional helicopter. He knew that the Osprey had twice the speed, could carry three times the payload, and had up to five times the range of traditional helicopters, and these capabilities were critical in helping to improve Japan's national defense. A fleet of Ospreys operating from the Kaga could land several companies of quick reaction forces within hours if needed, all under air cover from advanced destroyers and Japanese fighters. For an island nation like Japan, the technology offered critical advantages in supplying and, if necessary, defending the thousands of small islands and islets along an archipelago that stretched for thousands of miles from just south of the Kamchatka peninsula in the northeast to Taiwan in the southwest and Guam in the east.

"What do you think, sir?" asked his executive officer in a hushed voice. "It's coming together, don't you think?"

As was his nature, Okada remained outwardly impassive. He frowned slightly. "*Ibaru na...*" Okada responded, more to himself than to his EXO. "Let's not be too proud. Yes, it is coming together, but we have much work to do still. Now that we have acquired the aircraft, we have to integrate them with our task force, we have to ensure our pilots can land and take off just as easily at sea as they can here on land. We have to ensure jointness, that our ground forces feel at ease flying in these new platforms over the sea as they do flying in our old Chinooks over land." Okada looked at his executive officer and repeated for emphasis: "We have much work to do." He sat back and folded his arms over his chest. "Yes, much work to do." His face remained stoic, but his eyes lighted with passion that came from a deep sense of purpose.

"I look forward to serving under you, sir!" his new executive officer said, bowing.

Okada grunted, tipping his head forward slightly in return. Japan's road to a truly independent, even if limited, defense capability in the northwestern Pacific was virtually complete. Now Japan had a regional power-projection capability to ward off challenges to its territorial integrity and sovereignty. Okada was immensely proud. Neighboring countries would have to think twice before attempting to redraw territorial maps in the western Pacific.

•   •   •

Three men in U.S. Army combat uniforms stood atop a metal observatory behind the parade stand for the distinguished visitors. They relaxed now that the major event of the day had successfully concluded. The sun had just appeared over the horizon, the sky bursting into hues of red and orange. Steam from the hot coffee each held rose visibly from the disposable cups in the cool autumn air.

"You and your guys trained them well," declared the senior of the group, Colonel Stewart Bradley. He already knew how well the training had progressed over the past month based on the frequent reports from his trainers and, when he arrived, on his own observations over the past several days. He had said nothing until now, wanting to refrain from giving undue praise before the final demonstration exercise. He looked over the railing as Staff Sergeant Solberg, one of the U.S. trainers, gathered his charges at the training facility below to review the exercise. Bradley watched as some of the Japanese men horsed around with each other, a good sign of unit cohesion.

With Bradley stood Lieutenant Mark Newland. "The Japanese troops did well, sir, they have been eager to learn. They need to continue to train, they need more experience, but I think they're ready to be activated."

"That's good, that's good to hear. You and your men have done a fine job, Lt. Newland, Master Sergeant McCarty," Colonel Bradley said in response. He looked briefly and nodded approvingly at

Newland and then at McCarty, the senior NCO who had just arrived from participating in the exercise. He played the booby-trapped terrorist who killed one of the Japanese operatives.

"Thank you sir. They're a good group of men, very eager to learn," Newland said, repeating himself since he was unsure what else to say to one of the top men responsible for executing special operations for U.S. forces throughout the Pacific. Newland felt more at ease with his men in the field than schmoozing with brass at demonstration events, not because of a lack of experience, but precisely because of his already lengthy service. Newland had served two enlistments and had seen action in three war zones before going to ROTC at Texas A&M, and he was one of the few cadets throughout the United States to wear both the Army Ranger and Special Forces tabs, in addition to a combat infantry badge and combat patch. He did not know it yet, but he was weeks away from being selected for promotion to captain.

"I could tell today's final 'UBL' mission demonstration, which we augmented with a hostage rescue scenario, really impressed the Japanese brass," Bradley declared, chuckling. He watched the Japanese senior officers talk among themselves below briefly, then looked at Newland and smiled. "They eat this shit up, don't they?" he added. Ever since the successful May 2011 raid on Usama Bin Laden's compound in Abbottabad, Pakistan, U.S. special operations trainers featured a similar scenario for their foreign students to demonstrate to their respective leaderships in their home countries. Foreign military brass loved it, thinking that their new special operators could now penetrate deep into foreign territory to take down their country's most wanted terrorists. Bradley and all of his trainers knew such a capability was in reality much more complex, but it served an important purpose of building rapport and good relations with their counterparts, so in the end it was a worthwhile exercise.

Newland smiled back, and then asked abruptly, "Sir, when will we find out what our real mission is here?" Newland and his men were part of the 2nd Battalion, 1st Special Forces Group stationed in Joint Base Lewis-McCord in Washington state, and had been in-country for over a month training with their Japanese counterparts. They were used to training rotations such as these, since it was part of an annual training programs that the men conducted throughout the region. But this one felt different to Newland and to his men. For one, Bradley himself had taken a lingering interest in special operations capabilities in and around Japan in the past couple of months, which was uncharacteristic for someone who was more operationally focused at the strategic level.

"What do you mean by that, lieutenant?" Bradley asked. Bradley had wondered if his presence here would create questions among these men. Bradley was the deputy director for operations at SOCPAC—Special Operations Command/Pacific—and he normally did not attend training events such as these. Bradley's boss at SOCPAC, the chief of operations, was keenly interested in the planning and execution of this upcoming mission as well, but he sent his deputy, Colonel Bradley, to Japan to avoid the extra attention that always comes with being a general. The chief would instead arrive with the U.S. naval contingent that was scheduled to take part in a naval training exercise with their Japanese counterparts, although this was in danger of being delayed several weeks due to the snap national elections to be held later in the week. The SOCPAC commander himself was also kept apprised of the status of the mission, who in turn reported back to commanders of both Special Operations Command in Tampa and Pacific Command in Hawaii.

"We just finished the last of our joint training this morning, but our orders were extended just days ago," Lt. Newland further explained, "and we are now here for another couple of weeks. And we were told to prep full combat gear. The only time that happens is when we're about to go kinetic. So now that the exercises are over, the men have been asking, what's next? I don't have anything to tell them right now."

Bradley paused for a moment, thought, and then said, "right now, your orders are to lie low. We might have a mission for you from here, we might not. All I can say for now is that I'm due at the U.S. Embassy in Tokyo this afternoon for briefings on possible mission sets. We should know more in a few days, maybe a week or two. But the only thing to tell the men now is what is stated in the orders, and to stay ready, understood?"

"Roger that, sir," McCarty said, as Bradley looked at him and then back to Newland. Bradley knew that McCarty had more intimate contact with the men, as the senior NCO, so the order was directed at him just as much as it was at Newland.

"Do you think we'll receive our orders in the next 72 hours, sir? Now that this phase of training is over, Master Sergeant McCarty and I were planning to give the men some time off. We've been up here training for over a month now, and they're ready to get out, see some sites." And the more curves on those sites, the better, Newland did not have to add. Newland himself was ready to hit the town in Tokyo, while McCarty was looking forward to some downtime elsewhere.

"Soon, LT. The last-minute parliamentary elections later this week meant we had to reconfigure some aspects of this mission. But I think it'll be safe to plan for some R&R, just have to double-check that the pending exercise will start on time. I just hope events don't overtake us…" Bradley turned serious, picked up his binoculars and began to look through them, at what though, neither Newland nor McCarty could tell.

"Yes sir," the lieutenant said. He could see that Bradley was deep in thought, and he did not want to interrupt.

Colonel Bradley was silent for a moment and then added: "Give your men some time off, Newland, but make sure you can recall them immediately should the time come."

"Roger that, sir," Newland said, and nodded to McCarty to inform the men.

CHAPTER 2 – FIRST BRIEFINGS

Wilson Bennett arrived at the gate of the U.S. Embassy in a black Toyota Crown limousine. The vehicle's tinted windows hid dark leather seats softened only by the lace doilies draped over the headrests, which Bennett saw as a facile attempt to convey luxury. Bennett read through three morning dailies—two Japanese and one English—he bought when he arrived at Narita airport. It was now late-afternoon in Tokyo and the headlines were at least twelve hours old, but they would have to do. As luck would have it, the plane's inflight Wi-Fi went out shortly after takeoff, so he could not get any updates on developments around the region. That and the family of five with fidgeting twin four-year-olds and a whimpering baby sitting behind him in coach made for an excruciating 14-hour flight. He had already read through a stack of unclassified papers in his satchel hours ago. He would have to catch up on classified reporting once he was in station, perhaps after briefing the Ambassador.

Bennett glanced out of the window as the limo slowed and then stopped in front of the yellow-and-black-striped metal barriers blocking the main gate. Local police quickly surrounded the vehicle, sliding flat mirrors on rollers along its undercarriage for any explosive devices. The inspection was surprisingly thorough for a developed country such as Japan, but security was methodically enforced throughout this section of Tokyo where the U.S. embassy was just blocks away from the Prime Minister's residence and Japan's parliamentary building. Two other police officers stood on either side of the intersection looking guardedly at the passing traffic, their white-gloved hands leaning warily on their long wooden staffs in front of them.

The guards pulled back the mirrors, satisfied that no explosive devices were hidden under the vehicle. As a VIP limo, the guards did not check Bennett's credentials, however. Bennett glanced out of his window at the police officer who waved the limo through the main gate.

As the limo proceeded slowly forward, Bennett watched the strategically placed trees and shrubs lining the inside of the tall white fence surrounding the Embassy's main chancery building and the rest of the compound. They had both an ornamental and practical purpose, absorbing the noise from the busy Tokyo streets outside while gently obscuring the activity on the compound. It was late afternoon, and much of the regular daytime staff was walking in an orderly fashion past his vehicle toward the exit to start their commutes home.

The vehicle proceeded up a slight incline to the main entrance of the chancery building, avoiding office workers as they headed to the pedestrian gate next to the main entrance. A Japanese guard promptly opened the back door of the limo just as it stopped, and Bennett hurriedly tried to gather his papers strewn about on the seat beside him into a pile on top of his briefcase. He then placed the stack of newspapers and his shoulder bag under his arm in one clump as he exited the limo. He had to get out and stretch his legs after a full day of sitting. A young-looking man standing at the entrance greeted Bennett as he exited the Toyota Crown, offering to collect the papers and the briefcase. "Let me take that for you, Mr. Bennett," he said in a hurried voice. Another Japanese guard, this one standing guard at the entrance of the building, retrieved Bennett's suitcase and garment bag from the trunk.

Before Bennett could answer the young man, a woman approached him with an open hand and a stern, tight smile. "Mr. Bennett, a pleasure to meet you. Madeleine Tucker," she said as she looked at him through rimless, thin glasses. "Call me Maddy," she added, smiling faintly without breaking eye contact. She wore a sharp deep-blue pencil skirt and matching jacket over a white, crisply starched button-down shirt, with a thin gold necklace hanging closely around her neck. Her light chestnut hair was parted on the left and flowed along the side of her high and prominent cheekbones into a wave hanging just above her shoulder. The streak of gray in her hair gave her an air of wisdom.

"Thank you young man," Bennett said as he handed over his pile of papers and then promptly shook Tucker's hand. Her grip was firm and direct. "Yes, thank you Maddy, it's a pleasure to meet you in person."

Without pause, she promptly turned to the glass door, held a hand out to pull the door open and said without stopping, "right this way, I'll take you upstairs so we can talk."

She walked through the small entryway, briskly bypassing the metal detector and X-ray machine. The two locally hired security screeners said nothing as she passed. Bennett followed behind, similarly unhindered by the normal security protocol due to his rank. A Marine sergeant stood almost invisibly behind the mirrored plate-glass window on the far end of the small room. Neither Bennett nor Tucker could see him punch the button to activate the inner door to the chancery, but when a barely-audible buzz sounded Tucker pulled open the fortified door and held it open for Bennett, waving slightly to the Marine and mouthing "thank you" to him. She walked through the door after Bennett. The young man behind them fumbled with the pile of papers and briefcase under his left arm as he tried to take the briefcase handle with his right hand before reaching the door. It began to close, but he caught it with his still-empty right hand and had to thrust his shoulder into it to keep the heavily reinforced door from closing on him. He almost dropped the papers and briefcase as he forced himself through, and was caught off-balance by the weight of the door. The barely visible Marine smiled wryly at the closing door and then turned his gaze back to the multiple monitors of the Embassy compound hanging in his secure room.

Maddy Tucker led Bennett down the hall, and he had to increase his pace to catch up to her long and steady stride. "I'll take you upstairs to my office where we can go through your itinerary, and then I can show you where you'll meet the Ambassador," she said firmly.

"Thank you," Bennett said with a deeply furrowed brow. The unconscious expression was less a sign of concern than an attempt to fight the rapid onset of jet lag. Bennett had just arrived to Tokyo three hours earlier, and he did not have any time to stop by the hotel to freshen up. The two glasses of wine that he had with his meal over the eastern Pacific in a vain attempt to drown out the commotion only provided him with a few hours of fitful sleep. He was now both intensely groggy and anxious because of the two cups of coffee he drank before landing and the additional can of coffee he bought along with some morning dailies from the vendor at the airport before being escorted to the limo. He was approaching the most critical phase of a mission he set in motion many months ago, and he had to be as alert as possible.

The three went up several floors, and after walking through another set of secured doors Tucker escorted Bennett down the hall to her corner office while the young man went in the opposite direction to his desk to put the papers and briefcase in better order.

Tucker walked briskly into her office. "Come in, please have a seat," she said in a businesslike tone. She gestured to several seats arranged around a small round table, and as Bennett sat she closed the door quietly. Her office was spacious. In addition to the round table, there was a couch next to the door with several English- and Japanese-language picture books arrayed on a low-lying coffee table. Tucker's broad desk and leather chair were on the other side of the office. Two shorter leather seats faced the desk, but Tucker rarely used them except during particularly formal meetings or to reprimand members of her staff. Several computer screens sat on a side desk in the corner behind Tucker's main desk, with one screen showing a log-in box and the other showing the random designs of a screen saver.

"How was your flight?" she asked as she came around the table to sit on the seat closest to the wall, facing toward the door. Bennett sensed from her tone of voice she was uninterested in his flight. She surely wanted to press him for information before taking him to brief the ambassador, because he had not discussed with her his talking points for the ambassador. Nor did he have any intention of doing so.

A large flat-screen TV hung on the wall behind Tucker. The sound was off, but Bennett watched as reporters seemed to talk breathlessly on-location in what appeared to be a small pier in a rural area of Japan. The caption below the animated reporter read in Japanese: "Father, daughter killed in maritime smuggling incident! Japan Coast Guard, police suspect drugs..."

Bennett used his jetlag to play for time. He smiled tiredly and responded slowly: "The flight was fine, thank you, except for the kids sitting behind me. They kept tapping on the screen on my seat, playing games or something."

"Hmm, that's unfortunate," Tucker said in a tone that smacked of disinterest. Tucker followed his gaze to the television behind her. She pointed perfunctorily at the screen. "They've been reporting all morning about a maritime incident last night. The Japan Coast Guard was attempting to interdict a drug smuggling operation off the coast of the Noto peninsula when one of the boats fled, hit a fishing boat and then exploded," she explained. "The other boat was disguised as a fishing vessel, and it was heavily armed. It escaped, and did some pretty heavy damage to the three Coast Guard vessels chasing it. Word is, it fired an anti-ship missile, but we haven't been able to confirm that with our Japanese counterparts yet."

"When I read the headlines in this morning's papers it reminded me of the North Korean ship the Japan Coast Guard sank several years back," Bennett said almost to himself. "Is it the same type of disguised ship?"

"More sophisticated, but yes. The Japanese Defense Ministry and Coast Guard first observed some suspicious activities several weeks ago, but they lost it after some storms rolled through the area. They re-acquired it at the last moment, as it was approaching the Japanese coast to deliver its cargo."

"And they had some help from us too, I understand?"

Tucker appeared to weigh her words before responding. "We were able to provide some additional information on the network, so in that sense yes," she said.

"The smugglers must have learned a thing or two since their previous multiple encounters." Bennett considered the meaning of the last night's operation. He had read reporting on the Asia-based smuggling networks closely. "An anti-ship missile system, huh?" he asked. "If they had that type of weapon system onboard, it would be a serious escalation, and in Japanese waters no less," he added. "That's an act of war if it's traced back to North Korea. Several years ago when the Japan Coast Guard began pursuing the disguised boat then, it ignored orders to halt and fired back at the Coast Guard vessels with an anti-aircraft gun hidden under a tarp when they fired warning shots. When the Coast Guard finally hit the engine to stop the boat and then tried to board it, the crew fired rocket-propelled grenades. Ultimately, the crew scuttled their own boat to avoid being captured. Japan found the wreckage at the bottom of the sea and raised it the following year, and they discovered an arsenal of heavy weapons on board. It would've been a bloodbath if the Coast Guard had actually boarded it then."

"This time they didn't have a chance to board the ship," Tucker declared. "The Coast Guard called off the chase after it began firing anti-ship missiles. The boat was even faster this time, with a new radar-absorbing material even. Presumably more heavily armed. And with the election just a few days away, the Ministry of Defense didn't have the political cover to sink it in open waters, since all the politicians were back in their home districts campaigning. No one was around to give the order," she explained. "The shipment was probably timed for exactly this occasion." She then looked at her watch. "Your meeting with the ambassador is in a few minutes, so we should head over to the tank soon."

She paused, then leaned forward on the table toward Bennett. "So, what are you here for, really?"

"I'm not sure I know what you mean," he answered with guarded disinterest. He suddenly remembered what Sun Tzu wrote about working with spies: *One cannot use them without sagacity, and one cannot get truth from them without subtlety.*

"You're visiting on very short notice for an immediate meeting with the ambassador. Your cable included flight information, and that was it. Your assistant at the National Security Council had no response when I asked, in my official capacity, about the purpose of your visit to prep the ambassador. In fact, I've been disinvited to the meeting with the ambassador." She looked at him directly. "This is all highly unusual."

"The president asked me to brief a situation to the ambassador as a courtesy. I did not think it was necessary, in fact I argued against it. But you know how former businessmen are, they're connected and the ambassador helped get the president elected. So I am here to provide as short a briefing as possible and be on my way." He smiled slightly to convey levity, but he could tell from Tucker's furrowed brow that she was in no mood.

"This is not a 'situation' that you're briefing, this is an operation," she continued. "But I double-checked. There's no new code-word material coming through this station, no new compartments.

I checked with the mission center at Langley, there's no new op going on, certainly none that I do not know about here in Asia. At least, no new CIA operation..."

"Yes you are right, there is no new CIA operation, and we are going to keep it that way. Let's just say I'm passing through, and we'll leave it at that." Bennett knew Tucker and her compatriots well: Their careers revolved around knowing what others are secretly thinking and planning, what the truth was "inside the building"— whether a terrorist's lair or an in their own Embassy or headquarters—and for them, not knowing was deadly. Sometimes deadly for people, and certainly deadly for reputations and careers.

"The thing is, I checked with the other chiefs of station in Seoul and Beijing, and they have not heard of any new cases either, not of the type that needs to be briefed to the ambassador at the request of the president," she added.

"Well they don't need to know, and with all due respect, at this point neither do you," he answered more forcefully as he leaned now toward her. "This is being handled with utmost discretion, and after making the obligatory visits to my counterparts here in Tokyo for this trip, I'll be on my way."

"With all due respect to you, Mr. Bennett," Tucker said as she leaned further forward, "it is my job to know. Nothing should be happening in or around Asia without me knowing about it," she added. "You are a political appointee at the National Security Council, your purview is policy, not intel..."

"Maddy, I've been doing 'intel' work, of a sort, since before you were a twinkle in your daddy's eye," Bennett asserted. "The NSC is where intel and policy meet, and where White House foreign policy priorities are managed, and that is what I'm doing here now, managing the highest priority for this administration."

"Running bibles into communist countries is not intelligence work," she declared curtly. "Your 'strategic initiatives' group"—Tucker added air quotes as she said this for emphasis—"and an operational-ized NSC is not what the United Sates needs. For God's sake, leave operations to the professionals. History shows us what happens with an activist NSC."

"On the contrary, it is exactly the same thing. Bibles or bullets, it's all about winning hearts and minds to our side and supporting allies in enemy territory. And frankly, bibles are more effective at winning hearts than the crates of gold and cash your people throw around. Our work requires multiple and parallel logistics networks, networks of people who are willing to lie and fight and die for a cause they believe is right. Or I should say, righteous even. It re-quires the most profound levels of trust. Whether it's intel or the military running it or a church, it's all based on the same basic principles."

Bennett looked up at the clock and then at his watch, readjust-ing it. He looked back at Tucker. "Now if you'll show me to the tank, I don't want to be late for my meeting with the ambassador."

They both stood up. Bennett buttoned his collar and began to tighten the knot on his tie.

"I printed out some latest intel in the region for you." She hand-ed him a folder with an 8 ½ x 11 paper stapled to it. There was a thick red border around it, with "TOP SECRET" printed in bold red letters at the top and bottom. A list of other compartments and caveats followed the classification, but Bennett barely noticed them anymore. "You can use the terminal back in the main spaces for coms. I'll show you as we walk out."

"Thank you," he said, tucking the folder under his arm and ris-ing from his chair. He did not need to mentally prepare for the meeting. He had worked this case since before he was appointed the executive secretary of the National Security Council. A seem-ingly innocuous title, the position was critical in overseeing the day-to-day work, managing meetings and agendas, and approving policy for final White House discussion and approval. Although Bennett had been in the position for just a year now, he had worked in Asia most of his life, first as the son of missionaries and later as an academic. With a doctorate in applied linguistics, during his day job he had taught and conducted research at the Hoover Institute in California. Increasingly, contacts from his parents' many decades of missionary work came to him to consult on humanitarian relief work throughout Asia, and in particular in Northeast Asia. Aided by globalization, new communications, gradually liberating economies in Asia, and a general sense of humanity compared to the first half of the 20th century, Bennett found that missionaries and humanitarian workers especially had become ever more adept at helping those in need. He had been working to assist this particular case for over 18 months now, initially on purely humanitarian grounds. Upon his arrival at the NSC, Bennett began to shop this individual's case around due to his access to North Korea's most sensitive nuclear program in addition to the difficulty of his personal situation, representing what Bennett knew would be an intelligence coup that would open up additional policy options for the U.S. government. At least, that was how Bennett saw the situation. Others, such as Tucker's colleagues in Washington, disagreed. But they were by no means the only players in town.

Chief of Station Madeleine Tucker escorted Wilson Bennett along a narrow corridor and entered a portal with a large, vault-like metal door. They stepped from an office environment into an industrial one, with dozens of fiber optic cables running parallel to exposed duct work along the ceiling, and stacks of computer servers along the walls. They walked halfway down this narrow corridor, turned to an open, steel-reinforced door along the wall, walked up a slight ramp and stepped through a second set of doors into a low-ceilinged, enclosed conference room. High-backed and slightly worn faux-leather chairs surrounded a dark mahogany table. There was enough space to seat six comfortably, although more chairs lined the side walls.

On the far side of the small room hung two flat screen TVs, with a small camera on a swivel base pointed at the table. A computer terminal sat on a narrow desk in the opposite corner of the room, controlling the monitors and secure video teleconferencing system. The monitors currently showed a map of the region. When Bennett entered the room, he felt both a stillness and a low hum due to the additional insulation and soundproofing, quite unlike any other conference room in the embassy. Even his footsteps were muffled, as if he were walking on a cloud of feathers.

As he walked in, Bennett saw Colonel Bradley sitting on the far side of the table reviewing notes. Bradley rubbed his temple unconsciously with his thumb while he lifted his thinly framed glasses on the tips of his other fingers high on his forehead. Bradley looked up toward the two, smiled slightly as he placed his glasses on his leather-bound portfolio on the table and then stood to greet them.

"Good afternoon," he said. As he shook Bennett's hand, he added: "You don't look too bad for having just flown in, Mr. Bennett," winking slyly and patting him firmly on the shoulder twice with his free hand.

Before Bennett could answer, Bradley turned to the station chief and, pointing to the computer in the corner, said, "I loaded up my slide deck for our presentation, I hope you don't mind."

"Not at all, Colonel Bradley," Maddy Tucker replied. Following their conversation Bennett could see Tucker's thinly veiled resentment simmering beneath her calm and polite exterior at being excluded from the briefing. When it came to the ambassador and to U.S. operations in Asia, there were very few issues she was not intimately involved in. But as a career case officer and chief of several stations with decades of experience, she had long ago learned to mask her true emotions, and Bennett knew that as a professional she would never let her raw emotions show. "Very well, I'll leave you to it then," she said with a broad smile, and she turned to leave.

It was then that Ambassador George Robertson III walked into the room. An avid sportsman and athlete, Robertson was tall and ruggedly thin. He had the bronze skin of a southern Californian surfer, and the salt-and-pepper hair of a middle-aged corporate banker. His pearl-white teeth radiated from his tan and chiseled face when he smiled, and he always seemed to smile. He had to stoop slightly to clear the lower-than-normal metal doorframe, but he seemed to use that to accentuate his stature when he stood fully upright again. Robertson extended his hand to greet each of them.

"Maddy, you look just as fresh now at six in the evening as you did when you gave me today's intel briefing first thing this morning!" he said, flashing a smile.

Maddy introduced the ambassador to Bradley. "Mr. Ambassador, this is Colonel Stewart Bradley, the deputy chief of operations at Special Operations Command-Pacific, SOCPAC, he will be briefing you this evening along with Mr. Bennett, whom I believe you know already."

"Great to meet you, Colonel Bradley!" said the ambassador. "How did this morning's demo go with the Japanese brass?" he asked.

"Very well, sir. They are eager to expand their fleet of V-22s, and their special ops as well. Your defense attaché was there too, I believe he plans to provide an in-depth briefing for you tomorrow."

"Good, good to hear, I look forward to getting his read-out," Robertson responded. He then turned to Bennett: "Willie! Good to see you again!" Robertson declared as if he were meeting a long-lost friend. He smiled broadly and held Bennett's handshake for a few seconds while he patted him on the opposite shoulder with his other hand. "I hope your trip went smoothly. I'm looking forward to hearing about your efforts in the region, Maddy has told me nothing so far..." he said, winking at her. "She keeps saying she wants you to be the one to provide the briefing, so I've had to wait until now. Please, let's get started," he said with a broad and engaging smile as he sat down at the head of the table. He looked toward the flat-screen displays as Colonel Bradley pulled up the first slide.

"You're in good hands, Mr. Ambassador!" Maddy said cheerfully as she departed.

An aide who accompanied Robertson backed away and gently closed the vaulted door as he exited. The completely sound-proof room engulfed the group in a muffled silence. The room was the most secure within the U.S. Embassy and hosted the most sensitive discussions among U.S. officials, but despite this Bennett still felt deeply concerned. Not because he was paranoid that there might be a listening device planted somewhere in the room: Bennett was more concerned about Robertson himself. It was obvious that Maddy had kept him in the dark about her lack of knowledge or input into the current operation so that she could discreetly plug him for information afterward. Roberson was too new to the U.S. Government to know how many sides were trying to play him and ply him for information.

Ambassador George Robertson III was a wealthy southern businessman and, while he supported another candidate during the election primaries, he quickly demonstrated staunch support for the president once he became the party's official nominee during the election. After attending the University of Alabama in the 1980s and looking to travel, Robertson had come to Tokyo to become a bond trader at a major Japanese bank just as the economic bubble was at its height. With access to a wealth of data during his day job, Robertson made his first fortune by shorting real estate and the Nikkei stock market at night as the bubble burst, which media commentators would highlight endlessly decades later after his appointment as ambassador to Japan was announced. Once the most lucrative shorts had dried up by the mid-1990s, Robertson relocated to Silicon Valley to make his second fortune in software for sharing and editing music on Sony MiniDiscs, which were especially popular in Japan in the late 1990s. Few in the United States had heard of them, which made the niche particularly profitable for Robertson. After selling his company at the height of the market, making another fortune, he returned to his hometown of Montgomery, Alabama, where he became heavily involved in economic development for the state. He helped to lure major Japanese manufacturers to the region in the early 2000s. A sports fan, he also helped to win backing for a new minor league baseball stadium and a team imported from Florida. He was shocked when the owners accepted a fan proposal to rename the team after a breakfast food, but the team started winning soon after they arrived and that was enough for him. After finalizing a contentious divorce ten years later, he sold his ownership stake in the stadium, adding millions more to his wealth. He then promptly wed his mistress, who was over two decades younger than he and by all accounts a social climber. Robertson used his wealth for philanthropy—after paying off his ex-wife—and donated to political causes almost as a hobby and social outlet for the new couple rather than based on a deep interest in either charity or politics. He had spent a not-inconsiderable amount of time and money supporting another candidate for president but when he dropped out early in the primaries, Robertson switched to the front-runner for president, and spent even more social capital in connecting the president to his deep-pocketed southern business and venture capital contacts.

Bennett had never met Robertson but he paid close attention to the president's appointments in Asia for any hints of new foreign policy directions in the region that would impact his field work. Bennett himself was only distantly connected to the small group of foreign policy advisors during the election and in the first months of the new administration. But he was offered a position in the months after the current administration came to power and after the inevitable first firings that take place as most new White Houses struggle to find their footing.

Bennett conceded that Robertson's nomination was an interesting one given his multiple business ventures that seemed to profit during Japan's financial downturns. But Robertson's knowledge of baseball and Japanese baseball in particular quickly won over the Japanese public when he first arrived. Any time he traveled, he made a point of watching a local baseball game—pro, college, or high school, it did not matter—and he was often interviewed on sports channels about the latest developments. While politics quickly became boring whether in Yonkers or Yokohama, sports drew wide audiences, and Robertson used this to his and Washington's advantage.

But now, Bennett just wanted to be sure Robertson kept quiet about what would be briefed here today. Bennett did not trust that neophyte political types these days could keep the secrets that needed to be kept, either because they liked to brag about the juicy intel they received, or because they wanted to settle petty scores with rivals both in and out of government.

After his aide exited the briefing room, Robertson sat down at the head of the table. "So tell me about this secret contact of yours," Robertson asked Bennett congenially yet pointedly. "Maddy has been rather coy about him."

Bennett leaned forward in his seat, clasped his hands on the table in front of him and gazed steadily at Robertson to convey an air of seriousness.

"As you know, my association with missionary organizations in the region goes back many decades. I am not as active in any particular church as I would like to be, but I consult with several organizations working out of South Korea and along the China-North Korea border, as well as in other parts of Asia."

He paused for effect, and then continued. "More than a year before the election, before I joined the foreign policy team for this president, I received a call from the head of a group I've worked with in the past that runs an underground railroad, so to speak, along the North Korea-China border. The group is in the business for purely humanitarian reasons. There are many others along the border that help defectors, but many are run by organized crime syndicates, which are looking solely to make money off of human trafficking in the region. This group is legitimate, and most of its operating funds come from donations. It happens to also run a smuggling operation into North Korea, partly as cover since everyone along the border is looking to make money, but mainly to expand its in-country networks to deliver Bibles, hymnals, prayer books and such to underground churches in the north."

Bennett looked at Bradley for a moment, and then back at Robertson and resumed his briefing. "The head of this group informed me they were in contact with a recently converted member of a church established in the north-central region of the country. This individual, I was informed, had a sick child, and they needed treatment that is simply unavailable in North Korea. Based purely on humanitarian grounds, I wanted to help, but his son's condition complicated his ability in finding a way out for the family."

"How so?" Robertson asked.

"First of all, because of the sensitive national security work he does, he is essentially barred from leaving, even across the border to China. Even if he personally wanted to escape on his own, there would be bribes involved and other hazards along the way. Smuggling a family with a sick kid out of the country is something else entirely. Given his age and condition you can't conceal him for any length of time, he'd probably cry out and give himself and his parents away. Long-term sedation is very risky, because you don't know how long the journey will take."

"Well then, does it really matter?" Robertson asked. "I mean, it's tragic that he's sick, but ultimately, so what?"

Spoken like a man with no children, Bennett thought to himself. "Under normal circumstances, sure. But this is not just some farmer in a North Korean village. It became apparent that this particular individual happened to be one of the few engineers at the working level who had insight into DPRK's missile programs across the board as well as the nuclear program, because as the senior systems engineer he was in charge of ensuring the warheads could fit on the long-range variants such as the long-range, road-mobile KN-08 Nodong-C missiles, for example."

"So he would know exactly how far along North Korea's nuclear program is," Robertson interjected, nodding his head.

"Yes, and presumably how North Korean technology is developed, or where it is stolen. This would help our interdiction strategies immensely," Bennett added. Bennett consciously neglected to say that he was actually the chief systems engineer for the nuclear warhead project, a critical position that requires understanding not just of the explosives design within the warhead and how much nuclear material would be used, but also the guidance systems and mating used with North Korea's delivery systems, to include its medium- and intercontinental-range ballistic missiles. If this individual did his job right, North Korea could miniaturize a nuclear device, stick it on a long-range missile, and ensure that the device reached its intended destination, such as Japan, Hawaii, or even major metropolitan areas on the west coast of the United States, and yield a nuclear explosion of catastrophic proportions.

"His wife works as a technician at the facility as well, so she would be a valuable asset in her own right," Bennett continued. "They now want out to get their son the medical treatment he requires but can only get in a Western medical facility."

"How much information have they been able to provide us so far?" Robertson asked.

"That's one of the issues we currently face, Mr. Ambassador," Bennett explained, "and that's why we're here today."

Robertson looked at the empty seat next to him and then back at Bennett. "Yes, I noticed Maddy isn't here, what's that about?" Robertson asked.

"North Korea is not a permissive operating environment, so we have not been able to meet with him directly. We have teams working with my contact along the border as proxies to deliver messages to him, ascertain the veracity of his story, test him out, that sort of thing."

"'Ascertain the veracity of his story?' So you don't know if this guy is legit is what you're saying," Robertson said pointedly.

"To be honest, sir, the U.S. Government does not know if he is who he claims to be," Colonel Bradley interjected. "Some in the inter-agency process are of the opinion that this might be a dangle. The CIA is one of the dissenters on this operation." Bradley noticed Bennett's irritated look, and then looked back at Robertson. "It's important that all sides are represented in these briefings, Mr. Ambassador."

"On the other hand," Bennett said, recovering, "having worked with this particular group personally over the decades, I have not encountered a single instance where people were not who they claimed to be. As part of the many attempts to validate his story during my recent time in government—which has been a cumbersome and bureaucratic process, I have been surprised to find—we asked for and received a videotape of his son, shot to appear as a family video. We did this so cleared medical professionals could make a medical diagnosis, and the video happened to catch the view out of their apartment window that corresponded with their housing complex at the nuclear complex near Kusong. We did this because we obviously could not get our doctors to their location in North Korea, and also to ensure the videotape if seized by State Security would appear innocuous and not give away its real purpose."

Robertson turned to Bradley. "And what objections were made to the video evidence, as part of the inter-agency process?"

"There are some who say the video could have been doctored, or that it could actually be his family, but shot in a way to make us think he has the stated motives."

"They think the kid is faking an illness, you mean?"

"That's right. Their son, who is about the age of 10, has muscular dystrophy," Bennett explained. "We think it is probably Duchenne MD because of his age and symptoms, but it could be an early onset of the milder Becker MD. The doctors were able to examine the video and copies of a few medical records that our contact was able to provide, but at this point it is impossible to say which it is."

"But some are concerned that the child is faking, or that perhaps the child in the video actually has MD but is not theirs," Bradley added. He looked at Bennett again, and then to Robertson. "I'm not saying these are my opinions, sir, I'm only representing the full scope of conversations at the inter-agency level as far as I know them.

"This was not incontrovertible evidence, of course, but we wanted to see what access he had so we provided him with a covert communications capability once we were able to analyze the video," Bennett added calmly. "In one of our next attempts to vet him, we asked for the names of some of his co-workers, who we already knew worked at the facility. He provided the names of those we knew of, and the names of additional workers we hadn't known about until now."

Robertson turned to Bradley. "And what were the concerns about that?"

"We crossed-checked the names with other information, and the list of names consists mainly of janitors, the night cleaning crew, those sorts of workers," Bradley answered.

"So in all likelihood he's there, but he could be feeding us false information either as a dangle or in order to win his freedom and treatment for his son on the U.S. dime, is that what you're saying Colonel Bradley?"

"Some are raising that as a possibility, yes," Bennett quickly interjected, "but taking into account the totality of his story, and my past work with the facilitators in the region, there is a high probability that this guy is legit and well worth the risks."

"And that's what you told your bosses at the NSC, who somehow convinced the White House that this is worth doing?" Robertson added.

"We need to take more risks in order to be rewarded," Bennett responded. "And we *will* be rewarded."

"How does DoD fall on this?" Robertson asked Bradley.

"The decision was above my pay grade, to be sure," Bradley said. "I understand that some, most in fact, are skeptical, but we want to do what we can against the North Korea target."

"So if I'm reading between the lines then, what I hear you saying is that Bennett here engineered an end-run around the CIA and you're now on the hook to get this guy out, right Colonel?"

Bennett regarded Robertson's jocular smile as an indication that he still did not treat this with the importance and gravity necessary for a man in his position. This worried Bennett.

Sensing Bennett's concern, Bradley replied quickly. "The President signed a directive ordering us to take action, and it fell to me to plan and now execute this mission." Bradley looked back at Bennett. "And I look forward to carrying out the mission successfully. Failure is not an option," he declared, again looking at Robertson.

Bennett by now had leaned back in his seat. "I should add that I've worked with this network on multiple cases over several decades. The head organizer contacted me before my work for the presidential campaign was announced, so he and his associates had no way of knowing I would end up in my current position. And besides, there wasn't any talk of his actual position initially, just help for his son."

"To be fair, Mr. Ambassador, despite the perhaps lower probability of this particular asset panning out, the mere possibility of gaining access to the type of information he could provide certainly warrants extraordinary measures," Colonel Bradley clarified.

Robertson turned to him. "So that's why you are here, and Maddy isn't? Ok, so what are you planning?" Robertson asked both Bradley and Bennett.

"What we are about to brief must stay in this room, Mr. Ambassador," Bennett said forcefully. "The president asked that I convey this to you as a courtesy, just in case anything goes wrong. This is not to be discussed at all, under any circumstances, with CoS Tucker, any other member of the country team to include your deputy chief of mission, or anyone else outside the embassy." Bennett waited until he received a reply from Robertson, which was in the form of a nod. "With that, I'll turn the briefing over to Colonel Bradley."

Colonel Bradley motioned to the screen as he started speaking. "Sir, SOCPAC is in the process of dispatching two special operations teams to participate in an exfiltration operation. We will use the annual U.S.-Japan bilateral exercise 'Keen Sword' as a cover mechanism to position these teams between the East China Sea and the Sea of Japan…"

"'Exfiltration operation'? You mean you want to get this guy out already?" Robertson sat back in his seat for a moment. "So that's why the attaché was pushing for the exercise to continue as originally scheduled!" Robertson exclaimed.

"The attaché's office knew nothing about the specifics on why we were requesting at the highest levels that the exercise go forward. They were just instructed to ensure that it does. The exercise was supposed to begin within days, but after Japan's ruling coalition parties called for a snap election, Japan's Ministry of Defense requested that the exercise be delayed by three weeks so that a newly elected prime minister could name a new cabinet. This would have likely delayed execution of the operation by several weeks, and already Mr. Bennett's asset has had some close calls. And because of the deteriorating health of his son, we needed to act soon or he might change his mind, or worse, get caught," Bradley explained.

"His son has had some recent heart troubles and a recent bout of pneumonia due to weakening diaphragm muscles," Bennett clarified. "He just can't get the treatment he needs in North Korea for this type of debilitating disease…"

"I see," Robertson said. "Go ahead, colonel." Robertson was now transfixed on the slide showing the planned movement of units in delivering the special operations teams.

"Sir, the Virginia Class submarine USS Texas is scheduled to take part in the bilateral naval exercise, but on day two it will peel away from the naval exercise AOR to this location here…" Bradley pressed a button that illuminated a portion of the Yellow Sea near the Korean Peninsula. "The Texas will approach to approximately 12 nautical miles, here. The team will be aboard the USS Texas from the start of the exercises, and since this is a unilateral mission in international waters, even during the exercise itself, their presence on the Texas and mission will not be known to our Japanese partners. The Texas is equipped with a dry deck shelter and, using the newly developed Next-Generation Shallow Water Combat Submersible, SEAL Team 3 will disembark here," he said, tapping a button that caused an arrow to appear in the illuminated portion of sea, "and meet with the family who will be on a small watercraft at a pre-determined point." A circle appeared just above the tip of the arrow. "We were able to provide the asset with a beacon to use once they have successfully reached the pre-determined point."

Bradley clicked forward to the next slide, and continued. "The second special operations team will be pre-positioned on the air-craft carrier USS Ronald Reagan. This team, from the 1st Special Operations Group out of Joint Base Lewis-McChord in Washington state, will stand by as a Quick Reaction Force in case SEAL Team 3 is forced aground or otherwise encounters hostilities. Other assets will be available from the Ronald Reagan such as search and rescue if necessary, but these operations would have to be conducted un-der the cover of the exercise." The slide showed the planned posi-tions of each of the naval assets in the East China Sea the day the operation was scheduled to take place.

Bradley went to the next slide. "The family and SEAL Team 3 will rendezvous just southeast of this isthmus, here," Bradley said, pointing at a strip of land jutting out into the Yellow Sea. "We judge early-warning systems to be weakest in this area of the country. Seal Team 3 will collect the asset and his family at sea here"—an X ap-peared near the coast of the isthmus on the slide—"and then re-turn to the Texas."

"We'll then transport them to Guam and then back to the United States for extensive debriefings and medical treatment," Bennett interjected.

"Sounds simple enough," Robertson said of the plan. "So even my chief of station doesn't know this?" he asked in a surprised tone.

"That's correct, Mr. Ambassador," Bennett affirmed.

"For once I know something that she doesn't!" Robertson chuckled.

"She has an idea something is in the planning stages," Bennett said sternly, "and she'll most likely try to case you, that is to say, talk you up to see what she can get you to divulge. She's good that way, don't underestimate her even though she works for you. Remember, she works for *you*, not the other way around."

"Oh she's good alright, but don't worry about her," Robertson replied without recognizing his own overconfidence. He sat for a moment looking at the map, and his demeanor turned quizzical. "Why are the Spec Ops guys coming from Washington state?" Robertson asked. He then looked at Bradley. "Don't we have special forces units here in Asia, in Japan?"

"That's correct sir. But we suspect that North Korean intelligence has been casing those known locations for some time now, as part of their early-warning network. We wanted to play to this by having our special ops teams participate in some very public exercises with their Japanese counterparts at Camp Fuji in the run-up to Keen Edge, making it appear that they are fully engaged in the exercise. And they've been away from their base for some weeks now, participating is some public relations events prior to the exercises," Bradley explained. "Meanwhile, the Lewis-McChord special ops team will pre-position on the Ronald Reagan in the coming days, just prior to Keen Edge."

"Was that Hokkaido training part of the V-22 Osprey induction and counter-terrorism training you just returned from?" Robertson asked, secretly pleased with himself that he had remembered this information from a briefing several weeks ago.

"No, sir," Bradley answered. "That is a separate team that has been training with actual Japanese operators on the use of the V-22s and infiltration operations. Although that training has a longer timeline, it's been kept close-hold as well. No PR related to that exercise except for the Japanese brass, it's strictly real-world training. As I noted, the air and naval attachés here at the Embassy observed the exercise this morning with his Japanese counterparts, and they should be available to brief you later this week."

"I see, good, I'm looking forward to hearing more on that." Robertson turned to Bennett. "And I'll also be looking for an update on the ship incident last night, tell Maddy I want a full read-out tomorrow morning," Robertson said, taping the table as he stood.

"I know they are working hard on a thorough update as part of your intel briefing first thing tomorrow," Bennett replied, smiling.

"Great! Good to hear, I look forward to it." He looked at his watch. "Now if I hurry, I should be able to make it for the third inning of the Giants game," he said, referring to the Yomiuri Giants based in central Tokyo. "They're one game out of first place, and this is the second-to-last game of the season before the championship series," he said as he stretched. Bradley and Bennett stood up at the same time, with Bradley reflexively reaching to open the vault door for the senior in the room. "Very exciting times!" Robertson said as he left the room, patting his aide on the back as he turned down the corridor.

CHAPTER 3 – THE CAMPAIGN

The October air filled with the smell of acrid smoke. Farmers had dried their rice paddies and harvested their rice, and they were now burning the leftover stalks in the barren fields before the frosts of late fall set in.

The small crowd stood in the parking lot of the local farmers' coop and listened intently to the man standing on a small platform on top of a compact white Isuzu van. He held a walkie-talkie receiver close to his mouth, its black spiral cord curling down to a large megaphone slung over his left shoulder. He wore a charcoal gray, simple suit on this day, a similarly dark and unflashy tie askew around his neck from a long day of politicking throughout the countryside. His voice was hoarse from the long and loud speeches he had given in the chilly and damp October air in recent days.

"Japan is at a cross-roads!" Representative Seikichi Tadaishi, candidate for re-election to this local district in Fukui Prefecture, shouted in a barely controlled manner, turning from side to side as he broadcast his message across the crowd, his microphone wet from spittle. "Japan is a great nation that has fallen! But we have seen worse, and we have survived! We have returned from every trial, hardened and stronger, a better and more resilient people! And I will tell you why, I will tell you our secret..."—here he lowered his voice into his microphone, leaning slightly in towards the crowd, peering more closely into the eyes of those at the front—"What is this Divine Wind that breathes magic through this rural district of ours, and in turn through the nation, through this great country of ours? I have no need to tell *you*"—his voice rising—"standing before me, for *you* are that Divine Wind! *You* are the heart and soul of this nation, not those city-slickers in Tokyo and Osaka..." Tadaishi thrust his arm at an angle into the air as if to point at the surrounding landscape, causing the megaphone to swing at the upward gesture as he scanned the crowd again.

"Without *you*, this nation would be starving and impoverished like many other nations this very day! Yes, look around us, look outside Japan"—he tried to point behind him while still looking at the crowd, but ended up pointing up to the sky—"and what do you see? Japan has been at the apex of Asian civilization for centuries now while those around us starve and yearn for the life *we* live, the life *you* have built! I only ask to be, to continue to be, a mere servant expressing *your* voice, for your desires, for your needs. Together, we can build a new Japan, a 21st century Japan, a great Japan!" He pulled a handkerchief from his pocket and dabbed the beads of sweat from his forehead, conscious of the image of a hard-working politician it conveyed. He continued his speech as he held his kerchief balled up in his right hand, jabbing his forefinger for emphasis.

The residents here, no matter their profession or background, all had a deep vested interest in hearing their local representatives campaigning in the countryside. Most local farmers owned only a few hectares of land and worked their property in their spare time, a legacy of major land reforms after the war. Teachers, petty bureaucrats, small business owners, factory workers: Many in this rural region of Japan owned a tiny plot or two of fertile land handed down from their parents and grandparents. And that land produced income, whether from co-ops paying elevated prices for rice or from the government paying them to let the land sit fallow. Despite the high price of Japanese rice, the government paid a premium even for non-cultivation to control production each year. The logic was one of politics driving economics: Rural Japan for decades exercised clout that urbanites did not possess. The Japanese form of parliamentary democracy, established and solidified during the post-war political ascendancy of the Liberal Democratic Party in the 1950s, weighted votes heavily in favor of the rural voter, where power has resided until recently, as rural Japan ages and dies away. Even as demographics have shifted, the million-member small farmers' lobby, one of Japan's largest, fights mightily to retain significant influence in Tokyo.

Pork-barrel politics underpinned development in rural areas throughout Japan following the devastation of the war. Politicians brought in federally funded construction projects in the form of public roads, bridges, dams, and public halls. Ubiquitous rice paddies, cut in size with land reforms and with each generation's inheritance, lined the increasingly developed hills and valleys, visible as soon as travelers departed the Tokyo-Osaka megalopolis. One of Japan's most powerful—and perhaps most corrupt—20th century politicians, Kakuei Tanaka, built a political empire from his rural base in Niigata prefecture, a two-hour drive from this community. Among the many pork-barrel projects he secured for his rural constituents, Tanaka won public financing for a bullet train directly from Tokyo to the sleepy port town of Niigata city. His model of politics mixing with development was copied throughout rural Japan.

On this late afternoon in autumn, Candidate Tadaishi repeated the casual platitudes with this crowd as he had with passersby in the town square that morning, and at the breakfast with an elderly group at a small retirement home, and with the PTA he addressed in the middle-school auditorium. Each appearance would make for good evening news, depending on what the candidate-friendly TV producers chose to feature. Later there was to be a lunch with a group of small business owners, after which he was to meet with reporters from three local newspapers. And he would continue much the same that night at a local elementary school and later at the Kiwanis Club. He liked to finish with groups like the Kiwanis Club, since they always had several rounds of alcohol to go with the sashimi and tempura which he never had time to eat. But he was quite adept at talking and drinking at the same time.

An entourage stood beside a second white van stationed behind the crowd, almost out of sight. They watched Tadaishi, who for over 20 years represented this rural district in west-central Japan, campaign for re-election following the prime minister's recent call for snap elections. They watched intently, hawkishly peering at the crowd for any sign of a negative response to today's speech. They were older men, some of them portly. These were the leaders of Tadaishi's *Hakuzan-kai*, his local grass-roots support group named for one of the highest peaks in Japan for which Fukui was famous, Haku-san. Together with Fuji-san and Tate-san, Haku-san was considered one of the "Three Holy Mountains" of the country.

The leaders of the group were business-like and professional at what they did, which was electing candidates for the people who sponsored them. They were not consultants in the modern, Western sense, for they did not use focus groups or polls. These men preferred other tools of the trade that were sometimes blunt but quite often persuasive.

The older of the gentlemen stood to their rear, between the van and a smoldering pile of rice stalks in a local paddy and invisible to the crowd. Takada Kano scratched his chin slightly and squinted while taking in this particular campaign event. While he was not formally a member of the *Hakuzan-kai*, he kept in close, if discrete, contact. Kano had sponsored Tadaishi since his first days of campaigning, almost thirty years ago. Despite all the years of campaigning and politicking—and despite his other, more discreet extracurricular activities—Tadaishi still looked half his age. Kano was over two decades older than Tadaishi, though Kano's physique still held echoes of his days as a construction worker. Kano had kept a watchful eye on many of the promising youngsters in the area, and the young Tadaishi had caught his eye early. He was athletic, outgoing, and affable. He was also self-possessed enough to appear smart and capable, without actually having to do anything.

Kano recognized the perfect traits for a politician early on, and encouraged him. That included encouraging him to stay close to home during his college years: Talented kids growing up in the country are often eager for something bigger, something different, and Kano looked for potential talent among the young and still-in-nocent, when they were malleable and impressionable. If Tadaishi had left for college in, say, Kyoto or Tokyo, he likely would not have returned. The cities have a visceral allure, and their pleasures bring out passions in young people that are never quenched back home. Kids sometimes return, but never for long. Kano quickly found that while not especially bright, Tadaishi was eager, and sociable. Kano mentored him, guided him, suggested that he not go off to college in a big city, but to school locally, in Fukui City, the capital of the prefecture. He would get a taste of learning, earn a credential or two, but not be seduced by the big city. At least not yet. He did not need a college pedigree to go into politics in this region. Kano's expanding networks could facilitate Tadaishi's future in politics.

Of course Kano did not concentrate all of his attention on Tadaishi. There were groups of boys who went off to college or technical school every year from the area, boys who had qualities Kano found potentially useful. But Tadaishi made out well early on. Tadaishi returned and began to establish himself locally as a business man, running one of Kano's legitimate local operations, and making a name for himself in local circles. And at last, Representative Yamada finally passed away in office. Kano was grooming Tadaishi to be the youthful candidate to take over Yamada's seat, and he wanted a young man who was both energetic and slightly naive who would live a long life in office to help him in his other occupations, more so than that slobbering boob Yamada. Yamada's death had been long overdue, thought Kano, for he had that detestable quality most men of his age had who survived the war: Damn good health, and a damn sharp intellect to match. Kano had not been old enough or established enough to engineer Yamada's rise to power. But by Yamada's death, Kano was ready to take control of local politics by running his own man against the other factions' boys.

Kano was successful, and Tadaishi's rise in politics facilitated Kano's expanding business operations nationally, with funds from supplemental budgets earmarked for projects in which Kano's companies were especially suited.

We just might weather this, thought Kano of the recent shift in local sentiment. Kano watched Tadaishi and the crowd's reaction intently. Kano judged each reaction the crowd made, examined the careful attention in the eyes of the on-lookers, even as many seemed almost disinterested and listening passively.

Kano looked at the crowd, that October day, and he felt a certain energy. He saw the farmers hold their hoes and rakes and other tools more steadily, their attention drawn to Tadaishi as he spoke. But he was unsure *what* that energy was. They seemed...pensive, wary, guarded...

Buuutttzzzttt, Kano felt in his breast pocket. *Buuutttzzzttt*, again. All of his cell phones were set to vibrate. Kano was the only one in the group allowed to use his cell phone during Tadaishi's speeches, but even then only away from the crowd. He grabbed at his main cell, then his secondary one. *No, it better not be...*he thought, as he retrieved a third phone and quietly spun away from the crowd. He looked at this one in disbelief. This phone wasn't supposed to ring, not now, not today. *Bzzzztttt*. It vibrated again in his hand. The display showed only three digits of the one number it was used to communicate with.

He flicked open the case of the phone, open the settings, and pressed VPN. The pinwheel began to spin.

Bzzzztttt.

The pinwheel continued spinning as it attempted to find a connection.

Fucking inaka countryside, Kano thought.

Bzzzttt.

Damn it. Kano returned to the phone app and pressed the green *on* button.

"What?" he whispered angrily as he stepped into the back of the nondescript white van for more privacy. He quietly shut the door behind him.

"Why didn't you know our shipment was being tracked?" the voice on the other end asked in a barely controlled voice. Only one voice was as gruff as Kano's, and that was Kitagishi's—or at least, that was what he called himself in all his conversations with Kano.

"Why are you calling me now, here?" Kano demanded. "I told you, don't contact me at this number for three days until after our last…meeting. No matter what!" He said in a shouted whisper.

"The call is encrypted," the voice asserted.

"You idiot, I hadn't set up my private network yet. The time of this call isn't encrypted! The length of the call isn't! You're lucky I'm out of the office, but my location could be tracked too…" Kano nearly burst into a full-throated shout into the receiver, but then calmed himself down when he looked at the back of the crowed outside the small, tinted window.

"I didn't get paid for the product last night, and we didn't get the goods we had ordered either," Kitagishi interrupted in an even tone.

"Yeah, well I've got nothing now, *nothing*," Kano whispered again into the receiver. "If your idiot boat pilots actually looked over their shoulders, they might've seen the damn Coast Guard *right behind* them before they even got to the rendezvous point!"

"I thought you had a man on the inside to tell us when the Coast Guard was around. What happened to him? Was he too drunk that he missed the intelligence briefings? Or maybe he was just whoring around with those young sluts he likes in the capital?"

"Fuck you. My sources are solid." *And if they're not, I'll take care of that myself soon enough,* he thought to himself. "In case you didn't notice, there's an election going on so the bureaucrats have taken over, there haven't been any briefings for weeks. We'll have complete situational awareness next time. *I'll* see to that."

"You better. We need to get another shipment out, we want payment and we *need* our satellite receivers."

"And I need product. My suppliers in the region are running low..." *And I've got votes to buy,* Kano thought to himself. *This is going to be an especially expensive...* "We have new orders coming in from North America that are going unfilled, and we need to square things, return to business as usual. Get the next shipment ready, and call at the next number. *At the agreed time!*"

"You better be prepared next time. We need those receivers from Japan's new quasi-zenith satellite positioning system."

"I can get you all the GPS receivers you need..."

"No!" the man on the other end interrupted Kano. "We have those outdated pieces of shit. We gave you very specific orders to acquire receivers for Japan's new quasi-zenith satellite system, it is accurate to within centimeters. The GPS technology is decades old. And another thing," Kitagishi declared, his voice rising. "I hear the Americans are involved now too. Why are the Americans there, why didn't you tell us that? I had a lot coming in last night, because I thought it was safe!" the man on the other end screamed. "You told me it was safe *precisely because* there was an election going on! No one would be watching, you said. Now you better tell me, what are they doing on the coast? Are they patrolling? Where are they? When are they there? You've been holding out on me! This better not be a setup. I have to make this up, we lost a lot of product and a lot of time last night!"

"Just get the damn shipment ready. I'll handle it." Kano hung up, turned off the phone, and threw it at the man sitting in the shadow behind the front passenger seat. Although both he and his boss were wearing leather gloves, the man in the shadow rubbed the phone thoroughly with cleaning solution. He then took out the SIM card and smashed it and the phone with a hammer. He put the small pieces of the SIM card in his left jacket pocket and the shards of the phone in his right inside jacket pocket for later incineration.

Fucking Tadaishi, Kano muttered to himself as he looked out the small window, *you're getting harder to keep in line.* He looked back at the man in the shadows. "Tell Tadaishi I have to see him, *tonight.* He knows where to go." Without waiting for a response from his henchman, Kano hit the interior wall of the van with his fist three times before opening the side door and stepping out of the vehicle. He grabbed another phone from his coat pocket and dialed it. "Kensuke! Get ready to prep another shipment..."

CHAPTER 4 - WORKING IT OUT

"*Ich! Ni! San! Shi…!*"

At each number Master Oyama shouted, a unison of cracks from the students' Karate *gi*s echoed through the wooden rafters above with each practice punch. The uniforms of even the toughest students were drenched with sweat, from Master Oyama's intense workout and from the lingering heat in the *dojo*. Droplets of sweat exploded off of the students' fists with each movement and pooled at their feet as they squatted in deep stances to ground their *ki*, their spiritual energy, when they punched. Every technique they executed correctly ended in a crack of their *gi*, their Karate uniforms. Any lazy movement ended in a *whish* and was further corrected by Master Oyama with a sharp yell and, if he was close enough, a sharp slap down on the student's punching arm. "*Chikara hai'tte nai zo!*" "More power!" he yelled.

Sensei Oyama clapped twice in quick succession just as the students completed a set of one thousand punches and one thousand kicks, a warm-up. "Prepare for *kumite*! Find a partner! *Hayaku!* Quickly!" The instructor didn't shout his orders, but rather let them emanate from deep within his diaphragm. His voice was coarse and gravely. He was a stocky fellow, not short and not tall, but all muscle. He had short stubby fingers and always carried an intense scowl on his forehead. He wasn't angry, just deadly serious. Every move had a purpose, every word contained meaning. He didn't consider himself a teacher, but merely someone who showed others how to move in every way with purpose and awareness. Stay alert, stay alive, was his mantra. He was a man of action, and how does one teach action? Certainly not through words.

The students had to focus closely on maintaining balance as they moved quickly to face their sparring partners. The smooth wooden floor was dangerously wet from perspiration, and not a few students slipped as they moved in bare feet along the hall. Most caught their balance, while a few fell to the floor with a muffled thud but immediately jumped up to get into position. Oyama made no effort to have the floors cleaned, because the wet conditions made students focus on maintaining their balance as they moved.

"Face off, *rei!* Bow!" Oyama shouted gutturally. He approached two students as they bowed to one another, eyeing each other fiercely. He pulled the junior of the two gently and firmly aside with a hand on either shoulder. He then bowed slightly to the other, intoning under his breath, "*yosh…*" *Time to see what you are made of,* his eyes said.

Trinh Archer stood across from her new sparring partner, Master Oyama, and bowed respectfully but just as intensely in return. They had sparred many times in her two years at Oyama's *dojo,* and his large and solid frame did not intimidate her. At almost six feet tall, Archer was almost a full head taller than Master Oyama. She often lost, and sometimes she won, but she always gave her best and never allowed herself to become intimidated. Since shortly after she joined the school to add to her many years of training in other martial art forms, Oyama had been secretly impressed by her determination and skills. He had taught her a few tricks she had not known from her previous training, and she in turn had taught him a thing or two as well. He took his lessons and bruises silently, and she accepted her lessons uncomplainingly. He admired that of her.

As she took her fighting stance, Archer heard her cell vibrate in her bag, a faint but meaningful sound. For a moment she thought of cutting out of class early. *I could take the call and return back to work now,* she thought, but quickly realized that she was just looking for an excuse to avoid the inevitable bruising that would come of this session. Oyama-Sensei did not budge, nor did he look away from Archer's gaze. Archer did not flinch from his, either.

"*Hajime!*" Oyama-Sensei declared. He charged Archer, throwing at her thin frame a barrage of punches and kicks. Archer avoided the first set of punches thrown fast at her face and torso by half-twisting, half-blocking each attempted blow. She then blocked his kick aimed at her stomach, which was just a feint in an attempt to land another punch aimed at her left cheek. She ducked at the last moment and wedged herself under Oyama's elbow to catch him in the ribs with a right uppercut of her own, but Oyama caught her arm just as she made contact with his body, and he jerked her arm toward his body to catch her in an inverted elbow lock.

Instead of trying to pull away as most untrained students instinctively would, Archer lurched her body into him just as he started to pull her into a tighter lock. She checked his ankle at the same time with the insole of her foot, causing him to loose balance. His arms flailed outwards, releasing her from his elbow lock.

If this had been a street fight Archer would have rushed into him as he fell backwards, catching his head with one hand while throwing her body into an elbow blow to his face with her free arm. Instead she threw another uppercut at his solar plexus to further throw him off balance, letting out a sharp cry to intensify the power of her strike. She tried to reach around his thick neck to catch him in a sleeper hold as he stumbled, but Oyama caught her elbow coming around his neck and positioned himself to throw her over his hip in a classic Judo move. Archer sensed what was coming and quickly knocked Oyama in the back of his knee with her foot, unsteadying him enough to break free of his grip again.

They tumbled to the ground, Archer on top of Oyama. Oyama threw Archer to the side and mounted her, pulling at her *gi* near the neck in a modified chokehold. She placed both her hands on his clenched fists, clasping the top knuckle of his thumbs, squeezing the tips and wrenching them away from her uniform.

"Ahhh!" he intoned uncontrollably as his thumbs were forced against their joints. She released her right hand, straightened it and slammed her palm at his face in one fluid motion. "*Kiai!*" she screeched, her high-pitched scream echoing through the hall. The meat of her palm barely brushed the tip of his nose, and he knew that she was in full control of her strikes. He knew that he would have a severely broken nose now if this had been a real fight.

"*Yosh,*" he said again under his breath as he looked down upon her. They both were breathing heavily, and for a split second each wondered if the other intended to continue the fight.

Oyama slowly lifted himself up. Part of his *gi* hung over his tattered and well-worn black belt, untucked and askew, but before fixing his uniform he offered his arm to Archer to help her up. She quickly recovered, and they both returned to their original positions. They bowed to each other, this time a little deeper and a split second longer in a show of deepened mutual respect. They then turned away without uttering a word, Oyama to another group of sparring students and Archer to her cell in her bag.

Archer had realized, more by instinct than by intellect, that Oyama-Sensei usually approached his opponents in straight lines and acute angles. His style of Karate operated in lines and angles to an opponent, and he had become subconsciously accustomed to attacking straight toward an opponent, even if to the side. Oyama hit hard, yes, but he hit straight and did not circle. That was the key to defeating him.

Enough for today, Archer thought regretfully. She excused herself from her next partner and went to her bag to retrieve her cell and the message. She picked it up, and just as she expected: Nishi. Time to get back to work.

Archer was operating on adrenaline and coffee alone by this point after the drug bust went bad the night before. What was expected to have been a straight-forward seizure—catching North

Korean nationals in the act, no less—had turned into a fiasco. One punk tried to escape, and in the process he rammed his speedboat into a fishing trawler and killed a father who was squid-fishing with his young daughter. What probably would have been a record drug seizure for the year, and direct evidence of North Korean smuggling into Japan, literally went up in smoke and flames. This was supposed to have been the first big bust for the new Japanese counter-smuggling effort and a big media coup for the conservative ruling party ahead of this week's contentious elections. So much for that. Worst of all, the North Korean ship escaped in the fog of bureaucratic bullshit. No one had the guts to give the order to shoot at it, sink it if necessary, because there was no political top-cover this close to the election.

After nabbing the smugglers and the gang and seizing their shipment, Archer had expected to catch a red-eye from Kanazawa to Tokyo and get a few winks before briefing Embassy leadership. Instead she spent the night sitting with Nishi and his crew interviewing sailors and local fishermen to try to figure out what the hell happened. She still didn't know what that fisherman was doing at sea without his squidding lights on. Archer was lucky to make it back mid-day in time to draft cables back to Washington so analysts could read about it first thing in their morning stateside, but half-way through she decided to take some time for her early evening's Karate class. She probably should have skipped it to finish her work, but she was pissed. She wanted to work out her aggression, and she was thankful that Oyama stepped in as her sparring partner so that she didn't send one of the newer students to the hospital.

She wanted to soak her bruises and ego in a long, hot bubble bath, but she only had time for a short, luke-warm shower in the ladies' room at the gym. She stripped off her Karate uniform, her chest glistening with sweat in the bathroom lights. She finished undressing and lowered her head under the low-hanging shower faucet, splashed some of the cold water on her body and then applied soap as the water warmed slowly. She washed her hair quickly and then rinsed, towel-dried herself and then dressed. She glanced in the mirror to comb back her dark hair, tossing it over her head to comb it from the back side down. She saw blood-shot eyes with deep bags under them stare back at her from the mirror. She packed her bag with her sweaty *gi* and flung it over her shoulder, and she exited the auditorium that served as Oyama's *dojo*, hearing "*kiai!*" shouts as she departed.

Archer took out her cell phone and dialed Nishi's number. "*Moshi-moshi, Nishi-san?*" Trinh said in easy Japanese, "this is Archer, yeah, what's going on, Nishi?"

"Archer-san, I wanted to update you on the status of the operation," answered Nishi. Archer heard him take a draw from his cigarette and then exhale the smoke. She pictured him blowing the smoke away from the receiver on his cell phone, pulling the phone back as he turned his head slightly in the other direction. A chain smoker, blowing smoke away from those around him was Nishi's way of being polite while smoking, even when talking over the phone.

"Go ahead," she replied in anticipation.

"Remember the young tough who fell off the speed boat as it tried to get away?" he asked, continuing without waiting for a response. "The Coast Guard picked him up out of the sea, dried him off and took him into custody."

"That's great, what're they doing with him now?" *At least something might come out of this,* she thought.

"We just brought him in to Tokyo for interrogation. I came with him on the same flight, we just got in this afternoon. Wanna sit in?" he asked.

"Tell me when and where," she said, her pace quickening.

"We're at the Tokyo Detention Center. Meet me in the visitors' reception area per usual. It'll be closed by the time you get here, but I'll have the guards let you in."

"On my way," she said and hung up.

CHAPTER 5 - KUSONG

Pyong Hae Han sat at the table in the small kitchenette. The table stood next to the wall with a window directly above it. He glanced briefly through the small window and watched the farmers and laborers below laying out the harvested corn to dry on broad sheets of canvas under the overcast sky.

The TV was on. His was one of the fortunate households that had a color television. And this was no ordinary television: His rank and contributions to national defense resulted in an award of a new Sony high-definition TV. Engineers like himself received gifts every quarter or so, as long as the lab made progress in developing and modernizing the defenses of the homeland.

The technology awards, along with extra rations of food like white rice, soybeans, and fresh cabbage to make kimchi, were some of the perks of his position. Han knew that most people did not even have black-and-white TVs, much less color ones. Very few families have any way to acquire a "high-definition" television, even though they were on open display in stores in the capital, Pyongyang, to fool the few foreigners allowed to visit into thinking the country is modern and prosperous. The one national television network, KCTV, had even begun to broadcast in high-definition so that stores can feature the broadcasts to foreign delegations staying in the more posh hotels or allowed to walk the few commercial streets of Pyongyang. The programming is also broadcast to Koreans and Chinese in the region as propaganda and to compete with HD signals from abroad that some families of means secretly watch, even if watching unapproved foreign programming is an act of treason.

Three photos were hung over the television on an otherwise barren wall. The three radiant faces smiled into the room, all of them with short, cropped black hair and pearly white teeth. The youngest-looking one now hung in the middle, above the others. Red flags fluttered in the background with a crossed hammer, sickle, and calligraphy brush clearly visible in each picture.

The antenna on the shelf just above the TV was positioned to obscure the crack running diagonally down the wall, from the ceiling to the baseboard behind the pictures. Han had watched it expand over the years in this communal apartment, and he knew that similar cracks were growing in the foundation of the building as well.

He did not watch the television, however. He looked to the other side of the room across from the TV, where an arm chair once sat. In its place sat his son, immobilized in a wheelchair. Han's only child watched the television, almost lifeless except for his squinting eyes and a strand of drool that trickled from his mouth. There was not much else his son could do, in his current state.

Han then looked down at the open photo album on the table in front of him. The pictures were taken five, six, seven years ago, in a different era. His son smiled in each of the pictures, though gradually less so, Han could now see. He looked over the corner of the room, where his son slept lightly in a high-backed chair. He wheezed slightly with each breath, whether from the recent pneumonia or because of his deteriorating condition, Han did not know. Han had pulled enough strings to gain access to the Pongwha Clinic in Pyongyang, usually reserved for party department heads, ministers, and national leadership. The doctors might be able to get a respirator, they said, but after that there was not much they could do. They did not offer foreign medical treatment, and he did not ask. Scientists and engineers at his level were barred from leaving the country under any circumstances. To openly suggest such a thing when living in the "worker's paradise" that is the Democratic

People's Republic of Korea would be considered treasonous. A tear welled in his eye, and he blinked his eyes tightly and then rubbed them both.

At the age of eight, he beat me at chess, Han remembered. *Not just once, and he seemed to do it so effortlessly too. The boy is a genius trapped in a body that is failing him...*Han looked up toward the ceiling and clasped his hands together. *Why God, why? Why are we all trapped in this failure?* He lowered his head onto his clasped hands for a moment, and then he stood up to go to the wardrobe in the bedroom.

Han's wife, Mi Yong, had gone to the local market to get some additional, freshly grown vegetables for dinner. It wasn't a strictly legal market, perhaps, but the local authorities overlooked it because their own wives and mothers also shopped there.

Han opened the tall, narrow wooden wardrobe and pulled out a black umbrella. He then walked to the small terrace balcony and opened the umbrella. Instead of placing the handle down, he placed it top down so the handle pointed almost straight up to the sky. The tip caused the upturned handle to lean at a slight angle, but not enough to disrupt the signal burst to reach the satellite in orbit over northeast Asia. The high concrete siding of the balcony, which reached to Han's chest, obscured it from view from other balconies of high-rises in the neighborhood.

He unscrewed the bottom of the handle where the wrist cord was attached. He pulled off the cap to reveal what looked like more cord. When he pulled one end of the cord out of the base of the handle, it had a jack on the tip. He then pulled a small cellphone from his pocket, flipped it open, and inserted the jack as he powered it on. He scrolled down to the surname "Hwang," a common enough name in the north, and then down to the third set of numbers. He pressed "0" and "send" simultaneously. The phone displayed "..." as the message was being sent and then vibrated once to indicate the message had been sent.

He checked that the phone had downloaded any return messages, and then he took the jack out of the phone. He waded up the thin cord and placed it back in the umbrella handle. As usually was the case even now, after using the contraption over a dozen times, he had difficulty stuffing the cord into the handle, but finally he got enough in that he was able to start screwing the cap back on. He was careful to pull out the outer nylon cord as he screwed on the cap, which was more and more difficult to do with each turn because of the bunched-up cord inside. He finally got it attached enough that it held, even though a space was visible.

He then collapsed the umbrella, with the spindles hanging loose as he put it in the back corner of the wardrobe behind a winter coat. He had neglected to attach the velcro tab on the umbrella, which was worn and failed to attach most of the time anyway. The trench coat kept it in place in the back of the wardrobe.

He then pressed "call" and "9" at the same time. A text message appeared in Hangul on the phone's display. "Thank you for the news of your family! We look forward to seeing you soon. Your cousin."

As Han read the message, he heard the "click" of the lock at the front door. He looked up instinctively and furtively, froze for a second, and then shoved the phone into the pocket of a jacket hanging in the wardrobe. He closed the doors to the wardrobe just as the door to the flat opened.

"I'm home," came a soft voice from the main room as the door closed. Han peeked around the corner, relieved to see his wife at the door.

He stepped into main room and stood silently for a moment. She looked back at him expectantly as the door swung shut behind her, still holding onto the bags of produce and fish she purchased at the market.

"They replied," he said. "We leave tomorrow, according to plan."

She nodded once, then put the bags on the table and began to sort the ingredients for the evening's meal.

CHAPTER 6 - THE SAFEHOUSE

Kano waited in the back seat of his black sedan as the front-seat passenger and the driver exited the car. One stood next to the back door and looked first one way down the narrow street, then the other way. He smoothed the lapel of his suit coat slowly with his right hand to check that his suit jacket continued to conceal his sidearm from view. The other walked around the back of the car to the rear door. Before opening it, he glanced over the top of the car to the third-story rooftops of the houses and small apartment complexes bunched one next to the other along the street. He too held his right hand along the front of his suit jacket. Seeing nothing unusual in the dusk, he half-turned to open the door to the black sedan with his left hand, still scanning up and then down the street. Takada Kano stepped out and walked to the entrance of one of the nondescript houses.

This street was long and narrow and especially well-kept. Called Arimatsu, this section of town was located several blocks from the main thoroughfare that cut through Kanazawa, the provincial capital of Ishikawa Prefecture with a population of two million. The Allies largely spared the city of bombings during the Second World War, so that many older buildings and sites remained intact. It featured a beautiful year-round garden and castle ruins that were especially striking during Cherry Blossom season in early spring. It also featured an original—and still operational—Geisha district. Thus Kanazawa had long ago become known as "Little Kyoto."

Few tourists came to this sleepy and nondescript section of town in the suburbs of the city, however. With direct access to the major road, and another that forked from the main road and headed south of the city, it was ideally situated for one of Kano's many safehouses in the region. His generous gifts to the local *omawari-san*—the

Mr. Walkabouts, as the cops who walk the local beat are known—helped to keep this particular part of the neighborhood off the radar screens of law enforcement in general. In return, Kano kept his boys quiet and otherwise gainfully employed, in a manner of speaking. He paid his taxes and a lot extra, so there would be no need for cops or the local politicians not already on his payroll to take notice of the place in any case.

The facade remained silent when Kano stepped to the door. Motorbikes, roadsters, and even a few scooters stood next to each other outside the main doorway under a portico. Through his dark sunglasses Kano looked casually at the camera hanging from the awning, but the door did not open. He waited impatiently, then pushed the door open himself. It was unlocked. He unbuttoned the lapel on his Armani jacket and walked confidently and angrily inside, leaving the driver to survey the street after him.

Kano walked into the small foyer and removed his shoes before stepping onto the faux wooden hall in his black socks. He walked immediately forward into the short hallway. Just around the corner from the foyer, hidden from direct line of sight to the door, was a desk with multiple monitors on it and behind it. Kano saw his two toughs standing guard in the darkness outside in one of the video feeds displayed on the monitor behind the desk. At the desk, a young man sat hunched over with his head lying sideways on an open two-inch-thick comic book. A line of spittle hung from his mouth and dribbled onto the paper. The youth breathed deeply and audibly, almost snoring. His hair was a mangled mass, suggesting that he had neither bathed nor even thought to comb his hair for days.

Hrmph, grumped Kano, disgusted at the sight. He raised his hand and whacked the boy, a horizontal slap over the youth's scalp. "Wake up!" Kano demanded.

"*Naaa-ni shiteru no!*" the boy whined as he lifted his head from the comic book, rubbing the insult from his hair. "What the hell are you doing?!" he complained, wiping the sleep from his eyes. The boy was still groggy, and Kano noticed a scene from the comic was tattooed on the side of his face. Kano decided to slap it off his cheek.

Whack!

The boy's head spun to the side as he cried out. He looked back at the man in front of him as held his cheek. "Ah! *Sumimasen,* I'm sorry boss!" said the boy as he attempted to stand. The force was so strong that the chair he was on slammed into the wall immediately behind him and prevented the youth from standing completely up-right. His knees, caught partially under the desk, remained bent. The position merely made his obsequious bows seem lower and more humiliating. "I'm terribly sorry...!"

Kano raised his hand as if to slap him again. "Do I pay you to sleep on the job, huh? Why are you here, anyway? Are you gonna earn your keep around here, or should I throw you back out there on the streets?" He whacked the youth over the head with his palm, keeping his hand raised as if readying to strike him again with the back of his hand.

"I'll do better, I promise! I'm *terribly* sorry, please, forgive me!" sputtered the youth. He held his head low, partly in a half-bow, partly to protect himself from more blows to the meatier parts of his face.

"Hrmph!" said Kano aloud, and he rubbed his nose once out-wardly with his leather-encased thumb. Kano wore black leather gloves, which he rarely took off. The youth bowed again as Kano turned to enter the main part of the house from the hallway.

Kano surveyed the main floor. The decor was Spartan. The faux wooden hallway leading from the entrance gave way to an entire floor consisting of *tatami*, thick mats made from rice straw that mea-sured almost two meters long and less than a meter wide laid side by side. Thin futon mattresses, sheets and covers were strewn about a small room to Kano's left, while the TV was blaring in the living room corner to his right. A samurai suddenly hacked a man's head off with a vicious "Aaaaiiiii!" cry on the screen, and the camera cut quickly to a grimacing villager, terrified of the scene and scraping the ground desperately in obeisance. Kano walked closer to the TV, both drawn to the samurai scene and upset that it was on so loud. As he approached it, he tripped on a small pillow and lost his balance slightly. "*Chikushou!*" he muttered, and kicked it across the room. He reached behind the TV and tore the plug from the wall socket, and then lifted the TV over his head and flung it at the wall. It burst into pieces upon impact. He stormed angrily into the dining room.

Three young men sat around a low *kotatsu* table on futon pillows. They had been reading comics and smoking, but they dropped their comic books and cigarettes and scurried to stand as Kano charged into the room. Kano stood there looking at the three, seething with anger. All three bowed almost in unison. They all had long hair, un-combed from their recent reveille, their long bangs flopping down over their faces as they prostrated themselves. One wore only long underpants, his naked body bare of any distinguishing marks; the other two wore sweat pants and tee-shirts, one of which said "Levi Jeans" and "California" beneath it, though Kano knew the kid had never left the local Hokuriku region of Japan, much less visited the U.S. west coast.

"What the *hell* are you all doing here, huh?" he shouted. Kano kicked the nearest one on the outside of his thigh, who yelled "ahhh!" and clutched his leg as he fell. Kano grabbed the boy next to him by the back of the neck and slammed his cheek onto the table, and then lunged for the third, who had already backed away. Kano jumped over the *kotatsu* table and grabbed him by his shirt as he turned to run. It ripped in the back as Kano pulled the kid toward him. He grabbed his torso with both arms, lifted him up and hurled him into the nearest corner of the room.

"Why aren't you boys down at the racetrack today, setting loans for gamblers, huh?" Kano screamed. "Or do you just sit around all day like a bunch of fucking oafs?" Kano knew the answer, but he wanted to scare the shit out these *baka* neophytes. "Is this what you do all day? Sit around and read comics? Eh?" He reached down to the table and toppled it over, and all the comics, the ashtrays, and cans of coffee crashed to the floor. "I don't pay you to sit on your asses!"

"But boss, we were told to lie low today, after what happened last night..." the middle one said rapidly as he stood back up. He bowed again just as rapidly. They each had dyed their hair, one a dark red, the other a light brown. This one had the lightest hair, a blondish color almost as if he used hydrogen peroxide. The other two peeked up expectantly at Kano from a half-bow position, their hands on their thighs and butts sticking out. They were almost hiding behind their bangs.

Kano stood for a moment, starring at them for dramatic effect. "Hmmph." Kano snorted as he rubbed his nose with his thumb again. He continued to peer at them through his sunglasses, which he neglected to take off when he entered the building. If he were truly angry, by this point he would have grabbed them by their hair and pummeled their heads against the wooden doorframe. They had yet to see him truly angry. They would in good time, unless they cleaned up their act working for him.

"This place is disgusting!" he shouted, ignoring the kid's response. He picked up a pillow and threw it at one, then a soda can at another. "Clean it up!" he shouted. "It smells like *shit* here. Where are we, in some *inaka* pig sty, huh? Pigs live cleaner than you all do! Clean it up now!" Kano picked up the side of the dinning table and turned it over for good measure. "And one of you get that *baka* friend of yours up front to help too. I don't *ever* want to come here and see this place like this again!"

Kano knew they were keeping a low profile at the safehouse since he gave the order himself through intermediaries. This particular safehouse served as a repository of sorts for younger initiates who worked delivering whatever he needed them to, doing all the menial tasks for any of his many businesses, working the racetracks and gambling halls, making deliveries. Perhaps eventually they would graduate to roughing up people late in paying their loans, or evicting people from their property, but they were way too soft for such work now. They were *bosozoku* wannabes, wanting to join biker gangs that Kano controlled up and down the west coast. But these new initiates seemed to get softer and softer each generation. These three would need a lot of roughing-up to get them ready for the real work he needed done.

"Is it just the three of you?" asked Kano. "Where are your *sempais*?" Blondie, too afraid to move or talk, responded with a grunt in the affirmative. They remained in bowing positions at the far ends of the room, away from Kano.

Kano knew that no one else was at the house, but he pressed them anyway. They needed to learn to be aware of their surroundings and of the comings and goings of their superiors. "Where's Jun-kun, and Haru? How about Mori-kun? Eh?" The kids were silent, wondering how to respond as their gaze shifted from one corner of the room to the next. They were obviously unsure. But Kano knew, the *sempais* were working his pachinko parlors. He had already checked on them. "You must always know where your *sempais* are, always! Do you understand that? Tell them what happened tonight, and that I'll have a talk with them later. I'm going upstairs. Now get to cleaning, damn it!" At this, Kano threw a glass ashtray at Blondie, turned and went upstairs.

Those morons didn't see Tadaishi come in the back entrance, Kano thought as he climbed the stairs to the second and then to the third floor of the building, where he kept his private quarters.

Kano went into his private den, a room three tatami mats in size and more of a meditation room than a den. An alcove featured a scroll showing the Chinese character *Mu*, or "nothingness," and no other decoration was present. There were no books or bookcases, and only a small table stood on the far tatami mat with paper and an empty ink well. The brushes had been cleaned and stored in a drawer beneath, but Kano was not there often enough to practice his calligraphy.

Tadaishi sat on his knees next to the desk. When Kano entered, Tadaishi placed his hands in front of his knees and bowed deeply. "Kano-san, thank you for inviting me to talk with you tonight."

"*Seikichi-kun, hisashiburi desu ne...*It's been a while since we've talked in person..." Kano said in a guttural and menacing voice. He frowned deeply as he glared at Tadaishi. Even though he attended some of Tadaishi's campaign rallies, he did so discreetly to check on him and to gauge the general pulse of the crowds. He rarely spoke to Tadaishi directly, instead using intermediaries to conduct most of their regular business. This evening, however, was not business as usual.

Without stopping, Kano went to the alcove and pulled at the right frame board that bordered the alcove. It popped open and then turned toward the calligraphy on hidden hinges. Kano stuck his hand in the back of the wall, unlatched a hidden door from the inside, which in turn allowed the back wall of the alcove to open outward as Kano pulled on it. This revealed a small and well-worn wooden ladder. Kano entered the alcove quickly and began to climb up. "Come with me," he ordered Tadaishi, without looking back to him.

Kano climbed into the small attic that ran the length and width of the building. The frame of the roof was so low that neither he nor any visitors could stand up straight. Kano liked that this setup, since it reminded all his visitors of the lessons of humility. All were forced to bow to enter and to participate. The space was bare and without distractions, another sign of humility.

Kano sat at the far end of the space, watching while Tadaishi climbed into the attic space. Kano, still wearing his leather gloves, took out a handkerchief and brushed off the dust from his shoulders. He flicked the handkerchief once, took off his sunglasses with his other hand and then blew on one of the lenses so forcefully that spittle collected on the surface. He began to wipe the lens slowly as Tadaishi situated himself across from Kano.

"Wait there," said Kano as he put down his tinted glasses with one hand while pulling out a folded cell phone from his breast pocket with the other. He powered it on, pressed a number, and the beeping digits cut through the dead silence of the attic.

"*Moshi moshi*," Tadaishi heard on the other end.

"Kensuke! It's me. Tell me, what morons have you recruited for the organization this time?"

Tadaishi could hear the voice on the other rise to another octave as it answered, but he could not make out what was being said. Tadaishi had heard the name "Kensuke" before, knew him to be one of Kano's motorcycle gang goons handling some of Kano's more sensitive dirty work, but that's all he knew and even that was too much as far as Tadaishi was concerned. Aware that the phone call was as much for him as it was for Kensuke, Tadaishi made an effort to show complete disinterest and kept a steady gaze at the mat away from his benefactor.

"Those idiots are lazing around on *my* time and in *my* house. You need to whip them into shape, get them out there with some gainful employment!" He paused as Kensuke hurriedly responded. "Yes I know I said to lie low, but that doesn't mean they get to laze around all day in their shit-stained underwear watching samurai movies and eating mochi cakes, damn it! Now put them to work, and don't *you dare* talk back to me again, got that?"

Kano frowned deeply at the phone as he jabbed his finger at the "off" button. He watched as it powered down, and then he threw it into the corner behind Tadaishi. Kano then looked directly at Tadaishi.

"Now, Seikichi-kun." Kano took a long breath as he reoriented his attention to the issue at hand. "We had a recent...misunderstanding, I believe." Kano picked up his sunglasses, turned them over once to examine both sides of the lens, and began wiping the inner portion of the lens slowly. "I buy the votes that get you elected. I make sure you get on certain committees in the Diet, in our national parliament, and in turn you supply me with certain requested information."

Kano then lifted his glasses up to the light on the ceiling to check for any missed smudges on the lens he just cleaned. He then dropped his gaze and focused it directly at Tadaishi. "I've held up my end of our relationship, Seikichi-kun. But you seem to have forgotten your duties in return."

"I should not be here, Kano-sensei. Here of all places...I have a whole series of campaign stops. I need to prepare speeches, talking points. This has become quite a contentious election this year, with all the things Seitoh and her party has planned if they gain seats in the election and with the..." Tadaishi paused, unsure how to approach what he knew to be the central issue of this meeting, "with the, er, incident last night especially. People are protesting now, for, against, these days we're not even sure sometimes. I've never seen it like this before. Elections used to be such...orderly things."

"Seikichi-kun, just keep showing up. You do what you do. Make speeches, give platitudes at the debates about serving the people. You let me supply the votes. Now..."

"But Kano-sensei, this is different I tell you. I'm not so sure now, if you, er, if we can get the votes this year..."

Kano put down his glasses next to his knee, then lunged forward and slapped Tadaishi across the face. "Shut-up goddamn it!" he growled, pointing his forefinger directly in Tadaishi's face. "Focus, you understand me? For me to get the votes, I need you to get the information I ask for, understand? You failed me last night. You *did not* get me the information I needed, you did not tell me that they were planning a raid on one of my shipments!"

Tadaishi sat silently holding his check as Kano sat back down.

"I started to wonder some time ago whether this is still a mutually beneficial relationship. Why should I buy *you* the votes, why should I support those provincials in the *Hakuzan-kai* for you. Why not bankroll a new candidate, someone a little more...aggressive? Someone a little more appreciative, who remembers his duties in return? I wonder, what purpose do you serve? You certainly did nothing over the past several weeks to warn me of the coming raid. Do you know how much I lost in that one shipment? Hmmm?"

"I..." Tadaishi stammered, "Kano-sensei, no one told the parliamentary transportation committee that there was any planning underway for such an operation. The ruling cabinet has been very tight-lipped about security matters, they've really clamped down...I had no way of knowing!"

"That's no excuse! *Find a way*, Tadaishi. Get on your sources connected with the Ministry of Transportation, they're the ones that run the Coast Guard, after all! And see about your contacts on defense and police-related matters, while you're at it. And do it now, understand? I need to know what they have planned *now*, what routes they're following *now*. Understand?"

Kano picked up his glasses and began to clean the lens again. "Seikichi-kun, perhaps you don't understand me. Let me tell you of the consequences. This isn't just about supplying votes on this end of Japan any more. There are a lot of tabloids in Tokyo, you know. They would love a juicy story about a certain representative and his, shall we say, proclivities, eh? They would love to learn of your extra-curricular activities, understand? If they were to find out, you would quickly become convict Tadaishi, not Representative Tadaishi. Eh?"

Tadaishi gritted his teeth. "I wish in all humility to ask your for-giveness for my failure," and he bowed his head to the floor. "*Yarasete itadakemasu.* I will undertake to do my best to rectify this situation, sir." Tadaishi lifted his head from the floor and only slowly dared to raise his gaze from the space between them to Kano's eyes.

"Good. Now, you know what I really want to hear, hmmm? I want to hear the news from Tokyo. I want to hear what is going on, when these next raids might be planned, where they are patrolling. They can't be everywhere. Where will they be? I need schedules and routes…" Kano reached for his glasses and began cleaning the other lens.

"Certainly, Kano-sensei. Now if you'll forgive me, I have work to do." He bowed again.

"Get the information, soon!" Kano ordered, and he nodded his head once to Tadaishi in dismissal as he grunted. Tadaishi then backed his way to the ladder to descend to the floor below. After his head disappeared below the floorboard, Kano took out his hand-kerchief to wipe the beads of sweat that were beginning to form on his brow. *We need that next shipment, soon,* thought Kano. *This has become an expensive election indeed…*

One more shipment. Then Kano could settle accounts and make one final push, through the members of parliament he sup-ports and through other avenues, to legalize gambling and the construction of casinos. Then he could go mainstream, develop casinos along the Sea of Japan to attract the millionaires and bil-lionaires from China, Southeast Asia, and beyond. His construction companies could develop vast new tracts of land, expand airports and port facilities, to attract new tourists and gamblers, the interna-tional high-rollers who go to the Macaos and Vegases of the world.

No more mom-and-pop clientele, or pasty-faced teenagers trying to scam his machines at the pachinko parlors. No more financial authorities breathing down his neck looking for money laundering that until now was easy to hide. It was time to go mainstream, and in a big way.

This would cost money across the board, so this last haul had to be big to pay for it all.

CHAPTER 7 - INTERROGATION

Trinh Archer had visited the Tokyo Detention Center on many occasions. While serving as the duty officer during her off-hours, a role all embassy employees had to take turns filling in case any U.S. citizens got into legal trouble, she was sometimes called to the center to meet with detained Americans, hear their cases, and explain her role in the legal process. The interaction often ended by giving them a list of local lawyers who spoke English and their phone numbers, and wishing them good luck. They needed it. The Japanese legal system was not lenient on guilty foreigners, at least in the beginning, nor were the Japanese inmates. And most who ended up at the Tokyo Detention Center, Archer knew beyond any doubt, were indeed guilty.

At other times, however, she visited the center on official duty to interview drug dealers, organized crime figures, and smugglers as part of her work on illegal networks in Asia. Tokyo was the hub of the Asian financial world and Japan's high-tech industry. Thus it was the Mecca for Asian organized crime and the Medina of state-sponsored illicit activities. Archer's specialty at the embassy was following—and when possible, taking down—transnational organized criminal and state-sponsored smuggling networks.

That's how she came to know Ryutaro Nishi, for a second time.

• • •

"Get your cocktail dress on, Trinh, embassy's hosting a function tonight, and you need to get out for a few hours," Maddy Tucker said as she popped her head over Archer's cubicle wall unexpectedly.

"I've got some more cables to go through, and then I have to…"

"Don't worry about that this afternoon, it's Friday so consider yourself dismissed from your duties. Go change, and meet me in the lobby at 6 sharp. I need someone to ride shotgun at tonight's cocktail reception. That's an order!" Tucker said in feigned seriousness as she smiled at Archer.

Archer met Tucker in the lobby at the top of the hour, and they departed for the embassy function. They arrived at the Tokyo Ritz-Carlton fifteen minutes later where the function was being held. Once in the large banquet hall inside, they instinctively separated to work the room. Having just arrived to her new post in Tokyo a week earlier, Archer felt drained and did not feel like socializing tonight, so she went to the bar to get a Sprite. She avoided the glasses from any of the many passing waiters since they all contained champagne or wine, with beer flowing copiously from the taps at stations along the sides of the room. Without ice, and as a sufficiently bubbly and clear substance, no one would suspect her of avoiding alcohol. She scanned the room disinterestedly as she sipped from her glass.

While she stood a hair below six feet tall, she carried herself as if she were closer to seven. She had long ago ceased being self-conscious about her height, and in fact she had become comfortable enough in her body that she moved with a mixture of silent confidence and unconscious grace. She was toned without being muscular. Her shoulders were too wide and bulky to be a runway model, but not so wide as to look unfeminine. Her jet-black hair was thicker than most Asian women's, influenced by her half-Kaw Native-American lineage. And unlike many other young, trendy Asian women, she did not color it. She also kept her hair longer than was the style, but the soft and silky sheen accentuated and softened her tall frame. In Asia, even with Asian features, Trinh Archer stood out.

"*Aachaa-san*, is that you?" she heard a voice beckon from the crowd. She looked around but did not recognize anyone. Since the men mostly wore well-tailored dark suits, white shirts, and dark ties, the male Japanese attendees at first blended together in a sea of formality. And then a younger-looking man and his companion approached her out of the crowd. His face was flushed red from the third toast of the evening, and he was smiling broadly.

"Archer-san, that is you, I thought so!" he said. "It has been a while…" he said as he bowed to her.

"Eh…" she could only manage a surprised reaction from the suddenness of the man's approach. "Yes, it has been a while…" She bowed formally in return.

"Oh yes, you wouldn't remember me, of course," he said quickly to save face. "I arrived in Kabul before you departed. My name is Nishi. Ryutaro Nishi, of the Security Bureau in the National Police Agency. I worked at the Japanese Embassy in Kabul when you were the liaison between our and the U.S. Embassy there," Nishi explained.

"Oh Nishi-san, of course!" she half-lied in reply. She recognized him, but she did not immediately recall why. "Yes it has been a while, huh! How are you these days? You are back in Tokyo, I see…"

"Yes I am back. I did my duty and returned to a new post here in Tokyo…"

"Returned to a post?" his equally drunk Japanese companion scoffed. "You practically took over the whole damn office, cleaning up after that washed-up bureau chief! Don't be so modest, Nishi-san, you're the youngest to reach this position!"

Archer knew that normally even Japanese rank-conscious professionals would indeed be outwardly very modest about their position in any given pecking order, but that modesty among colleagues went out the door by around the second toast at any given social event. After that, everything became a fair topic of conversation, which made her work so much easier.

Nishi's talkative companion turned to her and half-whispered: "He's the deputy chief of the Security Bureau at the National Police Agency. For careerists like Nishi, that's the heart and soul of the NPA, just so you know…" He winked at her. "And they always have a fast track immediately to the top!" Some beer splattered out of his glass he held as he motioned toward the ceiling. He smiled at his social faux pas.

"Hmm, is that so?" Archer replied in feigned ignorance. She knew the implication of Nishi's position, but she wanted to see if Nishi's companion would say anything more.

"No, nothing like that, I am just honored to have the opportunity to fulfill the duties of the office to the best of my abilities…" Nishi interrupted, a little embarrassed by his friend's fawning.

Maddy Tucker joined the small group holding a half-filled glass of chardonnay. "Nishi-san, Murata-san, so good to see you both," she said as she bowed slightly but formally. "We are so glad you could join us on this occasion." She then looked toward Trinh. "And I see you have met Archer-san, a new arrival at the mission." A waiter started to refill her glass, but she waved him off after a just a trickle.

"Yes, we are getting re-acquainted. We actually worked together in Kabul. She was quite a legend among the Japanese community there…"

"Oh really?" Tucker said, obviously surprised by the sudden and unexpected praise. "How so?"

"She worked as a liaison between your people and the Japanese mission in Kabul. Her Japanese skills were impeccable. She even briefed the ambassador personally on several occasions."

"Well my Japanese skills have gotten rusty again, unfortunately," Archer said in her own attempt at humility.

"No, nothing like that!" Nishi declared. "She provided very useful intelligence quite often. I'll never forget, just after I arrived, she rushed to our compound late in the evening to brief us on a plot to blow up a Japanese aid convoy that we had scheduled to depart early the next morning. Six vehicles in all…"

"They were all thin-skin vehicles too," Archer added almost as an aside to Tucker, referring to the lack of physical protection for the vehicles.

"Yes, many of our aid convoys unfortunately lacked armored civilian vehicles, so it was especially dangerous for our people. At any rate, we delayed the departure until we could work out another route. By mid-morning, we had heard that another caravan had been attacked in that same location, and all the vehicles had been destroyed and any survivors were taken hostage by the local militants. It was very unfortunate for them, of course. But it would have been a huge problem for our government here had it been a Japanese convoy with Japanese casualties or hostages."

"We attempted to warn all of our partners about the impending attack, but sadly an unaffiliated NGO did not get the warning in time, so they were the unfortunate victims of the attack," Archer explained, looking into her glass as she did.

"Yes, my ambassador wanted to thank you officially, but unfortunately you left so soon afterward. We didn't have a chance to properly thank you."

"Thank you Nishi-san for the thought, but the ambassador did indeed thank me several weeks later, and I felt very honored," Archer replied.

"You know how we Japanese value ceremony, so a word of thanks was not adequate!" Nishi said animatedly. "Here is my card with my contact information. As an expert on the region, I want you to brief my people. I will also set up a meeting with some of the deputy cabinet secretaries, and maybe the chief of intelligence too. They are always looking for expert speakers to engage with."

"I am honored, Nishi-san. I am now working on illicit networks here in Northeast Asia, perhaps we can exchange information on them too."

"Yes, we will do that, excellent. Now I have to excuse myself, but it was a pleasure meeting you again, Archer-san!" Nishi and his companion Murata bowed and then disappeared into the crowd.

Tucker turned to Archer. "That was Deputy Chief Ryutaro Nishi, of the NPA Security Bureau. I was actually surprised to see him here tonight. I've only met him a few times. He's quite a legend in Japanese circles, for reasons I'm not quite clear about. You seem to know him though…"

"Yeah, it's coming back to me now," Archer said. "You know how officials in foreign missions came and went in the war zone, and the Japanese were no different. I remember now that Nishi was a very engaging man, really interested in improving things for local Afghans."

"It seems you really made an impression on Nishi, if he's not playing you. Doesn't seem like he is, so congratulations on that. I don't remember seeing that Ambassadorial recognition in your personnel file, though."

"It was a small ceremony weeks after the fact, due to operational issues, and I was wheels-up the day after the ceremony. To be honest there was so much going on at the time, and I don't even remember who from our office attended. That was usually the case since my boss, the deputy chief of ops, was a womanizing drunk and didn't know or care to know what we were doing anyway."

Maddy gave a knowing look and nodded, but she did not say anything in response.

"Plus, it's not like we completely averted the attack. People were still killed."

"Well, you provided warning, which is our most important function, and you saved some lives, at least. You kept it from becoming a major news item here, and sitting where I do now I can see how big a deal that really is, so congratulations," Tucker said warmly. "We haven't gotten this kind of direct access operationally with the NPA before. I'm sure you'll make the most of it." Tucker raised her glass to Archer and smiled, even as she scanned the room for other officials to engage with.

•   •   •

Like many bureaucratic terms in Japan, the name "Tokyo Detention Center" was understated to the point of being euphemistic. This was unlike any "detention center" in any other developed area of the world. It was a hulking multi-wing complex in Katsushika Ward, a suburb in the far eastern part of Tokyo. Some 12 stories tall, the building branched out in two wings on either side in an X pattern. Two smaller wings jutted out the front and back of the building, so that the entire structure took the shape of an asterisk as seen from the sky. Not only did it house recently detained individuals, but also corrupt politicians, repeat offenders awaiting trial, and hardened criminals. It also hosted a hanging chamber where many of Japan's executions took place. The facility therefore served many functions beyond that of a way-station "detention center." And despite its modern exterior, life was not easy there.

Archer approached from Kosuge Station through multiple gates to get to the main building. She also passed by a dozen media vans parked along the central access road. The loud sounds of generators emanated from the backs of the vans. Thick, black cables led from the vans to the half-dozen white media tents that had been set up facing the facility. The tents were arrayed so that the camera angles could feature the detention center complex in the background of each of the correspondents standing immediately in front of the tents. The tents protected the cameras, equipment and crew while the correspondents each stood in the open air, the weather adding dramatic effect to their reporting. Large, bright spotlights shone on each of the correspondents, and the scene from afar seemed almost as if the detention center itself was projecting search lights along the facade of the building for an escaped convict. The government had obviously given special permission to broadcast from there, Archer realized instinctively, to help amplify the story to the public for dramatic effect.

As she neared the walkway to the visitor center that ran parallel to the media tents, she made sure to approach from the far end. Archer pulled a black cap from her bag and pulled it down low, and then pulled up her hood over her head. A slight mist was visible in the spotlights, so wearing a hood did not seem out of place. It wasn't the rain she was concerned about, though. She did not want to be seen on camera.

Archer heard a cacophony of chatter from the correspondents talking to their respective television audiences as she approached the entrance. "The lone survivor of last night's dramatic incident, that claimed two innocent lives of a local Japanese maritime family who were just trying to get one last catch on the last evening of squidding, is now being held here at the Tokyo Detention Center," one correspondent reported. "The case is sending shock waves through the political establishment immediately ahead of the election…" he continued. She heard another declare that "perhaps because of politics, or perhaps because of timidity, no one at the Japan Coast Guard or Ministry of Defense was in a position to order the detention or sinking of the suspect fishing vessel that officials believe ultimately caused the death of two innocents, one a young girl…" A third told viewers that "last night's incident has dramatically renewed concerns about links to organized smuggling, and per-haps even state-sponsored terrorist operations targeting Japan…"

It should not have been like this, she thought to herself. *Operation Crimson Leaves would've been a success, should've been a success, had we just maintained better situational awareness. Why didn't we see that a fishing boat was out there, even if its lights were out? Now two innocent civilians are dead, and the perpetrators have escaped. Except for this one kid, left holding the bag…*

Archer dashed onto the walkway and turned to the entrance door as quickly and as unobtrusively as possible. She pulled at the door of the visitors center, but it was locked. She pulled at another door, and it too was locked. She glanced up to the corner of the entryway at the security camera, pulled back her hood and lifted her cap, and looked again. The door buzzed, and she entered.

Archer was greeted by two uniformed women at the security check point, one younger and one older. "I'm Trinh Archer from the U.S. Embassy," she told the women, "here to meet Deputy Bureau Chief Ryutaro Nishi of the National Police Agency." She presented her official identification.

The older woman scanned a list of expected visitors, then turned to the next page, furrowing her brow. Archer hadn't seen these two during her pervious late night visits to the center, but they change personnel often.

"*Aachaa-san desu ne?*" the woman said to confirm she found the right person on the list. "Please step this way," she motioned toward the body scanner, "and place any bags or other objects here." Archer laid her bag flat on the conveyer belt, which started as she did so. The younger uniformed officer examined the monitor as the bag passed through the scanner.

Archer stepped into the body scanner, which beeped. The younger officer looked up suddenly, as if panicked that this foreigner was about to try something. The older woman walked to Archer with her hand-held wand, and asked her to raise her arms. Archer had already done so, however, having been through this drill many times in a variety of circumstances. *What did I forget to take off now?* Archer wondered to herself.

The wand remained silent as the older woman motioned over Archer's outstretched arms and front torso. She repeated the motion on her back, and as she moved the wand downward to Archer's lower back, it buzzed loudly.

Damn, that's what I forgot, Archer remembered. The older lady began to tap Archer in that area before Archer could pull out the knife and explain what it was. The unformed lady pulled at Archer's pants to retrieve the flat, folded knife that was secured by a clip to Archer's waistband.

The lady held it up in front of her eyes and turned it slowly, wondering what it was. "*Ehhhhhh,*" the younger officer gasped involuntarily as she stood next to her colleague to examine the knife.

It was clear to Archer that these ladies had experienced very few instances when a visitor had so much as a wooden toothpick in their possession, much less a weapon of any sort. While many of the individuals held in the detention facility had rap sheets that included possession of illegal weapons, visitors were almost never caught trying to smuggle anything in or otherwise found to possess any weapons.

They began whispering between themselves, obviously sure that this was most certainly not allowed in the facility, but unsure whether it was illegal in Japan and if so, what they would have to do with this American from the U.S. Embassy for attempting to bring it into the facility. Archer could not quite make out their hurried discussion.

"This is *not* allowed in this facility," the older officer firmly asserted. She opened it to reveal a rounded, sharpened edge that would be deadly in the right hands. The ladies gasped even more audibly this time at the site of the curved blade of Archer's Karambit. Developed with Canada's Joint Task Force special operations group, its blade was shaped like a talon, and it would not simply cut but quickly disembowel any attacker with one slice. Archer was pissed that she forgot to better conceal this weapon, because it was expensive and she didn't want it confiscated. *At least they weren't paying attention to the Glauca B1 in the bag*, she thought to herself.

"Yes, certainly, I'm very sorry about this," Archer began to explain. "As a single woman walking in a major city at night, I of course want to protect myself from any..."

"It is *not* legal to carry this kind of weapon in our country," the lady declared as she continued to look almost in horror at the shape of the blade. Archer was certain that she was incorrect and overly sensitive, but she could also tell from her tone of voice that the situation had progressed beyond any sort of explanation or negotiation, and the two uniformed ladies were no longer open to discussing the situation further. *Ladies, you have no idea*, Archer wanted to shout at the naive women across from her, *the Taliban pick their toenails with knives bigger than this...!*

"I will have to report this to central security immediately," she said as she picked up a phone and pressed a button.

Just then, the main door to the facility opened. "Aachaa-san, there you are. I've been waiting for you inside for the last ten minutes," a man said as he entered the screening room.

"Deputy Bureau Chief Nishi, I'm so sorry to keep you waiting," said Archer, stepping toward him and bowing apologetically.

Nishi raised an eyebrow as Archer bowed deeply in front of him, unaccustomed to this display of obsequiousness from his American colleague.

"I was still going through security, and I am so sorry to have created trouble for your security personnel," she continued, bowing again to provide a face-saving gesture for the two uniformed ladies.

Nishi looked at the ladies holding the knife, and then he understood what Archer was doing. "I had told them to expect you, but it seems the new shift just arrived and was not informed?" Nishi said motioning to the ladies. "But I'm sure everything is in order here, right?" Nishi looked sternly at the two women, who did not know how to respond. "Ms. Archer is on your visitors' list, correct?" Nishi asked as he reached for the clipboard that the older lady held.

"Yes, she is, but..."

"But I unthinkingly brought a weapon to the facility, Deputy Bureau Chief Nishi, I'm so sorry to have caused a delay because of this..." Archer interjected. She bowed again in apology.

"I'm sure everything is in order," Nishi said. "Yes, here she is." He pointed to Archer's name as he handed the clipboard back to the older guard. "And is *this* the cause of the delay?" he asked incredulously as he picked up the knife. "My sushi-making grandmother has knives bigger and sharper than this!" Nishi said, laughing. He turned to Archer. "You have no need for this in the facility, of course," he explained to Archer, "and you may leave this here with the ladies for safe-keeping." He turned to the ladies, 'I'm sure that is alright with you, yes?"

The two looked at each other and then back at Nishi. "Yes, deputy bureau chief, we will hold it for Ms. Archer until she leaves," the older said as the two bowed in accepting the order.

"There now, shall we?" Nishi said as he motioned to the door. He opened it, and he and Archer entered the facility.

Just beyond the entrance, Archer walked past multiple rows of orange plastic chairs that were attached to the floor in the waiting area and immovable. Above was a screen showing multiple rows of different colors, corresponding to the locations where visitors would meet their loved ones currently being held in the facility. Only black spaces were visible where visitors' numbers would be displayed during operating hours. They passed under the monitor to the back of the empty visitors' center.

Nishi escorted Archer into the complex itself on the way to the interrogation room. "Given the high-profile nature of the defendant and his crime, we thought it best to have him centrally located here in Tokyo to undergo interrogation, which might take some time," Nishi explained. "I plan to personally head the interrogation."

"Convenient, if he is convicted, since you can carry out the death penalty here too," Archer joked. She was alluding to the center's role as hosting Japan's death row, where high-profile detainees including the Aum Shinrikyo cultists have been held while awaiting their death sentences. The doomsday cult had conducted a series of increasingly brazen attacks with chemical and biological weapons in several major cities, which culminated in a multi-pronged attack on the Tokyo metro that was meant to kill or maim many high-level officials commuting into downtown Tokyo. Shoko Asahara, the leader of the cult who was perhaps the most famous death row inmate, directed his followers to worship the center as a holy place while the cultists were held there, even as others conspired over the years to free him by force.

"No, certainly nothing like that," Nishi declared. While he had an amiable enough personality, even if a bit stoic, Archer noticed that he was always quick to defend official Japan from any possible slight, real or perceived. "Certainly he wouldn't be put to death here, since he was a mere bystander so far as we can ascertain. The system must take its course, too, but there is no reason to expect he will be executed for his crime. In the meantime, we must gain as much information from him as possible, to bring to justice those who were really responsible for last night."

They entered an elevator and went to the eighth floor. The doors opened to reveal a blue hallway. Archer immediately recognized it as the floor where Japan's death-row inmates were housed, and where the execution chamber was located as well. Nishi seemed, or pretended to seem, unaware of the irony of their conversation just a few minutes before. Despite Nishi's protestations, the national police had indeed decided to keep Taro Hatano on death row, at least unofficially for the time being. But Archer remained silent.

They walked down the hall. As if reading Archer's mind, Nishi stopped at a metal door and explained in a straightforward tone, "because of overcrowding we have to keep Hatano here."

Archer could not help but add: "And the psychological effect of being on death row helps the interrogation too…"

"That is an added if inadvertent advantage, but it is not the original reason for doing so…"

Yeah right, Archer thought to herself, silently admiring the added psychological impact this was sure to have on Hatano.

"…here, have a glance at the suspect," he said as he pushed aside the cover of a peephole into the room.

She saw a teenage boy hunched over, his hands clasped on the table in front of him. His longish dark hair obscured his face, but she could tell from his bobbing head and pool of tears and spittle dripping from his clasped hands onto the table's surface that he was sobbing, and had been sobbing for some time.

"I'll take you to the control room where you can observe the next interrogation, over here." Nishi said this with a restrained smile. Archer could see that he relished this fresh opportunity to terrorize a young wannabe tough into further confessions. From the boy's body language, Archer realized that the boy had already been broken and had most likely confessed the few details of his involvement hours ago. He probably didn't have anything else to confess about last night, since his handlers, or in this case his older brother, most likely didn't tell him much about their work at all except where to go and what to do once he got there. But having seen the needless death of an innocent family with her own eyes during last night's operation, and the destruction of peoples' lives because of drugs and the scumbags peddling the stuff throughout her career and before, she did not feel sorry at all for the boy. She almost volunteered to go in for Nishi herself to see what she could do with the boy.

Nishi escorted Archer to a room at the end of the hall where a monitor displayed most of the room. Nishi then left, and moments later she saw Nishi enter the interrogation room on the monitor, accompanied by a large and imposing man who took up a position in the corner behind suspect Hatano. Nishi in turn sat at the table in front of him.

Hatano looked up as they entered the room and glanced furtively at the man behind him and then back at Nishi. "No, no, not again, I told you all I know…" He then looked back at the man again. "Not him again, please!" He turned back toward Nishi, almost lunging across the table at him. "Please…!" he beseeched Nishi.

The man pulled him by the shoulders back down into the seat, and suspect Hatano put his head in his hands and began to sob. "Please, no, not again!" he whispered almost inaudibly. "I just need some sleep, please…!" he wailed.

"You have not told us everything, suspect Hatano. We know you are holding back information." Nishi then paused to gauge Hatano's reaction. "The driver of the boat was your brother, Taro, after all. You've told us very little of his involvement in all this over the years. You must know what he was up to, who he worked with. He was your brother after all."

Suspect Hatano jumped up and slapped his hands on the table. "What the hell more should I know, eh?" he shouted as spittle spewed from his mouth toward Nishi. The man behind him slammed him down again in his seat. "Like I told you before, my older brother was a member of a *bosozoku* motorcycle gang. He was away a lot, for days, weeks at a time. I would see him come and go, he didn't tell me anything. Yeah I wanted to go hang with him, he had a cool souped-up bike and awesome gear, but he wouldn't let me come. He never let me come. Not until a few nights ago, when he said I could start making some money so I could get a bike too, really learn to ride..."

"Taro-kun, where did he get his money? Who was he working for?" Nishi demanded more firmly now. "You said he had a custom bike, how'd a supposedly out-of-work teenage punk get the money for that?"

"Hell if I know, I never asked, he never told me, I didn't even think about it. I just figured he had connections and all, was doing some *'baito* part-time work..."

"Connections, eh?" Nishi asked rhetorically, and nodded once at his colleague, Menda, standing behind Hatano. Menda then grabbed the back of Hatano's collar and pulled at it, so that the front of his prisoner's suit began to cut off Hatano's windpipe. At the same time he lifted Hatano up from the seat and kicked it out from under him. Hatano began to cough hoarsely and flail at the man's grasp behind him, but he was unable to free himself.

Nishi came around the table and leaned directly into Hatano's face. "Who did your brother work for, suspect Hatano, eh? What kind of '*baito*' did he do? Where did he get his money, huh? You're lying, suspect Hatano! You know who he worked for, because *you too* worked for them!"

Nishi grabbed Hatano's flailing hand at the wrist, pulled it down as he pushed his elbow up, and then forced Hatano's arm behind his back. He grabbed Hatano's prison suit just below the grip of his colleague, who then let go. Nishi slammed Hatano's torso down on the table, being careful not to cause his face to hit the surface too hard as well. Last night's accident would be more than sufficient to explain any minor injuries in the coming days, but they couldn't inflict too much bodily damage here…

Nishi leaned down toward Hatano's ear and shouted. "Tell me where the money came from! Tell me who gave the orders! Tell me who you and your brother worked for!"

Hatano coughed and wheezed uncontrollably from Nishi's tightening grip.

Nishi then lowered his voice. "We have all night, suspect Hatano. If you cooperate, if you tell us all you know, you can rest. You can meet the rest of your fate in peace. But until you fully cooperate, until you tell us everything you know, you are mine. Do you understand, suspect Hatano? *Mine.*"

Nishi released his grip. Hatano continued to cough, and then slid off the table and slumped into a ball on the floor.

"The choice is yours, suspect Hatano."

Nishi left the room, followed by Menda.

A moment later, Nishi entered the monitoring room. He adjusted his shirt, which had become partially untucked. He pulled out a cigarette, lit it, and took a long drag. Nishi looked at the cigarette, as if to contemplate the possibilities with it, and then looked at Archer. "There is no need to report our session with suspect Hatano back to your government, correct?" Smoke flowed from his mouth and nostrils as he said this, and then he took another long drag as he looked at Archer.

"I only came here for consultations with you and other law enforcement personnel, Inspector Nishi. I do not know anything about how you have conducted any interrogations with anyone who might or might not have been associated with last night's incident," Archer stated matter-of-factly.

"Yes, good. So let us continue with our"—Nishi took another drag of his cigarette, squinting his eyes as he did so—"consultations, diplomat Archer." Smoke came slowly from his mouth and nostrils again. Archer suppressed an urge to cough, even as her eyes began to water. "When you left the crime scene this morning, we were still trying to locate the two responsible for the pick-up and transport on land. We actually traced them back to a small storage facility north of the accident, just outside a village called Monzen. We surrounded the place quietly, so as not to impose too much on the local population. And we waited most of the afternoon for them to come out. When we finally went in to investigate, though, we found them dead…"

Impose too much on the population, thought Archer, *how quaint*. "Were they murdered?" asked Trinh, trying to hide her sudden welling of emotions. In a perfect world the fishing vessel would have had its lights on like all the others, and the seizure and clean-up operations would have taken place without incident. There would be several hundred pounds of *shabu*—crystal meth—and fentanyl, the new drug of choice in North America especially, in police custody along with over a dozen suspects, and North Korea's connection would be proven beyond a doubt. But the stupid kid thought he could outrun the Coast Guard, and ended up blowing up his boat and all the evidence on it, and the Japanese bureaucrats who planned the mission failed to take into account the major explosion masking the escape of a suspect fishing vessel with even more horsepower and firepower than previous smuggling vessels. The Korean boat had escaped, the main pick-up man was dead, and there was no *shabu* or cash used to pay for it. All they had to show for it was a scared kid who's brother had died and an empty storage shed with two more dead bodies. One of whom was *her* responsibility, though she would never divulge that to Nishi.

"Suicide, apparently. Autopsy report is still days away. They'd been dead for several hours by that point." Nishi mumbled more than usually with the cigarette between his lips as he reached for his box of cigarettes. As he did so, Archer turned and wiped a tear away from her eye. Nishi took out another cigarette, unaware of Archer's sudden turn away from him. He used the lit cigarette to light the next one. He stabbed the old one out on a side table holding recording equipment, then flicked it to the corner of the room. He took a drag from the fresh cigarette and exhaled again.

"Damn, another dead-end then," said Archer, cringing. Her hand balled into a fist and hit the table next to her. She rubbed her eyes, feigning fatigue when in fact she could barely keep her eyes open due to the smoke and her sorrow at losing an asset. She lost her best asset in this case last night, the one who led them to the drug deal in the first place. A good kid. But the key to keeping anyone talking was to keep them relaxed in their own environment, preferably fiddling with something, so she tried not to react to either the smoke or to the death of her guy. "What about the storage area itself, anything there?" she sniffled, re-engaging with Nishi.

"Nothing. They cleaned it out pretty good before they left. There were others around last night, we can tell. We just don't know who yet. They probably bugged out just before we got here..." Nishi paused for a moment, then asked: "How about on your end, what have your people found out?"

"I haven't gotten the reports yet." She paused for a moment, knowing that no more reports would come since her main contact was now dead. "I'll keep you posted."

Nishi took this as a sign that she needed to get back to downtown Tokyo. "Very well, I'll take you back down to the entrance." He opened the door, and Archer took several deep breaths in the hallway as she allowed Nishi to walk in front of her. She rubbed her eyes, again feigning fatigue.

"You should get some rest, Archer-san," he said as they entered the elevator. "It's been a long couple of months."

"And you should too, Nishi-san. You've been working to take down this network longer than I..."

"Not until Hatano-kun talks."

"Do you really think he's hiding information? He seems pretty beat-up now."

"Yes, he's answered the initial questions. But I think he has more information for us, he just doesn't know it yet. We'll get him so mixed up with these interrogation sessions the next few days that when we start asking the real questions, he won't be able to stop talking."

The elevator doors opened and Nishi escorted Archer through the empty waiting room to the security screening room. "Don't forget your knife," he said to Archer as she walked past the metal detectors. "You might need it to fend off those reporters out there. They're like a pack of wolves, hungry for any leads!"

Archer took the knife, clipped it inside the waistband of her pants, and exited the facility.

CHAPTER 8 - A BAD BREAK

Kano sat silently in the attic after Tadaishi had departed. He heard muffled sounds of the vacuum cleaner and other activity below, but no one would bother him up here. He laid his sunglasses to one side and pulled his glove off his right hand, finger by finger. He then pulled off his left glove. Three short stumps appeared instead of fingers, and Kano rubbed the knuckles over each. Only his pointer finger and thumb remained.

He had long ago put inserts into the otherwise limp last three fingers of his left glove, slightly bent to give the appearance of a normally formed hand. While they did not move, most people did not focus here. These fingers did not pull the trigger or slash with a blade. Most did not think twice about fingers that did not appear to move much. Certainly no one dared to ask if they did.

He felt a dull, throbbing pain at the end of one of his knuckles. Doctors told him he would experience phantom sensations and pain from time to time along the stumps, and it took all his willpower to avoid rubbing them through the gloves when the pain suddenly appeared while he was at work. Here, alone, he allowed himself to absentmindedly massage the deformed tips of his shortened fingers with his right palm as he sat, staring into the distance. He thought back to the time his fingers were taken from him. Along with his last remaining innocence.

•   •   •

"Takada-kun, we have decided to return to the homeland."

The young Takada Kano had just picked up a large helping of kimchi from the communal bowl with his long metal chopsticks, and his arm froze in mid-air as he heard those words. He looked at his uncle as he stammered.

"But…but uncle, you have not been in Korea since the '20s, when you were a teenager…" His shoulders slumped as he sat back in his seat slowly, his kimchi dripping on the table in front of him.

"Yes, it has certainly been a while. Indeed, that is why it is time for us to return. Your auntie and I have decided this is best."

"Many of our friends have already returned," added auntie. "It has been almost fifteen years since the end of the war. The nation is much better off as its own independent country, run by its own people, after centuries of subjugation. We are now independent, a new Democratic People's Republic is being built at long last as a modern nation, a peer among peers, newly rebuilt cities are springing up everywhere. They just need more workers to help, more Koreans like us. There are many opportunities now, unlike here, where we will always be second-class citizens. It is the thing for us to do."

"But father…what of the parlors? What is to happen to them?" Kano's cousin Taiei asked. Kano could tell that he remained equally bewildered, despite having been told earlier. Taiei's parents had yet to convince him of the wisdom of their plans, apparently.

"You and Takada-kun have done well helping us to run the pachinko parlors. It will take us some time to get all of our affairs in order as we make the move to the Democratic People's Republic. Like auntie said, there are many opportunities for us Koreans, especially for those of us with modern skills acquired while living abroad. And there are sure to be opportunities for you too, even though you were born here and, unfortunately, speak very poor Korean. But that is our fault, we failed you in that respect…"

Auntie looked pityingly at her husband. "Don't start that again. We did all we could under the circumstances…" She turned to the boys. "The boys can learn Korean quickly once they come, after all, *neh?* Right? Just find young, pretty Korean wives and you'll be fluent in no time!" She smiled wryly. "We want you two to continue to run the pachinko parlors for now. Pay us a portion of the income each year, and once economic conditions improve here, perhaps we can sell them for a nice profit and you can think of joining us. Uncle or I can come back to help with the sale, and we can split any profit as thanks for helping us."

"But uncle, you spent the last decade on the parlors, first setting them up after the war, and you were just starting to expand them!" Taiei said, almost pleading. Taiei clearly felt as Takada did, completely unprepared to take on full responsibility for running the fledgling pachinko parlor business.

"Yes it is true, it was a challenging time for us, but when has it not been challenging? I came over just after the Tokyo earthquake in 1923, looking for a job, any job. I was just a boy then, just needed to find work. So naive. Little did I know how tough it was for us as Koreans here, and how difficult things would be in the next twenty-five years. But by then my lot was set…"

"We lived in the slums of Tokyo, on the outskirts, so we escaped the fire-bombings, mostly," auntie continued as Uncle Kano sat in thought. "We took you in, Takada-kun, when you were barely three, because…" her voice began to quiver, "…because your parents were not so fortunate." A tear appeared in her eye as she spoke. "Many of our friends and loved ones were not so fortunate, but they are surely in a better place now."

"So just as it was time then for us to relocate, after the war, to build a new life ever so closer to the motherland here in Kanazawa as the land and economic reforms were taking place, so it is our time now to look to build an even better future not just for ourselves but for our fellow Koreans in a new country, in *our* country, at long last!" Upon saying this, Uncle Kano smiled as if sensing how glum his demeanor had become. He suddenly looked giddy. "'*North of the 38th Parallel,*' hmmm? Just as that wonderful book suggests, that's where we will find true equality! Not with that bastard lackey of the Americans in the South, who didn't experience a day of hardship in his life…!"

"But father, where will you go, what will you do?" asked Taiei.

"I've already talked with Korean Workers Party officials. They've assured me that as a successful businessman, even if modestly so, I'm sure to have a proper position in the government hierarchy. They need functionaries with real experience like myself, they say. The North lost many good people in the last thirty years. We're to meet with officials in Pyongyang in a week, and we will discuss my duties then."

"In a *week*?!" the younger Kano gasped.

"So that's it, it's all decided already, eh?" Taiei asked, dejected.

"Son, Takada-kun, we need you to handle the parlors until it is a good time to sell. Of course you may come with us, as soon as the property is taken care of. Until then you and Takada-kun are capable of running the parlors. It should not be too long. But you've lived your whole life here in Japan, so the situation is different for you."

"We'll leave the house to you boys for now, too, most of the furnishings. We'll also leave some of the keep-sakes," auntie said.

"Yes, my pin collection, that'll stay here for now. I'm sure I'll get more pins of our Great Leader, the flag of our new country, and many more patriotic pins like them once we arrive!" Uncle Kano sat in apparent deep thought about his future prospects, and then he declared: "We leave in a week!" He pounded the table in delight, and chuckled gleefully.

• • •

Six weeks later, Taiei and Takada Kano sat in the back office of the pachinko parlor, calculating their winnings for the day.

Pachinko was a vertical pinball game played with ballbearings fired in rapid succession during which players tried to collect as many ball bearings in slots as possible as they fell to the bottom of the machine. Gambling was illegal in Japan, but players could redeem their collected ballbearings for prizes. The prizes themselves started out as hard-to-acquire gray market goods in the immediate post-war years, but they eventually evolved into trinkets such as costume jewelry, badges, small toys that could be "sold" at separate merchant kiosks that paid cash for them. It wasn't gambling in the strict sense, but pachinko was fast becoming an obsession in post-war Japan in large part because of the potential winnings involved.

And Taiei and Takada continued with the tradition of strategically—and secretly—placing magnets in each of the machines and turning them on in the mornings to increase the number of ball-bearings players collected. The polarity of the magnets hidden in the backs of the pachinko games could be changed later in the day, with the magnets imperceptibly nudging the metal bearings away from the slots. Thus the house could attract players early in the day with larger winnings, who might linger longer or attract more customers who would then gradually start losing their winnings as the day progressed. With the game's popularity and managed outcomes, pachinko was also becoming a cash-generating machine for those elements looking to exploit the legal loopholes.

Sitting in their office and counting their earnings after the parlor had closed, Taiei and Takada heard a scratching noise at the back door. They looked at each other, cigarettes dangling from their lips. A stray dog, probably, their gazes said to each other. They wordlessly went back to work counting their yen. This time there was a louder noise.

Bang bang bang. Taiei paused again while Takada sat up straight, stood, and went to the back door. It was metal and barred shut from the inside. Takada looked out the peep hole and saw nothing but darkness outside. "What the..." he murmured.

"What's going on?" Taiei asked, clutching two full stacks of yen in mid-count.

"I don't know, nothing's out there." Just as he said that, he saw an object swing toward the door, and another *bang*! rang through the room.

"*Oooiiii*! In there!" a muffled voice said. "Come on out! We want to talk with you!" The two could not quite place the voice, but they instantly knew what he wanted. Taiei grabbed his revolver and pointed it at the closed door, quivering. Takada shoved his wad of cash into a drawer and picked up a baseball bat kept in the corner for just such an occasion. They both stood at the back door. Taiei shouted back, "You better go away now or we'll call the police! And don't think of coming in, we've got guns!"

"Guns, eh?" A voice asked from behind them. "Well, so do we."

Taiei and Takada turned to find three thugs with raised pistols pointed at their heads. They did not have to wait for the next command to drop their weapons. The two boys did so almost by instinct and then raised their hands. "Nakajima-kun?" Taiei gasped. One of the thugs went around them and unlocked the door to let their compatriot in.

"Call the *police*?" The thug asked as he stepped in, slapping Taiei in the face. "You're going to call the fucking *police* on us?! You still don't know the rules of this game, do you." He then looked back at the leader of the group, who nodded once. "We *own* the police!" The men then pounced on Taiei and Takada, striking them with blows to the head and the solar plexus. As the two slumped, the thugs continued to kick and stomp, gaining strength after each whimper and sob coming from Taiei and Takada. With two swift kicks to the face, they both went limp.

"Ok, let's get them out of here. Leave the money, we'll get that later," Ichiro Nakajima said with a chuckle.

•   •   •

Takada Kano regained consciousness first. He opened his eyes slowly, groaning as his vision slowly came into focus. He could not breath through his nose, because it was caked with drying blood. Drool trickled down his check onto the *tatami* mat beneath his head. He tried to sit up but his head began to throb immediately as he lifted it. He winced in pain. He noticed that his hands were bound behind his back. He tried to move his legs but they too were bound. He continued to lie there as he heard voices.

"So at last you have come to. Lift him up!" Kano heard from somewhere inside the room. He felt two strong grips seize him under the arms as two men yanked him up to a kneeling position, his arms and legs still bound. His head throbbed mercilessly, and Kano grimaced. He kept his head down to avoid further pain, and to avoid facing his tormentors directly.

"Unnnnhhhh..." came another voice from just outside his peripheral vision. It must be Taiei, Kano thought. He heard shuffling.

"*Yosh*, good, they are both up now," said the voice in front of the kneeling Kano, almost to himself. "Sit him up too!" he ordered.

"Nakajima-kun, why are you doing this...?" Taiei managed to say. Kano glanced inconspicuously to the side and caught a glimpse of his mangled face, and winced. "Our fathers were partners. My father lent your family the money to start up his parlor, they divided the region so our parlors wouldn't compete..."

"Nakajima-*san*," Nakajima asserted. "Give me *respect*."

Taiei hung his head at Nakajima's admonition in a subconscious realization that a childhood friendship had for some reason been forever lost.

"They might have had their agreement then, or maybe not," Nakajima continued. "Maybe my father lent yours the money, after the war, hmmm? Who's to say. But where are they now, hmm?" asked Nakajima. "Well, my parents are here, and our family is actively contributing to the wellness of society. Where are yours?" Nakajima paused as he leaned in front of Taiei. He lifted up Taiei's face to look him in the eyes. "Your parents have left this country, they have defected to the so-called 'Democratic People's Republic of Korea,' right?" Before Taiei could respond, Nakajima grabbed Taiei by the back of the neck and pressed his cheek near Taiei's ear and shouted, "your parents are fucking traitors, and that means you are too!" Nakajima grabbed Taiei's shoulders with both hands and flung him down onto the mat with such force that he slide into the wall behind him.

"Ach!" cried Taiei as he drew himself into a ball and winced in pain.

Nakajima sat down slowly facing them as his thugs pulled Taiei back into a kneeling position.

"My father served on the front lines, you know. He served in Korea and then pressed into Manchuria. He was part of the great Japanese Imperial Army that helped establish Manchukuo. He was a sapper, before his injury cut his military career short."

Nakajima turned as he said this and pulled a long, brown canvas bag from a low-hanging and barely visible shelf behind him. He unsnapped the top of the bag and pulled out what looked like two wooden rods. He then screwed one into a metallic head of some kind, and then he screwed the two wooden rods together. He turned the device up and displayed it to Kano and his cousin.

"It is beautiful, isn't it?" he asked rhetorically. "My father used this to cut through barbed wire your people would use to try to block passage of the Imperial Army through the Korean peninsula, to Manchuria." Nakajima caressed the cutting edges of the wire cutter as he talked. "He used it on the front lines, cutting through wire barriers and clearing paths so that our infantry soldiers could move forward unimpeded. He liked to call this his 'Thunder Stick,' with each cut giving a loud and sharp clap of thunder that welcomed the arrival of Japanese Imperial Army troops."

Nakajima then looked up at Taiei and Takada. "Of course, when a family defects, they immediately give up all property rights in their homeland. This is common sense, right? They certainly have no need for the property any more, their departure is a de facto declaration as such. And this is of course both national and international law, right?" Nakajima looked at his henchman, who nodded smilingly and grunted in agreement, "unh!"

"Now, it is time to discuss business. Namely, the sale of your pachinko parlors. Now that your father has defected to Korea, your family loses ownership of the properties, it's just a matter of time."

Nakajima sat back as he continued to play with the wire cutters. "Yes, they're practically abandoned even now, is what I would say. The courts would certainly agree with me, but there's no need to go that route, time consuming as it is sure to be." He kneeled toward Taiei and tapped him on the knees with the large wire cutters. "Let's just make it official here and now. My partners and I will buy the properties from you right now, before the bureaucrats finally come around to take possession. This way, you at least get something to show for what is now greatly depreciated pieces of land."

Taiei's eyes widened in horror, but he said nothing.

Nakajima stood up and continued talking. "I mean, who would buy such a property once it becomes widely known in the community that they're owned by the family of traitors? Would you?"

He pointed with his wire cutters to his henchman standing in the corner.

"No, certainly not!"

"And you?"

"Not for a single yen," another one replied.

"Right." Nakajima looked back at Taiei. "Bring over the papers." With that order, the one in the corner grabbed a set of papers, unfolded them, and placed them in front of Taiei.

Nakajima then kneeled in front of Taiei again. "You stamp the papers here, here, and here with your personal seal indicating the transfer of the parlors to us, and our business is complete, hmm?" He tapped Taiei on the thigh with the large and heavy wire cutters as he looked him in the eyes.

Taiei paused momentarily as if trying to process what was being said. He slowly looked up, his face contorting into an expression of further horror.

"What?! No! My father worked fifteen years to build up those parlors, and he entrusted us to oversee them while he is away. I'll never transfer them over to you!"

"Yes, I figured as much..." Nakajima said as he leaned back to sit on his bottom, shaking his head slowly. "Really quite a pity..."

"You... you..." Taiei stammered, "you wouldn't take what both your father and my father partnered to build, they were friends!" Taiei pleaded.

Nakajima flashed his gaze menacingly back at Taiei. "They were 'friends'? My father hated Koreans, and he used yours just to buy time to expand his own business! Then *your* father defected! Now your father is a card-carrying communist!" Spittle sprayed from Nakajima's mouth as he shouted into Taiei's face. "I *hate* communists!" Nakajima pulled his hand back and then slapped Taiei across the face. "And you, *you* must be a communist too, eh?" He slapped him again.

Taiei began to whimper again.

"Stamp the god-damn papers!" Nakajima ordered, placing Taiei's *hanko*, his personal seal used to stamp official documents, next to him.

He waited, looking at Taiei. Silence filled the room.

Nakajima sat back and nodded once. At that signal, one of Nakajima's henchmen grabbed Taiei's right hand and slammed it down in front of him, beside the papers. The other one held Taiei's left arm behind his back and put Taiei into a modified chokehold. Taiei began to gasp for air.

"You are left handed," Nakajima said, patting Taiei on the left shoulder. "I will start with the right hand. This deal is simple. Each time you refuse to stamp the paperwork agreeing to sell the parlors, I will take a finger. You need only your left thumb and index finger to seal the document with your *hanko*. Those will be the last fingers I will take."

His henchman pressed down on Taiei's knuckles, forcing his fingers to splay further as Taiei struggled in vain to form a fist.

"You don't even need those two fingers," Nakajima added as he opened the wire cutters and leaned over Taiei's hand, "to stamp your *hanko*..." He placed the open pincers around Taiei's pinky and then forced his entire body down on the handle.

Snap.

Taiei let out a cry as his pinky plopped off his hand.

Nakajima's henchmen released Taiei, who writhed in agony as they stood up.

"But what of filing it at the local town hall? You need to have witnesses that the transaction took place, certified and notarized paperwork, all of that...!" Kano pleaded, trying to buy his cousin time to recover.

Nakajima leaned forward in front of Kano. "Let me handle that," he said, chuckling. "I've gotten this far, hmm? I have friends at town hall too, friends who could use a little extra cash. Maybe they'd like some trinkets from *my* new pachinko parlors to sell on the secondary market, eh? I'll be sure the games are *very* accommodating whenever they come!" Nakajima looked up at his henchmen. "We've made a lot of friends in town that way, eh boys?" They chuckled again and abruptly stopped as Nakajima nodded at them.

They grabbed Kano and this time slammed his left hand onto the mat while locking his right arm behind his back and placing him in a choke hold.

Nakajima leaned down in front of Kano and tapped him on the head with the wire cutter pincers. "The tax man doesn't question monetary gains from selling trinkets won at pachinko, very convenient with friends in special places."

Nakajima placed the wire cutters around Kano's pinky. "And *you* are right handed," Nakajima said, "so I will start with your *left* hand..." Nakajima threw his body weight onto the handle of the open wire cutters until the pincers cut through Kano's pinky.

Kano screamed in pain.

Nakajima sat back as both moaned loudly in pain in front of him. Nakajima's face was flush, with droplets of blood splattered diagonally across his forehead and cheek. He wiped it away as he declared to Taiei and Kano: "Now, let's try this again. Do we have a deal, or no?"

CHAPTER 9 – THE TEMPLE VISIT

The caravan of black sedans slowed as they approached a small parking lot off Highway 307 that ran through the town of Katsushika in northeast Tokyo. Uniformed and helmeted police officers standing on either side of a makeshift barrier lifted the mobile gate at the sight of the approaching cars. Three sedans pulled into the parking lot, while several others stopped on either side of the entrance on the highway.

A half-dozen men alighted from two of the parked sedans, while others stood along the narrow sidewalk and walkway to the temple. They all wore dark suits, starched white shirts, and dark, nondescript ties. Their short-cropped hair revealed transparent earpieces in their right ears with wires that snaked behind their ears and disappeared into their suits at the back of their necks.

A man in the passenger seat of the third vehicle stepped out and opened the back door of the sedan. A woman stepped out as the man bowed slightly. She was joined by two formally dressed men, but in contrast to the conservative attire of the bodyguards, they wore dark gray suits with faintly visible pinstripes and tails, silvery satin ties and matching cummerbunds.

The one woman in the group, Ayumi Seitoh, wore a button-down charcoal-gray suit jacket with the white collar of her blouse overlapping the jacket's lapels. Her knee-length skirt covered skin-tone and barely visible stockings. She walked confidently forward in her two-inch dark heels to the narrow and short stone walkway that traversed the front of the Buddhist temple.

The senior Buddhist priest, dressed in layers of formal white robes, stood at the front gate of the temple. He bowed deeply as Seitoh approached, and she bowed politely in return. The sounds and flashes of cameras clicked rapidly behind them as the two leaders greeted one another. A phalanx of reporters and tourists stood separated by guardrails and uniformed police mere meters away from the temple's entrance, constrained by the narrow approaches to the temple. The bodyguards looked warily toward the crowd on either side of Seitoh, and one spoke briefly and quietly into a microphone partially hidden by the lapel of his suit.

The priest and his staff led Seitoh and her companions onto the grounds of the temple. Several of her bodyguards accompanied them while two stood guard on either side of the gate facing the onlookers. Seitoh stepped first to the *tsukubai* washbasin directly to the left of the main gate, where she picked up a small ladle to perform a ritual wash of her hands. Cameras again clicked furiously as she unhurriedly performed the ablutions. The group then turned to the entrance of the main hall, passing under the sacred Zui-Ryu-no-Matsu "Lucky Dragon" tree as they approached. Carved guardian lions peered down on the visitors from the wooden rafters as the small group disappeared inside the ancient building.

Reporters continued to photograph and broadcast the visit from the gate. Originally built in the 17th century, the ornately carved wooden structures of the Shibamata Taishakuten temple had long ago been designated a national treasure, and a glass facade now encased the main wooden structure to protect it from the elements and to allow tourists and visitors more comfortable, and controlled, access to the wooden murals.

The onlookers watched as the small group appeared again in the glass-encased section of the temple to tour the carved wooden sculptures. Four main panels lined each side of the building, with minor panels depicting intricately carved cranes and other symbolic creatures on smaller sections below, and minor deities and forces of nature depicted in narrow wooden panels above. The priest could be seen pointing first to one section, then to the other, and then they moved down to the next section. A Buddhist deity was depicted riding an elephant in one, while in another, a Buddhist figure lectured to seated monks, surrounded by other powerful minor deities standing guard. In a third section, an intricately carved figure stood in a righteous pose holding a sword in his right hand, while his left palm was open and empty. Dragons peered from rafters overlooking this section of the temple. Candidate Seitoh nodded as the Buddhist priest explained the history and symbology of each of the panels. She looked focused and intensely interested in the conversation. Cameramen with zoom lenses could make out the occasional "*so desu ka...*" and "*heeeeiii*" in a soft and respectful tone to the priest as she took in the expansive tour of the centuries-old temple.

The group then disappeared from sight again as they rounded the corner to tour the backside of the building and temple grounds. Within ten minutes, the group rounded another corner and returned to the entrance. Seitoh and her companions bowed deeply to the priest, who bowed still deeper in return. Seitoh then turned to the gate and walked toward the throng of reporters, cameras, and other onlookers. The crowd stood silently as she stepped forward to make a statement.

"It is with great humility that I come here to visit this revered temple today," she began, her two bodyguards standing on either side watching the crowd intently and silently. "I have long considered the Buddha to be an important figure in the history of religion. He represents both wisdom and humility, values that I prize above all else. He became enlightened in realizing that life is both exquisite and fleeting. He stayed with us, with mankind, to teach us the ways of enlightenment, of wisdom and humility."

Cameras flashed as she spoke, but the crowd remained silent.

"Yet he could not do this alone. The Buddha himself knew that wisdom and humility needed to be protected in order to be passed on and nurtured by future generations. For this, for the assurance of his personal safety, he relied above all on his companion, Taishaku-ten, the deity Taishaku, for protection."

There was a murmur in the crowd, and cameras flashed more furiously.

"And that is why I came here, at this time, to honor the deity Taishaku, the protector of the Buddha, of wisdom, humility, and enlightenment. It is appropriate that the deity Taishaku is honored here, in this humble temple near the heart of the capital of Japan. Like the Buddha, I believe that the Japanese people are the embodiment of wisdom and humility. The Japanese people have experienced many challenges over the centuries, and have gained wisdom and humility as we have overcome those challenges together. And just like the Buddha, the Japanese people too deserve a protector like the deity Taishaku to ensure their safety and security."

One of Seitoh's guards spoke discreetly into his microphone as he eyed the crowd.

"Recent events have made me understand how fortunate we are, and yet how fragile our safety is. The maritime incident several nights ago was but one in a series of exceedingly dangerous incidents that we as a nation have encountered. Taken as a whole, the continued actions of certain of our neighbors constitute an increasingly grave threat to the security of our nation and to peace-loving people everywhere. We cannot allow the wanton violation of our nation's space, of our peoples' right to live in peace, to continue."

There was a sudden hush in the crowd, and for a moment, the flash of cameras ceased.

"Just like the deity Taishaku protecting the Buddha as his highest duty, I pledge to the Japanese people that if my party is re-elected as the majority, and if I am privileged to serve the Japanese people as prime minister, it will be my highest duty to take all possible measures to ensure the security and safety of the Japanese nation, such as young Ayako and her father, Mr. Toda, who died tragically and needlessly in this most aggressive act. I will not let these wonton acts of aggression continue without a concerted and appropriate response."

Ayumi Seitoh bowed slightly to the group of reporters and on-lookers to indicate that her statement had concluded. With that cue, the reporters then erupted in cries of "Madame President! Madame President…!" One cried out: "Does this mean you will introduce a security council resolution at the UN?" And another shouted: "What do you plan to do if it does happen again if you're elected prime minister?" A third interjected: "Will the Toda family receive compensation?"

"We have already begun to undertake diplomatic efforts to protest the incident, which our neighbor has denied, baselessly," Seitoh declared. "On the broader question of security, whether in the strictly legal or broader constitutional context, I pledge that I will undertake all efforts to see that this does not happen again. I would like the Japanese people themselves to decide what they want, and to express that will through the elections. I only ask to serve the people's will."

Seitoh looked at the reporters in stern solemnity as they continued to shout questions. Her gaze turned reproachful, as if to ask, *you focus on such small questions when the fate of the Japanese nation is increasingly at stake…* "Thank you very much," she said perfunctorily yet patiently, took a half-step back and bowed more deeply, and then she turned to depart along the narrow stone walkway to the caravan of cars waiting for her. She remained silent as reporters continued to shout questions at her.

CHAPTER 10 - BRIEFINGS

Bennett had arrived early to the embassy. While he had awoken before sunrise since his body had yet to adjust to Japan time, he felt refreshed from a short but solid night's sleep at the hotel. He spent the time catching up with messages and reading in to prepare for meetings in the morning.

He glanced casually at the television screen as he leaned back in his chair, stretching away from his computer terminal. He noticed that instead of morning chat shows, a live broadcast showed the prime ministerial front-runner Seitoh entering a vehicle and pulling away from what looked like a smallish temple in the suburbs of Tokyo. Bennett reached over to turn up the volume.

"…we're live from Katsushika Ward in Tokyo, where Ayumi Seitoh, president of the majority party and potential future prime minister, just departed the Shibamata Taishakuten temple in Tokyo…"

"Katsushika Ward? Isn't that where you were last night, Trinh?" Bennett asked Archer, who was sitting around the corner.

"That's where they're keeping Taro Hatano, the younger brother of the kid who died trying to run from the Coast Guard," she said as she rolled in her chair to look around the corner. "Why?"

"Because Seitoh just visited a local temple there. It looks like the major broadcasters interrupted their morning programming to report on it." Bennett turned to several different channels, which all appeared to be broadcasting from the same location.

"Prime ministerial candidates don't normally visit Buddhist temples," said Archer. "Not from that party at least. What's that all about?"

"Yeah, they normally visit Shinto shrines, like the main one in Ise southwest of Tokyo. Sometimes Yasukuni Shrine, but that's controversial since all of Japan's war dead are ceremoniously interred there, including World War II war criminals."

"Um-hm," Archer muttered in acknowledgement. "And she's already visited there several times, and gotten the usual flak for it too." Archer turned the volume up some more

"...This is the first visit of its kind to this temple in living memory, so it is highly unusual," one talking head, a professor from Tokyo University, declared. "At this stage of the campaign, with only days left until the election takes place, this visit has many symbolic meanings," he continued. "The Taishaku-ten, the deity Taishaku, as Ms. Seitoh said, was indeed in charge of protecting the Buddha. It is the Japanese name for the deity Indra, or Shakra, literally meaning strength or power, in Indian Buddhist cosmology. Taishaku-ten protected the Buddha along with the deity Bon-ten, or Brahma."

"Moreover," interjected another talking head, this one a retired Tokyo Police Department official, "it is located in Katsushika Ward, mere blocks away from the Tokyo Detention Center, where the young suspect Hatano is being held as part of the investigation into the maritime incident a few nights ago. He was the only survivor of that tragedy. There is certainly a connection to that, both symbolically and in Ms. Seitoh's statement. It is being reported that investigators are trying to determine if there is a state-sponsored angle to the incident..."

Bennett looked at his watch and then turned the volume down again. "Colonel Bradley should be in the conference room by now. You still up for meeting with him this morning?" he asked Archer. "We're interested in getting the latest on that 'maritime incident' as they're calling it now..."

"Sure thing, let me lock up." Archer turned to her computer console to secure it while she was away. Bennett waited for her by the door to their work area, and the two then went to the conference room.

As soon as they arrived, Colonel Bradley held out a folder to Bennett without waiting for pleasantries. "Take a look at this," Bradley said in a hushed tone as Archer arranged her materials. "This might throw a wrench in things."

Bennett opened the folder, which revealed several satellite images. They appeared to show a major weather pattern that had formed southeast of the Japanese archipelago. He flipped to the next page, which showed the typhoon's projected paths over the coming days, all but one of which showed the storm passing directly between Japan and the Korean Peninsula in the general path of the planned exercise.

Bennett grimaced. "This doesn't look good. When is it supposed to hit?"

"In just a few days, sooner perhaps. It formed pretty quickly and is gaining strength as we speak."

"Any word from the Japanese side on the exercise?"

"They're watching it closely. Depending on its trajectory as it passes over Shikoku, they might cancel it. Again."

"So what does that mean for our ships?"

"Well, aside from possibly having no reason to deploy to that area with the exercise canceled, they would also probably want to avoid the storm's path too. We can have the Texas proceed as planned, but..."

Bennett held his hand up slightly to stop the discussion from progressing any further. "Ok, let's watch it and discuss further once we have more information."

Bennet then motioned to Archer. "This is Trinh, Trinh Archer. She's one of our best working the illicit networks issue. She doesn't know it, but since coming to the NSC, I've been keeping a close watch on Ms. Archer's work in this area, among others working the region," Bennett said.

"Yes, we met briefly. You were in Afghanistan when I was traveling through a few years back..." Bradley said.

Archer looked at Bradley for a moment, and then her eyes narrowed knowingly. "Ah yes, you were the one with the beard!"

"Yeah, my entire team had beards back then, since we were operational..."

"Exactly. I met so many SOF with beards that y'all began to look the same after awhile...But yeah, I remember you."

"Well then I guess we did our job of blending in locally, huh?" Bradley responded.

"If you mean blending in with a bunch of white hicks at a biker bar, sure." Archer replied sardonically.

Bradley turned to Bennett. "I like this girl of yours, she's got spunk!" Most people treated Bradley was a mix of respect and fear because of his rank, so it was refreshing to meet someone who could banter with him.

"Ok, now that the pleasantries are out of the way, tell us the latest," Bennett said to Archer. He squinted one eyebrow at her to communicate to her that she should keep her composure.

Archer squinted back, and then pulled out her own folder of documents and slides. She laid them out on the table in front of her then pushed them toward each of the men.

"Together with the Japanese side, we've been tracking a number of smuggling routes into and out of Japan along the western seaboard," Archer began. "We are fairly certain we know the major players conducting smuggling operations into and out of Japan."

"Let me guess, North Korea," Bradley said.

"Well, yes, North Korea, along with organized crime syndicates operating out of the Russian Far East, China, and to some extent South Korea as well. The problem with North Korea is making out which operations are state-sponsored and run by the regime itself, or otherwise by rogue groups or new syndicates looking to exploit their connections along the North Korea-China border." Archer pointed to several maps of Asia showing clusters of known organized crime syndicates, their primary areas of operations, and smuggling routes.

"But the USG position is that it is indeed state-sponsored," Bennett asserted.

"Yes, that's right, the U.S. State Department says as much in its annual reports to Congress," Archer said. "For intelligence purposes that's fine, and we think the evidence is irrefutable, but for more legalistic purposes to engage diplomatically or, if it came to it, undertaking kinetic operations, we want hard proof to win over the public, both at home and the publics of our major allies."

"You can bet the North Korean public doesn't get a say in any of this…" Bradley said.

"That's the problem, ultimately, isn't it?" Bennett stated. "The North Korean people have no say and they are held hostage by an unaccountable regime. And that's what we're trying to change, whether by one dissident at a time, or through other means." Bennett winked slightly as he spoke.

"The thing is, most smuggling operations are partnerships between syndicates, with Japan-based ones trading with others in the region," Archer continued. "While we know most of the gangs operating in the region, we don't know exactly who runs the smuggling operations within Japan. It's the whole supply and demand thing, if there is a supply coming in, you can be sure someone is ordering it to fill a demand domestically or elsewhere in the region. You can also bet that they are also increasingly using Japan as a transshipment point to North America, now that authorities there are cracking down on deliveries from China."

Archer pulled out another series of slides. "So we figured, let's attempt to track both paths to the transfer point to get that hard proof and take down two operations at once. We partner with the Japanese military and Coast Guard to track suspicious traffic into Japanese waters—the supply—and we partner with Japan's National

Police Agency to track the stuff from the streets back upstream—the demand. That became 'Operation Crimson Leaves'..."

Archer sat for a moment in thought at the failure of the most recent attempted bust, but then collected herself and continued. "That's what we were hoping to find out when the collision happened, at any rate, which took out the main actor and pretty much all the evidence. My contact with the NPA, Security Bureau Deputy Chief Nishi, said his guys raided a storage shed in a rural area just north of the incident, but it was cleaned out by then."

"What were they trying to smuggle?" Bradley asked.

"Amphetamines and methamphetamines, most likely. That and other manufactured drugs such as ecstasy, and now increasingly, fentanyl, that sort of thing. Manufactured drugs are more popular in East Asia but they are quickly spreading and blending with the heroin trade to Europe and North America. The regime has also cultivated poppies for heroin, but that goes mainly west through Russia and on to Europe, or south. The trade ebbs and flows through Asia, depending on where it's easiest to get the product through, with illicit trade through Japan growing again. And we haven't even touched on the human trafficking problem in Asia, but it goes hand-in-hand with drug smuggling and money laundering."

"So what are the next steps?" Bennett asked.

"We now have the boy, the little brother of the primary guy we were after who is now dead." Archer showed mug shots of both of the boys. "I was just over there at the detention center, he doesn't know much at all, but Nishi seems to think he can get more out of him. Who knows, maybe he will but I doubt it. Japanese intelligence is scrubbing its recent collections for any signs of clandestine signals over the past week that might indicate anything..."

"And the smuggling ship?" Bradley asked.

"Our overhead guys lost it in the heavy cloud cover. We believe it returned to its home port." Archer pointed to a close-up of a port facility. "But we can't say for sure given the weather and some new facilities that appear to be covered ports."

Bradley turned to Bennett. "Are the Japanese making a stink out of this? Is this going to impact our…"

Archer noticed Bennett hold up a finger slightly toward Bradley as if to silence him from any further questions along that line. Before Bennett could respond, Archer interjected. "So far the National Police Agency considers this an active investigation, of course, and the public is debating the incident because of the deaths and with the snap national elections about to take place, but otherwise there is a political vacuum now with the sudden health issues of the incumbent prime minister, so nothing is imminent. Besides, there's not much the Japanese can or will do, without a smoking gun."

"That's pretty much what I've been hearing too," Bennett said to Archer, and then turned to Bradley. "It's too soon to say for certain, but Seitoh and her party have really surged in the most recent polls, and she's been talking things up as you saw this morning, so we'll need to keep an eye on her and the election closely over the coming days." He nodded almost imperceptibly.

Bennett turned back to Archer and smiled. "So, enough of this, and good work by the way, Archer. We're heading out to meet some of Bradley's guys who just arrived in town from exercises up north."

Bradley squinted for a moment, then added: "Yes, you should come out with us tonight, I'm meeting with some of the guys, who are on leave right now," Bradley repeated. "One of my top SOF guys is touring some Buddhist temples in the countryside, he's kinda into that sort of thing, but the others are in town and plan to go out tonight."

"Buddhist temples, eh?" Bennett asked. "I dabbled in that a little bit myself during my college days when I was minoring in comparative religions. Delving into human 'suffering', all that. I had some interesting experiences, but after visiting a few remote temples in some pretty impoverished areas, I began to realize how much liberal democracies and free market economies alleviate real suffering by giving people the economic freedom to lift themselves out of poverty. Of course free trade has to be *fair* trade," Bennett tapped the table with his finger to emphasize his point, "but this all came out of the Judeo-Christian tradition, not an eastern one, so I turned from an inward and personal emphasis to a, shall we say, more materialistic approach to alleviating suffering..." Bennett smiled wryly at his attempt at subtle humor, which missed its mark.

"I guess I'd agree with you," Archer quipped, "if my ancestors and I hadn't been forced from our lands and ways of life as a result of settlers and others espousing so-called 'Judeo-Christian values...'" She tried to maintain as collegial a tone as possible, while still making her experiences known.

"There have been problems, to be sure," Bennett said without missing a beat. He clearly had had these conversations before. "But we developed a system of checks and balances that is clearly codified in the constitution, and we are a nation of laws, not despots. So as a society that values freedom of speech, thought, religion, we can work through problems of the past. It's a painful process, to be sure, but it's unlike any other system on earth, and you can see the positive impacts of this open political and economic system here in Asia, comparing Japan and South Korea to North Korea..."

You can say all that academically when you're on the inside of an ivory tower looking out, but when you're the one trying to 'lift' yourself and your family from poverty, it's another thing entirely, Archer thought to herself.

Bennett stopped himself as he looked at both Bradley and Archer. "Sorry, I get a little animated when it comes to this sort of thing. Just an idealistic realist, I guess." Bennett said, with a shrug of his shoulders.

"By the way, I've been meaning to ask, and I hope you don't think this inappropriate," Bennett said, turning to Archer, "but your name 'Trinh' has intrigued me. Isn't that a surname used in Vietnam, dating back to the Trinh nobles in the sixteenth century?"

"I'm impressed, Mr. Bennett, you know your history," Archer replied. Only other Vietnamese had asked her about her first name. "It is, but the name is sometimes used as a first name especially among children of diaspora. In my case, it was a bit of an accident..." Archer paused, uncertain about how much to share. "My parents had a fight right before I was born. In fact, I was born six weeks early, in the early morning after the fight, which my mother blamed on my father. And because of the fight, or the circumstances, he was..."

Archer paused again to collect herself, and then continued. "... he was not there. He came later, when my mother was about to fill out the birth certificate. Her maiden name was Trinh, she was from that same area as the Trinh nobles, but during the war she and her family, the grandparents I never met, were displaced as 'bourgeois nobles.' That's where she met my father, a U.S. Army helicopter pilot. At any rate, he came to the hospital just as she was planning to give me her maiden name as a family name, or that was her plan. Her English wasn't very good, and my father walked in and they started fighting about it. He must've heard from someone what she was planning, there were a lot of nurses there with ties to the local reservation near the hospital. But they fought, and the administrator was there trying to figure out the names through all the fighting. He knew my father's last name, Archer, so he put that down, but my mother kept yelling at him to put down 'Trinh'. He didn't know she meant that as a last name, but he asked her to spell it, which she did, and he put it down as a first name. He left then, before double-checking the information, and then it became official."

"Wow, that's quite a story," Bradley said, mesmerized.

"So after all that, your mother started calling you by her own family name?" Bennett asked. "That must've been hard for her..."

"No, she never used that word. She had a pet name for me, which is private as I'm sure you'll understand. But since it was on my birth certificate that was used to register me at school, that sort of thing, all my teachers, other kids, they called me Trinh. So I got used to it, I suppose."

"And Archer?" asked Bradley. "Where's that from? Just out of curiosity..."

"That's a Cherokee name, well, sort of at least. It's on the Dawes rolls, to register the Cherokee tribe members back in the 19th century, but my father's family was more Kaw than Cherokee. They were displaced from northern Kansas back before the Civil War, when the transcontinental railroads were being built. They were resettled in Cherokee territory, first on the Kansas side and then again on the Oklahoma side. My father's family wanted to ensure some official membership in the Cherokee tribe so they wouldn't be displaced by the government again, so they took a last name that started with 'A' to be included at the top of the list. So I guess you can call me the result of a marriage between two lost tribes of the world," she concluded.

"It's a wonder that you ended up working for the U.S. Government then," remarked Bennett. "But we are the better for it."

"You'll understand why I sometimes bristle at neo-liberal jargon, but ultimately I guess you can say we all have our journeys that we walk," Archer replied, without directly responding to Bennett's question. The real reason she ended up where she did was another story entirely. "So, what about that happy hour?" She added, gesturing to the clock on the wall.

"Oh yes, look at the time," Bennett said as he turned to the clock. "Let me just touch base with Maddy," Bennett said, "but you can meet the guys here." He finished writing the location on a small corner of one of the slides and then ripped it off and gave it to Archer.

"I just need to check in with my office, then I'll head over," Bradley added. "So we'll meet you there?"

"I suppose so, I'll look for the meatheads with beards right?" Archer asked Bradley with a wry smile.

"Ha ha! Right, no, nothing like that, we're in Asia now so beards don't quite work in this environment..." Bradley grinned broadly, not picking up on Archer's pointed statement.

• • •

Bennett knocked on Madeleine Tucker's half-open door. "Hello, Maddy, I wanted to talk to you about schedules over the next couple of days or so..."

"Yes, Wilson, it's good you stopped by." Tucker got up from her desk and approached Bennett without smiling. "Please, have a seat," she gestured stiffly to the seat facing her desk and closed the door as Bennett stepped into the office.

Whether it was the tone of her greeting or the abruptness of closing the door, Bennett was now on guard.

Tucker came around Bennett to sit in her chair behind the desk. *This is certainly more formal than yesterday*, Bennett thought to himself.

"I know what you're planning," she said as she leaned forward and placed her crossed forearms on the desk.

"I don't know what you're talking about," Bennett feigned.

"Don't play coy with me," Tucker responded. "The operation to get your guy out of North Korea." Tucker looked at him with an expression of disbelief. "Are you insane?"

"I've respected your capabilities for some time now and figured you would find out soon enough," Bennett replied patiently. "I should be surprised you were able to do so in such short order, but I'm not."

"Platitudes will get you nowhere with me. You're jeopardizing covert assets, millions and potentially tens of millions in funding, the lives of U.S. servicemen and women, the White House's trust even, for a completely unvetted and unproven asset. One who is sketchy at best and potentially a con artist, a dangle, or both. Why the hell are you doing this? We don't need another 'Curveball' to appear in the annals of abject intelligence failures."

"If you're talking about that engineer who made up claims of chemical and biological weapons programs in Iraq, that's clearly not the case here. North Korea has a declared and demonstrated nuclear weapons capability and a history of making threats against us and our allies in the region. It's not a matter of *if* they have a program, but where it's at. Our highest duty is to learn about it and disrupt it at any cost necessary." Bennett tried to remain measured but forceful in his response.

"And who among the North Koreans doesn't know that, and who wouldn't use that as a pretext to get whatever they wanted from Uncle Sam's deep pockets? Just like 'Curveball'…"

"Did the ambassador tell you?" Bennett wanted to get at the source to find out what exactly Tucker knew, or if she was playing him to confirm any rumors she might have heard or hunches she might have. Agency types like her were experts at digging up "rumint"—so-called intelligence based on rumors and hearsay—among themselves about any given administration and the sensitive policy-making process at the White House and in Congress, and then ferreting out half-truths from insiders who thought they knew more than they did. Sometimes, Bennett thought, officers like Maddy spent more time collecting intelligence on activities within the U.S. Government more than targeting foreign threats.

"If you must know, I got it from the ambo's cable on your meeting."

"He let you see the cable? That is supposed to be eyes-only and extremely sensitive, even you know that, Maddy!" Bennett feigned indignation but was upset nonetheless. "That's a punishable offense, Maddy, you better be very careful in how you tread!" he declared, pointing at her to impress his point.

"Don't bullshit me, Bennett. No, I didn't see the cable, just the title. It mentioned your back-brief on the 'finding,' obviously a reference to the presidential finding that he must've signed to authorize your operation, but even that is code-word protected. I just asked the ambassador about how his conversation went with you on the 'finding,' and he said I wasn't supposed to know and that you instructed him not to talk to me about it or your briefing. Which was smart of you, but you had to know I would find out." She paused, looking at him directly. "How I found out is beside the point. Let's just say I have working-level contacts at the NSC just as you have them at the CIA. But I'll ask again, are you insane?"

"Yes, of course there's a presidential finding, I've no need to deny it at this point. So now you're plugging me for information about the finding, but it's a done deal Maddy. He signed it, we're proceeding with it. Don't obstruct it, because things are about to happen."

"I also asked around the mission center. My contacts at headquarters told me that they were against going forward with this guy because his story was so difficult to corroborate, and it went counter to other information we had on this facility and his potential involvement. We've assessed that he's probably a janitor, at best. I had heard some details at the time, saw the video myself. We might have ultimately supported a risky operation after a more thorough review, or perhaps we would have formally dissented in the interagency process had it reached that point, who knows..."

"But I didn't let it reach that point," Bennett declared. "Time had become critical and we didn't want to waste it on bureaucracy."

"There is a process in place, Wilson, for legitimate reasons, to include protecting us and the administration both from history-changing disasters. Because you thought we were against it, you went to the Oval directly to get the president to sign off on this half-baked scheme of yours. You are once again operationalizing the National Security Council, with potentially disastrous consequences!"

"I did not go to the Oval Office, my seniors did after we discussed all aspects of the case, and at any rate, DoD and others thought this guy was potentially valuable enough to work with. *You* aren't the only player in this, Maddy!" Bennett said angrily, pointing his finger at her again. Bennett could see that Tucker was livid, both about the operation itself and because she wasn't informed that the operation would take place in her own backyard.

"And he's legit, Maddy, you'll see when we get him out," Bennett added. "Even if he's not, we should be doing all we can to lure North Korean defectors, especially ones who have any connection at all with sensitive programs. We need to cause a brain drain, at a minimum, so that the north no longer has the skilled manpower to build this kind of weaponry. This is the real 'drain the swamp' at work..."

"Not with the potential cost of lives and treasury, we shouldn't!" Tucker yelled. *Is there more in that finding that he's not telling me?* she wondered to herself.

"Since when did a seasoned officer like yourself become so risk-averse?" Bennett wondered aloud. "You're supposed to be the tip of the spear. Is it just you who's lost your edge, or all your colleagues at the Agency?"

"Don't condescend to me, Wilson," Tucker replied with a sneer. "My colleagues and I have seen more shit and worked in more hell-holes in this world than you could ever possibly conceive. We know what works and we know when politicians and their hacks are taking major gambles with the lives of real patriots they've never met."

"Just remember, Maddy, you're not the only ones who are out there risking your lives for the greater good, so don't condescend to them either. And on this, remember too that if the president orders it, we do it. Period." Bennett stood up to leave. "The White House expects our full cooperation to make this a successful operation," Bennett concluded as he turned to the door.

"Don't question my professionalism, Bennett," Tucker said as he left. "And don't think that there aren't better ways to attack this problem, either, but that requires working *with* us."

You haven't done much on this for the past seventy years, Bennett thought as he walked away, *so why should I trust you'll do anything now?* He shut the door to Tucker's office, grabbed his coat, and left the vault for the day.

CHAPTER 11 – THE BAR

"Hey, look at that chick by the bar," the sergeant said just as he and his buddy walked into the mostly empty bar. "That is one hot ass on her!" The bar had just opened for the evening, and the two young soldiers were among the first to arrive.

"Damn, you got that right," said his comrade, gawking. "I knew this place was good for picking up, but *damn…*"

"Hey, watch this…"

"Ah com'on sarge, don't try it, man…" his wing-man said as he chuckled.

"Nah it's all good. She's gonna love me, that's my next girlfriend right there!"

"Yeah for how long, three hours, three days, how long this time?"

The sergeant walked around the few tables scattered along the makeshift dance floor between the entrance and the main bar area. It was still early in the evening, and most of the expats who frequented this area of Tokyo wouldn't arrive for hours. The sergeant approached the girl, who stood at the bar studiously looking through the pages of the menu.

"Konishiwa, babe, genki de-su ka?" he said in an unrecognizable accent.

She did not respond.

"Hey, lady, how ya doin'?" He said, this time putting his hand on her shoulder. "Ya lookin' for a good time tonight?"

Archer had pretended not to hear the conversation behind her, but now she was forced to act. She felt the large hand land on her right shoulder give a lascivious squeeze. She was already nauseated by these idiot Americans thinking they could have their way with any Asian woman. Now she had to teach them the responsibility of remaining polite in a foreign land.

In a split second, Archer assessed her new adversary's position: He had placed his left hand on her right shoulder, and he stood behind her and slightly to her right. Perfect positioning, she knew from instinct. Without turning around or making any other bodily motion that could signal her next move to this asshole, she reached up with her left hand across her body and grabbed the top of his hand short of the wrist. She lifted slightly but firmly while she took a half-step back. She rotated toward him at the same time, shoving her right hand up into the crook of his elbow while she squeezed his hand with her right hand. She yanked her left hand down and rotated his hand toward her at the same time as she pushed up with her right hand at his elbow into an upward-facing chicken wing. She twisted his hand toward him as she held onto his elbow, causing him to wince in sudden pain as she turned him away from the bar.

He was strong, but not strong enough to force her to release him from this position. Her abrupt motion and his now extremely awkward position sapped his body of any strength he might have had. He let out an uncontrollable yelp. "Lady, what the…"

Archer felt his body tighten as he struggled against her. Good, she thought. She pushed forward hard on the elbow to elicit his counter-response, a hard push back to get out of being put into an elbow lock behind his back. She expected his reaction, and she shifted her right hand down to his wrist in response.

The sudden shift in position meant he began to fall into the direction where he had been pushing his elbow downward. Now he was ready to fall, all he needed was some help from Archer.

With both hands holding tight to his wrist, she straightened her thumbs upward along the top part of his hand and forced his hand forward at a ninety degree angle. She then pulled it into her solar plexus and stepped with her left foot in front of him, and then swung her right foot and body around almost 180 degrees. The motion, together with his sudden fall to his left from struggling against her arm lock, caused him to flip over himself backward uncontrollably. He landed flat on his back and his momentum caused his whole body to swivel on the hardwood dance floor in front of Archer in reaction to the new lock she held him in.

She stood above him now, holding his wrist in the same lock with his arm now straight. She did not let go. Instead, she stepped over his head with her left foot and placed the back of her ankle over his neck. She kicked her right foot under his armpit and fell onto her back on the floor perpendicular to his shoulders, still holding his wrist and arm locked tight. With her left foot over his neck and her right foot tucked under his armpit, she forced his locked elbow against the inner part of her left thigh and pulled it into an arm bar.

He screamed in agony as she tightened the pressure on his arm.

"Is this what you wanted, huh?" she shouted at him. "Is this what you were after, to get between my legs? This feel good to you, asshole?" Archer pulled harder each time she asked a question, and she pulled in her left leg over his neck as she did so, cutting off more and more of his windpipe.

He yelped and coughed. "Ah! Let me go!" He looked up at his colleagues, more of whom had arrived and were now standing in a semicircle around them on the ground. "Jesus Christ, get her off me, damn it!"

The group, at first stunned into silence by the girl's swift movements, broke out laughing. "Damn, sarge, she tore you up!" one said, doing nothing to help his comrade. "I told you, man, don't try it!" said another. More of sarge's 'friends' had apparently showed up as he was hitting on Trinh.

"Touch me again and I'll break your goddamned arm, understand!" Archer said as she peered forward to look at him in the face. "And that goes for all of you assholes too!" she yelled at his friends standing around him.

"Holy shit lady, you're damn right we won't touch you!" one said, as they all held up their hands and stepped back from her. "In fact, we were just heading out, right guys...?" another said as they looked at each other. "Yeah, yeah that's right, we're just moving on to another club right now..."

Just as Archer let go, she heard a familiar voice approach the group from behind.

"My god, what the hell is going on here?!" came a booming voice.

"Attention!" one of the group yelled. Each one stood ram-rod straight, while the sergeant struggled to his feet. He doubled over again with a loud cough, and then tried to stand up straight again.

Colonel Bradley stood in front of him. "Soldier! Were you bothering this young woman?!" While Bradley did not know this individual, he could tell from his demeanor, his haircut, and the way they all talked that he was a U.S. military serviceman and, more than likely, in the U.S. Army. In his command position, Bradley had been briefed multiple times on what establishments military personnel frequent in most capitals in Asia, and this was one of those establishments.

The sergeant coughed and hacked again as he struggled to explain. "No, sir," he said in a scratchy, barely audible voice. "I mean, I was just introducing myself, sir..." He stood at half-attention in order to show some respect without being too deferential to this stranger who wasn't in his chain of command.

"Ms. Archer, is that correct?" Bradley asked Trinh. "Was this young soldier politely introducing himself to you," Bradly paused to look back at the sergeant, "or was he otherwise being a real jerk?" Bradley continued to look at the sergeant, whose eyes widened with surprise when he heard the colonel call her by name. He knew her, which meant this was personal for the colonel.

"I'd say it was the latter, Colonel Bradley. If this is the best the U.S. Military can muster, I'd say we're in trouble as a country…"

"Wheeeew, damn!" "Oh-ho-ho…!" she heard some voices say in the background.

"At ease!" Bradley yelled as he turned to the rest of the men. He then turned back to the sergeant. "What's your name and rank, son?" Bradley asked.

"Sergeant Joseph Edwards, sir. But I don't think it's fair that I just went over to talk to the girl…" Edwards said.

"Sergeant, you best apologize to this young lady," Colonel Bradley said, interrupting him.

Edwards thought a moment. "Ma'am, I'm really…" the sergeant stammered, "I'm really sorry to have approached you that way." His voice trailed off, not knowing how else to respond. He did not make eye contact with Archer, and looked back at the colonel as if to ask, "satisfied?"

"Don't look at me, son, look at her!" Bradley said in return.

"Sorry. No hard feelings, right?" He reached out to shake her hand.

"Sure, but it's not 'hard feelings' you should be concerned about," Archer replied, gripping his hand tightly as she shook it in one firm motion.

"Very well, sergeant, don't do it again!" Bradley barked.

"Thank you, colonel," Archer said as she turned back to the bar to pick up her glass of Coke, the ice now half-melted.

"Don't thank me, thank your coach or Karate teacher or whatever, they obviously taught you to take care of yourself. Now if you'll excuse me for a moment, I need to go over to talk to my lieutenant," he said, motioning to a man at the far end of the bar.

"Sure thing, colonel."

Sergeant Eric Solberg approached the bar where Archer stood, swirling the melting ice in her drink. "Damn, lady, those were some bad-ass moves. Where'd you learn to move like that?"

Archer looked at him, and then returned her gaze to her drink. "Don't tell me you're trying to hit on me," she said. "Not in the mood, certainly not now and not by someone in the military."

"Nah, just interested in your story is all. Don't meet too many girls who can knock a six-foot-two, 220 pound man onto his ass like that."

She sensed an earnest tone in his voice. "Ok, sure, why not," she said as she turned to him. "I learned them, believe it or not, in a little town in Kansas," she said, and looking back at him she continued curtly, "and before you even think about it, I don't do Dorothy jokes."

"You don't look like you're from Kansas," Solberg continued. Before she could answer, he introduced himself. "Eric. Eric Solberg."

"Trinh," she responded, shaking his hand once.

"What are you, Asian or what? I can't tell," Solberg asked.

She rolled her eyes. "I'm American, you asshole."

"Hey Trinh, chill alright? I'm one of the good guys," he said as he placed his hand lightly on her arm. "Let me buy you a drink to make up for what happened there, huh?" Without waiting for a response, he turned back to the bartender. "Two more of these, please," he said, pointing to Archer's drink.

"You're obviously with them," she continued, motioning to Bradley talking with another individual to Solberg's left. "Not with those other guys, huh?"

"Yeah, that's right, not with those guys," he replied, nodding to the two who had just left the bar. "Look, as a guy in the military, I really want to apologize for that, that was really uncalled for..."

"It happens sometimes with you guys, huh?"

"In the military, you meet some of the best people in the world, but also some assholes. I guess judges still give the option to either join the military or go to jail. But those were some wicked moves though, seriously," he repeated, "you should come train with us, we could use a sparring partner like you, no kidding!" he said, shaking his head in amazement.

Archer noticed a Japanese man approach Solberg from behind and turned just as he slapped Solberg on the shoulder. "Sergeant Solberg! Where are the drinks you owe me?"

"Chief Sato, my man!" replied Solberg as he held out his hand. "Oops, 'xcuse me," he said as he backed away from Sato and then saluted, followed by a deep bow. "Chief Sato, pleased to meet you again." The two laughed as slapped each other in a high-five salute, which Archer thought to appear somewhat awkward since it was obviously a new thing for Solberg's friend.

"Ms. Trinh Archer, please meet Chief Isamu Sato, pilot, Japanese Air Self-Defense Force."

".. *Dozo yoroshiku onegaishimasu,*" she said without thinking as she bowed.

"*Ah! O-Jozu desu ne!*" he said to Solberg, who did not know what was being said. "She speaks excellent Japanese!"

"*Iya, so de mo nai desho...* if only that were the case!" Archer replied, again without thinking. Archer had these types of introductory meetings multiple times daily.

Chief Sato stepped back and bowed deeply in return. "Welcome to my country!" he said, not knowing or caring that she had already been there for some time. She could tell that he was just poking a little fun at this foreign woman acting like a proper Japanese. She liked the sudden levity, and chuckled.

"We just completed some training and exercises with a team of..." Solberg paused, looking at Chief Sato and realizing their training mission was technically classified.

He didn't know that Archer was cleared to hear everything he could say about the training and more, and indeed she had learned as much as there was to know of the units involved from various contacts at the U.S. Embassy and at the Ministry of Defense already. She wasn't going to tell him that, however, just as she had not told Bennett or Bradley. She looked at him feigning ignorance.

"…well, they're a team of Japanese soldiers who can take on the best of 'em out there!" Solberg stammered. He looked down the bar. "Where are those drinks?"

Archer thought the sudden nervousness was cute, especially coming from such a big man. She smiled slightly. "You must've trained them well, I'm sure…from the look of those biceps I'm sure you know how to handle yourself just fine," she said as she leaned on the bar and casually inched closer to him. She had long ago learned how easy it can be to stroke a man's ego, in words and in deeds. And the bigger they are, the easier it is. What more could she learn about the training exercise from this sergeant? She wondered.

She timed her moves as the bartender put down the drinks, so she could redirect her attention immediately after her flirtatious compliment to enhance the effect. "Shall we toast?" she declared to both Solberg and Sato. "Oh my, Chief Sato, you don't have anything to drink!"

"Oh do not worry, Ms. Aachaa," Sato said in a deep accent. "I already ordered. In fact, here is my beer now!" He lifted his pint-sized frosted mug of frothy Sapporo beer just as another bartender placed it in front of him. He shouted "*kampai!*" and they all clinked glasses and took long swigs from their glasses.

"Yes, we're just starting our R&R now," Solberg declared with a wry smile as he placed his mug back on the bar. "In fact…"

Archer knew where this was going.

"…we were going to go out tonight, get something to eat and hit some clubs…Trinh, you should come, you've got some nice moves. What do ya say?"

Colonel Bradley appeared behind them from nowhere. "Sergeant Solberg, are you treating this young woman with respect?"

Bradley maintained a smile as he said this, knowing that all his men acted like gentlemen off the field of battle. He knew because he demanded it of them.

"Certainly sir! We were just talking about our plans for the evening…" Solberg declared, standing up straight in front of his senior officer out of habit.

"Good, take good care of Ms. Archer, she's a good…a good Foreign Area Officer." Bradley caught himself before he let anything slip. "Or maybe I should tell her to take care of *you!*" He slapped Solberg on the back and then turned to Sato. "Chief Sato, how are you? That was some good flying you did the other morning…" He was clearly working the room now.

"Foreign Area Officer? You're a diplomat?" Solberg asked. "What's a woman with your moves doing pushing visas all day?"

"Aww, thanks for the offer," Archer said before Solberg could push any further on the evening plans. *He may be kinda cute, but he's not too bright,* she thought to herself. "I have plans tonight, but it'd be great to go out with you boys some other time." She took another drink and put down a few coins to pay for the second drink. "I'm sure *you* have some good moves on the dance floor too!" She tapped him on the shoulder with her fingertip, smiled and turned to go.

Before he could protest, she inserted herself between Bradley and Sato. "Thank you for the invitation, Colonel. I need to head out now, duty calls! And nice meeting you, Chief Sato, it was a pleasure if only a brief one…!" She bowed deeply in jest.

"*Kochira koso!*" He said, bowing deeply in return. "The pleasure was mine!"

Archer exited the bar, only to see Sergeant Edwards on the corner with one of his boys. She rolled her eyes as he approached.

"Hey, lady, just give me a minute to explain. I didn't mean nothin' by it, you know. I was like, just approaching to talk, ya know."

"Whatever you say, G.I. Joe. I overheard you and your boys talk back there. Don't assume that people around you here are stupid and don't see your game for what it is, even if they don't understand your words."

"Look, it's a compliment, girl. You got a nice figure, so own it already."

"And damn, you got some *moves* too!" declared his friend, who had been silent until this point. "You took Edwards out like he was a rag doll or somethin'. Damn!" Sergeant Edwards shot him a look at his comment. "Wha? Just sayin' is all..." Edwards's friend replied.

"Well boys, let that be a lesson..."

"So anyway, what d'ya say?" Edwards pressed. "You and me, let's go somewhere, hang out and stuff..."

"Hey, what about me?" protested Edwards's friend.

"Don't worry, we'll find you a nice Jap lady..."

"Oh Christ not this again...Obtuse and racist too." Archer muttered. "You really know how to woo the ladies don't you."

They both smiled unwittingly at the sarcastic comment, which caused Archer to roll her eyes and sigh out loud.

"Look, fellas, you may think you're slick and all, but if I wasn't clear inside, let me be crystal clear here. *I'm not interested*, got it?"

"All right, all right," Edwards said, holding up his hands in feigned resignation. "Some other time then..."

Archer did not notice. She was already headed in the opposite direction.

CHAPTER 12 - KANO'S REVENGE

"I have something for you, boss," Kensuke had barely knocked before allowing himself into Kano's private study.

"Kensuke, what's the meaning of this?!" Kano said, annoyed at the intrusion.

"Take a look at this," Kensuke said, handing Kano a thumb drive. "This is the girl that's been following us for months now, trying to penetrate us."

Kano retrieved his lap top from a drawer, opened it, and inserted the thumb drive. He opened the first video and played it, with the volume on mute. A reporter mouthed words silently outside the detention center in Tokyo. She wore a jacket with the hood up to protect her from the slow rain falling in the background, and the lights from the camera lit up her face in the darkness and the rain behind her. Portions of the building were also visible behind her from the floodlights from other reporters next to her and from the detention center itself.

"There!" Kensuke said as he paused the video. "That's her." He pointed to a figure in the corner of the screen. "Walking from the building in the background to the left, right there."

"*So ka....*" Kano said, almost under his breath. He pressed play, and the figure pulled her hood tightly over her head.

"She's the one who's been trailing your guys?"

"Yes, the one who was secretly meeting with Hayashi, too."

"The informant in our midst?"

"Yep. And he paid for his treachery with his life after the botched delivery," Kensuke said.

"Hmmm, suicide I heard..." Kano said coyly. "So who is she?"

"I talked to our person at the detention center, who says she's there often. She's American, a diplomat."

"Diplomat, huh?" Kano's interest was piqued further.

"Says she goes there mainly to meet with Americans if they've been detained and need embassy assistance. But she doesn't just meet with Americans, she also meets with Japanese who've been detained on drug charges, that sort of thing."

"Oh?" Kano asked.

"She's seen quite a lot with a National Police Agency official, a guy named Ryutaro Nishi. The same Nishi who is interrogating Hatano as we speak," Kensuke said, looking down at Kano.

"I don't like this girl. I don't like Americans, and I especially don't like them mucking about in my business." Kano said. Kano looked at Kensuke. "Take care of her."

"With pleasure, boss!" Kensuke replied, bowing. "Excuse me," he said as he turned to leave.

"Wait, just a moment." Kano began to smile. "I think I know someone who might want to meet her. Get her, and bring her to me."

"Yessir!" Kensuke said again, bowed, and left. He seemed more pleased with this order.

This'll be a nice sweetener for the next shipment, Kano thought as he sat back in his seat. *And I relish exacting revenge on my enemies, just like so many years ago...*

• • •

The aspiring Mafioso Ichiro Nakajima stumbled out of the small *izakaya* pub, laughing. He leaned on a woman who smiled despite straining at his considerable weight. "Now you come with me, *neh?*" she whispered in his ear. "Dump your friends, we'll have some fun together, you and me," she ordered rather than asked.

After stealing his first pachinko parlors from the Kano cousins, Nakajima was celebrating the acquisition of his seventh pachinko parlor in less than eighteen months. He would soon be playing with the big boys.

"*Oooiiii*, guys, g'on now, y'all head...go home," Nakajima declared to his male comrades as he flicked his hand at them a couple of times. "I'm 'a go with this pretty lady, right here..." he stammered, falling forward. The girl caught him and he laughed, both at his inebriated state and at his good fortune in finding lovely ladies such as this one.

"Boss, you sure you're alright?" one asked. He looked at the lady they had just met. Unlike the others, this one was particularly forward in her interest in their boss, Nakajima. And she seemed to know a lot about him...

"Yeah, maybe you should come back with us," his friend said, equally concerned about the girl's sudden and flirtatious appearance.

"*Iyaaaa*, wha're ya talkin' 'bout," Nakajima stammered. "Thissshh is m'new lady-friend..." he started to say.

"Yeah, mind your own business!" the girl shouted, poking at the boys with her hand. "You're just jealous that none of the other girls took any fancy with you!" She turned to Nakajima, smiling. "Com'on baby, let me take you home, take care of you tonight..."

She opened the door with her free hand and helped Nakajima into the passenger seat of the car. She paced quickly around the car and got into the driver's seat. Without looking at the two men now standing in front of her car, she started the ignition and put the car into reverse almost at the same time and backed out of the parking spot. The wheels kicked up gravel as she sped away into the night.

As the car pulled onto a paved road, Nakajima slid next to the girl. "Baby, ya' r'dy fer some fun t'night...?" Nakajima said, smiling lasciviously at her. He leaned onto her shoulder as she drove, thrusting his hand between the buttons of her blouse.

She jerked the car to the left just as he was about to lick her cheek, throwing him back into his seat. "Hey, babe, slo d'n!" he stammered, attempting to return to her side.

She looked into the rear view mirror at the empty road behind them, and then the driver-side mirror. "All clear," she said in an even, angry tone.

"Hmmm hmmm," Nakajima chuckled. "All clear, eh? Za' boys a'n't here any more, hmm..." He leaned into her again, this time to lick the nape of her neck. He placed his hand on her breast to both fondle it and steady himself in the fast-moving vehicle as he tried to mount her.

She leaned her head away and grimaced out of disgust.

Out of the corner of her eye she could see in the rear-view mirror a figure rising up from the back seat. In one motion the figure reached around Nakajima's head with both arms, and with one hand the figure placed a chlorophyll-drenched handkerchief over Nakajima's face just as his tongue curled up the side of the girl's neck. The figure pulled Nakajima's head back onto the head-rest as he struggled only momentarily. Already inebriated, Ichiro Nakajima was out in seconds.

• • •

Nakajima woke to find himself pinned upright by wire mesh. He could not move at all, and he could barely talk with the wire mesh wrapped tightly over his face. He felt something cold and hard at his back, with jagged edges cutting into his shoulder blades and lower back.

"*Oooiii*, what is this?" he mumbled. Nakajima could only make out figures standing nearby in the darkness and the bright glow of embers as the figures puffed from their cigarettes.

He struggled against the mesh, but to no avail. "*Ooooiiii*, what's the meaning of this, what's going on?" he demanded again, this time with a stronger voice. "I'm a very important man, my people are looking for me right now. I warn you, you're in for it, trying to treat me this way!"

One of the figures flicked away the dying ember of his cigarette, and he stepped forward.

"Nakajima-san," said a figure still partially obscured by the darkness. "It's been awhile."

"What is this? Who are you?" Nakajima shouted as he struggled furtively against the wire mesh again.

"Yes, how long would you say?" another voice asked.

"Seventeen months, twenty-seven days," the other answered, stepping closer to Nakajima. "Don't you remember me, Nakajima, you son-of-a-bitch?"

"*Eh?* Takada-kun, is that you?" Nakajima asked, surprised.

"Give me respect, Nakajima, call me 'Kano-san,'" Kano replied, emphasizing *san*, He banged Nakajima on the nose with the bottom side of his fist to emphasize his point.

Nakajima cringed at the hit, but then recovered quickly. He licked gently at the blood that trickled from his nose.

"Hehe, very well. Ka*nooooooo-saaan!*" Nakajima said in a feigned and nasally voice that dripped with condescension. "My people will know that I'm missing, they'll come for me, this is very dangerous for you and your boys there," Nakajima continued. He attempted to nod to the other men behind Kano, but he could not move his head.

"We're here to discuss making a deal," Kano replied. "I know you like to make deals, and I have one you will not want to refuse..."

"*Oooiiii*, where's that cousin of yours?" Nakajima continued. "Let's see, one, two, three...and you make four. And then that cunt driver of yours who picked me up at the bar, still in the car." He paused for a moment for effect, and then declared: "Nope, I don't see him. He's not here, eh?" Nakajima smiled broadly.

Kano welled up in anger. *Does he know? How could he know that Taiei, my cousin, contracted tuberculosis less than a month after working here on road construction projects through the mountain passes of central Japan?*

"He'll join us soon, Ichiro-kun, don't you worry," Kano replied, barely able to hold back his anger.

"Hmmmm, that's not what I heard," Nakajima continued. "I heard he didn't do too well after he sold the parlors..."

"Who told you that!" Kano demanded, thrusting his face inches from Nakajima's.

"That was unfortunate, but not unexpected. He was a weak boy. But you, I knew you would do well for yourself..."

Kano gritted his teeth in anger, drew back his hand in a fist, and punched Nakajima on the side of the face. He did not consider how the wire mesh would interfere with his punch, and he drew back his fist in pain, blood trickling from his knuckles. He turned from Nakajima and began to shake his hand instinctively. "*Kuso!*" He muttered. "Shit!" He steadied himself and turned back again to face Nakajima. One of Kano's men handed him a rag, which he used to wrap his hand while staring at Nakajima.

Nakajima's nose was bleeding more profusely now. "Fuck you!" he shouted back at Kano, blood splattering from the top of his lip. He then gasped when he saw Kano's man handing him a pair of wire cutters. "Where'd you get those!?" he demanded.

"You recognize these, eh?" said Kano, holding up a pair of wire cutters. "I believe you inherited them from your father when he died, hmmm?" Kano slowly examined the handles and then the metal head. "They have quite a history, as you have explained." Kano looked back at Nakajima. "And they are very helpful in *business negotiations,* as you have shown..."

"Let's make this simple. I'll speak in terms you can understand," Kano said, approaching Nakajima. "You are right-handed.

I will cut each finger on your left hand until you place your seal on this document returning the pachinko parlors to me, the rightful owner."

Nakajima balled his hand into a fist, realizing what was about to happen. Kano motioned his men forward, who lunged at Nakajima. Despite being immobilized by the wire mesh, both of his hands were free at the wrist.

"Look, Kano, you're a survivor, I like that," Nakajima said, speaking more quickly now as Kano's men attempted to steady his hands. "Become my partner, help me manage the properties. You know them well. We'll forget all of this, start anew, right?"

"I know how you treat partners," Kano said, and he slammed the flat side of the wire cutter head onto Nakajima's fist.

"Ahhhhh!" screamed Nakajima, who released his grip slightly. Kano's men grabbed his fingers and forced them to splay out against the rock.

"And this is what you get when you renege on an honest deal, made between two families!" Kano grumbled as he opened the wire cutters over Nakajima's pinky, cutting it.

"Aahhhhh!" Nakajima screamed. "Stop, stop!!" Nakajima thrashed at the wire mesh, but he was barely able to move despite exerting all his strength. His screams echoed against the canyon walls of the desolate valley.

Kano did not pause. He put the wire cutters over Nakajima's next finger and then cut it too. "My uncle and your father had a *deal,* and they *you* reneged on it and *stole* my family's property!" He then a third finger.

"Ahhhh!" Nakajima continued to cry. "No, no! Stop! I'm sorry, I'm *sorry*!!" he screamed again and again, whimpering. As Kano positioned the wire cutters over his index finger, Nakajima blurted out, "Ok OK!!" he screamed in agony. "Give me the *hanko,* I'll do it!"

Kano took the *hanko* from his pocket, opened it, and positioned it in Nakajima's hand. He then took the papers, held them up to Nakajima's hand, and Ichiro Nakajima stamped all the necessary places on several pages.

Kano stepped back, examined the papers, and then folded them and placed them in the inner pocket of his overalls.

Nakajima whimpered. "You'll never get those filed at town hall. They know who I am and that I would never actually *approve* such a deal. I'm a *business man*," Nakajima declared, his voice gaining in strength. "I'm a big deal in theses parts, Kano-*san*"—Nakajima's intonation rose to a shrill scream on saying "san"—"and everything you do will have to come through me! It's just a matter of time, Kano-*san*!"

"Oh-ho!" chuckled Kano, mocking Nakajima with a wry smile. "Is that so?" Kano smiled broadly. "I knew you would come around," Kano replied, ignoring Nakajima's renewed threats. "Very well, it was a pleasure doing business with you, *business man* Nakajima," Kano said mockingly in return. He handed the wire cutters to his henchman. "*Sore de wa*," Kano stepped back, nodded slightly, and motioned to another man standing in the shadows to come.

"Hey, Kano-san, what about me?" screamed Nakajima, blood trickling down the side of the rock cliff. "Aren't you gonna cut me out of here now? I stamped it, you got what you want. I even lost some fingers. We're even now…what, are you gonna leave me here all night? Com'on, let me out of here…!" He began to struggle against the wire mesh again, to no avail.

Kano's colleague pulled a portable cement mixer to the group, then picked up the long tube and hoisted it over his shoulder to drag it to the side of the shear face of the cliff, frowning under the heft of the equipment. The others began to encase the mesh wire with a wooden border to hold the concrete. Kano, meanwhile, retrieved some items from the back of a small truck near the group.

"Hey, what the *fuck* are you doing? What's going on, let me *out* damn it!" he struggled so that the wire cut into his skin on his face.

"Our crew is reinforcing the sides of these cliffs tonight in our work to prevent mudslides and falling rocks in this area," Kano explained as he approached Nakajima again. "We're prepping for a proper road to be built through the valley. All of your obstinacy has meant that we are now delayed, so my workers are getting back to work to ensure we complete the job on time."

Kano raised the wire cutter and smashed Nakajima along the side of his face with it. When Nakajima screamed from the hit, Kano stuck a block of wood in one side of his mouth to keep Nakajima from biting down. He took the wire cutters and angled them deep into Nakajima's mouth. Nakajima screamed even as he tried to pull back his tongue. Kano separated the handles of the wire cutter, stuck the open pincers in deeper and then closed them forcefully. "Arrghhh!" Nakajima let out a guttural cry, and then he started to gurgle from the blood flowing out of his mouth and down his throat.

Kano repeated the operation two more times to sever the last connections of Nakajima's tongue from his jaw. He pulled out the severed tongue with a spare rag, wrapped it in a separate handkerchief, and then forced the rag fully into Nakajima's mouth to muffle his screams, which continued unabated.

The workers then began to fill the make-shift wooden barriers set up along the face of the cliff in front of Nakajima with cement, first up to Nakajima's knees, then to his groin and torso, and then to his shoulders. Nakajima continued to thrash about, at times screaming and at other times whimpering. They installed the last of the wooden framework over his head and poured still more concrete.

"Mmmgghhhh...MMMGggghhh..." came the panicked, garbled cries as the cement slowly subsumed his neck, his chin, his nose, and finally, his forehead.

As they slowly filled the embankment with cement, Kano wrapped the original handkerchief containing Nakajima's tongue and wrapped it again lightly and stuck it in his pocket. He took out another handkerchief, picked up the fingers and wrapped them lightly as well. The pinky still had a diamond ring on it.

Kano then looked at the cliff. His colleagues poured the remaining cement mix over Nakajima's head to the top of the last wooden barrier. Kano watched the last bubbles rise to the surface and pop. He then stood a moment to relish the quiet.

The workers gathered their equipment and loaded their trucks, and then departed wordlessly. Kano drove in the opposite direction, back to his hometown.

•   •   •

The next afternoon, Kano stood on the corner of an elementary school playground. The school had just let out, and children scurried everywhere.

Kano focused on one girl as she approached, laughing with her friends.

"Yumi-chan, Yumi-chan!" he shouted in a nasally and cheerful voice. He raised his hand palm downward at her and flicked his fingers several times toward himself to gesture for her to come to him.

She looked toward Kano, tilting her head quizzically. She approached him out of curiosity, thinking that she must know him from somewhere since he knew her.

Kano smiled broadly at the girl. "Yumi-chan, you remember me, don't you? I'm Uncle Kano. We met last year, surely you remember?"

She cocked her head further to the side in confusion. "Eh? Uncle Kano?" she asked, trying to remember the last time they met.

"Yes, that's right, I have something for you and your daddy. Can you give this to your daddy for Uncle Kano?" He took out a small envelope. "This is a present for you and your daddy, but you can't open it now! Tell your daddy it's from Uncle Kano, Uncle Takada Kano, ok?"

"Unn," she said in agreement. She did not think to wonder why he did not want to give it to her father himself. She snatched the envelope and ran with her friends down the street. When she turned the corner out of sight of Uncle Kano and had parted with her friends, she slowed and looked at the envelope. She turned it over in her hands several times and squeezed gently at the lumps inside. One was squishy, one was hard. She held the envelope loosely in her hand as she started skipping along the sidewalk on her way home. She did not notice Uncle Kano peek around the corner at her as she skipped away.

When she arrived home a few streets away, she yelled "daddy daddy! Uncle Kano gave us a present! Open it!"

"Uncle Kano? Who's Uncle Kano...?" he asked as he took the envelope.

"Uncle Takada Kano, he said we know him, from last year," the girl replied. "What is it?" she asked in an excited and curious tone.

He remembered that name, but from where? Like his daughter moments ago, he turned the envelope over in his hand, confused by the lumps.

He pulled the sealed tab of the envelope. Inside were two handkerchiefs that had been stained red. The pit of his stomach tightened.

"Yumi-chan, go see your mother."

"But daddy! What's in it? What's in the envelope…?"

"Go, now!" he shouted.

"…what's the present daddy? Let me see…!" Yumi jumped to peek at what her father was holding.

"Keiko-san, come get Yumi! I need to make a phone call, it's urgent!"

His wife, Keiko, entered the room. "What is it dear…?" She saw his ashen face, and then immediately grabbed Yumi by the shoulders. "Come on dear, I need your help in the kitchen."

"But mommy, I want to see!" Yumi shouted as she tried to turn back to her father, still holding the envelope.

"Later Yumi-chan, I'm sure your father will show you a wonderful present later. It will be a wonderful surprise for all of us!" She glanced at her husband, who she could see was deeply disturbed. She turned back to Yumi. "But first we have to get dinner ready…" She ushered Yumi quickly into the kitchen and slid the shoji door closed.

He dared not touch the stained handkerchiefs. He pushed aside the books on the coffee table, opened the envelope wide and turned it upside down. The two handkerchiefs fell out onto the table, and a finger tumbled from one. A diamond ring fell loose from the finger.

"*I know that ring…*"

He reached for a pen to unfold the other one, which looked like…

He pushed himself away, gagging. He doubled over at the side of the table, trying to maintain his composure…and his lunch.

He looked up to the table again and saw that there was a small note that had fallen from the envelope. He grabbed the blood-stained parchment and then sat against the wall on the far side of the room. He collected himself, and then he opened the note.

"I've returned to take back what was mine," it began. "You will ensure the deeds are transferred to my full and rightful ownership, or I'll be giving your daughter these presents from you and your wife as well…"

At those cryptic words, City Hall senior administrator Yamanaka recalled events of the prior year. "Keiko-san! I need to go back to the office, and I don't know when I'll be back tonight!" he yelled as he departed the house.

CHAPTER 13 - MEDITATIONS

Hisao Araki sat in the small room, motionless. His feet were folded on his thighs, his heels almost digging into his groin. Hemp cord looped tightly around each knee and criss-crossed along his back, over his shoulders and around his armpits and were tied off in the middle of his back, locking him tightly in a lotus position. His hands were cupped in his lap, left hand over right and rigidly motionless. His thumbs touched gently above the palms to form an oval shape, which served to channel his energy around and back into the base of his spine. For that is where energy springs, and to which energy must flow for a person to purify himself.

No matter the distraction, no matter the desire, no matter the drowsiness, the tightly wound hemp cord would keep him locked into this position and help him achieve *nirvana,* his guru had always preached.

He sat in a bare room on a simple Japanese tatami mat measuring a few meters on either side. The room itself could accommodate only four tatami mats, the size of a mere closet by some standards. Araki preferred the room small, simple. No ornaments. No decorations. No distractions. Training was everything.

There was a small alcove across from Araki, a *Tokonoma* built into the wall. Instead of the typical hanging scroll along with a flower arrangement of some kind to reflect the season, there was a hanging picture of a man in white flowing robes, long black hair and an untrimmed beard. He was Asian, but larger than the typical Asian, more rotund, beefy. This was the Beloved One, and Araki saw both power and a stern love emanating as an aura from him. The few others Araki knew who didn't practice the same religion dared to call the guru a fat conman, but Araki had experienced something like an awakening around him. The guru did not smile

155

in the picture, but rather seemed in detached contemplation of something *else*. It could be that the figure was trying to make out an object in the distance, beyond the range of the camera. The man in the picture was unconcerned with things physical, and seemed more entranced with things beyond the normal and the expected. His eyes were half open, half shut, and there was a hint of a smile beneath his beard.

Araki too felt he had similar glimpses of what his guru saw and *lived*, but they were just glimpses. Araki needed to practice exactly as his teacher instructed in order to become one with that *other*, and this was one of the practices. Araki had long ago cut ties with those who questioned the Beloved One, because they did not know. How could they know? They were Lesser Beings, as the Beloved One taught, blind as they were to their own karmic hell.

Araki sat across from the picture, and opening his eyes slightly he would switch from *kundalini* to simple prayer. He prayed to the figure. He prayed for enlightenment, for deliverance.

Araki could not move, the hemp cord prevented that. Physical bondage would lead the way to spiritual freedom, the Beloved One taught at *Satyam No. 7* near Mt. Fuji, the main devotion hall where he and other like-minded devotees practiced. This was the typical training method for mendicants in the sect, for the ones just starting out, to gain the proper spiritual education. Too many people in this world practiced incorrectly, the Beloved One would say. And too few in this world dared to practice at all. "You are the chosen," Araki could hear him say, as he sat in the unlit room, eyes slightly ajar. "Karma has chosen you, your past lives have chosen you, and the path led to me," the Beloved One said. "And I know the path away from hell, away from suffering and into the light and peace of righteousness, away from the sins of this world," *kono yoo* he would say, "and into the warm soft pedals of paradise," *ano yoo*. This world and that, the defiled and the purified. And how defiled Araki had been before he heard the calling of his Beloved, before his Karma grew strong enough to allow Araki to turn from the world of materialistic bondage around him and follow the ways of the righteous…

"Human beings are so dominated by desire," the Beloved One would teach, "that they are largely beyond saving…When our bad Karma accumulates, gods of terror force us to realize this truth, and their severe, wrathful judgment is actually an exhibition of the highest form of love, for they are delivering the damned to a new life, and a new chance to redeem themselves…"

"You, my children, *you* have been led away from this hell of judgment and love, *you* have been led away from the cycle of love and hatred, birth and death, the realm of forms. But the others, the outside world, they have not, and *you*, the righteous ones, will turn the cosmic wheel of their Karma that will again propel them to their next incarnation. This is for their own good…" the Beloved One would preach, before drifting into a deep trance.

*Knock knock knock…*Araki allowed himself to become dimly aware of a sound outside his room. "*Araki-san, Araki-san, are you in there? I brought you your lunch…*"

Araki's eyes remained transfixed on the figure in the picture, which continued to speak to him. "Thus, my children, I offer you this incantation, a *mantra* for deliverance to salvation, a *mahamudra* of the highest spiritual attainment. This incantation will help you overcome the cosmic habits of bad Karma, the darkness in your minds and the vileness of your souls, for we are all born vile into the world of forms, duped to believe that this world is *the* world, when in fact it is but a grain of sand on an eternal beach of reality…"

Araki's face was milky, his eyes sunken. He was a thin man, and his ribs showed through his tightly-drawn skin. A few random hairs poked defiantly from his exposed chest. His hair was cut bowl-shaped and remained jet-black despite his checkered and eventful history in the sect and a life on the run. Most men would be gray now, but Araki kept the youthful appearance of a 15 year-old. He could feel his pulse race, but knew that the time would soon come. The time now was to train, and *this* was the training. The desire was a manifestation of past Karma, the negative life force of what he was and how he acted before drew him back into a hellish abyss, but by recognizing it and watching it and letting it go, he could slowly achieve enlightenment. He would join the savior, the Beloved, *his* Beloved. He felt his life force strengthen with each heartbeat. Training was now, the *now* was the training...

Knockknockknock. *"Araki-san, I have your lunch, and medicine, may I come in...?"*

"We are in a constant struggle in this world, but that is ok. This is the world of forms, and is thus an illusion," Araki heard his Beloved One say. "We are entering a period of war and devastation, but this war will be a *spiritual* war, a war of souls...as enlightened beings, as beings on the road to ultimate salvation, we will have to meet the enemy of forms directly. It is all right in this war to sacrifice people utterly lost in the illusion, because they are forever defiled. They *believe* the illusions that you are awakening from. It is all right to steal, to kill, to commit adultery, to lie, because that will be their shortcut to salvation. They will be forced to *deal* with the shattering of the illusion of materialism, and for that, in their next lives, they will be thankful, and we will join in harmonious celebration in the afterworld together..."

"Araki-san, I know you are training now, but I have your lunch and meds, and it's important that I speak to you now." The voice paused, and then added: *"It is about completing your guru's vision..."*

Araki opened his eyes fully, and he looked toward the door. He lifted one arm up slowly from its resting place, and then the other one, and without so much as massaging feeling back into them, without dispelling the numbness, he reached behind his back to undo the knot in the hemp cord. At *Satyam No. 7*–"Truth No.

7"—he could not do that, he could never reach behind his back to untie himself. The elders would perform that task for him, because he was in training. He as a mendicant did not know enough to stop his own training. But here, he was alone. He could not practice with others, there were no others, not here. He continued the teachings as best he could, but it had been many years since the accusations and arrests, and Araki was beginning to forget how things were.

"This is what in Buddhist theology we call poa. This is the washing off of bad Karma with abrupt treatment, shock therapy, as the Diamond Sutra and the *Tibetan Book of the Dead* teaches us. For when a person is on his death bed, we perform a spiritual exercise called '*poa*' to help that soul attain a 'transference of consciousness,' a rise to a higher plane of existence. We in the material world guide the soul to its proper destination so that it does not get lost forever in the illusions and shadows of the earth plane. We *poa* to dispense this higher existence to those who are defiled. In this way, with the world in critical condition as it is, we must *poa* to save the world, we must do what is required for salvation of the world, we must practice complete *Vajrayana* as taught in the Diamond Sutra and the *Tibetan Book of the Dead*, we must *poa* all wrongdoers. Repeat the *mantra* for *mahamudra*, for salvation, after me…"

Knockknockknock… "Araki-san, I'm coming in now…"

Araki glanced in annoyance at the sliding door while tugging at the knot. He tugged for some time, his heart pounding at the effort and at what awaited him. His hands shook too much. *"Dette Ike!* Go away!" he yelled at Kano as he entered, unconsciously embarrassed at being seen in such a compromising position. Finally, with beads of sweat forming on his body, he reached up to his shoulder and pushed at the cord until it slid off his shoulder, leaving red welt marks there, but Araki took no notice. The rest of the cord slackened, and Araki pulled himself out of the other side more easily. He left the cord around his knees, forgetting about them. His attention was already on the tray next to him. Under his breath he began to repeat the mantra, *I will do whatever is required for salvation of the world… I will practice complete Vajrayana… I will poa all wrongdoers… I will poa all wrongdoers… I will practice Vajrayana without a care… I will join the whole army to poa all wrongdoers…*

Araki picked up a long rubber tie from the tray, twisted it around his arm above the elbow joint and held the ends in his teeth. Under his breath, his mantra stuck like a broken record as his teeth clinched tightly in anticipation: *I will poa all wrongdoers… I will poa all wrongdoers…* He picked up the syringe, already complete with a hypodermic needle and filled, and he flicked at his vein with his middle finger while balling his other hand into a tight fist again and again… *I will poa all wrongdoers… I will poa all wrongdoers…* He found the vein, and like a medic on a war-ravaged battlefield he plunged the needle into the arm of his suffering patient at exactly the right place, pulled up slightly on the plunger, and slowly pushed down on it, discharging the milky liquid into the netherworld of his soul. *I will poa…* He went slowly on purpose, as a way to train, to teach himself control. He stopped pushing for a second though his body and soul ached for more smack, and then he pushed slowly down again, and still again. He felt his veins accept the substance, he tasted it in his mouth, on his tongue. He salivated almost as if he was about to lick the smack from thin air. *I will…* The rubber tie slipped from his mouth as it fell open, and his eyelids drooped lazily as his torso went limp.

…poa… he uttered as his back fell onto the wall behind him.

Kano sat next to the hunched up body of Araki in the corner, a huddled mass in a fetal position. Kano plucked the syringe out of Araki's arm and placed it on the metal tray, pushing it away carefully with his foot lest he accidentally step on it. Araki was still only dimly unaware of Kano's presence even as Kano shook him gently. Kano sat him up against the wall and tapped him on the cheek.

"Master Araki? Master Araki, are you with us, master…?" Kano said placatingly.

Araki grunted slightly, shaking his head back and forth to avoid the strange touch on his face…

"Araki-Sensei, please return to us…" *taptap…* "won't you grace us with your presence, master..?" *taptaptap…*

Araki grumbled. "Uhhnnn…" His eyes were still closed, and he drew in a deep breath. "Uuuhhhhhhhhhhhnnnnnnnnnn…"

Kano waited as Araki came to. He then sat in front of Araki in *seiza*, on his knees with his hands on the floor in front of him slightly. He peered at Araki's eyelids inquisitively, observantly, and as they flickered open slightly Kano's facial expression turned from one of observation to obsequiousness.

"Ah, Araki-sensei, how wisely you sit…" Kano waited for a response. Kano then slapped Araki on the cheek.

"Hmmm?" responded Araki, shaking his head. Araki looked like he was waking from a fitful sleep, his eyes were darkly rimmed and his face was gaunt and pale. His hair was matted from lying so long in the corner and from a lack of hygiene, and he smelled. "Hmmm? *Eh? Kano-san desu ka?* Kano-san, is that you…?" asked Araki.

"Yes, it is me, Araki-sensei. I came to observe the master in meditation. I've been hearing things about the young master from some of my people here, and so I decided to pay Master Araki a visit, and how right they were!" said Kano, hunched over slightly as his hands remained on the floor in front of his knees. He smiled gently.

"You…you came to visit me?" Araki was now trying to regain his bearings.

"Yes, master Araki. I noticed your meditation, and I even sat with you for some time to try to learn by example. *Saaaaa*, alas, my understanding of your practice is so shallow, I felt I had to bring you out of your trance so as to instruct me further..." At this Kano bowed in front of Araki, "I sincerely apologize for so rudely awakening the young master..."

"Eh?" Araki was briefly surprised at the sudden sight of his benefactor bowing before him, but then Araki realized that indeed his long years of hard training and sacrifice were changing him, had indeed changed him, and that this was just a sign of his new-found power toward other less-enlightened ones.

"Yes, Kano-san, I am glad to see you. I am glad that you came, I've been wanting to talk with you..." Araki began to straighten himself, he stiffened his back and sat more erect. His eyes narrowed again as he induced himself into a state of introspection. "It is good of you to come, we shall finally have time to talk..."

"Yes, master Araki, we will. As you yourself are fond of quoting, the 13th Century Samurai Gokurakuji said, '*One should have insight into this world of dreams that passes in a twinkling of an eye...*' I can only hope that you will someday deign to pass on such insight to a mere layman such as myself one day." Kano forced himself to look upon Araki smilingly, tenderly, fatherly.

"Thank you for such kind words, dear Kano-san, and thank you too for your hospitality. You have been so dear to me over these past years, and I have prayed for you often." Araki's eyes became mere slits as his ego soared, projecting a deeper aura of wisdom much as his master did so effortlessly. His heart slowed... *I am becoming one with the Master,* he thought, *just as he expected, just as he said we would join, someday, in eternity.*

Kano's eyes narrowed as well, but in an observant and conscious way. "Araki-sensei, if I recall correctly, your master, your Beloved who is in jail now awaiting the carrying out of the last sentence for the subway incident decades ago, he gave you a final mission before he was caught, am I correct?" Kano leaned forward slightly, peering intently at Araki.

Araki's eyebrows narrowed, and his head drooped almost imperceptibly. "Yes, yes he did. I have a mission to complete before I can enter the final state of Nirvana, before I can inherit heaven on earth…"

"Yes, I remember reading around that time, before the plans became public, that the military here in Japan was plotting to raid your complexes, with mustard gas and VX gas, and then if there were survivors, they were going to send you to a stockade and give you blankets covered in smallpox virus. You were to die a slow and excruciating death, wasn't that so Araki? Wasn't that their plan? Your people had to protect themselves from these diabolical plots by striking first, by fighting fire with fire."

"Yes!" Araki exclaimed. "They attacked us with *their* chemical and biological weapons, and the Japanese cops helped them!" Araki's brow furrowed deeply. He held his eyes tightly shut, holding back the pain and anger. He muttered, *we must poa all nonbelievers… we must poa… I must poa the devils… I must poa…*

"What was your mission, Araki? What were you planning to do? If I recall, again, correct me if I'm mistaken, I'm so forgetful in my old age, but didn't that final task involve a helicopter…?"

*I must poa…I must kill nonbelievers… I must kill…*Araki didn't move.

"Do you want to complete your mission? I have a need for someone like you, someone ready to defend the land, our people, our pure spirit, our race. Are you ready to complete your mission, Araki?"

"*Yes, I am, I must poa… I must kill nonbelievers…*" Araki almost hissed. "…must…poa…" The words oozed out of his pursed mouth.

All Kano could hear was a murmur, a whisper in the wind, but a whisper is all Kano needed. "I have the supplies for your mission, now is the time for you to complete it!" Kano grabbed Araki's shoulder in anticipation.

Araki opened his eyes almost in surprise, and then shut them again as he smiled. "Karma has delivered you to me, Kano-san," Araki said.

"No, Araki-sensei, I'm quite sure that Karma has delivered you to *me*," Kano said in reply. Araki mistook Kano's excited demeanor as proof of his newfound devotion to Araki's—and the Beloved One's—teachings.

"I know that your guru, the Beloved, trained you to fly helicopters for your mission, so you shall have one for this mission," Kano explained. "And you were an assistant to your group's defense minister, if I recall correctly? You helped mix chemicals and toxins?"

Araki nodded.

"Good, we will need those skills. Be ready at sunrise tomorrow, we depart to prepare for your mission!"

Araki nodded imperceptibly.

"Also, we will need you to contact your fellow believer at the Communications Research Lab in Kashima City, in Ibaraki Prefecture. We will need two more sets of quasi-zenith satellite receivers..." Kano caught himself as his voice began to strengthen into a demand, rather than an obsequious request. "That is, to complete your next missions, we will need the ability to target some additional facilities with complete precision..."

"Ah, yes, that makes sense," Araki replied, haughtily. "I will contact him."

"Thank you, Araki-San. Timing is of the essence, as you know, and I will have one of my men pick them up immediately..." Kano paused to watch his response, "...within the next 24 hours..."

Araki smiled, nodded in supreme confidence that he could fulfill the task at hand with the end so near, and then he closed his eyes to meditate. Kano, satisfied, turned to exit.

CHAPTER 14 - PLEASURE BEFORE BUSINESS

Candidate Tadaishi took the 10:35 pm flight from Komatsu City, located on the Sea of Japan, to Tokyo. The flight lasted less than an hour and was practically empty. That suited Tadaishi, since he wasn't scheduled to leave his district during the campaign. The fewer people around to see him depart, the better. He enjoyed the flight for its anonymity, since the stewardesses—all young and quite attractive, Tadaishi noted—were from Tokyo and too young to follow politics. And the three or four men in suits on the flight were probably returning to homes and families in Tokyo from closing a deal or two, or working in management at some local factories in the prefecture. At any rate, they fell quickly asleep.

Tadaishi turned on the TV screen on the seat directly in front of him. The late evening news segment brought viewers up to date on events of the day: A female reporter updated viewers from the Tokyo Detention Center on the status of the suspect involved in the maritime incident, while another reported on the prime ministerial candidate Seitoh's visit to the Shibamata Taishakuten Buddhist temple earlier that day. The program then featured North Korea's reaction, showing a pert lady in a regal pink Korean dress and thick black belt declare solemnly on North Korean television that "military imperialist warmongers" were "slanderously and viciously accusing the DPRK of provocative acts that we had no part in." A world globe slowly turned in the background, with the Korean peninsula peering at viewers from behind her head. "But in turn," she declared, "the imperialist warmongers have exhibited a return to military nationalism, evoking sacred figures in Asian mythology to threaten the peaceful people of the Democratic People's Republic of Korea with outright war!" She then declared in a rising voice that "our strong and steadfast military, together with our advancements in defense technologies, will meet and defeat any attack upon us!" She emphasized the point by pounding on the newscaster's podium and pursing her lips tightly while mocking viewers with her eyes. "The Japanese people should think twice before they bring to power the imperialist warmonger, one who denies the atrocities committed by the Japanese imperialists!"

Summing up the North Korean reaction, the Japanese newscaster then switched to an extensive interview with party leader Seitoh following her visit to the Shibamata Taishakuten Buddhist temple. "But historical issues aside, what matters to the Japanese people right now, here in the 21st century, is our national security," candidate Seitoh was shown saying. "Our colleagues in other Asian capitals try to suggest that, based on this or that statement made by any Japanese politician, myself included, it is an indication of revival of a so-called 'militarism' in Japan, but that is farthest from the truth."

"And what is the truth?" the interviewer asked.

"The truth is that we, as a democratic society that protects basic human rights such as freedom of expression, are highly concerned about living next to a country controlled by a totalitarian regime bent on possessing an arsenal of nuclear weapons and using them to blackmail us and other peace-loving nations. We also live next to a country run by the largest Communist Party organization in the history of the world, which by the way has made no secret of wanting to dominate the Pacific rim. That impacts us directly, as an island nation in the Pacific. These same leaders accuse us of militarism even as they build the largest army and navy in the world with a defense budget larger than ours by a factor of five. They are merely trying to deflect the world's attention from this basic fact: As an island nation at the gateway of Asia and at the forefront of a modern 21st century, we have no interest in inflicting harm on our Asian neighbors, but their growing capacity in the Asian region is highly provocative even as they attempt to deflect attention from themselves by blaming us of nationalism..."

Tadaishi steamed at the sight of Seitoh and her harping comments. *She could not be further from the truth,* Tadaishi thought. *We are the ones who have not given adequate attention to peace in the region, we have been the destabilizers, and we still have not properly atoned for our historic transgressions, and your actions, Ms. Seitoh, only serve to illustrate how that militaristic mindset continues to this day.* Tadaishi clenched his armrests until his knuckles turned white at the words of the leader of the opposing party. He punched the button in front of him to turn off the TV screen in disgust, and he turned toward the window to peer into the darkness outside. *We are not the party that is attempting to turn back the clock to an imperial education system, attempting to recognize the Emperor as the official sovereign leader of the nation. How is this 'democracy'? We must stop this nonsense by winning back the parliament!* he declared to himself as he struck the arm rest unconsciously. His mind then wandered to his coming evening in Tokyo.

• • •

Tadaishi landed at Haneda airport less than an hour later. When Tadaishi disembarked and exited from baggage claim, he saw his driver standing in the back of the airport in his coal-black polyester suit, captain's hat, and white gloves. "Welcome back to Tokyo, Representative Tadaishi," he said as he bowed. Tadaishi barely nodded and continued to walk at a brisk pace to the exit. Tadaishi was in Tokyo only briefly, so he had no luggage to retrieve and carried only a day bag. The driver took Tadaishi's carry-on instinctively and followed a step behind him.

There was a small limo waiting for him at the curb outside the terminal's main exit, and two police officers stood guard nearby. There was no advanced notice of Representative Tadaishi's arrival, but they noticed the vehicle's special identification and automatically went to the vehicle as a precautionary measure. They had been standing there alert ever since it arrived. As Representative Tadaishi came out of the terminal they sprang into action. One officer took the bag from the driver behind him, and the other went to stand next to the door. They both bowed several times in rapid succession as Tadaishi passed around the vehicle to his seat. The driver opened the door for Tadaishi, who climbed in rapidly, and then closed the door. The driver then rushed to open the trunk, whispering softly to the officer at the back of the vehicle, "*chotto, chotto*...wait a second while I..." and he popped open the trunk. The officer placed the small bag in the trunk. The cop then turned his back to the vehicle and looked back and forth along the terminal for anything suspicious. The driver was already climbing into his seat and starting the engine. Tadaishi's car quickly sped away.

The black Toyota sedan had white lace for curtains in the back window, but otherwise the car was unexceptional and somewhat old. While his political fund paid for the transportation, Tadaishi had long ago forgotten that the car service, and its parent transportation conglomerate, were owned through a cut-out company by his main benefactor, Takada Kano.

Tadaishi had scheduled an early-morning coffee with a mid-ranking contact in the government, and a discrete breakfast with several members of his *Seichokai*, his Policy Affairs Research Council, to discuss issues related to the campaign as a cover for his trip. It was already midnight, and it would take about an hour to get to his destination assuming there was little traffic. In Tokyo, that was a major assumption. He would get little, if any, rest before his mid-morning return flight to Komatsu and then the drive to his district in Fukui.

"To Kabukicho," Tadaishi barked at the driver, who continued to look at the road.

"Yessir," the driver responded. He knew Representative Tadaishi was staying at the Ginza Tokyu Hotel, but he did not ask any questions. He had heard whispered stories about this politician, and he knew some of them to be true. But Kabukicho, the red-light district, could be a rough area late at night, full of thugs and Yakuza And Chinese Triads...*where's the bodyguard, the police protection?* the driver wondered, and he tried to convince himself that they would join the car on the way, or perhaps they were waiting for his arrival there in Kabukicho. At any rate, he would as instructed report this excursion to his superiors, who unbeknownst to the driver had been in turn instructed to report the representative's every movement to the owner of the transportation company—Takada Kano.

The drive went fast. For some reason, the traffic was lighter than usual. Perhaps people stayed in to avoid the coming storm, the driver thought. Already a few rain drops dusted the windshield. The driver pulled off the main highway, built several stories above the city due to space constraints and to reduce noise pollution, and began to weave his way through the busy Tokyo city streets. The atmosphere was already heady in this area of the city. He didn't need to glance back at Representative Tadaishi to feel his attention perk up. The honorable representative was quiet and subdued for most of the drive, seemingly deep in contemplation. But as the car pulled onto the local city streets approaching Kabukicho, Representative Tadaishi sat up and watched attentively out the window, almost entranced. He paid no attention to the driver, at any rate, which was fine by him.

Men in vibrant silk suits walked along the streets, their hair slicked into crooked spikes that was the style of the day for the younger generation, or matted to their head among the slightly older types. Others sported a more quaffed and fuller hairdo, often in light shades of brown or blond highlights or gray. But all of them had hairdos that were not your typical salaryman's conservative style. One talked on his cell, while another smoked listlessly standing on the curb, and yet another was in a heated conversation with a lady in a low-cut blouse and a short and shimmering-silver skirt. She shouted at him and then pushed him, as her friend tried to pull her away. He slapped her, and a fight ensued.

"Turn here, driver, turn right," said Tadaishi, startling the driver out of his reverie.

"Yessir."

"Let me out in two blocks, at that corner up ahead." Tadaishi pointed ahead of the driver at the desired corner.

"Shall I wait for you sir?"

"No, I'll take a taxi later tonight. Just pick me up at 10 am tomorrow morning at the hotel to go to the airport, and that will be sufficient."

"Yessir," replied the driver. As he pulled up to the corner, Tadaishi said curtly: "No need to get out, just pop the trunk and I'll get my bag." Tadaishi pulled up the lapels and buries his face as much as possible into his suit coat as he got out.

"Very well, sir,' the driver replied, and he waited as Tadaishi got out and shut the door. The driver hesitated, not wanting to leave Representative Tadaishi alone on a strange side street like this. What would they do to him if Tadaishi ended up mugged, the driver wondered, or worse, killed? That sort of thing happens more and more these days, especially in this area, with the Chinese Triad and other foreign gangs moving in. But orders were orders, and the driver slowly pulled away from the corner as Representative Tadaishi watched. The driver turned the corner, and still Tadaishi was there, almost as if he were waiting for the driver to be out of sight before he made a move.

The driver then reached for his cell phone with his left hand as he continued to drive with his right.

•   •   •

Tadaishi watched the car pull away and turn a corner, then walked along a smaller side street for a block, then turned left. A few drunkards walked by, older gentlemen who were going bar to bar. They were loud after a night of heavy drinking, and they hung on each other's shoulders and were hunched over by their shared weight. They stopped a moment as one stumbled, and they both laughed hard. "You are such a *clutz*, Hiro-*saaa*, such a *clutz*!" one slurred and began to cough. He hacked a bit and spat into the gutter. At that, they laughed again, rejoined and began to stumble forward together. Tadaishi side-stepped them, intent on getting to his destination.

In the shadows at the end of the narrow street there was a metal staircase that led up to a second floor door, unremarkable from the outside. It was made of coarse and cold metal and lacked any discernible window or sign. It seemed from the outside to be a side entrance to a warehouse of some sort. Tadaishi walked up the staircase and entered.

Without pausing, Tadaishi walked to the end of the long, narrow hall and turned left into a small and dimly lit alcove. A deep-mahogany, solid door stood a few meters away from the hall itself, so that the door and anyone waiting to get in were out of the line of sight from the hall and any casual passers-by. A bonsai sat on a short table to the right of the door, and a floor light under it cast a deep shadow onto the ceiling above. Another light from the opposite corner in the ceiling illuminated Tadaishi as he stood immediately in front of the door.

Tadaishi did not reach for the handle, because there was no handle for which to reach. He looked up to the corner of the ceiling to left of the door. A camera peered back at him, barely visible in the multiple shadows cast by the floor and ceiling lights. The door clicked imperceptibly ajar. Tadaishi pushed his way through.

He walked down another short corridor and turned right. Two ladies in dark pink silk kimonos bowed to him. "*Irasshaimase,*" they said, greeting him. Without uttering another word, one presented a silver tray to him with a small touch screen tablet on it. He positioned his fingers on it, and it turned green upon registering his membership. The second woman then retrieved from behind the counter another silver platter with a solid case positioned on a red silk kerchief. Tadaishi took it and walked wordlessly around the corner beyond the two ladies, who bowed again as he disappeared into the darkness.

Tadaishi sat at a table in the back of the small room. Music played in the background, and he looked around the room. There were patrons at two other tables, both of whom inhaled deeply from their cigarettes as they watched the young and scantily clad dancer on the small stage. She hung her head low so that her hair framed most of her face, and she bobbed slowly as if in a trance. She appeared to be completely engaged with the music, her string-bikini-clad body writhing slowly with the beat of the slow and hypnotic music. Deep blue neon lights lit the back of the stage, so that her figure appeared almost in complete relief.

Tadaishi saw that no one sat at the bar across from the stage. *Good*, he thought. Though already vetted and invited based on connections, prospective new members of the club were always seated at the bar, requiring members in the room to be extra cautious.

Tadaishi opened the small case and took out pair of glasses. He unfolded them and put them on, pressing a button on the top right of the frame as he did so. He looked again at the girl. Through the glasses he saw high on her right thigh what appeared to be an advertisement: "Drink Suntory," it read in a deep blue glow, as if it were a temporary neon tattoo.

A waiter stopped by the table. "Your menu, sir," he said as he handed a textured and ornate piece of heavy parchment to Tadaishi. The waiter bowed and stepped away in one fluid motion. Tadaishi went half-way down to the whiskey section, where Suntory was listed at the top: 400,000 yen. The amount was more than many teachers made in a month, but Tadaishi was unfazed. He looked at the menu posted above the bar, where the whiskey was more modestly priced at 4,000 yen per serving. He looked down at his menu again, at the other items available today. He then clicked the button on the frame of his glasses again to see the other menu items on the screen embedded in the lenses that corresponded with the prices on the menu. On "Bushmills Single Malt Irish Whiskey, 18 Years Old," an image of a bottle of whiskey appeared, and when he clicked again, a full-body image of a young-looking brunette appeared on the screen, which only he could see in his glasses. He clicked back to the whiskeys. He clicked on the "Glenlivet" Scotch Whiskey, and then again he clicked through the picture of the bottle to the next, which revealed a light-skinned redhead. He didn't feel like a brunette or redhead tonight, so he went to the vodkas.

In the vodkas section, he started with the cheaper selections. He clicked on a Stolichnaya, with a price of 200,000 yen. A somewhat plump blond appeared, who also seemed a little older than the others, perhaps in her 20s. She was taller, to be sure, and there was something about her that intrigued Tadaishi, but he wanted something a little classier tonight. *Stolis always left a bad aftertaste,* he thought ruefully to himself. He clicked out and then onto a 300,000 yen Finlandia. Again, a little too casual for him this evening. He scrolled down through the vodkas until he saw what he was looking for. "Ah, there is my choice for tonight," he thought to himself as he clicked onto Reyka, the Icelandic vodka. A girl appeared with slightly curly, almost white-blond hair that hung below her shoulder. She had just a few freckles on her nose and a set of pearly-white teeth. The crooked two front teeth that overlapped each other didn't bother him. Neither did the price: 600,000 yen. His gaze lingered on her for a moment, and then he looked at the icon in the bottom left corner and he blinked twice.

Within a few minutes, the waiter reappeared. "Your drink, sir," he said as he placed the glass of Reyka vodka onto a coaster on Tadaishi's table. "An excellent choice, sir," he said as he bowed deeply. "Enjoy."

Tadaishi took first one sip, and then a second as he watched the girl on the stage continue to dance languidly and lithely. He then took a longer swig, swallowed, and with one last gulp he sat back whispering to himself, *umai naaa.* He felt the liquid warm his esophagus and stomach, and then shook slightly as the alcohol hit his system. He moved the glass off the coaster and picked it up, glancing at the character on top as he did so. "*Ume,*" read the Japanese character for plum. He put it in his pocket as he stood up from the table and walked to the other end of the room and through another small corridor.

Tadaishi passed through a small maze of halls that featured a few nondescript doors, then went up a small stairwell and through another set of doors. He knew the way well, having been a client of this particular establishment for many years now. He entered what appeared to be a hallway for a local hotel. Over the hotel room numbers, however, someone had affixed Japanese characters. "*Matsu,*" read one, and then "*Biwa.*" Finally, he came to "*Ume.*" He took the coaster out of his pocket, and then split it in half along the barely visible perforation. Now the size of a hotel card key, Tadaishi held it up to the key reader. It scanned the nano-chip implanted in the card, and the door opened. He walked in and closed the door.

"Hello, stranger," said a girl on the bed in accented English. Tadaishi saw a pair of naked legs draw up slowly as the girl sat up. "Herro," he said back, unabashed by his inability to form the letter "L" in his English greeting. He was not here for a language lesson. He took off his jacket, dropped it on the floor, and went to the girl on the bed.

CHAPTER 15 - DEPARTURES

Kusong City was located over 100 kilometers northwest of Pyongyang and 40 kilometers from Yongbyon. It traced its development from the end of the Korean War in the 1950s. Strategically located in the mountainous interior of North Korea, it became one of many hubs for North Korea's military-industrial complex, driven by the "Juche Ideology" of self-reliance. The first factories produced Soviet-model rifles and machine guns. More advanced factories that built trench mortars and recoilless artillery followed in the 1960s, supplied by the Soviet Union and then, after the Sino-Soviet split, by China. By the 1980s, even more advanced plants began to produce tanks and military helicopter and aircraft engines.

Munitions factories were also an indispensable component of the region's increasingly advanced military industry, and particularly for the development of advanced machine tooling. This regional expertise served as the base for development of advanced detonators for use in nuclear weapons as well. The region's relatively isolated location in the mountains and its strategic distance from Yongbyon—close, but not too close—made it a natural location for the technical development of nuclear weapons-related technologies.

This is what brought Pyong Hae Han and his new bride, Mi Yong, to the region right after graduating from university over two decades ago. The work in the early years was steady, if a bit of a challenge due to a lack of steady procurement of the needed technology to fulfill the tasks assigned to his work unit. And then came a period of remarkably low productivity, when Pyongyang made heroic overtures to improve relations with the imperialists and their lackeys. He and his colleagues continued their theoretical work, they experimented as much as they could, but supplies and funding seemingly came to a halt. Still, as a systems engineer, Han rose quickly through the ranks to lead the development, integration, and testing of components necessary to fit advanced and survivable warheads to the various missile systems North Korean scientists and engineers had developed, sometimes with the help of others who were similarly targeted by the imperialists.

But then with a change in leadership in Pyongyang, access to both significant funding and supplies of state-of-the art technologies increased significantly. Han and his colleagues did not know how or why, and they knew not to ask. They were gleeful to be able to work to their true potentials again, however. Both talent and serendipitous timing propelled Han to a senior leadership position as the lead systems engineer. It was his job to ensure all the components would fit together and operate when they needed to, so he had to know the details of each component. It was historically the one weakness of the program, because each component was developed in isolation for security reasons. Only the top political leadership knew about the program as a whole, but none of the scientists and engineers did. But now it was Han's job to know, and to make it work. If he did, he would be a national hero. If he didn't, he would be dead.

The new rules of the game, or at least the newly reinforced rules of the game, became clear within a few months of the end of mourning for the Dear Leader. A political commissar, sent directly to Kusong by the Central Committee of the Workers' Party of Korea following a failed medium-range missile launch, gathered the scientists and engineers a short distance away from their lab.

"These are the patriots who produce the means to protect our homeland!" the political commissar shouted at the assembled crowd of scientists and engineers standing near a hill. The commissar pointed to a squad of uniformed soldiers holding rocket-propelled grenade launchers. "We can have faith that *these* rockets work," he said holding up a live rocket in one hand to emphasize the point, "because these patriots build them to work as they must to protect the homeland!"

The political commissar then pointed to a lone figure standing down-range. Despite the distance of over a hundred meters, Han recognized the figure as the chief engineer for the medium-range missile that had failed at launch days earlier. They had graduated from university together. "Let this be a lesson! Those who fail the motherland in their sacred duties to build the means to defend our lands from imperialists and their puppets will eat the fire and flames of those who succeed!" Han could see his colleague's gaunt and thin frame quivering in the cold, merciless air.

The political commissar walked with his rocket-propelled grenade launcher to the uniformed firing squad holding similar weapons. They formed a line across the field from the hillock. At its base stood the newly disgraced chief engineer, chained like a dog to a stake in the ground. The engineer sobbed and began to grovel for leniency. "Please!" he shouted between loud moans. "Please, let me try again! I will make it work, I promise! *Please...!*"

"Three!" the executioner shouted. "Two!"

"*Please, I beg of you!*" the man shouted as he raised his hands to stop the execution. "I will do *bet...*"

"One! Fire!"

The roar of multiple rockets launching was followed almost instantaneously by multiple explosions along the hillock. Some hit high, some low. One flew over the hillock into the distance, and one failed to fire at all. That soldier threw his weapon down in anger, but it fortunately did not detonate.

Once the dirt and rock settled, most of the hillock, and the chief engineer, were gone.

The political commissar faced the assembled group of scientists and engineers, who were stunned into silence. "Failure is unacceptable!" he declared, and he turned to leave. Members of the execution squad smiled and joked among themselves as they packed their weapons. They clearly relished any chance to have a live-fire target practice. Han and his remaining colleagues filed silently into the bus that had brought them to the location.

The work unit bus returned Han and his colleagues from the firing range to their main building in Kusong that afternoon, after the execution. "We shall re-double our efforts!" declared the work unit chief, Mr. Ko, a political hack with no science or engineering background, in the bus upon their return. It was as if a declaration was all it took to lead people to success. All of Han's colleagues remained silent, still absorbing the lessons from the death of their beloved comrade by rocket-propelled grenades. They returned to their offices, still not uttering a word.

Han, his head hung low in thought, trailed the rest of his fellow engineers down the stairs into their shared underground research center. Mr. Ko, his boss, greeted him as Han reached the second sub-basement.

"Mr. Han, come with me," the corpulent Mr. Ko said dourly. Ko led him to his office.

"Shut the door!" Ko yelled as he sat at his desk facing Han. Han was required to stand, unless he was invited to sit. This afternoon, he was not invited.

"You saw what happened today. Failure is not an option!" Ko shouted again, this time louder than he had on the bus. "We have a very important mission. In addition to finalizing the warhead mating design, we must build the new QZSS satellite receiver into the warhead design. This must be done at all costs!"

"Sir, I've already completed the GPS receiver integration..."

"No, this is not GPS integration. This is integration of a receiver for signals from Japan's indigenous, 'Quasi-Zenith Satellite System'. It is accurate to within *centimeters*," Ko emphasized.

"GPS is accurate to within meters, when it is not degraded...Isn't that adequate?" Han had the temerity to ask.

Mr. Ko cut him off. "Do not interrupt me! Don't you see, with this system we can target anywhere in the Pacific region, on land or at sea. No longer will China have the sole ability to target U.S. Navy aircraft carriers with ballistic missiles! And we can target anywhere in Japan or South Korea with other weapons, like chemical, *biological* weapons..."

"But if we have a nuclear capability, won't that be adequate?"

"Again, you are not smart enough to see the big picture!" Mr. Ko half-stood as he yelled at Han. "Pyongyang is very wise in this. They know that if a bomb does not go '*boom*,' then it's like it didn't happen, right?"

Han dared not move, much less speak, in response.

Ko sat back down. "Now, with integration of QZSS, we can target anywhere in the region with deadly biological agents, say, and what will America do? No big nuclear '*boom*,' no U.N. Resolution against us. Without a resolution, Washington will do nothing. And Japan can do *nothing*," Ko emphasized, "because they are too weak and too old to do anything on their own. They are pacifists governed by a pacifist constitution, and they *actually* follow it!" Ko chuckled at the thought. "They have no capacity to attack us, their so-called preemptive strikes would be like a mosquito biting a cobra, without the Americans. And let's say we conduct a targeted strike in a rural area along the coast, like Hamanaka village on the coast of Hokkaido, for example, or a passing Japanese cruise ship in the Sea of Japan, with a warhead containing our genetically modified *small pox*. With a highly accurate, mid-range ballistic missile, all we need is one launch. And of course there would be no big explosion because that would kill the biological agent in the warhead. By design it *can't* explode. It would be as if nothing happened, even as the agent begins infecting the imperialists. With no '*boom*,' no anti-DPRK Security Council resolution, and without a resolution, there will be no American military action. Not in time at least. By the time the disease has been discovered, it will have spread and incapacitated half the Japanese population and all those stupid American families living with their military bastard husbands and fathers on bases there. But it's too late! Our secret inoculation program means we are immune to the disease..." Ko sat back and smiled at the thought.

"Now *your* job," Ko continued, jabbing at the air toward Han, "and the work unit you oversee, is to integrate the QZSS receiver into our new warhead, along with a warhead for biological strains that will survive the heat and stress of re-entry. That is an order, and *failure will not be tolerated*! Or else, *you* will be the next person to stand before the firing squad! Dismissed!"

"I understand," Han said, and he left the office without saying another word.

• • •

There were two taps at the door, followed by another, and then a quick check of the doorknob. Han would have missed it if he weren't waiting for the pre-designated signal for this meeting. He looked through the peep hole, and saw who he expected to see: Jang, a work colleague.

Han opened the door silently and smiled at his guest with his embracing eyes. Jang stepped in, and Han closed the door. They waited only a moment until they heard another wrap at the door. The same signal: two taps, followed by another, and then one half-turn of the doorknob. It was meant to be unobtrusive, so any onlooker would probably miss the significance of it. Or else misinterpret it: A full turn and push, or more than one attempted turn of the doorknob meant trouble.

The congregants had all arrived within minutes of each other. The group met around national holidays as part of their cover. If anyone asked, they can say that they were marking whatever anniversary or holiday. In this case, tonight, they were celebrating the anniversary of North Korea's first successful nuclear test. A momentous occasion indeed!

Han turned to the wall where the photos of North Korea's leaders, past and present, were arrayed. He turned the top around, exposing the picture's blank back to the room. He then did the same with the other two portraits, one on either side of the top portrait, but he re-hung them horizontally. He then took a hanging scroll that was next to the main entrance, and re-hung it on a small nail at the bottom of the main portrait. The hanging scroll too was hung backwards.

Han then stepped back and, with the others, clasped hands in front of the newly formed cross now hanging on the main wall. "Let us pray," he said, hanging his head. "Our Father, who art in Heaven, hallowed be Your name..." the small congregation began to say softly and in unison.

• • •

"Peace be upon you," Han said, bowing to his colleagues as he completed the evening's service. "And peace be upon you," they intoned, bowing back. Han's wife wiped away a tear from a mixture of love, compassion, and terror at the journey to come.

"My brothers and sisters, we've been on a long journey together," Han started haltingly. "I, like you, have spent my life building a tower...towers to progress, or so we told ourselves, but I have only recently begun to count the costs. As it is written, we must not 'conform to this world,' but we must be transformed, by the Word, by the Holy Spirit, so that we can know what is the will of God. Of this, we can be sure, that the Kingdom of God is near. Peace to you all, brothers and sisters!" He wanted to tell his fellow congregants of his and his wife's decision to depart, but this was the closest he could come to communicating their intention to leave. He knew his fellow parishioners would understand.

"Please pray for my son, he is back now from the hospital, but his condition is such that he needs additional treatment. We will get him the treatment he needs, God willing..."

They embraced each congregant as they departed, one by one. It was just by chance that this was the Han family's turn to host this evening's congregation. That had been determined long ago, but the arrangements to depart, which no one knew about, were finalized just days ago. "Until our next meeting..." Han said to the last of his guests. The Jang family would host the next congregation in a few weeks, per the pre-planned rotation.

Han and his wife had already packed a few small bags the previous evening, and she sat listlessly on the couch as he checked through their few bags one last time. He triple-checked his satchel for their travel papers, acquired at great cost.

"*I need a pass to some of our facilities near the coast and Pyongyang,*" Han remembered asking the clerk the previous day. He stood at a booth in the administrative office of his building. Han had timed it so that he was the only one there. He was nervous, but he was following the instructions of his spiritual guide, the seemingly impoverished gray-market vendor Han met several years ago who nevertheless had many resources and connections to the outside world. He could only trust in him.

"*Show me your papers signed by your work unit supervisor and party representative,*" the clerk asked without looking at him.

"*I unfortunately, uh, lost those...*" Han stammered. "*I want to, uhh...*" Han was not sure how to proceed, even though he had practiced the conversation hundreds of times with his mentor and in his head before this approach.

The clerk looked up from his paperwork and examined Han. "*I see. You need a pass to travel outside the municipality, hm?*"

"*Yes, that's right,*" Han replied, his mood brightening at the apparent understanding on the part of the clerk. "*I need a...clean pass,*" Han added, based on his mentor's guidance.

"*How much do you have?*" the clerk asked, his eyes narrowing.

"*Ummm, well...*" Han said, now unsure how to proceed again. His mentor had told him what payoff to expect, but Han, unlike his wife, had always been uncomfortable negotiating prices. "*I have 10,000,*" Han blurted out before he could stop himself.

"*Dollars, or Euros?*"

"*Dollars,*" Han replied.

"*You're in luck!*" the clerk said in low voice, smiling. "*The going price for a clean pass is $10,000!*"

"*Er, that's not what I was told...*" Han stammered, suddenly nervous again.

The clerk waved his hand to stop Han from talking further. "*Do not rely on what you hear on the streets. I set the price, and you pay me the set price. Understand?*"

Han nodded, then placed his hand behind his back and under his suit jacket and dress shirt to retrieve an envelope stashed in his pants under his belt. He then looked to his right and then to his left, then bent over to retrieve another envelope from his sock. Sweat formed on his upper lip, not only because of his resort to criminality according to the laws of the DPRK, but also because these funds were to have lasted for the entire trip as bribes for officials along the way, if necessary. Now those funds were gone.

The clerk took the envelopes, looked at the contents briefly, then filled out the necessary forms. "Here you go," he said, handing them over to Han.

Han took them and turned to leave the office, but he noticed that his was the only name on the forms.

"*Umm,*" he hesitated in asking the clerk.

"*Yes?*" the clerk answered, annoyed.

"*I need forms for my wife and son, who are to accompany me...*"

"*Ah yes, of course, give me the forms.*" The clerk then waited.

"*Is there a problem?*" Han asked.

"*I need another $10,000,*" the clerk said in an emotionless tone.

"*Wha...*" Han stammered. He had no dollars left. "*I gave you all the money I have...*"

"*Hmm. That's a problem then, isn't it. Ok.*" The clerk waited, holding the paperwork.

"*I, uh, have North Korean currency...*"

The clerk snorted. "*That's no good here. Not for this,*" the clerk added, shaking the paperwork. "*How about Chinese currency?*"

"*Yes, well, I have a few thousands Chinese Yuan...*"

"*Since this is your first time, I will make an exception to the current pricing.*" The clerk held out his hand. "*Give me what you have.*"

Han reached into his other sock and retrieved another roll of currency. He hesitated, then he handed what he had to the clerk. Beads of sweat formed at his temple now.

"*What are their names?*" the clerk asked without looking at Han. Han told him.

"*Mr. Han, how are you!*" a jovial voice said behind him. It was his boss, Mr. Ko. "*Are you ok? You look pale,*" he added as Han turned toward him, having received the paperwork.

"*Yes, just something I ate. Some bad pulkogi, I think,*" Han replied, holding his stomach. He felt truly sick to his stomach.

"*Oh, you should stop getting your food at that local outdoor market, you don't know what you're getting! You'll surely get tapeworms, if you haven't already. Take some time off around the WPK Foundation Day holiday, I hear there are to be a lot of 'fireworks,' if you know what I mean!*"

Han nodded once, and then headed to the door.

"*I will do that...*" Han whispered, still in shock.

"*Next!*" he heard the clerk shout on his way out.

•   •   •

The sun had set below the horizon when Han sat down again after clearing the table. This was their last supper in the apartment, which had been prepared for them by their fellow congregants as thanks for hosting the evening prayer session. Three freshly baked loaves of bread sat on the counter, although neither Han nor his wife remembered seeing anyone put it there.

"I'm nervous," Han's wife Mi Yong said, sitting at the table across from him.

"I am too," replied Han. "We can only trust in God that He will deliver us. Now let's get the boy in the car before it gets too late. Remember our story to any friends we might encounter while driving out of town. We're taking him to the river for some physical therapy, as the doctors had prescribed."

CHAPTER 16 - THE COMING STORM

Bennett had just arrived to his hotel foyer when he received a call on his cell.

"Bennett, this is Bradley, you better come back to the embassy."

It was already late in the evening, and the alcohol combined with the lingering jet lag hindered Bennett's understanding for a moment. "Embassy?" Bennett repeated, as if to ask what the word "embassy" meant.

"There are a few developments that you need to be aware of," Bradley said more forcefully.

"Embassy? Yes, the embassy. I'm on my way." Bennett turned and exited the hotel. He climbed into the first in a line of awaiting taxis, this one with its back door already invitingly open. "To the United States Embassy compound," Bennett said simply as the door closed automatically, and the taxi zoomed away.

• • •

"Thanks for coming in, Bennett, I'm sorry to have bothered you," Bradley said while he ushered Bennett through the vault door. This time Bennett had instinctively come to Bradley's spaces in the defense attache's office. "I know you're probably exhausted now from all the activity and jet lag, so sorry about that."

"Duty calls," Bennett answered groggily.

Bradley motioned for Bennett to sit at a conference table in a small meeting room adjacent to the entryway. "We've been tracking the storm, and we are now confident that it is passing in a more north-easterly direction. So the good news is that the exercise will continue as scheduled." Bradley said.

"As scheduled? That's good, but what's the catch?"

"Due to the storm's progression, the exercise will now take place 250 miles to the southwest, here," Bradley said.

"Hmm," Bennett grunted as he looked at the map. "That location looks like a straight shot up to the rendezvous point here, right?" Bennett asked out loud.

"That's right, it's actually easier to get there from this area of operations than from the old one," Bradley replied, confirming Bennett's thoughts. "We had to divert the Texas farther southwest, but that has not been an issue. The team is onboard and the sub should arrive with the U.S. contingent to this new location within hours, ahead of the official commencement of the exercise at 0500 local."

"Excellent!" Bennett said, allowing himself to smile.

"And that's not all," Bradly continued. "We received the signal from our man in Kusong. He's ready to depart..." Bradley looked at his watch, "actually, he should be departing momentarily, also on schedule."

"Any problems?" Bennett asked.

"Nope, everything appears to be progressing smoothly," Bradley confirmed.

"So we can send the Texas directly to the rendezvous point once it arrives to the training area later tonight?"

"That's correct, sir. The back-up team is standing by on the Ronald Reagan, as well."

"More excellent news!" Bennett exclaimed. "This is proceeding even better than I had expected. Do all of your ops go this smoothly, Bradley?"

"No sir, none of them ever have," Bradley said, allowing himself to smile at their current good fortune. "So maybe we're due for a smooth one for a change..."

"Remind me to call you for my next one, you're my lucky charm it seems!" Bennett exclaimed with a smile, patting Bradley on his back. "I guess I'll head back to the room, for a few hours at least."

"I'll hold the fort down here, we have direct comms with our guys on the Reagan."

"Good, call when we have our man."

Bradley nodded once as Bennett left the vault.

Bennett retrieved his cell phone as he exited the Embassy and absentmindedly thumbed through his latest RSS feeds before leaving the compound. All benign reporting, and there was nothing out of the ordinary about the exercise or the region. Then Bennett opened a link to the latest installment of the Japanese "Kasumigaseki Confidential" column. Named for the administrative center of the Japanese Government, the column was an insider's account of all things official in Japan and in the region, including what many considered gossip from the diplomatic corps based in Tokyo.

"Speculation has risen after reports that the U.S. Ambassador's wife has posted comments seen to be related to a top-secret operation underway soon..." the column began. Bennett stopped in his tracks. *Shit*, he thought. *Not now, not right now...*

He turned and ran inside the Embassy building again, not even acknowledging the Marine guard who buzzed him in. He continued reading as he entered the elevator.

"...Apparently, U.S. Ambassador George Robertson III's new wife, who is his second and many decades his junior, posted comments to her Facebook account calling attention to the U.S.-Japan exercise commencing tomorrow, but adding cryptically that 'there is more than meets-the-eye to these exercises.' She added most interestingly that 'a lot goes on behind the scenes that aren't reported in the daily papers, and we should be grateful for the SILENT SERVICE of our men and women in uniform!'"

God damn it, Bennett thought as the elevator door pinged and the door opened. *Like no one is able to decipher THAT...*

"While high-level participants on the Japanese side assert that they have no plans for anything beyond the exercise," the column continued, "and no knowledge of U.S. plans in addition to what is scheduled to take place during the exercise, speculation is rising that Washington may be planning some sort of action against North Korea in the coming days..."

Bennett placed his phone in the cabinet beside the main door to the ambassador's suite. He buzzed several times in succession, looking directly at the camera hanging from the ceiling as he did so. The door clicked, and Bennett pushed it open. *How long has her post been out there?* Bennett wondered. *The column was just published, but surely others would've been watching her social media accounts too...*

"Good evening Mr. Bennett, we hadn't expected to see you here at this hour," the administrative assistant, Sally, said in an authoritative tone.

"I hadn't planned to visit tonight, Sally, but if you don't mind, I have something urgent to discuss with the Ambassador." Bennett struggled to keep his tone level and polite.

"He is getting ready for a teleconference with Washington now. I'm sure it can wait until he is finished with the telecon," she said, attempting to gently but firmly dissuade Bennett from an immediate meeting.

"Please just let him know I'm here, it's a matter of national security."

They locked eyes. Sally could see that Bennett's were sufficiently inflamed, and she knew that he was sufficiently senior, that this indeed required immediate attention. Sally lowered her gaze as she picked up the receiver. She whispered into it, waiting a moment for further direction, and then placed the receiver down.

"You have five minutes."

"Thank you, Sally," Bennett replied as he walked by her desk to the Ambassador's spacious office in the corner.

Ambassador Robertson was at his desk signing a document, and he did not notice Bennett close the door. "Mr. Bennett, I'll be right with..." Robertson started to say without looking up from his paperwork.

"How could you?" Bennett demanded as he launched himself at Robertson's desk. "I gave explicit directions that what was briefed to you *could not* be shared with anyone, *anyone!*"

"What are you talking ab..." Robertson said, looking up at Bennett who was now leaning on Robertson's desk.

"Don't you know that leaking this type of highly sensitive information is a criminal offense?" Bennett demanded again.

"What are you talking about?" Robertson demanded in return, now upset that this man was suddenly accusing him of criminal offenses.

"You told your wife about the impending operation, and she in turn blabbed about it on social media, and now all of Tokyo knows about it!"

Robertson looked at Bennett, then sat back into his leather seat as he folded his right arm into his left and pinched the bridge of his nose with his left hand. "Alright, what exactly is being reported," Robertson asked, now resigned to hear about the possible damage his wife might have caused to national security, and to his new career.

"A local, well-connected Japanese column is reporting that your wife posted a comment talking about the exercise commencing now." Bennett then relayed a gist of the article.

Robertson's mood brightened. "So she didn't actually talk about details of the operation?" Robertson said in apparent relief.

"Mr. Ambassador, let's be honest. Every intel officer this side of the Urals will know what she is hinting at. Your wife is saying that the U.S. side is using the exercise as cover for an operation to be conducted by a U.S. sub participating in the exercise, which happens to be taking place near the Korean Peninsula. The intel services of half-a-dozen adversaries, including without a doubt the North Koreans themselves, have read this report and will now instruct their sub hunters and other clandestine operatives to watch our units closely. One of which *is*, by the way, now *actively conducting an operation to secure a high-level North Korean defector!*"

"C'mon, Bennett, calm down now, that message could be read in many different ways..."

Don't be so obtuse! Bennett wanted to scream, but he contained his anger. "Your wife has jeopardized a highly sensitive operation, and if it fails, if we don't get our man out, his blood is on *your* hands."

"Now calm down, Bennett," Robertson ordered as he stood up, becoming upset again. "Sit down, take a breath."

"Mr. Ambassador, the teleconference will begin in one minute," Sally said, opening the door wide and stepping inside the office. Bennett figured she had heard shouting and wanted to ensure everything was ok, and that her boss wouldn't be detained any further ahead of the teleconference.

"Thank you Sally, I'm on my way," Robertson said as he closed his leather-bound notebook on his desk and picked it up to walk to the teleconference room. The notebook had the U.S. State Department seal stamped on it. He buttoned his suit jacket with his other hand and walked around the desk. "Listen, Bennett," he began, almost as a whisper, "I'll talk to the office of public affairs here, I'll have the director deflect the story, first thing tomorrow morning..."

"I hope it's not too late by then," Bennett asserted, and then turned to exit the Ambassador's suite. *And it's probably too late,* he thought to himself.

CHAPTER 17 – TOKYO DETENTION CENTER

The aged Michiko Fukuno slowly stirred a large vat of what she would only describe as watery gruel for evening meals at the Tokyo Detention Center. She maintained two cooking stations in her kitchen, one of many, at the center for decades. The one for favored inmates featured eatable, traditional Japanese food such as soba noodles and donburi. The other station prepared true prison food, such as a rice-based gruel that was usually light on rice, various bland rice cakes, and if inmates were lucky, some small pickles as garnish. Well-behaved—or more often, well-connected—inmates received the former, while new inmates and those under interrogation or in isolation received the latter. While she never admitted it to her fellow cooks, Michiko took greater pride in making flavorless gruel than in cooking the more traditional meals.

Michiko had seen countless scoundrels pass through the center during her many decades there. Some of the hard-core criminals, the murderers and rapists, were thankfully put to death. She indeed had the satisfaction of knowing when they were to die before they themselves did, and certainly before the public was informed after the fact. She cooked many of their last meals, and while she was never able to observe the death penalty carried out, she would personally volunteer to hang the noose around the condemned if offered the opportunity.

But others certainly deserving of at least prolonged sentences, if not death, were released before serving time befitting their crimes against society. They were the connected ones, the politicians and wealthy businessmen accused and then exonerated of embezzlement, briberies, engaging in prostitution, and other assorted "white crime" scandals. They were brought here, saw the harsh life on the inside, and then groveled sufficiently for forgiveness in front of the cameras and were let go. She despised these thieves and robbers more than the pickpockets who could be imprisoned for years. They lacked any honor, first in fulfilling their duties to their companies, families, and fellow Japanese, and second in repaying society for the damage they inflicted on the public trust and harmony necessary for the greater good.

The real victims were the ones who did not have the contacts to secure their release. They were perhaps guilty of the same things, too, but only at the individual level. Their crimes did not impact society as a whole. But because of their lowly stature, they couldn't buy or grovel their way out of their situation. They might be given a reduced sentence after fully admitting their guilt, but only after being humiliated by certain sadistic guards, staff, and judges in the process. She saw it everyday. Not only were inmates sent to solitary confinement for weeks and months on end for even the smallest infraction, they had to spend their days in *chobatsu*, sitting cross-legged in front of their cell door where passing guards could see them, "contemplating" their supposed transgressions. Perhaps they would gain *satori*, or enlightenment, in the process, the guards joked. Usually just before pummeling them again for the slightest movement.

Corrupt corporate executives and politicians robbing hardworking Japanese taxpayers needed *chobatsu* more than these petty thieves, Michiko had always felt. Not that pickpockets and thieves should get any more lenient sentences. Michiko merely felt that all convicted criminals should face the same lengthy jail terms regardless of background and connections. And that the sadist bureaucrats should be set upon them instead of the helpless.

Michiko's feelings hardened over the years as she witnessed case after case of severe sentencing and treatment of the little guy, and case after case of the connected getting off with little or any punishment, formal or otherwise. She kept her feelings to herself and continued to do her job. She was never overtly political, she came and went quietly as any loyal Japanese servant should, and she continued to receive her pay for her loyal and quiet service. To do otherwise would be unseemly. She was not paid especially well, but it was enough.

And then over twenty years ago, she learned what real human generosity was. Her only daughter had just started college near Kobe, and only months later a terrible earthquake struck the region that devastated the entire city. While her daughter's dorm building survived the initial earthquake, it was severely damaged, and an after-shock later caused it to collapse. Her daughter escaped just in time. But the earthquake had struck in January, so those buried in the rubble or left homeless—those like her daughter—suffered in the blustery cold and wet conditions in the days and weeks that followed.

Neither the local nor the national Japanese government could reach her, much less provide shelter. The destroyed roads and railways prevented or slowed first responders in the city from assisting the needy. Hospitals were destroyed or were about to collapse, and those that survived were filled beyond capacity. The national government spent days just trying to formulate a plan on sending teams to the region, but practically every ministry wanted to take the lead—and the glory—in managing the rescue operations. The resultant bureaucratic in-fighting led to critical and deadly delays. Local officials bickered with the central government on the "legality" of sending uniformed personnel to help, yet they were the only ones who were equipped and prepared to conduct a true national disaster response effort. But troops had never been deployed on such a wide scale before, so such a rescue effort would be unprecedented, and a further rise in the stature of the defense forces. Sending in American troops stationed around Japan was certainly out of the question, and for that matter, why should Japan need to rely on the Americans? The Japanese could do it themselves, they just needed a strong leader to cut through the red-tape and give some proper orders to do so. Japan sorely lacked strong leadership, Michiko thought.

Phone lines were down too. Yet, all Michiko wanted was to hear that her daughter was safe, after seeing fleeting glimpses from images broadcast from helicopters hovering in the sky of what was her dorm among all the other ruins of Kobe. She sat in a state of barely subdued panic for days, watching the television for any sign of her daughter. She tried to call directly and to local hotlines set up in the days after the earthquake with names of known victims, but she either could not get through, or was kept on hold for hours, or the harried telephone operators knew nothing. Michiko tried to work through the few contacts she had in the Ministry of Justice, but they too were swamped with similar requests.

And then, not a week later, she received a call through what was a just-restored phone line.

"Mom? This is Keiko. I'm safe."

"Oh thank goodness!" Michiko screamed gleefully. "How did they rescue you from under all that rubble? Those fire brigade personnel must have worked so diligently to reach you in the suburbs!"

"We got out of the dorm just before it collapsed, so we were spared any injuries…"

"Oh my!" Michiko exclaimed. "So where did you go? The college must have found another building for you to stay in, or perhaps the fire brigade found you shelter?"

"Mmmm, well, no," Michiko's daughter hesitated. "The fire brigade wasn't able to come for days, and the administration staff was busy with the initial rescue efforts of those who couldn't escape from the dorms in time…"

"I see, so where did you go?"

"Actually a local group of..." Keiko hesitated again. "A local group of, I guess, volunteers, you could say, helped us..." Keiko's voice trailed off,

"A group of volunteers? I knew someone would come to find you!" Michiko said excitedly. "I'm so relieved!"

"Yes, sort of. They were volunteers..." Keiko hesitated again, and then whispered into the receiver, "Ma, they were *yakuza*. The local branch of the *yakuza* family rescued me...."

"*Yakuza*, you say? Ehhhh..." Michiko muttered.

"They're really quite nice, I suppose," Keiko said more excitedly. "For *yakuza*, I mean...I've never met one until now. In fact, I've met quite a nice one who has been really good to us..."

Michiko thought for a moment, and then declared: "Keiko-chan, I'm just glad you are safe no matter who rescued you. Where are you now?"

"I'm staying in a shelter they built for some of us. We have a small heater, blankets and some food and water. We're waiting for the roads to be cleared so we can be transported out of here..."

With that phone call, Michiko's image of so-called organized criminals changed forever. *They obviously could do things that incompetent government bureaucrats couldn't,* she rationalized. *They knew the locals and what they needed. Perhaps some needed loans—loans that zombie banks couldn't or weren't willing to provide. They were expensive loans, to be sure, but hey, they filled a need, right? Some wanted to gamble, too, and what's wrong with gambling? Japanese laws are too restrictive on gambling,* Michiko thought to herself, *or they monopolize any gambling that is not illegal. Organized...families,* she started calling them, *helped fill a natural human urge that the central government had long ago outlawed. That some in the government also gambled just showed their hypocrisy. Same with sex. So what if they ran brothels? If they kept young punks off the streets and away from respectable girls like her own daughter, all the better. The girls were all whores from outside Japan anyway,* Michiko thought.

Michiko would be forever grateful for the assistance provided her daughter. And she, in turn, would provide all the assistance she could to her new family. For Michiko's only daughter Keiko quickly became engaged to a young member of the *yakuza* family, Hideo. She was pregnant, Keiko confided to an already suspecting Michiko. They were to be married that summer, and Michiko had never seen Keiko happier than that spring, despite the difficulties.

But one day, as she and Hideo drove down a newly cleared street months after the earthquake, a quake-weakened building that building inspectors had declared to be safe collapsed onto their passing car, killing them and several other passers-by instantly. That the inspectors had been bribed to declare the building safe added insult to injury. A devastated Michiko attended the funeral in Kobe along with her new, extended family. She had barely met them, but she felt a burning kinship with them that she had never experienced before. The funeral hall director later told her it was the largest funeral he had hosted since the earthquake, and he had run funerals every day.

In the years since, Michiko proudly provided any assistance she could to her extended family. Michiko provided information on certain inmates, delivered information to others. She gave extra portions to specific inmates when asked, and she made portions particularly inedible for others, to the point of sending some to the infirmary. And at times, for a few high-placed inmates, she delivered items or money. Some would call it smuggling, but she always considered it as returning loyalty to those who were supremely loyal to her. It was simply another sign of bureaucratic incompetence that she was able to do so freely, Michiko thought.

And now, the poor Ayako, the young girl who was killed in the boating incident days ago, reminded her desperately of the granddaughter she would never have, and of the daughter whose life was taken from her many years too soon due to all the bureaucratic incompetence that the earthquake simply served to expose, and which she witnessed ever more acutely since.

"There's a bounty on his head," her "cousin" told her late one night at a dinner he treated her to. "Someone wants him dead," he said bluntly, long ago forsaking any coded language for cold, hard truth with Michiko. The family had come to trust Michiko as much as she trusted them. "We can't say who, of course. Let's just say it's not us. But we work with this individual, and it's in all our interests that this particular boy does not live much longer," he explained.

Her benefactors from many years ago, her only family now, did not have to convince her or bribe her or pay her to kill detainee Taro Hatano. She wanted to kill him herself, and now she was glad to have a reason.

He handed her a small vial. "This is carfentanil, an extremely dangerous substance. It is 50,000 times more potent than morphine."

She looked at it. "There's only one small speck that I can see in here…"

"That's right," her cousin replied. "And that is enough to kill an entire company of soldiers if necessary. Do not touch it, do not mishandle it. Put it in his food as necessary, but make sure *no one else* comes into contact with that food, anything that cooked that food, or with this vial. *You included,*" he added. "Now, this is for your troubles…" he said as he slid a thick envelope toward her.

"Keep the money," she said. "You've done enough for me. And I don't want this traced back to you in any way, if they ever can trace it. I'll take care of him myself. Thank you for giving me the means to do so."

She placed the capped vial he had given her in her small purse, and left the small restaurant with a new mission.

•   •   •

Nishi opened the door to his small and temporary office, entered, and fell onto the aged leather couch. He slouched involuntarily, weary from the long days and nights. The couch had conformed to his various slouching positions long ago, and Nishi felt briefly comforted. He let out a deep-throated sigh as he took off first one shoe, then his other. He crossed his leg to rub the sole of his left foot, his plantar fasciitis becoming inflamed again.

A television sat on a tall metal filing cabinet across from him, turned on to the public broadcaster, NHK. A clock appeared on the screen, counting down from five seconds, four, three... Nishi picked up the remote control to turn up the volume just in time to hear the final second ticking off and then a high-pitched *beep!* that signified the beginning of the news hour.

"Good evening, and thank you for joining us. Our top story tonight: The suspect in the attempted narcotics trafficking case will be arraigned on charges of narcotics possession and aiding and abetting criminal activity. Our correspondent reports from the detention center in Katsushika Ward."

The camera cut to a youngish man in a dark gray suit and navy blue tie, his hair blowing slightly in a soft breeze. Two bright spotlights shone on him from either side of the camera, tracing his shadow at two angles on the fero-concrete wall in the distance behind him. He stood steadily and with an air of importance, a crease etched in his brow as he squinted into the camera through the bright lights. On the screen above him were the characters for "Live". *"This is Takahiro Endo reporting from outside the Detention Center, Ministry of Justice, Tokyo. The suspect arrived to the detention center here..."* Endo gestured to the building behind him, *"...yesterday after being transported directly from the scene of the crime in rural Noto peninsula where he and fellow gang members attempted to import illicit narcotics into Japan..."*

The screen cut to a taped scene showing a row of blue vans arriving to a side entrance, three of them pulling up to an entrance that had been cordoned off with blue tarpaulin material hung to hide the suspect from view. Men from the first and third van jumped out quickly to surround the door of the middle van. They held up blankets as the door opened, and the camera caught a glimpse of jeans and a sweater beneath the blankets. The figure jumped down from the van to the pavement below, and the group dashed as a single mass behind the blue awning into the entrance of the building.

"*The suspect is a minor and has yet to be identified by the police or the Ministry of Justice.*" The screen then showed a close-up of a break in the tarpaulin that appeared to reveal the profile of a teen boy's face, but the picture was sufficiently fuzzy so that viewers could not fully identify the person, further reinforcing the program's description of the situation. "*Sources indicate that he was working with at least one other person as they conducted a transfer of some sort with another vessel in the Sea of Japan. As authorities approached the suspect vessels, the two vessels separated and attempted to flee in different directions. The boy reportedly fell as his companion—my sources tell me the companion was his brother—attempted to flee the area. In the ensuing chase, the fleeing vessel collided with a fishing boat, killing himself and two innocent civilians onboard the other boat. The two who perished, a local fisherman and his daughter...*"

The smiling face of the girl and her father appeared on screen, and with that Nishi decided to mute the volume. *Our calculated leaks to the media, and the dramatic arrival of Hatano, is sure to arouse the passions of the Japanese public,* he thought to himself. *We can string this out for days for maximum drama...*

Nishi reached for the phone on the Korean War-vintage drab-green metal desk and pushed the intercom button. "Menda-san, has the suspect finished eating yet?"

"Yes sir, Deputy Chief Nishi, we're about to pick up the plates right now..."

"*Yosh.* I'm coming up now."

"I'll inform the guards."

Nishi put on his shoes and stood up haltingly. All the standing during the night operation, the lack of sleep, and the travel from Ishikawa made his sciatic nerve act up again too. It was an old injury that caused the demise of his more active career as a detective. He moved into management, which some aspired to but not Nishi. He missed the action, knowing the pulse on the streets, the pride he took in protecting the public order, solving crimes... Luckily the opportunity to serve in Afghanistan came along, and despite no one else volunteering Nishi had to fight for the posting because of his past injury. He would've burned out years ago had he not left Japan for an overseas assignment. And Afghanistan led to other opportunities and then his current work, and more opportunities to take down major criminal outfits while at the same time contributing to Japan's national security. *It is truly a new era,* he thought to himself. He rubbed his right lower back as he stood motionless for a few seconds. He then placed his right foot closer to the door, testing his hip as he put weight on it even as his left foot twinged a bit from the fasciitis. He opened the door and walked down the hall with a strained but forceful stride.

Nishi rounded the corner in time to see an older woman carrying a tray of a few small, empty bowls from the holding cell, slightly stooped from her age and from a steady gaze on the tray. Two guards in uniform and helmets stood erect behind her, their truncheons out and ready to strike at any sign of trouble. Neither they nor Nishi had noticed that the old lady had given Taro Hatano an additional treat of sweetened rice cake this evening. "*An extra something for you to keep up your strength, young man,*" she whispered soothingly in his ear as she handed to him. "*Don't tell the guards...*" she said as she watched him hungrily devour it and the poison that it contained.

The elderly woman backed out slowly but in a self-satisfied manner, as someone who appeared to Nishi to take pride in her work, however menial it might be. She turned and walked away from

Nishi in the opposite direction down the hall, unhurried, and she disappeared around the corner. The guards stepped forward as if to close the cell door, but then stood back again when Nishi walked to the entrance. He ignored them as he entered the cell.

"Suspect Taro Hatano, how was your meal?" asked Inspector Nishi abruptly and kneeled down in front of him. Taro sat cross-legged on a thin mattress on the floor. "Have you decided to tell us what you know, now that you have a full belly?"

Suspect Hatano sat there with his head bowed. Nishi put his forefinger on Hatano's forehead to force his head up, but as he raised his head Taro Hatano looked away from Nishi. The boy's eyes were bloodshot, and a tear streamed down his cheek.

Hatano had already been in interrogation for several hours that day, and that combined with the constant questioning the night before and a lack of sleep made him a tired boy indeed. In his initial state of panic from almost drowning, and after being arrested on what was unknowingly his first meth run of his life, he had already shown himself to be quite eager to apologize profusely for any and all transgressions of the law and in general provide everything he knew of the operation. The trouble was, he knew entirely too little of the operation to be of use to Nishi. So it was time to squeeze him for other information, about associates, about locations, about how his brother did what he did, possible code words, when he was absent and patterns of life. Hatano did not know it, but now the difficult interrogations would begin.

"What was that, Taro?" Nishi demanded. "What did you say?" Nishi wanted to get the boy talking about something, anything.

"I didn't say nothin'…" Hatano mumbled, and sniffled loudly.

"Well I tell you, Suspect Taro, you better start telling us what you know, because this is a most serious offense. It is not like you are playing hooky from school, though we know you've skipped eleven times in the last year. Eleven times! And then the late-night disturbances on the scooter you were working on, night after night." Nishi looked at Taro and then began to shake his head. "Yes, we know that too. The local police were informed about that a few times, too. You were holding out that information, weren't you Taro-kun? You've been quite a bad young man, almost as bad as your brother. But you've entered the big time now, suspect Taro. People get the *death penalty* for smuggling the stuff you two had, and for *killing* people in the process…"

Nishi looked at Taro's down-cast head, which hung even lower than when he walked in. It was hanging over his crossed legs, and Nishi saw a puddle collect on the single sheet covering his thin mattress. Spittle hung from his mouth, visible below the bangs of his hair that covered most of his face. Hatano snorted, causing the spittle to jiggle slightly even as his matted hair remained stationary.

"We…I didn't have nothin'," Taro whispered.

"What was that?"

"I didn't have *nothin'*!" Taro yelled at Nishi. He lunged forward. "My older brother, Ikeda, was collecting some boxes, but he ran away from me, left me in the sea. So *I* didn't have *anything*!"

"What did *your brother* have, then, suspect Taro!" Nishi shouted at him.

"Fuck if I know! I was just along for the ride, he wanted another person to help, so I helped. That's all!"

For the first time since arriving to the detention facility, Taro looked Nishi directly in the eyes. Nishi recognized this as the point when criminals harden their intentions to resist interrogation.

"Well, Suspect Taro, we caught that other boat, too. The suspects are here, just down the hall, and they both told us everything—they told us about all the drugs they brought here, about giving it to you and your brother, how *you* had a central role in the planning and execution of the operation, about the exchange of money. Yes, they told us everything, and now they are feasting on *donburi*. Wouldn't you like some hot *donburi* now, Taro-kun, to fill you up? It's really good, you know. That nice lady who was just in here makes it fresh. Not like that gruel they served you earlier. It looked quite disgusting, wouldn't you agree? I wouldn't know though, since I don't have to eat it. It certainly looks disgusting, but that *donburi*, though..."

"Unh." Taro's reply was barely audible as he slumped down again. His stomach ached.

Inspector Nishi of course knew that the Coast Guard had not in fact caught the other vessel, and he was quite dismayed about it. He wanted a smoking gun, a source of the stuff from outside. He wanted the Japanese Government to act in a more aggressive way against the source of the drugs, against the people who perpetrated the kidnappings of innocent Japanese, but without proof, final and irrefutable proof, Japanese politicians would only act in a 'diplomatic' ways, in ways that would not antagonize their neighbors, but also in ways that would not dissuade them either. Nishi felt that the politicians almost didn't *want* to catch the boat or any other vessel in the act of smuggling, since that would complicate their delicate balancing act. They would no longer be able to avoid the obvious. There would be calls for action, for effective responses to stop the madness, but Nishi feared his leadership lacked the stomach for what would be required. Why else did it take so much convincing to authorize the operation several days ago? But if one white lie could elicit more information from Taro, a confession even, that would be enough to press the case.

"Cum'on, Taro-kun, stop telling me you know nothing of the smuggling operation your brother and his gang had going in the hills just above the site you were to land with the stuff? Don't take me for a fool, Taro-kun. I know you were bringing in finished stuff, repackaging it, using your boss's trucking operation to deliver it to other ports, the drivers using it themselves sometimes…Come On! We know the entire operation, and it'll be easier for you if you just admit to your role, tell us what exactly you and your brother do in the operation. At heart, you are a good young man, I can tell. I've talked to your mother, she tells me how you did your chores very well, you did well in school, until recently. You're a good boy who did wrong this one time. But good boys don't do well in prison, I will tell you that. Now make it easier on yourself. Tell me the truth, no more lies. Talk to me, Taro." Nishi maintained a soothing voice despite his growing frustration and impatience.

Another sniffle, this one quite loud. Taro raised his head slightly and yelled to the ground in front of him in a hoarse voice, "I've told you already! I don't know anything more! We, my brother and I, we were going to pick up some bags of stuff, he said…I didn't even know what was in it, but he said it was a good-paying job and that I'd make some good dough. I wanted to buy a bike of my own, that's all, replace that shitty scooter…I didn't know what it was!" Another sniffle. His hair was matted to his forehead and the side of his eyes from the combination of sweat and tears. His checks glistened red under the harsh light of the room. He no longer looked at Inspector Nishi. "All my brother said was, we were going to get the stuff, take it to shore, drop it off to some people, and I would get paid. That's all. He was going to take off somewhere, like he always does, but I never knew where since he never took me along. And *that's all!* That's *all* that I know!" Taro's head drooped low again, and he wept loudly.

Nishi turned around for a moment, considering his next approach. In that moment of thought, Nishi at first did not notice that Taro's weeping had stopped, nor did Nishi hear the slight gurgling that emanated from Taro's throat. While thin, the mattress muffled Taro's fall.

When Nishi turned back, he thought that suspect Hatano had fallen asleep. He'd been up for days, and it was not unusual for suspects at this point in an interrogation to fall asleep suddenly, to utterly pass out, if allowed.

But Nishi realized that what he thought was drool from the mouth of an exhausted prisoner was in fact foam from an unconscious one. Nishi reached down and shook his shoulder. "Suspect Taro, this is no time to rest," Nishi said, unable to consciously accept the sudden turn in Taro's health. He shook his shoulder again, more forcibly. "Suspect Taro…" Nishi shook him harder. Nishi then noticed a spasm and another gurgle causing more fluid to flow from Taro's mouth. Nishi pulled open Taro's eyelid and saw his upturned eye and dilated pupil.

"Shit!" he said to himself. He turned to the door and shouted "Menda! Guards, get in here now! Call the medics!" He listened for breathing, but heard none. Nishi then ripped Hatano's prison suit open along his torso and began compressions on the center of his chest. After the first set, Nishi cupped Taro's neck and was about to clear his mouth to begin administering rescue breaths when a hand reached down to stop him.

"I'll do the breaths, you keep doing the compressions," Menda said, pushing Nishi aside. Menda knelt down, cleared Taro's mouth, and gave two quick puffs, and then looked up to Nishi. Nishi then continued with the compressions on Taro's chest, timing them with Menda's puffs.

We make a good team, Nishi thought to himself as they continued CPR for the three minutes it took the paramedics to reach Taro Hatano's cell.

CHAPTER 18 - KAWASAKI

Archer drove her Honda hatchback along Highway 1 from Tokyo to Yokohama. Called the "Zest Spark," it was the turbocharged version of the three-cylinder light models. "Turbocharged" in this case was relative, as it still only had four cylinders to run on.

But Archer was a trained driver, and she knew how to apply high-performance driving techniques to maximize even vehicles such as her Zest.

Archer reached Kawasaki, the mid-way point between the major metropolitan centers. Kawasaki was known historically as the industrial underbelly of the region, with its factories devoted to shipbuilding and facilities for processing industrial and municipal waste. Archer had a sensitive sense of smell, and she closed the vents in preparation for the onslaught of fumes.

Archer was unsurprised by the car she saw speeding toward her in her rear-view mirror from the toll booth they had just passed. Many Japanese youth liked to speed along this stretch of highway or otherwise show off their souped-up cars and motorcycles, revving their engines, and at times harassing other drivers late at night. And the police seemed surprisingly disinterested in patrolling these major thoroughfares despite the obvious reckless driving and noise pollution. As long as it took place late on weekend nights, when family vehicles were not on the roads, the police let the kids flaunt their rides.

Instead of passing her, however, the car veered into her far-left lane and slowed to trail her. She had seen these young idiots harass other drivers, but she had yet to be on the receiving end. She remained unconcerned, but she instinctively checked that her doors were locked and otherwise drove a steady speed. She watched the car behind her, but she could not see the driver because of the tinted windows and bright headlights.

A group of six motorcycles roared by immediately to her right and left, gunning their engines as they passed too close for comfort. Archer sensed that this was not coincidence, since these punks always rode in packs of both cars and motorcycles. They continued to speed forward.

As Archer watched the bikers move ahead of her, she caught a glimpse in her rear-view mirror of yet another car speeding up behind the one that trailed her. It remained hidden for several seconds, then cut over to the next lane, sped around them, and cut into her lane again immediately in front of her. It too had tinted windows and an obscured license plate.

A third car sped up next to her, boxing her in on the right. More motorcycles sped by, and two slowed to take a position ahead of the car next to her along the right forward corner of her Zest Spark. One rider threw a bottle at her car as he pulled into position, hitting and cracking her windshield. Archer ducked down in surprise, but not in panic. The biker pointed to the left several times, obviously indicating that they wanted her to pull over.

Archer reviewed in her mind the exits along the highway and the various routes available to her. As she was trained to do, she had mapped out this trip in advance for emergency situations, and she knew the next exit was not one she wanted to take because there were too many narrow, unlit streets and dead-ends. The group of cars and motorcycles began to slow and veer in unison to the left to force her toward the approaching exit.

These fucking punks think they can intimidate me, she thought angrily, *but they've never met someone who can hit back like I can.* She looked immediately to her right, stuck up her hand and thrust forward her middle finger toward the window. Despite the tinted windows, she was sure the gesture would be recognized in the spirit given.

Archer then took her foot off the accelerator, down-shifted and pulled on the emergency brake half-way. She didn't want to come to a complete stop, but she wanted to slow quickly enough to surprise the driver behind her without taping on the brakes and causing her brake lights to flash red.

The car behind slowed suddenly as well, bumping into her rear several times. The others on her side and in front slowed less immediately, leaving almost a car length of open space to her right, but not enough to speed through as she had hoped.

The brake lights shown brightly on the car in front of her and the car next to her began to slow even more than she had, leaving a half-open space to her front right. This was the next opportunity she was looking for.

Archer had already released her emergency brake, and she hit the accelerator just as the car behind her hit her a fourth time in an attempt to nudge her to the exit ramp. Archer sped forward and veered slightly right. She made contact with the car to her right but did not try to force it aside. She instead nudged the car next to her and she accelerated further into the car in front of her. She hit it on its back right bumper with enough force to cause it to lurch to the left. She maintained contact as much as possible with the lead car's bumper, the driver of the car trying to maintain control with Archer right on his tail. She saw her objective approaching.

The bikers sped forward toward the exit ramp on the right, obviously expecting her to be forced in that direction too. Archer had other plans, however.

Immediately beyond the exit ramp, Archer saw that the safety wall that ran the length of the highway began again. Instead of immediately veering right and away from the group, she began to nudge the car in front of her left toward the barrier. Despite the driver applying his brakes as he tried to make the turn toward the exit, the forward momentum of both vehicles together with Archer's continued acceleration was enough force the front car beyond the exit ramp toward the barrier.

Archer turned to the right and accelerated as much as she could on the approach to the barrier. The driver had been caught off guard by Archer's continued pushing that he overcompensated in turning first to the right, then to the left, causing the car's wheels to skid. Archer urged all of her Zest's momentum into the leading car's back right bumper, and then accelerated to the right and away from it. She cleared the car just as she made it spin out of control and hit the concrete barrier with its front left corner, and the slight incline of the base of the barrier caused the car to rise up on the barrier and onto its side. It slid back toward her as she veered toward the right hand lane, and she just missed it as it slowed to a stop. The car teetered back and forth, the wheels spinning in midair.

Archer glanced at the wreck in her rearview mirror as she sped away. She had hoped, and half-expected, that the cars would stop to help their fallen comrade, but they slowed only momentarily to avoid colliding with the wreckage. The two cars sped around it, one to the left and one to the right.

They're not just trying to harass me, Archer now knew. She looked forward again and noticed red brake lights appear across the highway, from right to left. She was rapidly approaching what seemed to be a phalanx of motorcycles.

Archer figured that they were more surprised at this situation than she was, and she therefore had the upper hand. They only knew that she was coming toward them, and that they probably wanted to slow her down until the cars could ram her off the road, probably toward the left shoulder. She drifted left to make it appear she was heading in that direction, but as the motorcycles began to converge in front of her on the left side of the highway, she sped up again and veered right, clipping one of the slowing motorcycles on the back wheel and causing him to skid to the ground. She quickly sped to the right side of the highway so that the far-right barrier was next to her. It would keep her pursuers from approaching her on the right and would offer some additional protection of the driver's side of the car where she sat.

Despite their seeming vulnerability to collision, the motorcycles swarmed around her, probably to draw her away from the right shoulder and barrier that protected her. One sped up along her left side and smacked her passenger side window with a crowbar. The window cracked but did not brake, and she veered toward him to push him away. She dared not pull away from the right-side barrier and the limited protection it afforded, however.

Another sped in front of her and threw a bottle at her right bumper, and then another. She tried to avoid the resultant shards of glass but could tell she went over a few. One of the trailing cars drove up behind her and bumped her, and then did so again, while another motorcycle came up alongside her and hit her already-cracked passenger side window with a crowbar. This time it shattered, and the chill night air rushed into the vehicle. She could smell the waste processing plants and incinerators in the distance.

I can't continue to drive much more through this, she thought to herself. She dared not try to dial while driving, she needed all of her attention on the road. She then remembered that a hospital was located near the exit ramp two exits away. They would not harass her there, at such a public place, and she could contact authorities and her office and file a complaint.

Archer's left tire blew, which caused her to lose control momentarily. As she slowed the car behind her hit her again, causing her to swerve again.

Fuck it, she muttered, and she jerked the car to the left. She knocked down an unsuspecting biker coming up along her left side, while two others parted to allow her between them for their own safety rather than for hers.

She drove as hard as she could given the flat tire, but she could sense that her car was about to give out. *Only a few kilometers away,* she thought to herself. *I'll have to take this exit and try to shake them on the backroads to the hospital.*

The trailing cars obviously intended the same. They merged once again on her right and began to forcefully nudge her toward the exit while the few remaining motorcycles zig-zagged in front of her to slow her down further. She attempted to resist the nudging car with what power her Zest had left in it as far past the exit as possible, which wasn't far at all. She then turned away abruptly and headed directly to the exit ramp. The sudden move caused the still-speeding motorcycles in front of her to miss the exit ramp.

She sped down the ramp to the local road. The lone light at the intersection flashed red. Not wanting to end up in a head-on collision Archer initially hesitated but, seeing the lights trailing quickly behind her in her rearview mirror, she had to take the chance that this late in the evening traffic would be nonexistent. She didn't see any lights from oncoming cars, so she accelerated down the off-ramp.

As she approached the intersection, she pulled on her emergency break again and then applied the breaks with enough force to slow the vehicle but without locking the breaks. She was almost through the intersection when she turned left suddenly. She had slowed enough that she did not roll her Honda, although her back tires slid on the damp pavement, and sparks flew from the blown tire. She fishtailed into the far curb but otherwise was ok, and she released the emergency break and began to accelerate again, returning to her proper lane on the left as she sped away from the intersection.

The larger pursuit car behind her was going too fast and turned too soon. It lost traction and slid into the small building beyond the intersection. The second pursuit car turned more slowly, but Archer lost sight of the vehicle when she turned the corner.

Archer drove along a deserted street that was lined with small warehouses and trash compactors. Large columns supported the elevated highway running parallel with the street. The pungent stench of refuse forced her to gag.

The second car turned the corner behind her. She forced her Zest forward, but it began to sputter. A car then turned the corner in front of her, causing her to veer away from it at the last moment. Her Zest jumped a small curb and crashed head-on into a concrete pylon. Airbags deployed all around her, which pissed her off because they now blocked her rapid exit from the vehicle. She grabbed her Karambit knife tucked in her pants at her right hip, opened it, and slashed the still-half-inflated bags in front of her and on her driver-side door to deflate them while at the same time unbuckling her seatbelt.

Archer stepped out of the vehicle and stood, waiting. It was too late to run, and she was seething now. Besides, the heft of the Karambit felt good in her hand, and she wanted to use it. The first thug approaching her took an involuntary step back in surprise at the sight of the towering woman in front of him. The sharply curved blade of the Karambit twinkled at him under the sole street lamp near the pylon. She lunged at him once, making a slashing move toward his belly. She wanted nothing more than to disembowel him, and he could see that in her eyes. He stepped back two more steps and was about to run. *This should be easy,* Archer thought to herself, but then caught a glimpse of another figure running toward her.

This one was angrier, Archer could see. He had pulled up on his motorcycle, jumped off and ran toward Archer and the boy in front of her. *This one wants to fight,* Archer thought. *Good.* He took out his collapsible rod from a side pocket on his leather chaps, flicked it open, and pushed his underling out of the way.

"Move aside you god-damned coward," he grunted, then lifted the metal rod over his head.

"Kensuke, I just..."

"*Damare!*" he shouted back at the boy as he charged Archer.

But instead of stepping back in fear of the rod, as Kensuke's other victims have always done, Archer leaped into him and grabbed his hands holding the rod with her left hand at the apex of the arc and jammed the bottom of her knife into his right tricep as she secured the upper part of his arm. She then forced her hip into Kensuke's torso and pulled his hands down as she lifted his arm and torso up in the air. She then pivoted her body under his as his forward momentum caused his body to fly over Archer's now crouching figure through the air. She then slammed him down on the ground with her own bodyweight and pounded her elbow into his solar plexus at nearly the same time. "Hmph," she heard him grunt, the air now knocked out of him. As she stood up, she backhanded him in the cheek and nose while still holding her knife, blood splattering in an arc as he rolled away from her. He writhed in pain at her feet, unable to catch his breath.

She could either continue the carnage and finish this guy, or escape. Her instincts wanted the former, but her training instructed the latter. Archer looked at the other punk and pointed her knife at him. "*Kabi dase!*" she shouted. "Give me the keys!" He hesitated, and she lunged at him again. He threw a set of keys at her and ran away.

Archer picked up the keys and then turned toward the car, but four motorcycles suddenly appeared behind it. They dismounted, and given their numbers they too were unintimidated by her significant height advantage. They swarmed her, and while she thrashed at them with her knife, their leather suits and helmets meant that she scored superficial flesh wounds at best. One kicked her knee from behind, while another tackled her. They fell to the ground, and his helmet smacked her in the nose. She lost her Karambit and involuntarily reached for her now-bleeding nose with one hand while pushing her attacker away with the other. In a last, desperate attempt to get away, she grabbed the attacker's helmet with both

hands and yanked it off, and she slammed it into the knee of another attacker who was about to kick her on the ground.

"Ahhh!" he yelled and fell back, grabbing his knee.

The one on top of her lunged at her with a punch, which glanced
off her cheek. He then slammed into her neck with his forearm,
causing her to choke. She pushed at him, but another kicked her
in the side with his boot, and she yelped in pain. Her last memory
was of the man on top of her grabbing her collars with crossed arms
and squeezing her arms across her neck. Archer blacked out.

CHAPTER 19 - ACCESS DENIED

Han had successfully avoided any run-ins with either acquaintances or security personnel as they drove out of Kusong. They reached open road, and were about to pass through a hilly area on their final approach to the shore, where they would take a "cousin's" fishing boat out to sea. But as they rounded a corner to enter the low-lying valley, they found themselves forced to come to a sudden stop. Multiple barriers blocked the road in front of them. Guards milled about near Korean War-vintage troop trucks and rusting armored vehicles.

One robust-looking guard approached the vehicle.

"Why are you driving this way at this time of night?!" the guard shouted gruffly. "You can't go this way, the area has been sealed off. Present your identification and travel permits at once!"

"What's the issue, what's going on?" Han asked, attempting to keep a calm but commanding tone of voice. "How dare you treat me like this! Don't you see the plates for this car!" He handed over his state lab ID and travel permits for which he paid the office clerk handsomely prior to departing. The documents and the red star on his license plate of his lab vehicle indicating "VIP" would normally have provided him access to most areas along the western seaboard, given the number of secret labs and testing facilities in this region, but Han was slowly coming to realize that this was a special circumstance.

The guard inspected the ID closely, held it up to the light, then turned it over to inspect the back. He then looked at the travel papers. "What's your business here?" he demanded.

"I am visiting a site north of Kwokson ahead of tests there," he answered in the most haughty voice his slight, five-foot two frame could muster. It was not haughty enough.

"This area is closed, there are military exercises taking place now," the guard barked at him.

"I know that! I am to be there for the tests! How long must I wait? I've been ordered here to conduct the inspection immediately, we have a very tight test schedule, directed from the highest levels in Pyongyang!"

"How long is classified, it will be over when it is over. We have strict orders not to let *anyone* through. Now move along back from where you came!" the guard barked.

Han grunted, nodded once as he put his vehicle into reverse, and backed away. He did not want to press his bluff any further. He did a U-turn and drove slowly down the road in the opposite direction of where he needed to be.

After driving another five kilometers, Han pulled next to a forested area along the side of the road, partly concealing his vehicle from oncoming traffic, of which there was none. Han could tell by the silence that his wife was worried. "We planned for this," he said. "We knew this could happen, now we just head to our second departure point."

She nodded in response, and then looked at her hands absently as she kneaded her palms with her thumbs, first one and then the other.

Han sat for a moment in silence. He then opened the door and got out, surreptitiously grabbing his umbrella. "I need to piss," he said coarsely, and he went further into the tree line. He was worried too. This was the easiest route, but it was blocked. As an engineer, he never wanted to face a situation that had featured a single point of failure. There would always be systemic challenges, and to prepare for those one had to build into the system multiple failsafe mechanisms to ensure the system performed as planned. Han had built in multiple failsafes for their departure, but each became exponentially harder.

Han finished relieving himself and retrieved the phone from his pocket. He powered it on, typed out a few letters in a text message, and then retrieved his umbrella. He opened it and pulled the cord from the base. After attaching it to his phone, he turned the umbrella upside down, paused for a moment to ensure everything was in place correctly, and then hit "send." He waited, looking back at the car holding his wife and son. The air blew through the tops of the trees, causing them to sway. He heard wood creak, and then a crack in the distance of a tree falling.

The phone vibrated once, and "sent" appeared on the display. He then returned to the car.

"We should've thought this through, Han…"

"We thought this through very thoroughly, Mi Yong. We have multiple contingency plans. We will make this work."

"That's not what I meant. I mean, why are we doing this at all? We can still go back…"

"And what of him?" Han pointed to their son, asleep in the back seat. "He dies if we go back, Mi Yong. He's brilliant, but he is stuck in a body that is failing him. In the west, we can get him treatment," Han assured his wife. "He will not only survive, he will thrive. He could be the next Stephen Hawking!"

"Or his brain could be dissolving into mush for all we know!" Mi Yong countered. "We have a comfortable enough life. Maybe we just live it and let come what God wills…"

"God wills us to leave, Mi Yong, we both feel that in our hearts," Han replied firmly. "We have options. We have our fallback plan. We just need to get to the next rendezvous point in time." He then started the car and headed back along the winding road they had traveled, slower now as he looked at the gas indicator.

CHAPTER 20 – BACK TO BUSINESS

Tadaishi sat in the back corner of the cafe, sipping his coffee. It was black and scalding, which he needed this early in the morning. Rays of sunlight began to appear around the adjacent buildings. A pedestrian walked by, one of the few on the streets at this early hour. Most of the city had yet to wake up.

A man in a navy-blue business suit entered the cafe and walked directly to Tadaishi in the back.

"Ahhhhh, *Nakano-san, 'sashiburi desu ne!* It's so good to see you!" Tadaishi said softly, as if not wanting to wake up the sleepy barista at the bar. Tadaishi bowed and gave the appearance of being glad to see his friend in the city despite his fatigue. He gestured toward the open seat at his table. "Here, I have a coffee for you."

"Oh, Tadaishi-san, yes, it's been too long!" Nakano replied, bowing in return and then sitting.

Tadaishi slid back into the booth and adjusted himself next to Nakano facing the barista at the front of the cafe. The pillar next to them and the high seatbacks conveniently blocked much of the line of sight between the cafe's front door and their table. It provided an extra sense of intimacy and confidentiality in the still-empty cafe. Many in the press would be interested to see a ranking member of the opposition in Japan's parliament meeting with a deputy director of the Public Safety Investigation Agency on the eve of national elections.

The conversational pleasantries quickly passed, and Tadaishi came around to the point. "You know, Nakano-san, members of my constituency have been asking me about that drug raid off Noto peninsula the other day…"

"That was something, wasn't it? People here in the capital have been talking about it too. There is a theory making the rounds that one of the Japan Coast Guard boats was firing on the little dingy that tried to get away, but instead hit the fishing boat and killed that father and daughter. They're saying the Coast Guard actually captured the little dingy, but in order to cover up their incompetence they're telling the public it ran into the fishing boat instead."

"You don't say?" Tadaishi asked inquisitively, taking mental notes now.

"Which helps them out, people say," Nakano continued, "since they don't have to have a trial or anything, they can just interrogate or torture them as they like. I of course don't believe that nonsense, but it was unfortunate that my agency was cut out of the operation, unjustly I might add, since we could've provided some significant assistance, maybe even prevented whatever happened the other night. But we can only go on what we hear from our counterparts at other ministries and agencies on this."

"Yes, I'm sure you would have been very helpful. I'll be sure to press other members of the transportation committee to ensure that your agency is included in the future." Tadaishi paused a moment to look at the front of the cafe as if to check for any patrons, and then looked back at Nakano. He sat forward and whispered. "I've heard similar rumors in my district, to tell you the truth, which is why I've come back to Tokyo. I need to know the facts of the incident, and what we can expect next. It wasn't my district, but my district is just south of the area and my constituents are of course concerned that they too might be targeted in some errant mission..."

Nakano interjected. "Really? And I thought you just missed the entertainment!" At that, Nakano laughed. "You country bumpkins don't have things as good as we do, eh Tadaishi-san?" Nakano nudged Tadaishi mischievously, who looked back at him quizzically. "Come now, don't tell me you didn't make a special visit to the entertainment district when you got to town last night, eh? Don't play ignorant with me now, Representative Tadaishi, y*ou're* the one who introduced *me* to the club, after all!" Nakano smacked Tadaishi in the chest with the back of his hand.

Tadaishi tried to hide his sudden anger. *And I pay for it too, Nakano, don't forget that...* "Oh, Nakano-kun, you know how I love that club, just like you do!" he replied with a thinly veiled chuckle, pressing back at Nakano with his index finger almost as a warning. "It certainly is expensive, remember that too...But no, Nakano, really, what gives? What's the deal with the Coast Guard taking on those thugs at night like that, and why weren't we in parliament informed of the impending operation?" He leaned in further and asked, "Why wasn't *I* informed, Nakano-san? They had to know it was dangerous, huh? My people, er, constituents want to know, is it safe to go out in a boat at sea or are they going to get rammed or even fired on by a Coast Guard cutter? Eh?"

Nakano thrust himself forward with a serious look on his face. "Representative Tadaishi, we've been asking the same questions. My agency feels that we can offer significant assistance in these operations and we're looking for channels to get additional information, but it goes all the way to the top, to the *Kantei*, the Prime Minister's office. They're the ones orchestrating this directly through a special task force run by the Japan Coast Guard and the National Police Agency, and now, I'm hearing, the Maritime Self-Defense Force is going to be involved too. They now have blanket permission to fire on and sink any unidentified vessels..."

"That's madness!" Tadaishi interjected. "At a minimum, they might fire on some unsuspecting Japanese fisherman whose radio is malfunctioning, or they could fire on a Russian, Chinese, or Korean fishing boat by mistake and create a huge diplomatic issue! Are they serious?"

"They've had that permission legally for a while now, but what has changed now is both the political and bureaucratic will to use force, deadly force if necessary, especially after they got away yet again. But we've been trying to communicate through our channels the danger inherent in that, and so far no one is listening to us. So I'm glad you've come to talk to me, Representative Tadaishi. Perhaps you can help us get our message out…"

"Well there is only so much I can do with a party in opposition, but perhaps tomorrow the Japanese public will choose a different direction."

"It's funny, because if they were really after drugs, if they *really* wanted to crack down, they would start just down the road"— Nakano gestured to the cafe door and the road outside to emphasize the point—"since we all know this is where the stuff ends up, right down the road there in Kabuki-cho. Here in Tokyo, whether fueled by the increase in foreigners, or trafficked out to other countries…"

"Well aren't they? What, they aren't doing anything here in Tokyo?"

"Oh, sure, we're going out more, we're getting more baddies, we're finding them on the streets, but they're the little guys, you know? Not the big fish. And the Chinese. My God, why aren't we going after the Chinese? I mean, *they* are *ruthless*! It's like they don't play by any rules! And they are slowly taking over this town, they're taking over Kabuki-cho, slowly…"

*What are you going to do when that happens, huh Nakano-kun? You can kiss your take good-bye then, when the Chinese clear out the Yakuza around here…*Tadaishi chortled at that thought as he looked closely at Nakano. *And no more hanging out with little girls either, that's one thing I can't pay for…*

"No, I'll tell you, I think it's the Americans. Yeah, it's the Americans, *that's* your conspiracy for ya! Some Americans got involved, and six months later, suddenly, all hell breaks loose. We had things under control until now, huh? Things were in balance…"

"How do you mean, when the Americans got involved? Who became involved? Are you talking about the new ambassador?"

Hmph, Nakano grunted. "The new ambassador. I doubt if he even knows half the story. No, there's a girl in town, an American diplomat, Asian features but tall, you can't miss her. She was at the site of the accident a few nights ago, and she's been hanging around the TDC lately too, with one of the leaders of the new task force. And a few others have shown up too, coming to the Embassy at odd hours, that sort of thing. Stuff is going on, and probably the Americans are behind it."

"What do you think they're up to, Nakano-san?

"There's talk that they are here to take down some North Korean ring. They got some network they're trying to roll up, supposedly one that we in the PSIA haven't been following." *Hmph*, Nakano grunted again. "Like we don't have plenty of networks we're following too, Russians, Chinese...It's those Americans who're pushing the agenda, and it's not about drugs, they don't give a *damn* about our kids getting high, or our girls taking too many diet pills, they don't care about drugs at all! They're going after someone to make themselves and the new administration look good at home, and this is an excuse. They don't care if Japanese get caught up in the crossfire..."

"Who cares if there are Koreans in Japan?" Tadaishi asked pointedly. "That's no secret, there've been Koreans in Japan for centuries! They obviously don't know their Asian history."

"And the ruling party here swallowed it whole, to play the national security card with the public right before the election. Got a nice bump in the polls too, I'm sure you saw. What's more, there's word that they're planning another operation..."

"Hmm," was Tadaishi's only response. Nakano did not see Tadaishi's piercing glaze at this as he continued to talk and watch out the window at the same time.

Several pedestrians walked into the cafe at once and lingered in front of the front counter, looking at the menu above. Nakano leaned in again. "This time the intelligence intercepts say there's to be a shipment arriving off the central-west coast. They're preparing to send units to that area imminently. And I'm sure some of the American units participating in the exercise are involved too. That's the rumor throughout Tokyo…"

"I see," Tadaishi responded. "Did they say where exactly? When?"

"It's not in your district, so I'm really not at liberty to discuss further, but still, it shows you how the Americans are involved in this. One operation right after the other, and around an election too. They're really forcing the issue this time."

"But Nakano-san, it is so near to my district," Tadaishi pressed. "You know how fishermen are, they launch from one port and then travel up the coast. It's not a matter of political borders at that point. If something happens to one of my constituents, like what happened off the coast of Noto peninsula, I'll be blamed for it and could possibly lose my seat at this delicate time. I really must insist, Nakano, what are you hearing?"

"Yes, I see that you are right," Nakano said. "And we need all the allies we can get in the Diet these days…" Nakano sucked in a breath through his clenched teeth. "*Saaa,* very well then…" He leaned forward and began to detail both the intelligence and the rumint his office had gathered on the potential raid.

Tadaishi took notes. "Any other operations in the coming days? Er, near my district, that is?" Tadaishi asked casually. "You talked about the Americans…"

"No, not that we have heard. But I'm sure they'll use units from there like during the last raid, and from the American units taken from the exercise perhaps. We won't know those operational details until we read them in the papers, though." Nakano looked sullen upon saying this.

"Yes, I suppose so." Tadaishi glanced at his watch. "Well, I'm sorry to have kept you this long, Nakano-san! This is definitely an issue that we will take up in the new legislative session after the elections!" Tadaishi declared. He didn't want to appear too anxious to leave, but he stood up to indicate that their conversation was at an end.

Nakano rose too, and they walked outside together. "Thank you for taking the time to meet with me, Nakano-san!" Tadaishi stood and bowed slightly. Nakano paid his respects, and turned to go to the metro. Tadaishi hesitated slightly as Nakano turned, and he purposely went the opposite direction of Nakano. Tadaishi turned the corner, glanced back to ensure Nakano had not returned to within earshot, and he then took out his cell phone and dialed Kano.

"Yes?" the expectant voice demanded.

"I have information for you."

"It better be good," replied Kano.

"It is," said Tadaishi, and he rapidly began to relay his conversation with his unwitting informant.

CHAPTER 21 - THE PEN FACTORY

Kano hung up the phone as his car pulled up to a small industrial building in a suburb south of Kanazawa City. Weeds had grown through the cracks in the pavement and along the foundation of the building. A crack in the tinted window was covered with duct tape. The building was dark inside, and Kano's vehicle was the only one in the parking lot.

The door to the warehouse in the back of the building opened, and the car drove in. Kano exited the car as the door closed.

"We arrived at just the right time!" Kano declared as he got out of the car. "Araki-san, take a look around," Kano said with a flourish of his outstretched arms in the middle of the small warehouse. "I believe this is what you said you needed, correct?" Large metal barrels lined the wall with markings "HCl" and "Thiodoglycol" on them.

Araki first poked his head out of the car, looked at the storage containers and then up at the ceiling at the ventilation. He then opened the car door and slowly climbed out. "And the equipment?" he asked with no sign of emotion.

"Oh yes, the equipment. It's a little old, this factory shut down years ago, but we checked it, the equipment runs fine. I even had it tuned up before we arrived." Kano flipped the light switch to the adjacent room, where mixers fed into a machine that in turn filled ball point pen cartridges with ink. The conveyer would then carry the cartridges to another that inserted them into pen casings, and then another would place them into boxes for packaging. They would be stored in the warehouse, next to the materials needed to make the pens: The cartridges, the casings, the precursor chemicals needed to mix the ink, and the boxes and packaging.

Araki began examining the equipment.

"There are still some supplies and materials from the previous owners, left here after they went bankrupt," Kano said as he watched Araki inspect the equipment. "The ink precursors were too old to use, so we dumped those along with some other industrial waste we were contracted to dispose of. It's all safely buried at sea." Kano let out a snort as he slapped one of his silent henchmen on the back, unable to contain the humor he found in being paid to dispose of barrels of chemicals in the open sea.

Kano saw Araki look quizzically at the labeled barrels along the wall.

"And when will the new chemical precursors arrive? You didn't drive me out to tour just an empty factory, did you Kano-san?" Araki asked. He rubbed his finger along the inside of one of the mixers, pulled it out and rubbed his fingers together. He looked at Kano.

"The shipment should be arriving soon, no later than this afternoon. The old licenses to purchase thiodoglycol in bulk transferred with the sale, so the paperwork is all in order, and in your name." Kano motioned to one of his men, who handed him a thick folder. "Wasn't easy to get in the quantities you need, Araki-san," Kano said in a grave tone. "Thiodoglycol is a Schedule-2 chemical on the Chemical Weapons Convention and is a controlled substance. Sure, it's used to make inks and dies, but the Japanese Government monitors this stuff closely. And the Hydrochloric acid...well, let's just say if the Japanese Government knew both of these substances were here together, under one roof, they'd raid it immediately."

"At any rate," Kano continued in a more upbeat tone, "this business is now officially yours, and the supplies are being delivered to this new pen-making enterprise. In fact, here is the prototype, if you are asked." Kano reached in his coat pocket and pulled out a heavy gold pen. "Here, sign your name to see how smoothly it writes..."

Kano placed a sheet of paper on the hood of the car as Araki looked at the pen and felt its heft. He then signed the paper.

"Not bad, eh Araki-san?" Kano chortled again. "You are going to make a wonderful businessman!" Kano then leaned in to Araki and said, as if in secret, "You will now be able to fulfill your guru's vision."

The self-contained Araki could not help but smile at the sight of the equipment and storage area ready to receive the industrial-sized vats and barrels of chemicals in the warehouse. While it was a relatively small factory for the mass production of ink pens—which is why it went out of business, because it lacked the economies of scale necessary to compete in 21st century Asia—it was the perfect size for Araki's operation.

Kano handed Araki the keys to the small factory. "You can begin your work now." Kano turned without waiting for a response, knowing that none would come from Araki, who was already preoccupied with planning for his first batch of gas production.

Kano did not notice, as he climbed in his car, Araki laying out the pins he had taken from the safe house. They were his good-luck charms.

●   ●   ●

Araki had spent more than two decades under the care of Kano and his extended "family." He could no longer recall exactly how he fell into Kano's protective custody, but as he had worked with one of the cult's chief scientists, he had learned that Kano had met many of the 'medicinal' and other chemical needs of cult leaders over the years. Araki at some point became the main interlocutor with one of Kano's lieutenants, who took the group's increasing orders and provided supplies on a regular schedule. They did not want to deal with typical *yakuza* for their supplies, since the leadership found them to be too provincial and, unfortunately in many areas, in close enough communication with local police that those contacts could prove a liability down the road. The group found in Kano a supplier who was a bit more self-interested and not too nationalistic. They knew him to be ethnically Korean, and while they presumed to know where he got his supplies, they did not ask. There in fact came a point when the leadership believed that Kano's supply chain was itself becoming a liability, because they came to rely on him too much. They began to expand their own supply chain to acquire precursor material, which led to a break in relations with Kano and his group.

Their break in relations probably had saved Kano from further scrutiny after the cult became more openly militant. But now on the run, following the police raids on their many facilities, Araki had nowhere else to turn, so he sought out Kano through his trusted henchmen. Araki remembered that a few members of a local *bosozoku* motorcycle gang transported supplies for him, and he was able to make contact with them in the gritty industrial town of Kawasaki, one of their operating hubs just south of Tokyo. In short order, he was at one of Kano's safe houses on the other side of the country. Neither he nor Kano had expected the situation to last this long, and had Araki not kept to himself as he had in continuing his spiritual training, Kano would have thrown him out long ago.

Kano did not realize the extent of Araki's explorations within the confines of his safehouses, however. Kano had grown accustomed to Araki's intense training sessions, to the point that he started to forget he was in any given location at the time. Araki, finding himself virtually alone for stretches at a time, broke from training to explore. He would wander through the halls and empty rooms late at night and in such silence that even if others were staying in the residence, they were unaware of his activities.

Araki had a particular interest in Kano's badges and pins from the 1940s and 1950s from North Korea, which he discovered in the back of a bottom desk drawer one night many years ago. Araki himself developed an interest in pin collecting when he took his one trip to the United States to visit Disneyland. He found he could acquire a pin for his favorite rides and characters, and later they reminded him of the memories of that magical time away from the growing pressure to constantly excel in school. Pin collecting became his one outlet as he struggled to adjust socially in school. He secretly kept his pin collection even when he joined the cult, despite their demands to "let go" of all worldly possessions to cult leaders. Indeed, he did not even consider them in the same category of "possessions," since they were decorative memories of a world of innocence, a netherworld of make-believe. And apart from having to leave the cult behind following the government crack-down, his one great sorrow was having to leave behind his pin collection.

When Araki discovered the collection as he secretly inventoried the possessions contained in the house, he assumed that Kano's interest was similar and genuine. Kano seemingly kept his interest to himself, hidden behind his tough-man exterior. Araki now felt a kinship with Kano, believing that they secretly shared a passion together. Araki saw the hidden collection as a reflection of Kano's desire to keep his interest to himself, and Araki would never shame Kano by asking about it. Araki would never know, and Kano would never have divulged if asked, that they were left behind by his uncle and aunt prior to their departure for North Korea to help build a new socialist society.

Instead of allowing them to gradually collect dust in the lower shelves of one of Kano's many desks, Araki determined that he himself would tend to the collection. Kano would never discover that a few pins would disappear now and then because Kano himself had forgotten about them, just as he tried to forget about his aunt and uncle's idiotic disappearance decades ago.

Now Araki kept them as charms as he prepared for his upcoming mission.

CHAPTER 22 - A TRAIN, EAST

Han looked at the needle on the gas gauge pointing toward "E." They were running on fumes now.

There, there it is! Thank goodness! Han thought to himself. He dared not speak his true feelings to his wife, for fear of worrying her even further.

Han pulled into the "Air Koryo" gas station. He exited and presented his gas voucher to the attendant.

"We're not taking those now," the attendant said bruskly.

"What do you mean, I just got this two weeks ago," Han asked, startled.

"Haven't you heard? They're rationing gas now. You've already used your allotted share for the month."

"But I haven't bought gas in weeks!" Han declared.

"According to this you bought five litters on the 1st." The attendant then looked at the license plate on his car. "And according to where you're from, Kusong, that's your quota."

"Don't you know who I am?!" Han blurted out a phrase he had vowed to never use in his lifetime. "You see the red star on the license plate. Here, take a look at my ID!" Han waved his state identification card in front of the attendant barely long enough for him to catch a glimpse of Han's photo. "Now give me gas!" Han demanded. His anger was real and not feigned.

The attendant looked back at the license plate, and then smiled. "Oh yes, I'm so sorry to have overlooked your situation, sir! We will be happy to honor your vouchers here. Of course, a man in your position can certainly afford the recent rise in costs associated with providing gas to out-of-towners…" The attendant added.

"What's that?" Han asked, taken aback.

"There is a surcharge in cases like these."

"Eh? Surcharge?"

"Yes. Surcharge." The man was quickly losing patience with Han.

After a moment, the attendant blurted out: "Do you have cash. Euros or dollars. You will need cash to buy gas here."

Han patted his empty coat pockets, first on his chest then at his side. "Er, I do not. Not with me…"

"What of Chinese Yuan then? If you have nothing, then move your car or I will move it for you. There are other vehicles waiting for gas," the attendant said, motioning to the line of cars cuing behind his.

Damn it, Han thought as he looked both ways to see if anyone was looking. He kneeled down as if to tie his shoe, and then drew out the remaining foreign currency he possessed, which was actually his wife's remaining savings that he was holding for her.

"Here, now give me gas!" Han half-shouted as he thrust the wad of cash at the attendant.

The attendant looked at the bills, and then back at Han. Without speaking, the attendant began to fill the tank. Han returned to his driver's side seat. Less than 30 seconds later, the attendant pulled the pump from the nozzle and taped the top of the car. "*Move on,*" he ordered.

Han started the car and began to pull forward. He watched the gas indicator needle rise. It barely reached a quarter of a tank. He stopped and rolled down the window. "Hey, what's the meaning of this, I didn't even get half a tank of gas!"

"You've used your rations for gas, now move along!" the attendant said loudly. He was already preparing to fill another vehicle, a black Mercedes 500E with tinted windows. Han didn't need to look at the special plates to know that he should not make a scene in front of whomever sat in the backseat of the vehicle. He sat back in his driver's seat, rolled up his window, and immediately pulled out of the service station.

Han frowned, but with no other option, he drove down the street in silence.

"What now?" his wife asked.

"We need more gas to proceed south. I don't know if we can make it to our facility in Pyongyang. If we can, I should be able to get some extra fuel, tell them we are headed to the testing grounds in the northeast, and then proceed south to our second point of departure. I've done it before, shouldn't be any questions asked there," he added.

"But with the rationing, and all the lock-downs, will our facility be able to provide us any more fuel…?" Mi Yong allowed herself to wonder aloud in a whisper.

Han pretended not to hear her, and he did not answer.

• • •

Han remained silent as he drove slowly south toward Pyongyang. The needle on the gas gauge pointed perilously close to empty again. He began to despair. As he surveyed his surroundings he saw a farmer light a pile of debris ablaze in a field in the distance. The fire sent a column of smoke up the in air. The blaze was suddenly obscured by a sign they passed on the road that read "Sundok," with an arrow under it that pointed left that read "Sunchon." The column of smoke rose from behind the sign. Han pulled over immediately prior to the turn. He felt a chill and goosebumps rose on his skin. He thought for a moment, then looked at his watch.

"We might make it in time," he muttered to himself.

"What?" his wife said.

"It might be our only option now, if we can't get gas."

Han turned at the intersection.

"What are you doing?" asked his wife, surprised at the turn. "This isn't the way to Pyongyang!"

"No, and we won't be able to make it there. We have no gas, and no money to buy gas. We'll surely be picked up by authorities when we run out of gas, who will see that we have forged papers. They will start to question us. Our only way now is to get to the train station in Sunchon, where a contact of mine should be passing through right about now..."

"Contact? Who?" Mi Yong demanded.

"You'll see. Trust me. I've planned for this. And God will deliver us…"

Mi Yong took out a white handkerchief and wiped tears from her eyes as their son moaned in his sleep in the back.

• • •

Han pulled into a small parking lot off of the main road and adjacent to the Sunchon railway station. The car seemed to die as Han turned off the ignition. "Wait here," he told her as he climbed out of the vehicle.

Han walked to the ticket vender at the main counter, displayed his ID, and said: "I need to get through the gate to talk to the engineer of the military train over there." Han pointed at the military cargo train parked alongside the far platform, where machinery loaded large crates into empty boxcars.

She waved disinterestedly, and he walked through the gate.

Once he reached the far platform dedicated to military transports, Han flashed his ID again and then hopped down to a walkway that ran along the tracks. Black ravens pecked at the ground in a futile search for kernels of corn from the recent harvest as he passed by. He stopped half-way down the train where a man checked the connections between the cars.

"Hello, Comrade Kim!" Han shouted over the movement of machinery that loaded and unloaded cargo.

"Ah, Comrade Han! What an unexpected surprise!" Engineer Kim said warmly. "What brings you here of all places?"

Han flashed a sheepish look away from his friend. "I'm embarrassed to say this…" His voice trailed off.

"Yes?" Engineer Kim said as he cocked his head slightly to one side.

"I did not realize the degree of rationing taking place now for petrol. I was on my way to stop briefly at my office headquarters in Pyongyang and then on to Hamhung to observe the latest launch, when I realized we were too low on petrol to reach the capital even…"

"Oh, it is a very strict rationing, yes. Luckily I do not have to put up with such rationing in this!" Kim said as he patted the side of the train and chuckled.

"You are headed to Wonsan, yes?" Han asked. Wonsan was the major junction on the eastern coast of North Korea, south of the next major city of Hamhung.

"This is our normal route, you know that from riding along before…"

"Would it be possible to get a ride? I'm to observe the missile launches in conjunction with the firing exercises, and it would a dereliction of duty if I were to miss it…" Han did not actually know if there was a firing exercise or not in Hamhung, but he assumed there were many taking place on both coasts because of the date and from the guard who blocked their passage to the coast the previous night.

"Why didn't you take the bus to the launch site, or the VIP train?" asked Kim.

"The truth is, I am taking my wife and son to see the momentous event!" Han said, straining to project an energetic demeanor. "It has been difficult getting permission for my only son to attend these events, however, due to his…condition." Han looked away at the thought of his son and fought back genuine tears. He tried to smile through the pain when he looked back at Kim. "I want him to experience the next test, whatever it takes, before the…the…eventual happens," Han added in complete sincerity. "And unfortunately because of the snap exercises and gas rationing, I'm not even sure if I could get back to Kusong, much less to Pyongyang and certainly not to Wonsan or Hamhung, where I'm sure all the truly spectacular firing exercises are taking place. So I have no way to get my wife and son there…" Han said, his voice trailing off.

"Hmm," Kim grunted. He looked at the supply car, and then back at Han. "We're headed that way, you've traveled with us before to escort your test warheads to the site," Kim said and paused, looking again at the box car. The car was many decades old, and the metal frame holding the rotting wood together was visibly rusting. "We wouldn't be able to accommodate you and your family in the passenger car, that's for military personnel only and full now."

"Certainly not. I would be very grateful to you if we could get a ride in the boxcar. Er, at least to the east coast, that is," he stammered. "I certainly don't want to impose on you…"

"You're cleared to ride in the compartment, but I'm not sure about your family…" Kim looked at the empty car again, toward the guard sitting in the back corner, and then up and down the tracks. "We're just transporting munitions to the firing exercise, nothing strategic, so I suppose it won't be a problem going across to Wonsan. But we have a shipment to pick up there going north, with a tight deadline…" Kim trailed off.

Han smiled in gratitude toward his friend and bowed his head in appreciation. "Thank you very much. We can take the bus north from there to Hamhung, I'm sure my colleagues will not have departed Wonsan yet." Han had no intention of traveling north to Hamhung, but he did not want to leave any clues of his actual plans to defect if anyone started to inquire about his whereabouts, which would surely be soon.

"We'll depart at half-passed the hour," Kim said looking at his watch.

"I'll get my wife and son immediately." Han returned to the main station and gathered his wife and son.

Once back at the boxcar, Han motioned to his wife to climb up the steep steps at the back. He would hand their son to her and their few bags once she boarded.

Kim leaned forward. "We should probably keep them in the back corner, behind one of the racks," Kim whispered to Han. "You know, just in case…" He motioned almost imperceptibly to the guard.

"Certainly, we will not be an imposition on you!" Han replied. He lifted his son to his wife and one other worker who had been loading crates onto the adjacent boxcar. They carried him to the far corner of the empty boxcar, and the worker went back to Han to help with the boy's medical equipment as the boy's mother steadied him. Mi Yong comforted the boy as Han finished loading their things.

The young guard sat at the far end of the car watching the scene unfold. He picked up a piece of wood, opened the cast-iron potbelly stove next to him, and shoved it inside. He then inserted a metal rod with his other hand to stoke the fire, and closed the door. He sat back down next to the stove and rubbed his hands together near it, his breath visible in the cool morning air.

"If you don't mind, I'll go to the latrine before we depart," Han said quietly to Kim.

"That's fine, you know where it is, but you better hurry," replied Kim. "The train waits for no one."

Han jumped to the ground and ran to their van. He grabbed the umbrella, which he had almost forgotten about with the rush to the train, and he held it close to his body in what he hoped was an unobtrusive manner. He ran back into the station and directly to the restroom near the platform.

The restroom was spartan and featured a short wall to one side that served as a urinal and three commodes lining the other side for defecating. The dripping of water echoed along the dirty-white tiled walls, and the stench of stagnant urine mixed with chlorine filled the still air. Han walked to the first commode, which was merely a porcelain hole in the ground over which a person squared to defecate. It was clogged and filled almost to the brim with shit. Han went to the second commode, but its door was jammed and he could not close it. The third commode was occupied.

Han returned to the first commode and stood over the shit-filled hole as he closed the door. Light still shone through the sides, but this would have to do. He hung his suit jacket on the door to cover the opening as much as possible. He retrieved his cell phone, squatted over the excrement and tapped out a line. *Running late,* the hurried message started. *Will meet you near the buried kimchi for breakfast.* Han did not have time to recall all the coded terms, but he hoped the half-coded, half-open message would be understandable to those on the other end, and that it was coded enough not to give away his ultimate plans if the message were intercepted by the state security.

Han retrieved the cord from the handle of the umbrella and connected it to the phone. His hands were shaking, and it took three tries to fully insert it. He lost his grip on the umbrella as he placed the phone in his jacket pocket, and it fell tip-first into the excrement below. *Damn it!* Han blurted as he picked it up. He unfolded the umbrella as much as he could in his squatting position and steadied it with his knees, trying to keep the dirty tip of the umbrella from brushing against his suit pants. He then retrieved the phone from his pocket, prepped the message and waited for the signal that communications had been established.

Bang! Bang! "Hey, what's taking so long! I gotta crap!"

Han looked at the door and then back at the phone. He could feel beads of sweat gather above his temples despite the cool air.

"." ".." "..." the screen displayed as it searched for a signal.

Uuunnnnnhhh, Han grunted to suggest he was having stomach trouble. He felt like he was, but either he was unconvincing or the other man did not care. "Com'on! I gotta go!" The man shouted from the other side of the door.

Bzzzttt. Han felt the phone vibrate once. A link had been established, and he hit "send." He waited as "..." displayed again. Then another *bzzzttt* followed. The message was sent.

Then the screen went blank. It had run out of power. Han stared at it in disbelief, wondering how he was going to signal to his rescue team his location at the departure point, or for a final rendezvous.

Bang bang bang! The door almost came off the hinges. "Hey, hurry up!" the man shouted again.

"Just finishing!" Han said as he rushed to fold up the umbrella. The man peeked over the door as Han stood and opened the door.

"Eeeewwwww!" The man said looking at him in disgust. Han could only hold his stomach and nod to acknowledge the state of the commode, which he did nothing to create. "*Hey, clean up you're own damn shi....!*" Han heard the man shout as rushed out of the restroom.

Han jumped from the top of the platform directly onto the ground below. He saw the train start to pull away. As Han ran, he saw a head peek out of the door half-way down the train. He could just make out Mi Yong's worried expression as she gesticulated for him to hurry. The black ravens along the train looked alternately at Han and at the departing train, and then took flight in unison.

They flew in front of Han along the length of the train, as if urging him forward.

Han reached the end of the train as it began to gather speed. His lungs began to burn as he continued to sprint to the head hovering in front of him. A hand waved for him to hurry. With three cars left to pass, he felt a sudden pull in his left quadriceps, and he began to limp slightly as he ran but he dared not slow down.

Two cars to go…one…

The train lurched forward with a "clang" as the engineer prepared to accelerate further. Han had no other choice but to jump for the railing on the car behind the one his wife and son were on. He grabbed the railing first with one hand as his legs flailed below him, then with the other. He lifted first one leg to the doorway, then the other and steadied himself before opening the door. He entered the box car, which was empty but for a cold pot-belly stove and a small but empty seating area for a guard. He went to the far end and opened the door. He looked below as the ground passed more quickly now under the two cars. A sudden *screeeeeech* rang through the air as the metal wheel below scraped against the railing when the train began to round a corner. Han winced at the sound.

The train straightened out, and Han reached for the other door while holding tight to the railing. He could not reach to the other side, but he could see Mi Yong look at him through the cloudy glass. She seemed helpless. He looked down again at the ground passing below, and he suddenly became dizzy. He stepped back into the portal and held his chest with one hand while he held onto the railing with the other. He looked again at the relative distance between the two cars, and he dared not even think of jumping.

Then a figure approached from behind, ushered her aside, and opened the door from inside. It was the guard. Without speaking, he reached for Han with one arm while he held to the side railing with the other. Han grabbed it, but he dared not let go of the railing himself.

"Jump!" the guard seemed to say. Han could not be sure over the din of the metal wheels below. "Jump!"

Han looked back at the box car he was in, and then at the guard and nodded. He closed his eyes as he leapt through the air, and he felt a pull on his arm. He caught the platform of the other car with only one foot. The other dangled below, and Han began to flail with his free arm. He felt like gravity was pulling him inexorably downward to the moving wheels below.

Screeeech! The metal-on-metal noise rang out from below through another turn.

Mi Yong appeared in the door, kneeling, and held out her hand. Han mustered just enough strength to thrust his flailing arm forward to hers. She grabbed him and together with the guard pulled Han into the car. The guard shut the door as both Hans fell to the floor, gasping. The guard walked back to his chair, without uttering a word.

When they had caught their breath, Mi Yong explained that Kim was not able to accompany them. "He said we'll 'meet in Hamhung,' have a meal together, sing some karaoke to celebrate all the achievements we've made in these last few years…" she relayed.

Han gave a knowing nod, but was too tired to talk. They moved to their seating arrangement behind an empty rack used to transport munitions to depots throughout central and eastern portions of the country. The racks were currently empty, so the three were only partially concealed from the gaze of the soldier sitting in the corner opposite of them. Sunlight from the rising sun shown through spaces between the wooden slats onto the soldier's well-defined and chiseled face. Han tried to nod at the soldier in thanks once he had collected himself, but he could not tell if the guard saw him. He seemed both wary and disinterested at the same time. Han could see that he was well-built and well-nourished, which was one of the privileges of serving in a unit devoted to guarding the country's strategic assets. A faint flickering of a burning ember of coal was visible from the small slat on the door of the potbelly stove. The guard sat motionlessly and seemingly stared fixedly toward Han, his wife, and their son.

Han had taken this route several times before to escort his and his team's test devices to areas in the central mountainous areas of the country. During each of the journeys to the test sites, he could have traveled in the train's VIP car, where high-level dignitaries traveled to observe some of the tests. But the devices were his babies. He wanted to see them from birth to their final cradle in the mountains, and would marvel at their technical sophistication. That is how he came to be close with Kim. As one of the chief engineers for the special transport trains, Kim shared with Han a special interest in ensuring systems ran smoothly and like clockwork. They often talked about their approaches to their respective work, the challenges posed by the bureaucracy and security apparatchiks, and with great discretion, ways to improve the condition in the country. Han wondered what Kim would think of his true plans…

Han and his wife fell back suddenly as the train jerked forward again and gained more speed. Their son, partially asleep from exhaustion of the trip, curled up next to his mother. He readjusted his sitting position as his mother angled them both to face slightly forward, in case of further sudden movements.

"Here we go," Han said when his wife sat down next to him. She grabbed his hand and squeezed it.

A company of ravens led the train on their eastward journey.

CHAPTER 23 - SHIPMENTS

Il Jin Kwon stood on a craggy embankment overlooking a simple wooden dock. What appeared to be a fishing boat came alongside the dock, and several port attendants threw ropes to men on the deck who then tied them down as the other crew jumped from the ship and walked briskly to the small building on shore. Kwon watched the scene unfold then descended to the building along a steep set of stairs carved into the rocky embankment.

Kwon burst into the building where the sailors were being debriefed. "What the hell happened out there?" He walked to the tallest individual in the room, the officer who commanded the mission, and slapped him in the face. "We lost tens of millions worth of product on this mission, and you came home empty-handed!" Kwon shouted at the crew standing motionlessly at attention despite the abuse. "Our motherland needs these shipments, but now you've raised your profile unnecessarily! I should order all of you to take your cyanide pills immediately for such incompetence!"

Kwon scowled as he walked in front of the crew members arrayed in a line, standing stiffly. He looked at each one as if to inspect them. Once he reached the last of the crew standing at attention, he punched him in the stomach and then looked back down the line again. "You are confined to your quarters until further notice!" he barked. "You shall soon see how incompetence is rewarded in this unit! Dismissed!"

The crew turned in unison to the rear door through which Kwon entered, and began to trot wordlessly out. As the final crew member approached the door, Kwon charged him and kicked him in the lower back, sending him careening into two other members of the crew in front of him.

"Mmpphh," Kwon heard him utter involuntarily, but rather than turn back to Kwon in reaction, the crew member ran faster out of the door once he had caught his balance. Kwon slammed the door closed behind them.

This trick of disguising clandestine vessels as fishing boats to blend in as they conducted smuggling operations was already old, Kwon knew. It had worked in the past for decades, until the Japanese finally got smart and sank one of their boats. They discontinued the practice for a time, but with new leadership and a new need for hard currency and technology that was readily available in neighboring countries, Kwon's masters had decided to recommence operations, with Kwon in charge.

Kwon was honored, and he enjoyed the perks that came with smuggling operations. In addition to satisfying his leadership's new appetites, he could satisfy some of his own as well, and those of mid-ranking officials by adding some additional items to his men's international shopping lists. It worked splendidly for a time, if only because the countries in the region had stopped patrolling for these types of smuggling activities after the thawing of relations in the waning years of the Dear Leader.

But the Chinese themselves began to send more intelligence-gathering vessels around the region even as they increasingly detained Kwon's troops in their own disguised boats, and maritime activities again grew increasingly perilous, and expensive. The bribes to free his men took up almost half their profits in recent years. He switched to Russian vessels for a time, but that too quickly became a challenge when the Japanese cracked down on Russian poaching, and the Russians themselves grew increasingly belligerent toward Kwon's men despite the bribes they doled out on that end as well. The increased North Korean presence in waters off the Russian Far East made the Russian regional authorities sufficiently nervous too, and their maritime patrol and combat capabilities were quickly being modernized after years of neglect. The trigger-happy Russians showed a tendency to shoot to kill first and ask questions later, which raised the stakes there. The Japanese didn't, at least not until two days ago, and *that* began to concern Kwon as well.

Not that Kwon was worried about the welfare of his various crews working the smuggling routes throughout the region. He could find plenty of impressionable and hungry kids from peasant villages who would do anything to escape their dire circumstances in service to the motherland. Kwon was solely concerned about delivering product and maintaining access to hard currency and supplies for his leadership, and for himself. Each lost or detained crew cost him time and effort in recovering his losses, reconstituting crews, and re-establishing routes.

Kwon picked up the black receiver off the black phone in the corner, and began to dial a number. Unlike many other phones in the country, this one had a line to the outside world.

He heard a deep, male voice on the other end say simply, "talk."

"I've been waiting for your call," said Kwon in a calm and even tone.

"We're ready for immediate delivery. Double it this time," replied the man on the other end, without hesitation. While Kwon knew him to be Kano, Kano on the other end only knew Kwon by his assumed name, "Kitagishi-san."

"Double? Are you sure?" Kwon sneered. "I can't trust you after the last botched delivery."

"I am very confident that route 3, with a modified drop-off point and using your new means of transportation, will be successful."

"Confident, eh? That's what you said last time."

"More active measures will be employed this time. I've been waiting for this opportunity for a long time now, and I now have reason to implement them."

Kwon could hear the seething anger in Kano's voice, and he believed Kano was truly prepared this time. "Very well then, we will double our shipment. We will expect cash and equipment, including the QZSS receivers, as payment in full upon delivery of this double shipment and the losses from the last one, understand? Don't shortchange us again."

"Fuck you. You'll get your money and your toys. Just be there on time at the designated spot. This is more complex so your guys better be good."

"It's your people I'm worried about, Kano-san. Send the final location, and we'll be there. Just make sure you are too, alone this time."

"One other thing," Kano said. "I'll have a special present for you along with the shipment."

"A present?" Kwon asked incredulously.

"Yes, and I'm sure you'll be able to elicit a lot of information from her on U.S. plans in the region. And I'm sure after that, she'll make a nice plaything for your leadership."

"Hmmm," Kwon grunted, intrigued. "This better not jeopardize the shipment."

"It won't," Kano said, "it's being handled like we handle all these cases."

"Very well, just send the exact coordinates," Kwon said, and then hung up.

Kwon stuck his head out of the entrance to the small building that overlooked the dock. "Oi! Let's load up now!" Kwon shouted to the dockyard manager standing on the pier.

The manager then pointed to some workers and motioned for them to return to the small warehouse to begin moving boxes to the pier. The dockworkers half-trotted in a small group to the warehouse and then walked out one by one, placing the boxes on the pier, next to the half-submerged midget submarine moored to it.

Kwon sat and turned up the volume on the radio that was playing softly in the background. North Korea's official Korean Central Broadcast Service began its mid-day news bulletins. "For the glorious anniversary of the founding of the Worker's Party of Korea on October 10, in two days the DPRK will launch Kwangsangmyong-4, the most glorious 'Bright Star' satellite!" the announcer declared. The announcer enumerated the many festivities planned throughout the country for both October 9, to mark the anniversary of North Korea's first atomic test and for October 10, to mark the founding of the Worker's Party of Korea. "Festivities begin tonight, when the Dear Marshall himself will attend a mass test of tank and artillery fire off the coast of Wonsan in what has become an annual show of the steadfast strength of the people of the Democratic People's Republic of Korea!" the announcer concluded with a deep and prideful bellow of his voice.

The broadcaster then turned to the topic of Japan, ostensibly to report on the beginning of elections there but which quickly turned into another warning to Tokyo: "We reserve the right to defend our interests in the region, at a time and at a place of our choosing. We will make the Japanese warmongers fully accountable for the catastrophic consequences that may be brought about by their high-handed and outrageous words and deeds. We are prepared for war with the Japanese warmongers and their imperialist masters. We have perfected a powerful nuclear deterrent that is already in our hands, and we certainly will not keep our arms crossed in the face of Japanese warmonger threats of a preemptive strike!"

Kwon listened intently. *Fucking Japs, we'll suck them dry and then nuke their capital and all the imperialist bases there*, he thought to himself. He felt a deep pride in how far the Democratic People's Republic of Korea had come in such short time, and the central role he played in that development.

CHAPTER 24 - ELECTION DAY

"I'm never going to get any sleep on this trip, am I Bradley..." Bennett grumbled as he arrived to the embassy early in the morning. Bradley had called him in for an update on the latest developments.

"It does not look that way, no. We just received this flash message. Our man was unable to reach rendezvous point alpha, he is en route to rendezvous point delta but expects a twelve-hour delay."

"Wait, what?" Bennett asked through a groggy haze. "He can't get to the rendezvous point? Did he give a reason?"

"Only something about blocked access. It was just a short message, I would say hurried even. Something must've happened. He just says he can't make it, and that he is en route to rendezvous point delta."

"What's happening in that area? Any updated imagery?"

"Nothing over the past 12 hours, but there are now reports of snap firing exercises up and down the western coast of the country."

"Shit. Do you think it was related to the Ambo wife's leak about the exercise?"

"Perhaps, or just coincidental given all the rhetoric and the anniversaries now. But that said, it's a lot of fire power that is essentially pointing away from us," Bradley added. "Not their usual M.O."

"So rendezvous point Delta, code name 'orange'. That's the fourth and least viable of the rendezvous options, from what I remember," Bennett said, trying to jog his memory of that part of the operation.

"I didn't even want to include it as an option," Bradley added, "but he insisted and ultimately we all agreed that it was best to have two identified areas off of both coasts. Smart for his part, but a royal pain in the ass for us." Bradley looked back at the map. "He must've had to abort because of North Korea's snap live-fire exercises off the coast in this area, here," Bradley muttered. "But what happened with options Bravo and Charlie?"

Bennett looked at the map, first at the west coast, then at the east. "Shit!" he said, pounding the table. "What does this mean for retrieving him?" he asked Bradley. "Delta is way over here." Bennett circled the location in the western Sea of Japan. "There's no one there…"

"That's what we need to discuss. Now that the exercise location has changed, the Texas is out of range to rendezvous at location delta, since it's on the other side of the peninsula. The original contingency was based on the exercise taking place here," Bradley pointed at the map, "directly between the East China Sea and the Sea of Japan, but now that we moved it over here, closer to rendez-vous point alpha, we are pretty much out of range."

"Can we say that the Texas is no longer able to take part, and send it directly there now?"

"Too late. It is already on station awaiting pick-up of your friend. It was then to proceed back to the exercise, complete a last portion of the training, centered around counter-sub operations, and then return to Yokohama surreptitiously to drop off our guy. I can look into withdrawing it, but it'll be difficult now that we've confirmed participation in that phase of the exercise. Besides, the Ambo's wife leaking details of the operation means that the entire exercise is being watched closely now, even more so than before."

Bennett nodded in resignation. "What are our options?"

Bradley looked at the map again. "We need other assets to de-ploy immediately to this area here," he said, pointing to the area around rendezvous point delta. "I have a team still on reserve, which I kept available just in case. I can have a two-man unit make contact at sea, which is why we were able to accept this as a final op-tion. But that was based on the ability to have a quick reaction force operate from the naval task force that was originally supposed to exercise in closer proximity to the area," Bradley said. "Now, they're out of range too, and we don't have any other platforms in the area. I just don't like the several potential single points of failure if we're discovered as contact is made and the recovery operation begins. I need more ways to get to them in case of trouble, I'm not going to leave them dangling like that. I need a place to station another quick reaction force."

They both looked at the map. "So, what's that there?" Bennett tapped at a naval unit stationed mid-way between Japan and the Korean peninsula.

"That's the Kaga task force, of the 3rd Escort Flotilla," said Bradley. "The Kaga is one of their newest and biggest flat-tops, which just replaced the smaller Hyuga on patrol there, and it's accompanied by the Atago, an Aegis-equipped destroyer for air- and missile-defense, on alert in case North Korea attempts to fire off any more missiles over the Japanese archipelago. They were sent there as a precaution during the election, since Pyongyang is issuing increasingly harsh statements these days with the anniversary of their worker's party founding taking place at the same time, and all these snap firing drills and missile tests. The ASDF is also quietly conducting short take-off and landing exercises with their new F-35s." Bradley looked at Bennett. "Are you thinking what I'm thinking?"

"Yep," Bennett said as he nodded once to Bradley. "But do you have enough men for a QRF now, in addition to the rendezvous team?"

"I certainly do. They just went on leave but they know they're on call now. We'll have to improvise a bit, and we'll need to get Japanese permission to station some of our people there as back-up…"

"We'll work through the embassy to set up an emergency meeting with seniors at the Ministry of Defense," Bennett said. "But give the order now to deploy your team to the area in preparation to make initial contact," he continued, "and we'll work on the Japanese option for your QRF as they deploy."

"I'll get a Gray Eagle UAV up there too to get some initial recon," Bradley added.

"Good, let's get to it," Bennett responded. "Hopefully our man can get to the area within the designated window. It's getting dicey now, with all the snap firing exercises and missile tests."

•   •   •

"No, absolutely not, we cannot do this. Out of the question!" yelled Madeleine Tucker. "Already it was a risky mission, but this is crazy. Do you realize that this could spark a war in the region, with Japanese forces potentially involved?"

"Maddy, I just need to work with our counterparts to get this in place," Bennett said. "I don't need to go through you, but it would be helpful to have you on board. If we went in with a united front, representing the U.S. Government, we can get this done. I already have support from the defense attaché's office, with the approval of Robertson and my own higher-ups."

"The alliance with the Japanese hasn't been tested to this extent, Bennett. Apart from our severe doubts about this supposed asset, how much would we tell the Japanese about the mission? You know how deliberative the Japanese are, and how each contingency is spelled out and codified in detail. Black operations and rescue missions don't fit neatly into what they consider a 'contingency operation'."

"The way I see it, it's a perfect opportunity to approach them with this proposal. There's an election going on, and they've already been ordered to deploy to the area. They would not be involved in any 'operation,' like you say, but just serve as a platform for our people to be stationed on, *just in case* something were to happen. And lack of political leadership is a two-way thing. The military leadership perhaps has some leeway to make a decision on this as the election takes place. They've gotten beat up in the press for not doing so during the maritime incident, and the frontrunner in the election wants to cede additional authority to undertake operations when time does not allow a political decision, such as now."

"I just don't see this happening, Bennett," she said, without providing a reason.

"Our guys are already deploying, Maddy, to get this guy. We just need some additional cover, some additional help in case something goes wrong." He paused for a moment to look closely at her.

"Maddy, why are you so against this, really?" he asked her. "Why do you keep throwing up roadblocks to this? You can surely see this issue as a clear and present danger, for us and for our allies in the region, and any partners we can get in the fight is worth the effort. But they'll only join if we ask." Bennett watched her body language, and then he pressed her: "You've lost your edge."

"Don't you dare say I have lost my edge, or that the Agency has lost its edge!" she replied, pounding the table. "I've seen more action, served in more war zones than you've had time to contemplate your navel in that ivory tower of yours in Palo Alto!"

"Then what is it, Maddy. What keeps you all from even considering some additional options? The decision to go has already been made at the highest levels. Either we have some additional insurance in case things go wrong, to get our guys out, or we fail if things go badly, which could itself spark an international incident. But it's certainly in all of our best interests, yours included, to get some additional support on this."

Maddy sat, starring at her folded hands resting heavily on her lap.

"And to show you I'm approaching this sincerely, I'll offer you a promise in return for your help," Bennett said. "If this goes according to plan and we get this guy out, whether we need our back-up response forces or not, and if he turns out to be a liar or doesn't have any information of value, you will never see me operating in your backyard here again."

Maddy thought for a moment, and nodded once. "Thank you for that, Bennett," she said. "But frankly, you should never be operating in *my* backyard at all. Leave that to the professionals who are trained to take risks and who know how to mitigate risks when they need to be taken." She returned a forceful gaze back at him.

"Let me give you just one example of how lives can be at stake, Wilson, and how quickly even the best planned ops can go to shit," Tucker continued. "Ten years ago, I was an operations officer in Iraq. I was working to vet a potential high-level informant, said he had a lot of information he was ready to provide to us. He gave us some useful stuff initially, and we wanted to vet him more fully, verify his story and bona fides. Ultimately, to do so we needed to meet him at one of our safehouses. It was owned by an elderly couple, childless. They were salt-of-the-earth types, who only wanted the best for their country. They wanted peace. They had seen a lot."

"So the main vehicle arrives," Tucker said, drawing from a clear and focused memory. "I'm watching from a building across the street. It was a good vantage point because we had visibility down multiple roads converging near the house. We watched as our informant got out. The owners were inside the house, waiting, while the two guards, our GRS guys, watched from under an awning in front of the house. The interpreter was with them, a young kid. Good kid, almost naively innocent. The informant got out, and the car drove off before our team approached, per instructions. We knew the driver, we had vetted him, but we didn't want to take a chance that any explosives were surreptitiously planted on the vehicle."

"GRS went up and checked him," she continued, "with the interpreter close behind to calm him. He was a bit agitated, both nervous and upset that he was getting a pat-down. And our guys were thorough, as they had to be. But he was clean, so they gave the all-clear signal. The elderly owner, Omar, came out. He obviously could tell that the guy was angry, plus he wanted to be a good host. They greeted each other, at first warily but then they warmed up to each other more quickly than I expected. Maybe they had distant tribal connections or something, I don't know. I'll never know."

Bennett watched as Tucker looked into the distance beyond him.

"It was only later, after the scene unfolded, that I remembered seeing another vehicle stop at the corner in the distance, up the road. It was partially obscured by a small truck parked on the street, a dirty white Toyota. A young boy got out, he was maybe ten. He took a few steps in the direction of the meeting, slowly. The car that delivered him sped off into the distance, kicking up dust around the boy. He didn't react at all to the sand and dirt swirling around him, he just continued to walk forward. I don't know if he was drugged, or if he had a mental disability. That's been one of their primary weapons for years now, kids with mental disabilities. It's disgusting, the fucking cowards…"

This was the first time Bennett heard Tucker curse. It wasn't the first time he had heard someone in her position, male or female, use salty language of course, but it was a surprise coming from someone like Tucker who maintained a studied and professional poise.

Tucker balled her hands into fists as she continued. "It was only then that he, I mean the owner, Omar, saw the boy. Omar gave the boy a big smile, knelt down, motioned for him to come nearer. He pulled a date from his pocket and offered it to him, as if he knew the boy was on his way. Sweet men like Omar always have a little something for the neighborhood children. I'll never forget that smile, it was so warm, so inviting, so sincere. The boy thought for a moment, hesitated, and then he rushed to Omar with the faintest smile. It wasn't a smile of joy, or happiness, but one of relief in a way. Omar's wife came out too, and walked eagerly to them as the boy hugged him. It was such a tight, warm embrace. But from our vantage point, we could see what was happening and were radioing down to GRS to get them separated, to get the informant inside, to get some distance between the group and the kid. I saw a bulge on the kid. I stood up and tried to wave them down, to wave them back into the house. GRS began pushing the informant into the house, who didn't know what was going on and who started to resist at the sudden use of physical force. It was too late, anyway. The boy squeezed, and when I kneeled back down to look again through my binoculars I could see tears welling in his eyes. Omar at that point was trying to push the boy away. He could feel it now, the bomb strapped to the boy. The boy quivered as he sobbed, refusing to let go of someone who, probably for the first time in months or even years, showed any sincere love toward him. And then, the explosion. It was deafening. Even though we were kneeling behind a brick wall at an open window, we were thrown back into the room…"

Tucker's voice wavered as she attempted to collect herself. She wiped the corners of her eyes with a tissue that she had concealed in one of her balled hands until now. Bennett hadn't seen her retrieve it.

"The elderly couple never had kids," she continued. "They so desperately wanted them. They volunteered to take in an orphan, several orphans in fact. We advised against it, for precisely this reason. Only indirectly of course, anything more would've been cruel in its own way. But there would've been more attachments, more collateral damage if something had happened to them. It's cold, I know, but something we had to think about."

"But I'll never forget the boy, looking in our direction at the very end as if watching for the trigger man, and then squeezing his eyes shut. He looked so innocent and helpless. He knew what was about to happen." She wiped her eyes again, and then looked directly at Bennett. "So yes, it's true, when I saw that young boy in the video, the Hans' only son, I saw the same innocent eyes. I didn't want him to be a pawn in some greater political drama. I didn't want him to be used like children are throughout the world by evil and manipulating groups…"

"And you didn't want to be a factor in placing him in greater danger than he otherwise might have been," Bennett added. "Maddy, that wasn't your fault. The boy in Iraq…" Bennett offered as he reached for her hand. She pulled back abruptly.

"I put them in that position, Wilson!" she said, glaring at him. "They were there because of *me*, because of us! The *boy* was there, because of me and my mission, our mission there!"

"No, they were there to help their country. They knew *you* were trying to help, that *we* were trying to help them build a better life for their countrymen and their children. One free of tyrants and terrorists. The boy was an innocent bystander, who was used by evil people for their own twisted ends. This was one of the evils in the country, yes, but *you* did not cause that bombing to happen. You were fighting for them, for the Omars, for the children and their children's children. Never forget that!"

Bennett leaned forward toward her. "Things are better in Iraq now. And we're doing the same for this country, for the people of North Korea. We want them to have a better life, a free life, and not be prisoner to an evil, murderous, terrorist regime, one with the ability soon to annihilate whole cities. This is one way to help, even if nothing comes of it. The stakes are high, yes, the resources necessary are significant…"

"Resources that are taken from other ops for something that might not pan out..."

"It might not pan out, but if this guy is the real deal, if we're able to get any additional insights, Maddy...we need all we can get." Bennett watched for a reaction. "And if this *doesn't* pan out, I will never try to engineer an op from the NSC again, promise."

"So you admit it finally? You *have* operationalized the NSC? You've circumvented processes that are in place for a reason, Wilson. We've had many fuck-ups in the past, we don't need more. Either on the front end of an operation, or afterward."

"On this, we would take the heat in case anything went wrong. *I* will take the heat. Not you, not the Agency, not the military."

Yeah right, thought Maddy.

"But all the pieces are in place right now. Our contact is on his way out now. The retrieval team is en route now. We need to have additional resources in place, because the weather and timing caused some challenges that we did not expect. At this point, we need Japanese assistance."

"Very well," she said. "Let's go to the Defense Ministry HQ."

CHAPTER 25 - THE CALM BEFORE THE STORM

Kano had gradually grown accustomed over the years to not knowing the fate of his aunt and uncle.

At least he had closure upon the passing of his cousin, Taiei. As his only remaining living relative, and his only friend, Takada Kano made the funeral arrangements and took his few remaining possessions from the hospital.

He was unable to inform Uncle and Auntie Kano of Taiei's passing. They had written once or twice in the weeks after their departure that they had arrived, and that they were settling into their new lives. The letters made many allusions to their bright new future, but no word about an actual position working for the regime, or where they would live once they settled into their routine. In fact, the letters were strangely devoid of details at all, like where they were writing from, for example, or how they were meeting their basic needs.

Over the ensuing years, after he had re-established himself as the rightful owner of his first pachinko parlors, Kano expanded into a regional chain of pachinko parlors in the Chubu region of Japan. Though he knew just the basics of money laundering in the beginning, Kano quickly found how easy it was to move major amounts of cash through his chain of parlors. He started as he had before, by cheating his customers on cash payouts, while over-reporting those payouts to the government. He kept the proceeds. He also over-reported the losses at his parlors. He had fun "losing" some of cash himself, on his own machines.

Unlike others in the business who funded lavish, even gaudy, lifestyles, Kano invested his proceeds in new businesses. He expanded his operations to include a regional transportation and shipping company, a construction company, and he dabbled in the distribution of soft-core porn videos in the back of his local video rental outlets along the coast and along the highways at truck stops that his own drivers frequented. And he continued to expand his pachinko parlors.

He invested locally in other ways as well, by liberally sponsoring local politicians' campaigns and by giving bureaucrats and police "VIP" access to specially configured pachinko machines in his parlors.

Word of Kano's handling of Ichiro Nakajima had quickly spread, giving him time to entrench himself in the regional power dynamics of the northwestern Chubu region of Japan, that included his home prefecture of Ishikawa, and the neighboring prefectures of Fukui and Nagano. While *yakuza* and major construction firms affiliated with them were competing in the major metropolitan areas of Tokyo, Kyoto, and Osaka, Kano consolidated his hold over the regional grey economies without fully embracing the *yakuza* underworld. And while he used his connections with the sizable ethnic Korean communities to their fullest, he could not embrace their attachment to the Motherland without knowing what had happened to his aunt and uncle, and indeed, to countless other Koreans who had returned and then disappeared in the north.

His memories of his uncle and aunt gradually faded. So he at first did not recognize the voice on the other end of the phone. "Takada-kun, this is your uncle, Uncle Kano."

"Eh?" the younger Kano intoned in a deeper, gruffer voice than he had when he last spoke with Uncle Kano twenty years ago. "Who is this?"

"Takada-kun, it is me, uncle Kano." The voice on the other end was rushed and did not pause to allow Takada Kano time to absorb the sudden contact. "I don't have time to speak right now, it is not safe. It is a long story, but I am back to work now, after a long absence. I'll send you a letter detailing more, by courier."

"Uncle Kano?" Takada finally uttered. "And what of Auntie…?"

"Unfortunately auntie has passed. The conditions were…more severe than we anticipated, but it is all for the best. I know that now." Before Takada could ask more questions, the elder Kano said simply, "I have to go now."

"But uncle, what about…" before he could finish his question, the line was dead.

Kano lingered in a state of suspended shock for three days, until the letter uncle Kano spoke of arrived.

Three Korean men walked into his main pachinko parlor, and went straight to the main desk.

"We need to talk to Kano-san," the main interlocutor declared in a thick Korean accent.

"He's not available," the receptionist said, "I will need to take a message…"

The man reached over the counter and grabbed the receptionist by the lapels, lifting her from her seat. She screeched and tried to turn away as he peered into her eyes. "I *know* he is here, and I *need* to see him now. He *will* see me." He then released her.

The attendant looked to the side as two bouncers rushed to them from the front of the pachinko parlor. The three Koreans drew revolvers from holsters hidden inside their jackets.

The bouncers stopped and then slowly backed away, their arms instinctively raised in submission. Strict laws in Japan forbade ownership of handguns, so the sight was extremely rare. It also meant the owner of a firearm was a hard-core criminal who meant business, and these bouncers did not have the firepower to match.

The three looked back at the lady. "Take us to him, now," they ordered.

She nodded and stood. "This way," she responded as she turned slowly toward the stairs. They walked up the stairs, and she knocked at Kano's office door.

"Kano-san, you have visitors," she said timidly, as she eyed the man standing behind her.

While Kano had waited impatiently for a letter from his uncle, he had expected it to arrive at his residence by post and not at work. "I said no visitors!" he yelled from behind the locked door.

"They say they need to see you now," the receptionist pleaded. "They say it's urgent…"

"*Tell him we are here to deliver a letter,*" the man behind her shouted in her ear.

"*Eh…*" She peered toward him from the corner of her eyes without turning and cringed at the smell of his thick breath.

"Just tell him!" he said as he nudged her with the revolver.

"They say they have a letter," she shouted through the door.

After several seconds of silence, the group heard the clicking of locks being disengaged. The door opened, and the Korean stuck his revolver at Kano's face through the opening.

"Kano-san, can we enter?" he said in a tone that would not take "no" as a response. He pushed open the door, and the three walked in and closed it behind them.

"What's the meaning of…" Kano began to ask.

"Shut up. We have a letter for you!" He threw an envelope at Kano, who missed catching it. He fumbled at it as it landed on the floor in front of his feet. Kano quickly picked it up and opened it, now unconcerned about the three armed men in his main office. He began to read.

"Takada-kun, it has been a long time. I know you have many questions. Let me just say that I was away for some time, studying the true importance and core values of socialism and Juche ideology. I thought I understood before I came, but I was misled by the defiled imperialist regimes that imported corrupt Western values to our societies. The Democratic People's Republic has undertaken heroic efforts to fend off these attempts to corrupt our Nation. I see the errors of my ways, and I want to be at the forefront of efforts to defend the motherland from all enemies."

"I know you have done well for yourself since I have been gone," the letter continued. "Some gentlemen will visit you to discuss op-portunities. Please make every effort to work comradely with them."

"It is unfortunate that Taiei is no longer with us. I wish he could be around to undertake these efforts together with you. Auntie, too, departed us for her final journey several years ago. But I have utmost confidence that you will undertake every effort to fulfill your duties to me, to auntie's memory, and to your compatriots in these matters."

"Yours, Uncle."

A mix of grief and rage surged through his veins. He crumpled the letter and threw it down to the floor. *Auntie departed for her 'final journey' years ago? How? And he has nothing to say of his only son's death from tuberculosis?* Kano clenched his fists and pounded them on his desk. His knuckles turned white under the strain of his weight as he continued to press down on the surface. He looked up at the inter-lopers in front of him, who had yet to leave. *They've been watching me almost since the beginning*, he realized.

"Well, now what?" Kano barked at them.

"Now, we enter into a business relationship," said the sneering man standing in front of him in a thick Korean accent.

You may have gotten to my uncle, but you will never be my 'compatriots,' Kano declared to himself as he listened to the "opportunities" be-ing presented to him.

• • •

"Done. We are ready." Araki stood alongside tightly sealed vats that lined the wall of the small warehouse. "We'll load this onto the back of the lorry and transport it to the site soon." Araki tapped the side of one of the containers several times and then stroked the surface of one as he admired his work.

"How long should that take?" Kano asked. "We're on a tight schedule."

"Several hours to load, then about four to drive to the departure point. These are very delicate containers, and we must proceed with utmost caution. Presuming everything goes well, it should be in place and loaded before dawn tomorrow, assuming you have supplied the necessary final equipment for delivery," Araki deadpanned, referring to the means of delivering the gas to its ultimate target.

"It is ready, Araki-san. We look forward to your arrival!"

Araki hung up without replying. He carefully wrapped up the set of pins and placed them in his satchel.

CHAPTER 26 – AN ESCAPE

Archer heard voices as if through a block of ice. She slowly came to, but she dared not open her eyes. She did not want to give any sign to her captors that she was aware of her surroundings.

"…it's better if she's still out when we move her…" she heard one voice say. "The guys said she's a slippery one, feisty."

"Some clients will like that where she's going," the other voice said, snickering.

"But they'll beat that out of her real fast," the first one replied.

"That's why they like 'em feisty at first, gives 'em a reason to beat the shit out of 'em! Makes it fun."

"Hey, what do you think if we..."

She heard the other snicker. "Yeah, why not…" Archer heard the ruffling of clothes as pants fell to the floor, and deep, panting breaths. One of them took a step and then another toward her, squatted down, then placed a hand on her shoulder. Just as he was about to pull her on her back, Archer heard a muffled voice from outside the room. "*Oi, what're y'all doing, get out here! We got work to do!*" Then she heard the two mutter "shit" under their breaths, and more rustling of clothing, zipping, the tightening of belts. They quickly opened the door, stepped out, and closed it behind them.

She heard footsteps shuffle down a hall, then what sounded like stomping on stairs, and finally shuffles of feet on the floor above her. Archer surmised they were going up a staircase, which meant she was in the lower part of a building. She opened one eye, peeked around briefly without moving, then closed her eye again. The room was empty of furniture but it was in a *wafu* style, Japanese with tatami mats and textured light brown walls. A *shoji* paper screen tempered the light coming in from outside. She was probably in a house of some sort, probably in the basement judging by the high position of the one small window in the room, and by the footsteps that she thought she could hear from time to time above her.

She opened her one eye again, this time moving slowly to look at the wall closest to her feet. There was a shelving unit attached to the wall, and on the middle shelf she saw a tight circle of red lights peering at her. A night-vision camera looked down at her.

Archer slowly laid her head back down and listened, motionlessly, for the sounds and rhythms of the building. She knew she could hear beyond the door, because she had heard the two men walk down a corridor after they closed the door behind them. She had earlier heard faint footsteps on the floor above her, and outside the one covered window in the room, she thought she could hear the faint sounds of vehicles in the distance. But the building was silent now.

The camera faced down on her feet and front part of her legs as she lay on her side. It therefore could see little of her hands behind her back. Since she heard nothing outside the door, there did not appear to be any roaming guards. She doubted anyone was sitting outside the door, since no guard would sit silently for so long unless they were asleep, and at any rate the two who had left did not seem concerned about or to otherwise acknowledge anyone outside the door. So most likely, no one was watching through a peep hole in the door behind her, and she would hear any roaming guards if they came to the door.

Thus she surmised that she could move her hands behind her back without being seen. She slowly began to move her hands to work some blood back into them, and then she slid her forearm along her belt along the hip. No knife. She then remembered trying to fend off the gang with her Karambit somewhere near Kawasaki, and then dropping it. Damn.

She then moved her legs slightly to work some circulation back into them too. Her legs were bound together at the thighs and at the shins. And then she remembered: Her boot.

She would have to make a grab for the inside of her boot, and the motion might cause someone to check on her if they were watching the monitor closely, but she had no choice.

Archer bent her knees as much as she could so that her feet curled up toward her bottom, but she could not reach them with her bound hands. She then kicked her bound legs back and forth toward her bottom and tried to grab one of her heels with one of her bound hands. She was only able to touch the back of her boot on the first kick, and with the second kick she hit the knuckle of her other hand, causing it to sting. Finally she grabbed the bottom of her right heel and held it for a moment while she caught her breath. Her ribs felt bruised, and it was difficult to breathe.

After a pause to collect her breath, she tried to inch her hand up the long leather boot, but she lost her grip. Finally after the fourth try, she grabbed the heel and then pinched the back part of her boot with her other hand before letting go with her right to reach higher on the boot. She could not reach the top of her boot directly, so she pulled her hands one by one up the side of the boot, moving the pant leg up as she went.

Archer reached the plastic tie holding her legs together at her shin and could go no further. She rubbed her legs together as much as she could to try to loosen the tie, and she could feel the knife at the top of her right boot as she did so, inches away. The left leg was tied slightly behind the right, so that it covered most of the area where the knife was.

She thought for a moment as she held on to the bottoms of her pants with her hands. If they hadn't noticed her in this new position by now, they certainly would soon.

Archer then began to inch one finger up the left leg, in the small opening at the side of the leg. She couldn't go up the right leg this way directly to the top of the right boot, but she might be able to reach the top of the left. She held onto the bottom of her pants with her left hand as she slowly felt her way to the top of the boot with her right.

There it was. The top of the zipper on her boot. She felt the top stop, then the zipper itself. She pulled at the pull tab on the zipper with her finger, but she couldn't grip the tab. Her finger slipped off the tab once, then twice as she tried to pull with one finger on the tab. She then felt for the top clasp of the zipper. She pressed down on the mechanism then pulled at it. She felt it give slightly. The top tooth unlatched, then another. She placed her finger over the top, giving her leverage to pull down on the zipper to beneath the tie over her leg. She then grabbed the tab and pulled the zipper to the base of her boot.

Archer now had a few extra millimeters of space to move her legs despite the tie. She shifted her left leg forward slightly, so she could reach beneath the pant leg to get to the inside zipper on her right leg. She slowly shimmied her finger up beneath the tie, this time with the left hand, and she could feel the top of the zipper. She pulled at it, but the leg was still bound tightly to the left leg. She pulled at the side of the zipper to get a better angle. It caught on the inside seam of her pant leg. She felt herself becoming more impatient.

Archer thought she heard footsteps on the floor above. She pulled her finger out of her right pant leg, stopped, and took a deep breath. She waited for a moment to collect herself and then reinserted it on the other side of the seam, repeating the upward motion. This time she had a better angle along the zipper, and she was able to reach the top of the zipper on the right boot with the tip of her finger. She started to pull at it, and the top tooth of the zipper unlatched. Then the next.

She then heard more footsteps above her. She was sure of it this time.

Archer then pushed in on the zipper and tugged at the top at the same time. It began to unzip more readily now. She pulled it down beneath the tie, and then pulled on the tab to the base of the boot. She was now able to move her legs up and down against each other slightly, just enough to force the heel of her right boot onto the base of the boot on her left. She felt the top of the boot pull down slightly beneath the tie. She repeated, and the boot slid down more. She then pulled at the heel with her bound hand.

Archer heard multiple footsteps now head to what she thought was the direction of the top of the stairwell.

She tugged at the boot as she tried to gain any additional leverage with her other foot to force it off. She felt one side slide fully under the tie, and she was able to pull her foot out of the boot. With one last simultaneous pull with her hand and push at the outside of the boot with her foot, the boot came free. She threw it to the side with her still-bound hands. She then straightened her body as much as possible and rolled over to face the door.

As she listened to the footsteps running down the stairwell, she pulled at the other boot. The door opened.

"What the hell do you think you're doing?!" exclaimed one of the young toughs she thought she remembered meeting on the road in Kawasaki.

Just as he had opened the door, Archer had pulled off the other boot and had secured the Glauca knife from its latched position inside the top of it. She opened it but concealed the motion as much as possible, staring seemingly motionless at the young tough as he berated her. The Glauca had a specially designed plastic cutter, and she quickly sliced through the plastic tie on her hands in one swift motion. She did not think he was one of the two individuals who had left her in the room before, but she was uncertain about that.

He reached down to grab her. With her now-free hand, she plunged the blade into his lower rib cage. She twisted it, pulled it out again and slashed at his belly with the blade again, drawing a long gash from his belly button to his bottom rib. He grabbed at his wound as blood flowed from both cuts and let out a high-pitched cry.

"Wha tha...?" cried the other kid, who rushed to see what had happened to his comrade.

Archer sat up and cut the bottom tie around her shins, and then the tie around her thighs. The other kid looked at her as she stood, then backed up instinctively to the corner as she flashed the knife at him.

Seeing the open door, and sensing no immediate danger from this kid, she ran out of the room and up the stairs that she now knew was at the end of the hall. Once on the main floor, she ran down the hall and out the main door, and she continued to run down the narrow, wet road from the house.

CHAPTER 27 - THE CALL-UP

Master Sergeant McCarty sat cross-legged on a thin tatami mat, staring at a bare wall ahead of him. It was early morning, and McCarty listened to the slight fall breeze blowing through the trees outside. The small charcoal heater behind him lessened the chill in the air. He felt the crispness deep in his lungs as he slowly breathed in, and he saw a plume of white vapor escape from his nostrils as he exhaled.

McCarty concentrated his gaze on the wall ahead, and he noticed a shadow pass slowly in front of him from right to left. The shadow loomed above his own reflection on the wall in front of him, cast by the glowing embers emanating from the charcoal heater in the center of the room. The shadow was the shape of a man, except for the long object extending above the shadow's head. The shadow past, and McCarty relaxed slightly.

Seemingly within seconds, he was tapped on the right shoulder. McCarty was startled awake at the touch, although he remained in a sitting position. He tilted his head slightly to the left, and at this the monk standing behind him gave him three quick whacks with the long, flat wooden stick he held in his hand. The whacks from the stick, a *keisaku*, stung just a little, while the sound echoed in his right eardrum waking him further. The exercise was not to hurt students, but to ensure they remained awake and aware of their surroundings as they meditated. Enlightened never came to those who slept, after all. McCarty rotated his head back to an upright position, and he noticed the shadow walk slowly to the left again, holding the *keisaku* vertical again.

McCarty's interest in meditation came when he joined his first Special Forces unit in the late 1980s. He had not yet earned his Green Beret or Special Forces tab when he had arrived to his first assignment as an intelligence specialist, but he was eager to prove himself and eventually complete the Q-course. An intriguing six-month training opportunity came along as he waited for the next running of the Q-course. A psychologist and martial artist had gathered a small team of specialists to run a trial program to train special operators in various forms of Asian hand-to-hand combat, as well as in biofeedback and other meditative arts, called the Trojan Warrior Program. This was the tail end of the 1980s build-up under President Reagan, when many non-traditional programs were funded, including this one. While McCarty was at first most interested in training in hand-to-hand combat and martial arts, the week-long session on meditation coupled with various courses on biofeedback became by far the best training he had received in the military.

His time in Asia allowed him to explore different practices, when duty permitted. Even before the most recent maritime incident he had been looking forward to visiting the small Buddhist temples on the Noto peninsula, maybe even practice *zazen* in some if possible, during his leave following the most recent round of joint training. He had almost a month of leave available, and he needed to use it up before the next leave year. He had just arrived at the current one, Myojo-Ji, located half-way up the peninsula, and this was his first morning session with other practitioners.

But as had often happened in the past, duty today would not oblige further exploration.

McCarty felt a vibration on his right hip, and then another. *Shit,* he thought, *what now?* He was obviously being recalled, but for what? Colonel Bradley had just personally approved leave a few days ago. Now McCarty would have to excuse himself from the meditation room to make a discreet phone call, no matter how much the monks there frowned upon breaking with practice half-way through a session. He took some solace in having seen local residents of the monastery using their own cell phones when not busy with chores or meditating. But he was here to practice.

He slowly and quietly rose, collected his duffle bag, and bowed to the monk making the rounds. "I'm so sorry, I must leave," he said as he bowed again.

The monk merely nodded, and whether he was expressing disappointment or knowing wisdom, McCarty could not tell. He exited the meditation hall and headed to the parking lot.

"Yep, talk to me," he said on his phone once he reached his car.

•   •   •

McCarty pulled up to the gate at Komatsu Air Base. The Japanese Airman at the gate checked his credentials, and let him pass.

Komatsu Air Base was a major airfield hosting both a regional, commercial airport, and Japanese Air Self-Defense Force aircraft patrolling the Sea of Japan separating the Japanese archipelago and the Korean Peninsula. It was also conveniently less than two hours down the coast from Myojo-Ji, and near the location of the maritime incident that happened just days ago. The airbase had maintained its heightened state of alert in the days since.

The airbase also hosted U.S. aircraft transiting the region, so the local airmen did not think twice about refueling two U.S. Ospreys and a P-3C patrol plane that had landed there nearly an hour ago.

After getting directions at the main gate, McCarty parked his rental and walked into the nondescript hangar. Solberg met him just inside the doors.

"Master Sergeant McCarty, you made good time. You were pretty close, eh? We're assembling on the flightline by the Ospreys." Solberg pointed through the hangar doors to the two V-22s that sat on the flightline. "Colonel Bradley is in the hangar's main break room, he'll brief you on our mission," Solberg said as he began to walk in that direction. McCarty followed.

"It's gonna be a cool one!" the talkative Solberg continued. "Don't worry, we got all of your gear ready in advance. Tight timelines. We'll get a targeting package to study before we're wheels up, after the colonel's briefing. He'll give a more general briefing to the QRF afterward, once we've departed."

"Just to prep them in case our asses are in trouble and needing rescuin', eh?"

"You know it won't come to that, master sarge! We're professionals…At least, I won't let you screw up this mission enough for that to happen!"

"Thanks for the support, Solberg…"

"Master Sergeant, we haven't got all day!" a clearly impatient Bradley yelled from a room to the side of the main hangar. "Let's get a move-on!"

"The old man's getting cranky, I better go now," he said to Solberg. "We'll talk after I get the full briefing," continued McCarty, patting Solberg on the back before heading to the break room inside the hangar.

•   •   •

Colonel Bradley gathered both teams in the hangar for a final mission pre-brief.

"Blade One will fly alongside the P-3C to deliver the payload. It will then return either to this base, or directly to the Kaga pending permission from Tokyo. Blade Two will fly to the Kaga with our quick reaction force once we receive permission to use it as a forward operating base. Again, pending permission from Tokyo, you will be accompanied by two Japanese Black Hawks, flown by Warrant Officer

Hisao Taguchi and Warrant Officer Isamu Sato"—Bradley pointed at the two pilots, who instinctively raised their hands—"who you worked with in the previous weeks at the Ya'usubetsu training area in Hokkaido. They are on an observation mission only, and they will be part of the general debrief team once the mission concludes."

Bradley scanned the assembled teams of U.S. and Japanese soldiers. "All right, let's load up!" Bradley shouted.

Amid a few scattered claps and cries of *let's get this done* as the men went to inspect their gear, McCarty and Solberg went to the waiting V-22, with Chief Warrant Officer Kirby already warming up the engines.

"Can I get a lift?" McCarty asked the crew chief.

"That'll be ten grand per mile," the chief responded with an outstretched hand.

"Hey, Lyft charges half that! I guess you'll have to charge my expense account," McCarty said, chuckling as they clasped hands and slapped each other on the shoulders. "...I pay extra for good in-flight entertainment. And add a tip for yourself and the drivers up front too," McCarty added, flipping a thumb toward the pilots in the cockpit.

"Oh-ho! Mister big-shot now, eh? Traveling on an expense account! Well if that's the case we're gonna charge you *double...*!"

Colonel Bradley walked out of the hangar after them to watch Blade One take flight. *Good luck,* he thought to himself as he gave a silent salute upon their departure toward the horizon.

CHAPTER 28 - ARCHER ESCAPES

In the distance Trinh Archer saw a spinning red light that seemed to glow in the fog. It was a *koban,* a police box. She immediately ran there and began pounding on the door.

A sleepy police officer opened the door half-way. "Wha...wha?" he exclaimed, more annoyed than concerned.

"I'm an American diplomat and I've been kidnapped! I just escaped from them, please, you have to help me!" Archer barked at him as if to order his help instead of pleading for assistance.

"Hmmm?" the cop wondered aloud. "An American, you say? A *diplomat?*" The officer cocked his head to one side. "Why would a diplomat be here of all places?" he muttered under his breath to himself. He looked down the street behind her, then in the other direction, perplexed. He had almost never seen any foreigners in the area, much less diplomats. "Is this a joke...?" he asked.

"No it's not a joke!" Archer commanded. "I'll provide my credentials when we contact the U.S. embassy, just let me in, please!"

The officer hesitated a moment, still groggy and uncertain what was happening. He saw that she was not wearing a coat and that she was shivering. He looked down and saw that she wore no shoes. "Yes, certainly, come in," the officer said more resolutely, deciding that this was not a prank. The girl was obviously a foreigner, spoke with a certain accent, was underdressed for the outdoors and was running from someone or something. She didn't seem intoxicated or under the influence, but he would have to make a final determination inside his small *koban.*

He opened the door for her. "Come in, please!" he said again. "Get out of the cold, wet air. My goodness, you're half naked! Let me get you some clothes." He rummaged through a footlocker and pulled out a deep-blue jumpsuit with a long zipper and a black belt.

"These are men's, probably won't fit you well, but they're the largest I have and for the moment they'll do..."

Archer put them on as the officer started to heat a pot of water for tea. He motioned for her to sit in a chair at the edge of his small desk. The *koban* was cramped, with room for no more than four people. There was a door to a back room, but the light was turned off so Archer could not make out what was in there.

"Now, explain to me more what happened. Did you say you were *kidnapped?*"

"That's right, by a group of young men, gang members I would say, you know, *bosozoku*, a motorbike gang..."

"Where did this kidnapping take place?" He asked further.

"I was driving down the main highway from Tokyo to Yokohama..."

"Tokyo to...Yokohama...?" He asked, shaking his head. "*Saaa...*" he muttered as he sat back in his chair.

"Yes, and I was forced off the main highway by this motorcycle gang. They chased me through the streets of Kawasaki..."

"Kawasaki?" he asked again, sighing more loudly.

"That's right, why do you keep asking me that?"

"We're in Ishikawa Prefecture, south of Kanazawa City. We're nowhere near the Kanto region of Tokyo." He slouched in his chair as he folded his arms on his chest. "*Hen da na...*This is very strange," he muttered again under his breath.

"Well they must've drugged me and brought me here," she said. "Please contact the U.S. Embassy in Tokyo, they will be able to confirm my identity. I can give you some numbers."

He continued to look at her, perplexed. He then sat straight up on his swivel chair, turned to his desk, and he began writing notes to himself. "Certainly. Let me make a few phone calls." After jotting down a few lines he swirled back to her. "Here, why don't you take a few minutes to relax in the back room," he said as he stood up and turned on the light to the room behind him. The room was

Spartanly furnished with a low-backed armchair, a small side table, and a disheveled cot. The officer was probably sleeping there when she started pounding on the door, Archer surmised. To her relief, the room featured only one small window above the cot. No one pursuing her could see inside.

Archer went inside and sat on the armchair, feeling more at ease since she was more concealed from the street in the back room. "Thank you," she said as he handed her a cup of steaming tea.

"You stay in here and relax while I call for further guidance," he told her. He smiled hesitantly and shut the door.

Archer closed her eyes for a moment, satisfied in her newly won freedom. She heard muffles in the *koban's* front office as the patrol officer seemed to be reporting the situation on the phone to his superiors at headquarters. Archer looked around the room more intently. She saw a safe in the corner, a pair of reading glasses lay on an open newspaper on the table next to the arm chair, and the paper was open to local ads section. *He seems to have been lazing around for most of his shift,* she thought to herself. *That's not like most cops I've met...* She then began to wonder about the proximity of this officer's duty station to where she was held captive. She didn't remember running too far...She knew that police in Japan often conduct *junkai renraku,* or personal visits of homes in any given neighborhood to build relationships with local citizens. Most neighborhood cops spend years, decades even, in the same area and have deep connections with the locals. Which is usually a good thing. Her kidnappers would have to be really good at concealing themselves and their location, or else the police in this area were just lazy, or...

She crept silently to the door to listen. "...yes, that's right, a young woman, claiming to be an American. An American diplomat, no less." He chortled at the response from the other end. "Yes, certainly, she's secure in the back room now..." he answered, and then another pause. "Yes, very well then, I'll wait here," he said in a resigned voice. "When should I expect you...?"

Archer stepped away from the door. Both because of the casualness of the conversation and the terms used, she felt a sudden distrust toward the cop who had taken her in. She instinctively knew the word "secure" meant she was less than free. She looked down at the door handle. It had a silvery sheen and stuck out parallel to the floor. She touched it, felt its sturdiness. She tried to force it gently downward to avoid making a noise. The handle moved slightly and then stopped. She pushed downward more forcefully, but it did not budge. The door was locked. She was prisoner again.

Archer looked around the room. She certainly could not fit through the small window above the cot. She wasn't even sure if it could open. She stood on the cot and felt for a latch of some sort. Nothing. She then looked down and around the room from her high vantage point. The door on the safe appeared to be slightly ajar. She stepped down from the cot and approached it. She examined it for any alarms, but it appeared to be a basic, ordinary safe. She pulled at the latch, and it opened. She looked inside and immediately saw several rounds of bullets and an empty holster, but no gun. She brushed aside the empty holster and reached into the back of the upper shelf, but felt nothing. Then she reached into the back of the lower shelf. She felt something solid in the back, and she pulled it out. A taser stun gun. She examined it, felt its weight in her hand, and then held it by the grip. It was on safe, so she flipped the safety switch up to arm it, and then looked at the information display. It remained black. *Damn it*, she thought, *the battery is dead.*

She felt around the back of the safe again, and found another battery pack. She placed the weapon on safe again, released the old battery from the bottom of the stock and inserted the new one. She armed it again and looked at the display. It began to boot up, which was a good sign that there was some juice in the battery. Once it had completed its boot-up sequence, she armed it again, and this time a "01" appeared on the display. She could not recall if that meant the battery had one full shot remaining, or one second of charge before it was depleted. Either way, it did not look promising. But it was something. She then flipped the safety switch again, and disabled both the laser site mechanism and flashlight on the taser to preserve as much battery as possible.

She heard gruff voices enter the main door. She quickly and silently closed the door to the safe, and then she noticed it in the shadowy corner behind the safe. A *keijo,* a walking stick-like wooden staff, almost like a long, wooden kendo sword that was over half her body length. Police throughout Japan, and in many other parts of Asia, often armed themselves with these seemingly innocuous sticks while standing guard, but in the right hands they could be deadly. Archer grabbed it and looked it over. Judging by the dust on top and general disuse, this particular cop hadn't used it in a while. But why would you if you're on the take?

She heard the main door open, and then voices approached the door. She put the *keijo* on the bed and covered it with the blanket. She then tucked the taser shallowly into the pocket of her policeman's trousers, sat on the arm chair, and grabbed the paper.

The cop fumbled with the latch and then walked in. "Alright, young lady, I'll take you to headquarters now."

She looked up at the cop, stood and then strained to see around him. "Alone? Sir, I know I heard voices in your front office…"

"Huh?" he answered. "Oh, yes, some local citizens stopped by…" he stammered. "But it is time for us to go to police headquarters now."

She did not move. "Where is the patrol car? How will we get there, and who will be on duty while you are away?" she asked in a forceful voice. "Surely you don't want to leave your neighborhood without a police officer on duty?"

The officer became flustered. "Certainly not. But, er, it is time for us to go now, anyway..." he reached for Archer's arm, but she jerked it away. "What is going on, sir? Why hasn't your headquarters sent a patrol car directly here to get me?" Archer demanded.

"Enough of this!" Shouted a man said as he stepped into the doorway. "You are coming with us now!"

The cop tried to detain her by holding on to her arm as the man stepped into the back room, but his many years on the take had caused him to grow timid and weak in physical altercations. She pulled her arm away and slammed her elbow into his face, and he fell back onto the safe in the corner. She then pulled the taser from her pocket and pointed it at the man as he entered the room with two others behind him. He paused at the sight of the weapon, at first unsure what kind of gun it was. The two others ducked for cover on either side of the door.

She armed it and fired it at him. The probes struck him on his torso where his jacket hung loose. He cringed as the taser gave off a last second of charge before it died. He looked at the wires that connected the probes to the taser, and then grabbed them as he looked up at Archer. He frowned in disgust as he pulled the probes out, grunting in anger. He charged at her.

Archer threw the discharged gun at him, striking him on his forehead. She ran at him, taking advantage of his momentary disorientation. She slammed the palm of her hand into his nose and drove it forward, screaming *aaaaiiiii!* as she made contact. His head snapped back at the blow, and he crumpled to the ground. Archer pulled away the blanket on the bed as he fell and grabbed the *keijo* staff, picked it up, and slammed the tip down onto his solar plexus at the same time as he hit the ground. *Aaaaaiiii!* she screamed again as she did so, this time as a warrior cry to disorient the thugs she knew to be waiting just beyond the door.

She rushed out, but instead of confronting the two thugs she went immediately to the front door of the *koban* to escape. She tried to turn the handle, but the door was locked. She looked back, and in either corner stood a thug, watching her but surprised at her speed. A window was just beyond one of them, its shade closed to prevent those outside from seeing the confrontation taking place inside. She needed to reach that window.

"*Aaaaahhhh!*" she shouted as she charged the one nearest to the window. She raised the staff over her head, planning in advance to use the motion as a feint to distract him.

No longer surprised at her extreme aggressiveness, the thug smiled as she charged him. He held up his closed fists, the brass knuckles twinkling from the overhead light. Expecting her to strike down at his head, he stepped forward to pop her in the mouth. He didn't want to damage her too much, since the boss had plans for her. But he was nonetheless eager to teach her a lesson…

As he lunged at her with a wild right-handed punch, Archer stepped left and forced his punching arm to the side with the tip of the staff and spun around 360 degrees away from him. She threw the top part of the staff down upon completing the spin, making contact with his right calf. Continuing the motion, she forced his leg up in the air, causing him to fall onto his back. In one smooth motion, she lifted the staff up again and slammed it down again onto his torso.

She turned to the other thug, who now cowered in the corner of the other side of the room. "*Aaaaahhh!*" she shouted again as she charged him, whipping the staff over her head and smacking the side of his head with the tip of the staff. She then flipped the staff again over her head to deliver another blow to his shoulder in a downward motion as he crumpled to the ground, his clavicle now broken.

Not wasting a moment, Archer went to the desk near the window and grabbed the chair. It was metal and heavy. Too heavy to pick up on the first try, she bent her knees a second time for additional leverage. She lifted it over her head and fell back a step because of the weight. She pushed herself forward and was about to swing the chair into the window, when a club came down onto the back of her head.

Uhhnnn, she grunted as she suffered another blow. She lost her left grip on the chair, and the arm fell into her shoulder causing her to crumple underneath. She hit her head again against the side of the desk behind her, and the back of the chair tumbled onto her side as she hit the ground. Her last memory was of the bloody-nosed cop raising a short billy club over her head, and then everything went blank.

CHAPTER 29 - A NEW PASSAGE

"What do you mean I can't pass through?" Han said, exasperated and exhausted. "I just need to get to the pier to get some personal belongings from our family fishing boat," he said pleadingly.

The large and well-built guard snickered. "No you don't, there's a Combined Fire Demonstration that's about to take place this evening off the coast of Wonsan, at sunset. With all the live-fire that's about to take place, you don't want to be anywhere near the pier or the shore. You should go up there," he said, pointing at the peak overlooking the shoreline, "and watch for yourself. It'll be historic. Your son will be telling his grandkids about it 70 years from now!"

Han turned to the peak. "Up there?"

"That's right, all the kids from the 6 December children's camp are there. They were invited to watch by the Marshall himself." And by "invited," he of course meant ordered.

Han thought for a moment. He barely noticed the ravens pecking at the barren field across the dirt road take flight into the sky toward the hill in the distance. He turned back and replied, "yes, that's what we'll do then." Han attempted to mask his anger at not being able to get to his cousin's small fishing boat for the final journey to sea. *We're so close*, he thought to himself, *but so far away*.

He turned back to his wife and son. "Come along, we're headed to the peak!" Han declared to them so that the guard could hear.

"Eh?" Mi Yong whispered in surprise as her husband took her by the elbow.

"Come along now, it will be an historic event, as our comrade said!" Han picked up the pace. Once they were out of earshot, he whispered to her. "We're going to the 6 December children's camp on the other side of the peak. They have a small pier with boats for the kids. We're going to get one of those."

"But surely it's closed!" she said, fatigued by the constant road-blocks thrown in their way.

"Yes, surely it is," he said in response. He then picked up the pace again to almost a trot. "Come on now, it's a ways away and we need to get there before it is too dark."

•　•　•

They reached the perimeter of the 6 December children's camp just as the last van of children departed through the main gate. Named for the DPRK founder's birthday, the children's camp was an oasis along the shore for the children of North Korea's connected and powerful. Its modern facilities were featured on TV broadcasts to international audiences as a showcase of Juche ideology and modern life in the Hermit kingdom. It was not, however, broadcast to domestic audiences. No sense in showing the poor masses the luxuries they and their children lacked. Han knew about it because they sent their son to the camp when it was first opened, before his condition deteriorated as it had this past year.

Han and his wife were still partially obscured by the line of trees in the approach to the main gate. After the van disappeared around the corner, Han began to rummage through the wooded area near what looked like a small pile of rusting scrap metal that was out of sight and long forgotten. He picked up a large fallen branch and swung it a few times, and then dropped it in favor of a sturdier one. He pounded it on a tree, but seemed dissatisfied and threw that one down to the ground too. He began to kick up the leaves, feeling his way as he did with his other foot.

"What are you doing?" Mi Yong whispered as she looked up and down the path.

Han did not answer. He continued to rummage through the foliage, kicking and then picking his way through the fallen leaves. Then he felt something. He knelt down and began digging around the area. He then pulled up a pipe, caked in mud.

"What is that?" Mi Yong asked, growing annoyed that her husband was playing in the dirt instead of looking for a way off the peninsula.

"Just as I thought," Han said to himself. "Remember when our lab was built? All the rubbish and random construction pieces strewn about the place?" Han cleared the mud from the pipe as he talked. "Well, this place is no different," he declared, pointing to the half-visible pile of old construction material and rusted metal fittings.

"Yes, but what do you need a pipe for?"

Han stuck the pipe partially down the back of his pants. "Lets go to the gate now. Stand a few paces behind me, and let me do the talking," he ordered. He set off without waiting for an answer. She had no choice but to obey, since she could barely keep pace with him.

"Hello there!" Han shouted as the lone guard stepped toward them upon their approach. "Sorry we are late, our car broke down at the station so we had to walk the rest of the way."

"Hmmm," the guard said, looking first at Han then at his wife and son. "We're full now, we aren't expecting any additional guests…"

"Well you can see my son, we're to undergo an experimental procedure at the hospital in a couple of days and then stay here to recuperate," Han explained hurriedly. "The director called us at the last minute and suggested we arrive early to watch the firing exercise." Han then strained to look at the low peak where most of the town was gathering. Dark clouds hung low in the sky over the hill. Han thought he felt a drop of rain, but he ignored it. "We aren't too late are we?"

"Hmmmm," the guard grumbled again. "This is highly unusual…"

"Well certainly you remember me from our past stays," Han demanded haughtily. "Why don't you just check with the director himself?"

"The director led the group of children to watch the firing exercise. He's not here now. No one's here now except for me."

Good, Han thought to himself, *just as I had hoped.* "Well then, just check the guest roster, surely we're on there," Han insisted.

The guard cocked his head slightly out of confusion. The only ones who talked to him in this manner were indeed frequent visitors, and Han seemed to know the place like he'd been there before, even though the guard knew that he had never seen him before today.

"Alright," the guard said hesitantly. He looked at Han again, and then at the woman and boy behind him. He nodded to them slightly, and then turned to the small guard house by the gate where he kept his paperwork.

Han pulled the pipe from his pants, and he struck the guard on the back shoulder.

Ummmph! The guard cried as he dropped to his knees, grabbing at now-injured his shoulder.

Han did not wait to strike again. This time the guard's head was in perfect position for a swing, and Han took advantage. He swung with all his might, and he made direct contact with the guard's temple. The guard crumpled to the ground, blood oozing from both his nose and eye next to the temple. His body convulsed a few times, and then it lay still.

"Ahhh! Ahhh! Ahhhh!" Their son cried out at the sight of the splatter of blood from the fresh corpse caused by the sudden violence perpetrated by his father.

"Shut him up! Take the boy inside!" Han demanded as he ran to Mi Yong and the boy. Mi Yong cupped her hand over the boy's mouth as she embraced him, soothing him with shushes.

"I'll take care of the body," he whispered. "Get the boy inside, hurry," he repeated as he opened the gate from the guard house. She looked at the body as Han knelt over it, transfixed by the scene and the sudden violence perpetrated by her normally meek husband. Her mouth quivered, and she pulled her son close to her body.

"Come on, Mi Yong, we've got to take care of things before everyone returns," Han repeated as he rolled the body flat. "Take him inside, I'll meet you there in a minute." He began to drag the body toward the wooded area. "We'll go inside," he said in a grunting and halting voice as he pulled on the body, "and get some food quickly…" *hmph*, he grunted, "…from the kitchen to take with us…" *hmmmph*, "…but we can't waste any time."

Mi Yong took her still-startled son through the gate and headed to the main door. Han placed the body behind the small pile of scrape metal, covered it with leaves and then hurried down the path to the main gate, furtively glancing up and down the path as he went. He entered the building soon after his wife and son.

"Good, now go to the kitchen for some food, it looks like it is here." He pointed at a room adjacent to the cafeteria as it was labeled on a map hanging on the wall near the entrance. "I'll head this way, to the pier." Han looked up and down the quiet hall, checking for any straggling students or faculty. "Grab what you can quickly, and meet me there." Han glanced at his wife and then kissed his son on his forehead before turning to run down the hall. As they parted, they heard the sounds of huge "booms" roaring from the beach on the other side of the hill, directly south of the children's camp.

Han exited the main building and ran down the pier, where he saw the flashes from a hundred muzzles of tanks and artillery cast the forested hill separating them in relief. The sounds of firing echoed along the shore and throughout town. Undistracted, he ran to the end of the pier where several small sailboats were moored. They bobbed up and down as waves crested around them. He went to the far boat at the end of the pier and looked it over. Some water had collected at the bottom but it otherwise looked seaworthy to his half-trained eyes. He boarded the boat and examined the outboard engine. It looked to be operational. He pulled the cord once, but nothing happened. Again, and nothing. He tried a third time, and finally the engine turned over. Han looked back at the building, and he saw Mi Yong scurrying out. She held a small bag as she guided her son to his location on the pier. Upon seeing her, Han untied one of the two ropes holding the boat to the pier.

Han became more conscious of the roars of the tank and artillery fire upon seeing his son's startled expression with each sound.

"This is it! This is our chance!" Han shouted over the booms. He grabbed the sack first, placed it in the middle of the boat. "Pick him up, hand him to me, let's go!" He stepped onto the pier with one foot to help his wife to place him in the boat, but the unsecured section of the boat began to float away from the pier. Han almost lost his balance, but he caught the side of the pier and steadied himself. He moved to the secured side of the boat, and with a wave motioned his wife to that side too.

Mi Yong had already started to move the boy, and she struggled to reposition him by the secure side of he boat. Finally she was able to hand him over to her husband, who pulled him over the side of the pier and placed him in the boat itself. The boy grabbed at his mother, crying out and not wanting to let go because of the steady violence erupting all around him. "No! No!" He cried, again and again as he clasped at his mother.

"Come on, come on!" Han yelled at both at them. "Get in the boat!" He wrapped one arm around the boy's waist as he pulled at his arms, forcing them from around Mi Yong's neck. As the boat bobbed in the waves, the wind now increasing in strength, he lost his balance and fell forward onto the pier. He caught himself with one hand while still holding onto the boy's waist with the other, but they tumbled to the pier and the boy's legs fell between it and the boat. The boy began to panic and flailed with both arms and legs. "Pull him up! Pull him, pull him…!" Han grunted as he attempted to pull the boat closer to the pier with his one leg while he tried to steady himself on the pier and pull his panicking son up at the same time with his other arm. Mi Yong grabbed his arms and fell backward onto the pier, but she did not let go. His legs cleared the side of the pier just as the boat slammed back into its side, causing Han to lose his balance once again and fall into the boat.

Han stood, grabbed the unsecured rope and wrapped it hurriedly around the anchor on the pier a several times to steady the boat. "Ok, hand him to me!" he shouted above the din and reached to Mi Yong. She half-pushed and half-picked him up as he continued to flail at the side of the pier, and Han grabbed him and lowered him quickly into the boat. Han knelt down with him in his arms, hugging him closely and caressing his head as Mi Yong lowered herself into the boat. "It's ok now, it's all ok now…" he said, watching for Mi Yong to be settled before he handed him back. He did not want to let go. He glanced toward the dark horizon and a tear rolled down his cheek as the adrenaline began to wane and fear appeared in its place.

"Ok, I'm ready," Mi Yong said as she pried their son from Han. "Let's go," she said firmly.

Han unlashed both ropes securing the boat to the pier, and now they floated and bobbed freely in the water. Han lowered the outboard engine into the water, and the boat lurched forward now that neither it nor its occupants were tethered in any way to the peninsula. Despite the waves crashing against the bow, Han regained his confidence as he piloted the vessel out to sea. The bursts of light grew brighter beyond the hill to their right as they went.

CHAPTER 30 - EN ROUTE

A P3C patrol plane flew at a lower altitude than normal, and closer to the North Korean coast as well.

The V-22 Osprey shadowed the P3C with matching speed and direction as it flew to the patrol craft's starboard side. Any radar from the North Korean coast would see one image on its primitive screens instead of two.

Pyongyang had unilaterally declared areas off both its west and east coasts as no-fly zones due to the firing exercises planned for the next 48 hours, and while commercial airlines heeded the declaration, neither the U.S. nor the Japanese military adhered to it. The P3C maintained its regular patrol schedule, flying ever closer to North Korea in international airspace, if anything, as a show of resolve.

Flying in blackout mode and with radio coms silenced, at the predetermined point, the V-22 dove at a steep angle toward the surface of the sea below. Warrant Officer Kirby pulled out of the steep dive as his Osprey rapidly approached the angry sea below. "Twenty meters," he announced, starting his final checklist on his approach to the objective. "Fifteen..." He rotated the bird's nascells to a hover configuration. "Ten, five..." His V-22 stopped at a hover, it's tail angled down toward the sea surface. "Open cargo door," Kirby said. "Three meters, one..."

"Cargo door open," the crew chief responded.

The waves from the sea almost leapt into the cargo hold once the cargo door was fully lowered. "Whoa, what was that?" Kirby asked over the intercom after a wave swept over the cargo door, its crest splashing into the cargo bay itself.

"Just some sea spray hitting us," the chief said laconically. He was tethered at the rear cargo door, and he was now soaked from his thighs down.

"Roger," Kirby replied as he steadied the V-22. "Green light!"

"Green light!" the crew chief repeated. "Let's deploy the StingRay and get to altitude," he told his junior crew member, who released the clamp mechanism securing the StingRay to the cargo bay floor, the mini-sub's crew already secured inside. They watched the two-man submersible, with McCarty at the controls and Solberg sitting prone next to him, slide down the cargo door and into the choppy sea below.

"Package deployed," the crew chief reported, as he secured the cargo door.

"Returning to altitude," Kirby announced. The crew felt the V-22 lift into the air at a steep climb on a return trajectory to rejoin the P3C on its patrol mission paralleling the North Korean coast. Even an attentive and trained radar operator would have missed the divergence of the two targets on their scopes, which lasted mere seconds.

McCarty and Solberg, dressed in combat wetsuits and gear, did not linger to watch the V-22 ascend. They immediately submerged and headed west-northwest. The StingRay, a newly deployed two-man semi-submersible designed for special operations insertion, reconnaissance and retrieval missions, was the outcome of an earlier, failed project to develop a special operations tactical delivery vehicle in which the pilot, copilot, and cargo could be kept dry. The famous "SEAL Delivery Vehicle" required its operators to be submerged in the same conditions as the SDV itself, which limited both the duration and distance the vehicle could operate. The prolonged exposure to underwater environments impacted operators' combat readiness over time. A longer-range, "dry" minisub program sought to solve this, but it was over budget and at almost 20 meters long, too large for many tactical applications. The program was cut, and in its place came the StingRay, slightly larger than the SDV but enclosed, "dry," and deliverable by a variety of means, including the

V-22 Osprey. It resembled a backwards-turned Chevrolet Stingray, from which it got its name, with the crew cabin forward of a tapered tail-like cargo compartment. Stabilizing fins deployed on the sides of the mini-submersible above hydrojets with steerable nozzles that provided vector thrust for high maneuverability in shallow waters. While designed to operate in dry configurations, it could also operate fully submerged and "wet."

McCarty, now submerged at five meters below the surface of the Sea of Japan, placed the StingRay on autopilot. The StingRay was pre-programmed to head to its designated spot. The craft was propelled with the help of storm currents, almost doubling their speed.

CHAPTER 31 - DEFENSE HQ

Bennett and Tucker sat at a long mahogany table in a large conference room, across from three men in dress-white uniforms. They were on the 13th floor in the main "A" building of the Ministry of Defense's Headquarters in Ichigaya, located several kilometers from the U.S. Embassy. Multiple monitors on the far wall displayed Japanese deployments in the region and local and regional news channels, all on mute.

"I don't know if it is appropriate at this time to allow your units to use our ship as a base of operations. We conduct exercises all the time, of course, so the presence of U.S. troops on Japanese vessels is not a new thing, but…" Chief of Naval Operations Admiral Nakamura sucked in air audibly through his pursed lips and tilted his head, taking time to consider the situation. "What is the purpose again?" he asked as he leaned back and crossed his arms while looking again at the group through quizzical eyes. Nakamura sat with his chief of intelligence on one side and his chief of staff on the other, each with stern looks chiseled on their faces.

"We are requesting to establish a forward operations cell on the Kaga, with a small special operations team to support a classified operation taking place in the western portion of the Sea of Japan," Bennett explained on the other end of the polished, deep-mahogany table. "They will most likely not be needed, but the timing is critical."

"It would be a good training opportunity for your special operations personnel who most recently conducted a demonstration of their skills in Hokkaido," Colonel Thomas, the defense attaché sitting next to Bennet, explained. "In fact, that can be the reason for the presence of our personnel on your ship, a routine training mission involving your new Ospreys and sea-based special operations capabilities. If asked, of course."

The defense attaché also did not know the details of the mission, just that one was taking place somewhere in the Sea of Japan and that they needed to station a response force nearby in case the the operators needed additional assistance.

"The *western* portion of the Sea of Japan, you say? Hmm, that is intriguing..." said the Admiral. "I'm not sure if we have the authority to..."

"The election results will be in soon, and if your political leadership objects, we can pull back our units immediately," Bennett said in an attempt to buy time. He calculated that it would take days, maybe even weeks, for the new political leadership to be in place and fully up to speed, and by then the mission should either be completed or called off.

"I thought your forces were conducting an operation in the *Yellow* Sea, on the western side of the Korean Peninsula, not the Sea of Japan," Nakamura added. He watched the three Americans for a response.

"That report was not entirely accurate," Bennett said, referring to the "Kasumigaseki" article.

Hmmmm, Nakamura grumbled in a subtle sign of chagrin at not having been informed of an operational matter so close to Japan. "Will our forces be in any imminent danger?" Admiral Nakamura asked.

"The U.S. operation will remain in international waters, certainly, Admiral," Bennett explained. "We would in fact expect that your units would continue with their original mission, to monitor and shoot down if necessary any ballistic missile that is fired toward the Japanese archipelago. We just need a platform from which to operate our Ospreys, and to station a small tactical operations center."

The admiral looked to his head of intelligence, and then to Madeleine Tucker.

"You will of course share all intelligence from this mission with the Government of Japan, correct, Ms. Tucker?" Nakamura stated rather than asked.

Tucker looked to Bennett, then turned to the admiral and smiled wryly. "Presuming it is successful and we secure what we need to secure, you have my word that I will share everything I learn with the Japanese Government."

Admiral Nakamura looked again at his chief of intelligence, who seemed to have a permanent frown etched onto his face. His head bobbed imperceptibly and his brow furrowed as the two communicated without uttering a word.

"Very well," said Admiral Nakamura. "You may station a small maritime unit on the Kaga. This will be a joint search-and-rescue exercise, and you will of course provide additional training opportunities for our units that will accompany yours during your deployment to the western Sea of Japan." Nakamura then motioned for an aide, who approached and bowed. "Inform Admiral Tetsuya Okada that he will be taking on additional personnel in short order. I'm sure he will not mind."

"On behalf of the United States Government, thank you, Admiral Nakamura," Bennett said while the group stood to depart.

As they exited the conference room, Bennett overheard Admiral Nakamura tell his aide in Japanese: "Get me the Chief of Operations for the Air SDF, we need to coordinate additional air patrols between us and the Korean Peninsula. And turn up the volume on screen three, it looks like North Korea is giving another statement."

Bennett caught a glimpse of North Korea's Vice Foreign Minister on the screen on his way out, but he would not have a chance to hear his statement until later.

Admiral Nakamura's aide increased the volume after the American group departed. "...We will go to war if they choose," a man on the screen declared in Korean with simultaneous interpretation into Japanese. "Now we are compelled to take notice of the Japanese ruling party's belligerent statements toward the DPRK and compare them with the U.S. administration's, and we have concluded that the two imperial powers are working hand-in-glove in ever more vicious and aggressive ways." It was North Korea's Vice Foreign Minister giving an interview in Beijing to a crew from Fuji TV.

"Whatever comes from Japanese politicians, once the results of the election are clear," he continued in answering the interviewer's question regarding Ayumi Seitoh's potential appointment as prime minster, "if their words are designed to scare or interfere in any way with the DPRK system or government, we will categorically reject them. If the reconstituted and now clearly emboldened Japanese military engages in reckless military maneuvers, as it is showing currently, backed by its U.S. masters or on its own, then we will respond to provocations with the DPRK's pre-emptive strike capability."

He continued, waving off the interviewer's attempt to ask his next question: "Not only do we have a powerful, million-man army, we've got a powerful nuclear deterrent already in our hands, and we have other special deterrent forces as well. We certainly will not keep our arms crossed and sit in silence in the face of aggressive Japanese pre-emptive strike rhetoric and belligerent maneuvers."

"The United States is always making provocations with its aggressive words, and now the Japanese are adding to those words like gasoline to an already-lit fire, and they are only looking for trouble in doing so. It is not the DPRK but the U.S. and Japan that make trouble, in concert and to the great consternation of the peace-loving people in the DPRK."

We better deploy additional missile defense units, Nakamura thought as he digested the North Korean Vice Foreign Minister's lengthy statements. *And perhaps it's time to test our new air-based missile defense capability...* Nakamura's aide approached the admiral with a phone. "Sir, the chief of air operations is on line two." Nakamura placed the interview on mute and picked up the receiver.

•   •   •

Two F-15s roared down the runway, their afterburners visible in the early dusk. Behind them, two additional F-15s taxied to the edge of the runway, and waited for the final direction from the control tower to take off.

The first two F-15s flew to their air patrol station over the Yellow Sea. An Air SDF KC-767 aerial refueler met them as they approached their patrol station and refueled the lead craft, then the second, in preparation for a long presence on-station. The KC-767 then turned northeast to refuel the second set of F-15 aircraft. The pilots began patrolling the skies west of Japan and south of the Korean Peninsula in a long figure-eight pattern.

The scene repeated itself at three other air bases along the Sea of Japan. Their comrades arrived to patrol areas west of Hokkaido, northwest of Kyushu, and along the Tsushima Strait that featured the narrowest distance between Japan and the Korean Peninsula.

CHAPTER 32 – THE KAGA

The Japanese team deplaned from their transports at Komatsu airfield laden with gear. The team was directed to the break room near the hangar area, where the American soldiers had spent most of the day. A local airman sat at a table eating okonomiyaki, watching the television intently. NHK interrupted to update viewers on the latest results after polls had closed earlier in the evening.

"Our exit polls indicate the ruling party will enjoy a significant victory," the announcer intoned. "Representative Ayumi Seitoh, who was just elected the new head of the party a month ago following health complications causing the incumbent prime minister to step down early, is expected to be elected the next prime minister following a special session of the Diet," the newscaster continued. Some of the arriving Japanese team members gathered around the large-screen TV to see the results. "Assuming she is elected, Ms. Seitoh will become the first female prime minister, and she has come into office with a hawkish outlook on security. North Korea is quickly presenting itself as the first major test of her administration, and Ms. Seitoh has already vowed to quickly form a national security team to deal with the critical challenge."

The U.S. team had gathered in the large break room for the afternoon, since the retrieval team departed. They took little interest in the reporting on Japanese television, but variously rummaged through the food and snacks in the kitchenette and played tabletop games with origami-like folded shapes and balls.

"Hey, Sato, Taguchi, how ya doin'!" Chief Kirby said to the two who just entered the break room. Kirby pulled a can of iced espresso from the vending machine. "Looking forward to having you on this mission!"

Sato happily greeted Kirby, while Taguchi acknowledged Kirby while reaching for a cup of ramen noodles on the counter.

"I always look forward to maneuvers at sea," Sato replied. "It is great training, attempting to land on a ship at sea. It'll be even more fun in this weather, with a typhoon moving through the Sea of Japan!"

Kirby could see that Sato looked genuinely thrilled to take part in the operation.

"Gentlemen, if I could have your attention, please." Colonel Bradley stood to address the assembled group of U.S. and Japanese service members. A large map of the Sea of Japan between the Korean Peninsula and Japan's main island of Honshu was visible behind him.

"As most of you saw or heard during our earlier mission pre-brief and checklist review, our advanced team departed earlier to the rendezvous point to retrieve a potential high-value North Korean defector," Bradley began. "We don't know his status at this point, because we have lost communications with him. Should the advance team, Marine One, make initial contact at or near the agreed upon location, their mission is to lead them to a secondary extraction point, here." Colonel Bradley then turned to the large map to point to the general rendezvous area.

"We have just been granted permission to deploy to the JMSDF Kaga, where we will establish a temporary Tactical Operations Center for this mission," he continued, turning back to the group. "Whether Marine One makes contact with the high-value target or not, we will support extraction of the team and any accompanying civilians at this secondary point well within international waters, or elsewhere as necessary. And if there is a shooting match, well, that's when we really get to have fun..." Bradley smiled at the assembled group of warriors.

"*Hoooaahhh!*" the Americans shouted, while the Japanese, feeling the energy in the room, smiled and slapped each other on the back.

"For this mission, because their V-22 Ospreys are not operational yet, Chiefs Taguchi and Sato will pilot their current UH-60JA Black Hawks, accompanied by their quick-reaction team, to observe our deployment and establishment of the TOC at sea," Bradley informed his men, who turned to see both pilots standing at the back. "While our actual mission is operational in nature, we are ostensibly conducting 'search-and-rescue training' in a joint exercise with our Japanese colleagues." Bradley scanned the room. "Under no circumstances are we to talk about anything other than our 'search-and-rescue training' outside this room or other operational areas, hoo-aah?"

"Hooo-aaah!" the group replied in unison, with several of the Japanese service members joining in the shouts.

Bradley turned to Newland. "Over to you, Lieutenant."

"Alright, we ran through our check-lists already, so let's gear up, men!" Lieutenant Mark Newland declared to the excited group. "Our Japanese partners are ready to see some action, so let's get this circus on the road and show them a good time!" Newland began to secure his own equipment, while Bradley opened the main door of the conference room. The loud roar of the engines on the just-returned Blade One greeted them when he did so.

Within a matter of minutes, both the American and Japanese teams were suited up, and they began to form up outside the hangar facing their aircraft. They inspected each other based on the buddy system, while the team leaders performed spot-checks.

"Let's load up!" Newland shouted over the noise of the flight line, and the team made their way to their respective aircraft. The pilots had completed their preflight checks, and the team members went to their designated spots, with Colonel Bradley sitting down last. They lifted off for an uneventful flight to the Kaga.

Newland and his men looked closely at the Kaga as they approached the newly designated flagship of the Japanese 3rd Escort Flotilla. They saw a long deck measuring almost 250 meters in length, longer than two American football fields. The island, a five-story superstructure containing the bridge, air operations and combat information centers, rose up from the deck on the starboard side, leaving plenty of room for aircraft to move along the length from bow to stern. They saw a SeaRAM missile launcher jut up from the deck in front of the island, as well as Gatling guns and other armaments arrayed along the sides of the deck on either side for ship defense. Behind the bridge, an elevator on the starboard side slowly lowered an F-35 down to the hangar below. Another elevator, this one in the middle of the flight deck, returned to its position, having presumably lowered the last of the aircraft on the Kaga's deck to clear room for the arriving V-22s and UH-60s. Several landing signal officers of the Kaga guided the V-22 Ospreys to their designated landing spots on the flight deck of the Kaga, and pilots Taguchi and Sato landed their aircraft a short time later.

When they landed, Colonel Bradley disembarked first, followed by Lt. Newland. Both saluted Admiral Tetsuya Okada as he approached. "Thank you for hosting us, sir," Colonel Bradley said.

"You are most welcome, Colonel Bradley!" Okada replied, returning the salute and then shaking hands with Bradley. "We are delighted to have you on board," the Admiral said in crisp, clean English, having studied for several years in the United States at Brown University and, later, at the U.S. Naval War College just down the road. "Let me show you and your men where you can set up your TOC. I've designated a spot in my own Flag Information Center, on the gallery deck one level below." Okada pointed to an open portal at the base of the superstructure. "This way, if you will please..."

· · ·

"Finally, the firing has stopped," McCarty said to Solberg. "Keep a look-out for the boat."

"Man, that was a *long* exercise, Solberg said in response. "Wish we had that much ammo to blow shit up with down-range. Do they have anything left?" he wondered aloud.

The two watched and waited, taking shifts in taking cat naps. They patched into the Gray Eagle in regular intervals to check the surrounding waters. While they were briefed on the specific signal they would receive from the Han family, they knew from past experience that sometimes those signals could get crossed, or not come at all. And they wanted to ensure they were not surprised by any fishermen or adventurous maritime patrols.

"What's that?" Solberg asked, pointing to a blip on the scope.

"Hmm, looks like something, but it's pretty small whatever it is. Could it be some debris on the surface, maybe from the firing exercise? Some destroyed maritime targets, maybe?" McCarty replied.

"Something tells me that's not debris. Its contour seems too regular, even as it bobs up and down."

"Yeah, those are choppy seas up above, that's for sure," McCarty said. "Let's keep watching, see where it goes..."

They observed the small craft bob up and down in the heavy winds and waves on the surface. They had the Hawk's camera zoom in as close as possible. It leaned almost 45 degrees to one side, they could see, from the single mast that jutted from the middle of the boat. There was no sail attached to it, however, so the occupants must have some outboard engine to propel the boat forward,

McCarty and Solberg surmised. As much as possible, at least, since the aft portion was out of the water as much as it was in it due to the high and undulating waves.

"Should we head that way?" Solberg suggested rather than asked.

"Hmm, I dunno. Still no signal. We don't want to come alongside an unsuspecting group out for a joyride," McCarty answered. "They're off course if that's them."

"A joyride, out here in this weather? Seems like they've been out at sea for a while, way out here. They could've been blown off course, I suppose, but..." Solberg continued to doubt that a boat like that would be out in this kind of weather for any reason other than that they were running from something.

"I've had to talk my way out of stranger situations in the past, when waiting for high-value defectors," McCarty said casually. "I wouldn't be surprised if they were an unrelated group that got caught adrift at sea for whatever reason. Maybe they were out here watching the firing exercise, and got blown off course like you said? We don't want to get involved in some rescue when we have a mission to accomplish."

"What if our guy can't signal?" Solberg pushed. "My gut tells me something's wrong, that they can't signal..." McCarty could sense his impatience.

"Easy, Solberg. Let's give it a little bit longer, just see how things shake out. At the very least, we can turn in that direction, even if it is beyond the agreed rendezvous point. But we also don't want to get too close for now, in case there are other ships in the area."

"Roger." Solberg remained silent for a moment, then added: "Maybe we should get a wider-angle shot toward the coast, to see if the Koreans are mobilizing anything..."

"Makes sense, switch cameras and see what's out there," McCarty responded.

Solberg re-programmed the cameras, and another image showed the coast. They both watched intently.

"There, what's that?" Solberg asked, pointing at the screen. "Looks like a vessel is pulling away from the pier."

"Yep. Not big, but are those guns on the deck? I don't think that's a fishin' boat."

"What d'ya think?" Solberg asked, looking at McCarty.

"I think we oughta get a close-up look of that small sail boat out there, is what I think," McCarty responded, attempting to conceal a heightened sense of attention. *Solberg might be right, that might be our guy...*

"Heading there now," Solberg hurriedly took over the controls.

CHAPTER 33 - TAKING FLIGHT

The Bell 206L helicopter sat on a high grassy knoll overlooking the Sea of Japan. Short, quick waves splashed along the shore line, the large concrete, jack-shaped barriers absorbing much of the early morning tidal energy. The wind blew from the northwest sharply, but the rotors were anchored to the ground, preventing them from whipping around unexpectedly. A tube extended from the belly of the helicopter about five meters to either side, flapping up and down slightly with each gust of wind. Nozzles hung in pairs along the tube to the tips, while under the belly of the helicopter hung a large tank.

"*Erai, na, Araki-kun!*" Kano declared to Araki. "I'm impressed you really know how to fly this thing!" This was the first time Kano had seen the bird up close. "It certainly looks pretty complicated..." Kano watched for Araki's reaction to check for any signs of self-doubt now that the mission was about to commence. He saw none.

Araki looked longingly at the bird and seemed absorbed in his thoughts. Without looking at Kano, he said, "yes, I trained many hours in helicopters in worse shape than this one. Yes, she is a beauty." Araki touched the nose of the Bell to feel its smooth contour. "I miss flying..."

"Where did you train, anyway?" asked Kano. He suddenly realized that he did not know the details of Araki's training. *What if Araki is wrong for the job?*

"We had what we called 'military drill tours'..."

"Military drill tours? Can you do that in this country?" Kano was surprised to hear that.

Araki smiled at Kano's genuinely surprised reaction. "No, we had them near Vladivostok."

"*Ehhhh?* Vladivostok...in Russia? What were you doing there?"

"Our religion touches peoples' hearts in many parts of the world, Kano-san. Some of our brothers had established a *Satyam* in a small village outside the city. We purchased a helicopter there for training, a MIL-17…ohhhh, I loved flying that machine." As he said that, Araki looked wistfully to the sea. "The Russians make such powerful machines."

"MIL-17? Isn't that a military helicopter?" asked Kano.

"Yes, it is. You could buy almost anything in Russia in those days. After Russia's military stopped ordering military equipment, all the factories set up around the country had to find customers. They would let you test out all sorts of equipment if you looked at all serious. It was just a matter of walking to the front gate and asking what their price was. They would train you and everything. We visited the Kazan Helicopter Plant in Tatarstan Republic, southeast of Moscow. In the 1990s, they were only too happy to oblige. We then shipped it to our new Vladivostok-based *Satyam* via the trans-Siberian railway, and conducted our 'military drill tours' there. Many in this world simply do not have the vision to see what we see, Kano-san. That is why we are the chosen."

Despite the religious rhetoric, Kano was surprised to hear Araki say something pragmatic for a change. *You have quite an operational mindset when you need one, Araki-kun. It's too bad you have to die. I could've used you in my operation, if I could ever have trusted you…*

"What were you going to do with it? Just take a joyride?" Kano teased Araki.

Araki looked at Kano and smiled at his naivety. "No, we weren't there to go joyriding. We were training, Kano-san. Just as I have been training these past years. We were training for a mission, just like the one you and I are about to undertake…" *Karma willing…* "All of our orders were destined for Japan. We had the helicopters ready, here in Japan too. We couldn't send the MILs directly from Russia, of course, that would've aroused an unacceptable amount suspicion. We had to route them through Azerbaijan to Slovakia, then on to Austria and the Netherlands, and finally to Yokohama port. You see, each port had different import and export laws, and we just adjusted the documentation as we went."

"And the armaments to use with them?"

"Yes, in separate shipments of course…"

*I really could've used you, Araki-san…*Kano looked to sea, as if to reconsider his next moves. *You were invaluable in the beginning, with your knowledge of chemistry and connections to chemical suppliers. But then you got hooked yourself, and you became too much of a liability…*

"Now, Kano-san, the half-moon is high. I'd like to fill the tank and fuel the bird before dawn." Araki opened the nozzle for the tank on the underbelly of the helicopter. "Please…?" he said, half escorting, half pushing Kano back to his vehicle. "It is very danger-ous, please go back to the vehicle in case anything happens…"

Kano complied without question. This was indeed the first time Kano had seen Araki take a truly commanding role toward anyone. Certainly Araki had never commanded Kano so self-assuredly. He'd condescended to Kano many times, yes, but never commanded.

Japan has been consumed with this nonsense about the death of the young girl and her father, as if kids don't die in boating accidents all the time, Kano thought to himself angrily, standing by his truck and watching Araki get to work. *But your attack, Araki-san will change the conversation…'A cultist attacking with weapons of mass destruction!' the headlines will blare, taking national attention and police resources away from my operation, and in the meantime, I will complete the biggest transfer of weapons technology, drugs, and cash in decades, right under their damn noses…!*

Kano watched as Araki donned his protective mask and protec-tive gear. He then pulled the hose from the small tanker truck to the helicopter and began the final preparation for his mission.

• • •

The night following the firing squad and his subsequent conversation with his boss Mr. Ko, Han could not sleep. Han rose early the next morning to take a long walk. He wandered aimlessly through town, and he found himself walking the narrow streets of the local, and technically illegal, farmers' market on the outskirts of Kusong. Vendors were just starting to put out their food and wares.

Han saw three street urchins in worn clothes scurry across his path, disappearing around a corner into a narrow alleyway. A woman walked in the same direction, holding a young baby. She looked weary, and her baby whimpered hoarsely after what was probably a sleepless night, whether from hunger or illness, Han could not tell. She too disappeared around the corner just as the street urchins emerged from the same alleyway. Moments later, the mother too emerged from the alleyway and walked down the street, away from Han. She held a bag of some sort, and her baby was now somehow comforted.

Han stopped at the intersection of the small road and alleyway, but he saw nothing. He turned the corner and took several steps into the alleyway, but he only found one vendor in tattered clothes unpacking jars of some sort from a worn canvas sack, out of sight of the street itself. Besides the three or four small jars he placed in front of him, the vendor seemed to have nothing else to sell. Han took little notice of the stooped old man, and he looked up and down the alleyway again. The rest of the alley was quiet. Returning to his gloomy thoughts, Han turned to continue his directionless journey.

"Would you like some fresh milk, or some honey perhaps, my son?" an elderly voice asked behind him.

Han turned in surprise. The street vendor squatted behind his jars, which were alternately small and large. The vendor gestured to one of the jars.

"It is rare around here, and so few have actually tried it. But put a little honey in your black tea, and it cuts the bitterness..." the vendor said as he gazed up at Han. The vendor had a soft and inviting look, unlike the other vendors who were hardened by their hand-to-mouth existence. "Here, have some hot tea," he added, holding up a small white porcelain cup. Steam wafted from the surface enticingly.

Han was surprised and could not see from where the vendor had retrieved the fresh cup of tea. He strained to see around the vendor for anything else he might have missed.

"You are saddened by the event yesterday, I can tell," the vendor added, before Han could reply to his invitation. "Many of us are. He was a good man, your colleague..."

"Wha...how..." Han uttered in astonishment.

"Yes, many of us heard what happened yesterday. We can only know that he is in a better place now." The vendor bowed his head in silence for a moment, and then looked back at Han. "Do not worry, my son, the day of reckoning will come," the vendor added with a calm and patient resolve in his voice that Han had never heard before. He felt strangely comforted by the vendor's words.

The vendor then put his jars of milk and honey into his worn sack and stood with some strained effort. "Come, my son, join me inside for a bit of tea," the vendor said, motioning to a door that Han had not noticed. "I feel as if we are long lost cousins, just reuniting again after a long journey, and we must get reacquainted..."

"Wake up, wake up!" Mi Yong half-shouted to her husband. "How can you sleep at a time like this! The waves are almost cresting over us!" She motioned to water collecting at the bottom of the boat as it bobbed to and fro. A wave crested against the side of the boat, almost causing it to pitch over. She grabbed onto her husband with one hand to balance herself, even as she clung to her son with the other.

Han shook himself fully awake from his dream, water splashing on his face from the sea. He felt a profound longing for advice from his spiritual mentor, but he was now a world away.

"What kind of man are you, putting your family in such peril?" she sobbed as the boat stabilized, overcome by her emotions. "We're going to die out here!"

"I am a man of faith!" Han boomed in response. "Better to be on a journey of righteousness, than to live in depravity and sin, serving the evil whims of a tyrant!"

"You and your sin, I want to live! I want our son to live, not die out here in this God-forsaken sea!"

"But God has not forsaken us," Han replied, calmly cupping Mi Yong's face with his hands as the boat steadied itself. "There is a plan, this is his plan," he whispered softly in her ear and gesturing to the horizon. "Perhaps He sent the winds and the rain as cover for us. But please have faith, do not lose your faith at this most critical time, as we wander through the proverbial desert," he pleaded.

CHAPTER 34 – THE CRISIS CENTER

A satellite moved silently into an orbit 350 kilometers over the Japan Sea. On a side panel, a large red dot painted over a white background, the *hi-no-maru*, would be visible to the casual observer. There were no casual observers in space, however. The satellite just finished firing small jet nozzles to position itself at a new angle east of the Korean Peninsula as it orbited the earth. It had repositioned itself from the usual 490 kilometer orbit to get a close-up of the peninsula below. Clouds obscured the target from visual images, but even the thickest cloud cover posed no obstacle for this satellite.

Two giant solar panels stretched out from either side of the main body, while a 9-meter-long panel was tucked along its underbelly. The panels provided 3 kilowatts of power, enough to generate a concentrated PALSAR phased array synthetic aperture radar wave directed at the eastern coastline and inland areas as it orbited over the north-eastern portion of the peninsula.

The panel vibrated imperceptibly as it sent its signals through the storm clouds to the earth below, while almost simultaneously receiving the echo signal that read its target like a blind man's fingers brushing over Braille.

The digital signals were immediately sent to a relay satellite in orbit far above it, which then sent the signals to a receiving station in Tomakomai, Hokkaido. A light-green dome covered the receiving dish to protect it from the elements, since its extreme northern location meant that the area received a lot of snow carried by cold winds from Siberia. Much of the work was automated, so only a few people staffed the two-story building. The real work took place in Tokyo.

A dedicated fiber optic cable connected the facility with the Satellite Intelligence Center in Tokyo and the government's crisis management center at the Prime Minister's Office. While most images from the reconnaissance satellites were normally sent for analysis to the SIC, in a building adjacent to the Defense Ministry Headquarters in Ichigaya, the present situation was different. The Prime Minister's Office, staffed by career security and intelligence professionals, had a pressing interest in security matters given recent events, and the PMO was thus at a high state of alert. The images were thus sent directly to watch officers at the PMO.

"There they are, pictures of armor and artillery units amassing for the Combined Fire Demonstration," said the imagery analyst as the pictures came into focus. "Located just north of the city of Wonsan."

"*Waaaa, sugoi na*, the senior duty officer said in reaction to the hundreds of tanks and self-propelled artillery pieces lined up along the coastline, pointing out to sea. "Look at the impact points along those small islands from past exercises, there," he said, pointing to the scene on the screen. "Judging by how many pieces are there, this is surely the biggest exercise yet."

"*Zettai*," the analyst agreed, "it sure is." He flashed through the satellite images up and down the coast. "Hey, look at this small port facility here," the analyst said as he pointed to another area north of Wonsan. "Zoom in. Right there, you can see activity at the port. And here," he pointed again at another image taken moments later, "is that the wake of a small ship of some kind, a small submarine perhaps? Looks like it's just submerged, you can kind of make it out, here…"

"Hmm," retorted the duty officer. "Small vessels often launch from there, don't they?"

"Perhaps, but North Korea unilaterally declared the zone closed to all air and maritime traffic. Why would they send a sub out from that location when a live-fire exercise is about to commence?"

"Maybe they're using it as cover so that they can launch it undetected, with our vessels steering clear of the area," the duty officer wondered. "Good catch, we'll need to keep an eye on that one. Load the images to the tablet, the deputy chief cabinet secretary wants to see these personally. Also add the shots from the Saeho missile launch facility. Looks like they're about to launch another rocket, purportedly a satellite launch but we need to keep a close eye on it."

The duty officer checked with other watch officers for final updates as he finalized his briefing materials for the deputy chief.

"Here are the latest intercepts from the suspected North Korean proxy servers," a collection analyst informed the duty officer. "Some additional collects than what we observed in the previous week, maybe some additional information here that might be useful."

"Good, make sure the NPA and the North Korea task force have received it and that someone is analyzing it for patterns." The senior duty officer tabulated the morning's intelligence on his specially configured Sony tablet and then walked down the hall to the office of the Deputy Chief Cabinet Secretary.

Eiichi Tokuda sat at his desk reading one of many secure faxes that had come in overnight and were piled on the corner of his desk. He took an audible sip from his bamboo-emblazoned *rakuya-ki* porcelain tea cup from his days at Kyodai University in Kyoto. Though his staff was unaware, Tokuda always ensured that the bamboo motif was turned to him as a reminder of their symbolic meanings of endurance and modesty. At just before 6 am, it was his second cup of tea that morning.

"*Shitsurei shimasu.* Good morning, sir. Today's intelligence."

"Good morning, SDO," Tokuda said as he greeted the senior duty officer. "I'm sure you heard the preliminary election results. We shall soon have a government in place again, so we must spend the coming days finalizing briefings for the incoming administration." As the administrative deputy chief cabinet secretary, Tokuda served as the senior career government official for national security and other administrative matters for the Japanese government during the election season when the politicians were campaigning in their home constituencies.

Tokuda tapped through several slides and satellite imagery. "What of the planned space launch?" the deputy chief asked as he looked closely at the satellite imagery of the launch site.

"We assess that the space launch is indeed intended to launch a rudimentary but nonetheless effective reconnaissance satellite, which will be able to transmit images to the Pyongyang regime in almost real-time, at least for the Asia-Pacific region."

"Hmmmm," the security advisor said as he looked at the imagery and other intelligence reports. "When is the launch scheduled?"

"Within the next day or two, sir. It is to coincide with the KPA founding day."

"This is a very dangerous development," the advisor asserted. "Not only is North Korea planning to conduct a so-called 'space-launch' of a missile"—his inflection and tone conveyed his suspicion of the event—"using technology that is clearly applicable in further developing an intercontinental ballistic missile and in contravention of all UNSC resolutions forbidding such launches, but it is further broadening its reconnaissance capabilities that would enable real-time intelligence collection and targeting of the entire region, including Japanese and allied bases." He turned to the next satellite image and then asked, "what is the expected trajectory of the launch?"

"From Saeho launch station, south over the East China Sea, most likely."

"Over the Ryukyu chain of islands, near Okinawa?"

"Yes, but there is a chance that North Korea could launch over the mainland itself," the SDO added.

"They may want to demonstrate both a satellite launch capability and the fact that they can target locations throughout the

Pacific," Tokuda responded. He paused, motioning for the SDO to shut the door, and then he continued. "Last night, once the initial results were in that the ruling party had indeed expanded its number of seats in the Diet, I received discreet inquiries from senior ruling party officials about conducting a test of the modified SM-3..."

"*Ah? So ka...*" the SDO uttered in surprise. "I do not know much about the program, but it is still experimental, I thought."

"It is, but what better time to test it?" Tokuda asked, stifling a smile. "It's the most advanced of the three classified projects under development. If it is successful, we know it works and we will have prevented the launch of their satellite and embarrassed the regime. If not, we will know that we need to continue to refine it. But either way, no one need know about the launch."

"Pyongyang would certainly know as they tracked it on their long-range radar. Beijing too..."

"Yes, but we have plausible deniability, publicly at least. We have air patrols currently flying along all probable flight paths currently. And we will have privately served notice that we will shoot down anything that flies over Japanese airspace without the permission of the Japanese Government and against international law. Now is the time to undertake a *tai no sen* strategy: We wait patiently for the opportunity to take initiative when the adversary thinks we are weak..."

"And what of the *ken no sen* direct attack strategy?" the duty officer asked.

"In this day and age, only a young and impetuous fool engages in a *ken no sen* strategy, but that is what we are facing, eh?" Tokuda said, taking a rhetorical shot at the young North Korean leader.

"And the *tai tai no sen* strategy?"

"We'll leave that to the Americans, the counterattack after the attack. We must be ready to take the initiative even here too, however." Tokuda let the implications sink in. "At any rate, we need to understand all options, and their implications. This is an especially delicate time for us, during the election period. It could take a week or longer for a special session of the Diet to convene and formally choose a new prime minister, who will then have to form his," Tokuda paused here to correct himself, "...or I suppose, her new national security team. Meanwhile, that man-child of Pyongyang is unpredictable, so we must be prepared for any eventuality, including the use of this launch as a cover for a missile attack on the Japanese mainland. These national security challenges do not wait for domestic politics to sort themselves out...I need you to contact the MOD. I need to discuss this with them within the next hour. I've been assured that we have political cover to do so, now that the election has concluded."

"Ryokai shimasu," the SDO said. He bowed and then exited the room.

As he left, Tokuda remembered the words of the great swordsman Miyamoto Musashi, whose strategies he just referenced. *When you are about to die, you must make fullest use of your weaponry. It is false not to do so and to die with a weapon yet undrawn...*

CHAPTER 35 – MOVING TO THE ATTACK

Araki readjusted the seatbelts in the pilot's seat to accommodate his thinner figure, despite wearing chemical protective gear. The rubber gloves, a light shade of green that matched his protective suit, made manipulating the controls somewhat difficult, but Araki knew he could manage. His protective mask sat in the seat next to him.

"Are you set, Araki-kun? Do you have your gas mask?" asked Kano-san. He had just walked around the helicopter pretending to inspect it, opening the cargo compartments to look inside, tapping on the storage containers, and peering closely at the nozzles. While Araki was looking the other way, Kano placed a package in one of the small cargo holds. If Araki had spotted him, he would have explained that the package contained extra literature from his guru, for luck. But Araki was so focused on preparations that he paid little attention to him. Kano was eager for Araki to take off so that he could prepare for arrival of the shipment.

"I am ready," replied Araki, as the roar of the engine became louder. The rotors began to whoosh above them. "*Sore de wa,* it is time, Kano-san."

"*Yooooosh,*" Kano said, and he couldn't help but smile. "We will meet back here after your mission, understood?"

Araki's stern face masked the glee he felt inside. "Yes, I will see you after the mission!" he shouted while looking at the controls. He turned back toward Kano and saluted awkwardly. Araki reached for his mask, grabbed the straps in the back, and lowered it over his head. He pulled the straps tightly, adjusted the nozzle, and cleared it so that the mask was sealed. "*Itte-kimasu,*" he said in a muffled and serious voice. "I'm off."

Kano saluted abruptly, turned, and ran back to the Isuzu mini-truck before Araki's lifted off. As he watched from behind the truck, the helicopter lifted slowly into the air, wobbling first left then right. The helicopter steadied, then lifted higher in the air. The helicopter's nose dipped forward as Araki departed for his final destination.

Kano placed his hand in his pocket. As he watched Araki depart, he subconsciously fiddled with the filters from the protective mask. *Good-bye, Araki-kun, You will find your paradise today*, he thought ruefully. *I hope you are not too disappointed.*

• • •

Araki from his new vantage point saw a ray of light glimmer orange from over the hills to the east. He flew low and steady along the coast, and then turned his helicopter inland to cut through the narrow peninsula on a direct flight to the base. This was the first time he had been outside, near the coast, in decades. The wind blew aggressively through the green vegetation below, and the surf was choppy, remnants of the storm that was surging north. The control stick fought him as he flew over the land below, where the wind transitioned from sea to land and then to out over the protected bay again. *I'll have to adjust for the wind on my approach*, he thought to himself.

Araki tapped his breast pocket, and felt the pins inside. He felt comforted with the good-luck charms from his benefactor in his outer garment pocket.

He saw the landmark in the distance—an outcrop of giant concrete flood barriers followed by a small wooden pier. The base was just a few kilometers away. He looked at his watch: He was right on time. The seabees would be mustering for calisthenics now. *Just as I had planned*, Araki thought to himself.

Araki cleared the peninsula and then hugged the coastline along the protected bay on his final approach to the base. He rose slightly and then went into a steep left bank, gunning the engine. The wind died down as he zeroed in on his target. He straightened his bird, the nose dipping as the Bell rapidly picked up speed. He now saw them: Hundreds of sailors had gathered in the crisp and blustery morning air for their calisthenics. One section started jumping jacks, while another did whirligigs, and a third began to jog around the perimeter of the field.

Araki passed over the first fence surrounding the compound, and he flipped the switch to the sprayers and decreased his speed. A few sailors near the fence stopped and looked up at the sudden sight of the helicopter coming low toward them, but most of the sailors continued their morning workout.

Araki saw a mist rise in a vortex on either side of the helicopter as he flew through the air, a sure sign the sprayers were distributing their payload properly.

After a few meters, he began to see sailors run to either side of the compound as if a sea were parting. Though difficult for him to make out with his protective gear on and the roar of the helicopter engine, he thought he could vaguely hear a siren sounding in the background.

Araki turned to make another pass. He flew alongside an open hangar building toward which he saw a large group of sailors running, and he re-engaged his sprayers. He looked down the long, open field from which he had just come, and he was pleased to find dozens of sailors on the ground, apparently writhing in agony. Some grabbed at their throats, others tried to wipe their exposed skin of the chemicals, their comrades in some brave cases attending to the fallen. Araki felt a sudden burst of excitement, and he pressed the bird forward, faster, to spray other groups of running sailors.

Araki paid little attention at first to the acrid mustard smell he sensed through his protective mask. He half-expected to smell some sort of mustard, after all. But the acrid smell intensified, and it began to burn in his mouth and nostrils, his trachea, and in his lungs. His eyes watered. He turned for another pass, this time along the shoreline. He saw the ships moored at the port, but he paid little attention to the activity on their decks and the blare of the sirens. He engaged the sprayers again for his next pass, his tearing eyes now beginning to sear in increasing pain.

Araki began to pull at his protective mask, readjusting it back and forth but to no avail. His throat and nasal passages burned, he could barely see through his tearing eyes. He felt a searing sensation on his face along the seal of the mask, and then on his cheeks, nose, and lips. He could stand the pain no more, and he tore the mask from his face and half-screamed, half-gurgled. He grabbed at his throat with both hands, not caring as the helicopter began to spin first left, then right toward the ships arrayed along the port. The sprayers continued to spew droplets of poison gas as the Bell helicopter spun out of control.

Araki grabbed at the stick as he began to careen toward the Echigo Coast Guard cutter, in port with the MSDF-Coast Guard counter-smuggling operation. Araki tried to pull up, but his Bell helicopter rolled left at a 45 degree angle and the blades began to dig into the deck as they continued to spin rapidly. The cockpit then spun back toward the superstructure and crashed into the side, creating a huge fireball and spilling the remaining mustard chemical onto the deck of the ship.

Sirens continued to blare throughout the base and on each of the ships, while screams could be heard from the field and from the deck of the Echigo.

CHAPTER 36 - FIRST MEETINGS

McCarty and Solberg headed toward the small sail boat for what seemed like an eternity.

"I think we're close enough to take a look through the scope," McCarty said as he examined their position relative to the last plotted position of the sail boat. He slowed their speed.

"Sending up the periscope now," Solberg replied. Another screen between the two of them lit up, and they could see the surface interspersed by splashes of water and waves on the scope.

"Man it's choppy up there," McCarty said. "Turn, turn, there, there it is." McCarty pointed at the screen. "Zoom in."

"Zooming in now…"

"I can make out a man, kind of small in stature it seems," McCarty said.

"And there, you can't really see it but there's a head…Is that a woman?" Solberg wondered as the head turned toward them. "Can't really match the faces to the couple of photos we have…"

"How about a kid, do you see a smaller one on board?"

"Nah, can't make anything out, we're both bobbing up and down too much. Looks like they're struggling though, tired too," Solberg added.

"Alright, let's do it, let's make contact. We'll assume at this point that they can't establish positive contact with us or otherwise signal for whatever reason."

"Roger, heading there now."

Within minutes, the mini-sub pulled along side the small sail boat and surfaced. Although they were within several meters of the boat, the waves forced them first together, then apart again as the waves hit them separately.

"Here we go," Solberg said to McCarty as he opened the top hatch. He rose up, weapon in hand. While he did not point it at the family, he made sure they knew he was ready to take action immediately if circumstances required.

He saw three figures looking back at him huddled in silence Their eyes were wide and unblinking. The small craft undulated as the waves crashed alongside. They held each other closely, shivering.

"Han-ssi? Dr. Han?" Solberg asked. He looked along the small interior of small vessel from bow to stern for any surprises as he asked. There were none.

The man staring back at him nodded once.

"All clear," Solberg half-whispered to McCarty below, without taking his eyes off the family.

"Roger, I'll send an update," came the muffled response from below. Within a few moments, McCarty called out, "sent."

"Roger, going over to the boat now." Solberg secured his weapon on his back, climbed out of the mini-sub hatch and stood on the back compartment of the StingRay. He steadied himself with one hand and timed the undulations of the boats to first grab the side of the sail boat and then step over its side. At a lull in the bobbing, he stepped onto the sailboat. It swayed as he did so, and he grabbed the mast and the far side of the boat to steady himself.

"This is a smaller boat than we expected," Solberg yelled back to McCarty as he poked his head through the hatch. "I thought the plan was for them to go out to sea on a family fishing boat?"

The couple looked at each other, then Han said haltingly: "Could not get fishing boat. We take small boat, from there." Han pointed back to shore, invisible through the clouds and the distance. "From camp, for children."

"Holy shit, you mean to tell me this is a kid's sail boat?" Solberg blurted out. "Y'all are a brave family, to be in this thing in this kind of weather..."

Solberg then turned to McCarty on the mini-sub. "McCarty, can we even pilot this thing back to the rendezvous point? Its outboard engine is..." he paused as he examined it more closely, "...tiny to say the least." The waves continued to splash against the side of submersible and the boat, forcing them to rise up and fall at random intervals. "It's a miracle this thing is even still afloat..."

McCarty peered out from the sub. He looked down the short length of the boat to the outboard engine. "Yep, that's small alright," he said, suddenly feeling the pit of his stomach tighten. "This thing's not built for the open sea, and definitely not for stormy weather like what's coming."

The two vessels bobbed up and down as the two soldiers considered their options.

"First thing's first," McCarty declared as he put his head down on the side of the hatch to collect himself. "We gotta get some more distance from shore. Let's tie that rope there," McCarty pointed to the forward portion of the boat, "to the sub here, and together with what power we can get from the outboard engine, we'll tow it as much as possible to the secondary rendezvous point. Then we can call in for air evac."

"So you don't think we can fit everyone below?" Solberg asked. His tone of voice indicated that was his first choice.

McCarty covered his mouth as if to stifle a burp. He waited a moment for the feeling to pass, then he looked at the small boat and then at the boy. "No, too dangerous. It's way too wet and the rocking is too severe to get all three onboard..." McCarty then grabbed the side of the hatch to collect himself again, as the family watched him. "If it were just Han, probably we could, but the wife and the kid especially, no way..."

Han's boy whimpered loudly and burrowed into his mother's side as both McCarty and Solberg looked at him.

"...not sure if we have room below..." McCarty said haltingly. He stifled another burp with his hand.

"Roger," Solberg replied, and he tossed the rope to McCarty, who secured it to the sub. "Should we dive and drive, or stay on the surface?"

McCarty looked at the boat and at the waves around them. As he did, the StingRay crested a wave and then fell as the small sail boat crested a wave, so that McCarty went from staring down at the boat to looking at its side. He bent over the side of the submersible and threw up.

Solberg waited until McCarty collected himself again, this time wiping off his mouth with his forearm and spitting several times. "You go below and pilot the StingRay, close the hatch, and get just below the surface to smooth out the ride a bit," Solberg commanded. "I'll stay in the boat here"—he looked at the sail boat, calculating the added weight—"and will keep in contact as we head to the rendezvous point."

McCarty could only nod once before he bent over to wretch again. He usually did not experience seasickness, so the sudden nausea surprised him. He wiped his mouth again, glanced at Solberg and nodded more resolutely again. He watched as Solberg secured the rope, ensured he was ok, then withdrew into the sub and secured the hatch.

The Hans remained silent as they watched the stranger tie a rope to the front end of the boat. They knew that speed was of the essence at this point, and they dared not interfere. Han's son whimpered, but he kept his head down in his mother's lap.

Solberg then motioned Han to sit next to his wife immediately forward of him so that he could man the outboard engine. His added weight would also help to counter-balance the submersible's forward pressure as it pulled the forward section of the boat. Or so he hoped.

"Rope secured, let's go," Solberg said in his mouthpiece.

"Roger," came the reply in his earpiece.

They felt a tug at the front of the boat, which caused it to dip into the surf.

"Whoa, slow slow slow!" Solberg shouted into the microphone. The boy started screaming as the boat pitched wildly.

"Not sure I can go any slower," McCarty responded. "Cutting engine now."

"We might have to do this the hard way," said Solberg as McCarty rose through the hatch again. "Sorry, buddy, but you might have to be up on the surface too."

"Right," McCarty replied slowly. The submersible rose onto the surface, and continued to chug forward. "I guess this is what we get paid the big bucks for," he added ruefully.

The boy glanced back and forth between the StingRay ahead of them and Solberg, whimpering in terror. "Hey, sarge, hand me the the medical kit from below. Let's give the kid something to take the edge off," Solberg said as Mi Yong tried to comfort the panicking boy.

"Good idea." McCarty handed the medical kit to Solberg, who filled a syringe with liquid, sterilized the boy's arm as his mother held him tightly, and then injected him without pausing. The boy screamed again at the pierce of the needle, but within seconds he relaxed into a languid state in his mother's arms.

The two boats gained some slow but steady speed, and Solberg instinctively looked over his shoulder. He saw several lights on the horizon. He could not tell if they were emanating from a distant shore that he could not make out due to the low-lying clouds, or on the water itself. But then he could see from the changing angle of the lights that they were at sea as well.

"Sarge, you're not going to like this, I think we have company coming our way."

McCarty stuck his head out of the StingRay and held up his binoculars to their rear. "Yep, there they are. Surprised it took them this long to get out here, given that the Hans probably stole their sail boat." He turned to Solberg. "We're not going to make it to the rendezvous point. I better call it in now."

"Roger that." Solberg watched McCarty go below. "Marine One to Base, we're not going to make it to rendezvous point orange. Multiple contacts approaching from west and northwest," he heard McCarty say.

"Roger that Marine One, we're monitoring your current position and heading," came the response. "We're sending units your way."

• • •

Trinh Archer stood in the back corner of the playground facing other kids in her class and with her back to the brick outer wall of the school. The only teacher on duty during recess was around the corner on the other side of the playground, tending to a first grader who had fallen from the monkey bars and scrapped his knees.

"Hey Poca*han*tus!" one boy taunted Trinh. He had pushed her into the corner first by his incessant taunts, and then by actual force. His two buddies stood close by, and they were joined by other kids behind them, attracted by the spectacle.

"Now what're you gonna do, Poca*han*tus?" He tapped his hand on his mouth and began to whoop, *wah wah wah wah*!

"Yeah, and what kind of name is *Trinh*, anyway?" His buddy shouted, joining in with the taunts. The boy stepped forward and pushed Trinh into the brick wall behind her. She lost her footing and fell to the ground. "What are you, an *Indian* or an *Oriental*, any-way?" the boy yelled.

"You're not from around here, that's for sure!" the third boy added from behind them. "You're not one of *us!*"

Oooohhhhhh, some of the other kids whispered as they watched.

Archer was disoriented and scared. They were all classmates in school. Why were they doing this to her? She was new, she had just moved to the area with her mother. She looked behind the boys and saw two other girls who she thought were her friends. They were Asian too, like her. Part of her, at least. Her Vietnamese mother and their parents, also Vietnamese who emigrated after the war, and had just started working together. She thought they liked her, a little bit at least. They had celebrated the Day of Wandering Souls together just a few months ago, after Trinh and her mother first arrived to the area. They had fun. Why did they stand by and do nothing?

The second boy began to tap his open hand against his mouth and made "woo woo woo" sounds like his friend, and he stuck his other hand behind his head to portray a feather. The three boys began to skip in a small circle, taunting her as if at a powwow.

While Trinh Archer was merely in fourth grade and this boy was in sixth, her growth spurt had started and she was as tall as he. She was gangly and uncomfortable with her changing body, she felt clumsy and did not know how to move in it. She was new to this small school in Dodge City, and all she wanted was to make friends. Trinh's mother moved them here just a few months ago to work with the Vietnamese immigrant community in the local meat pack-ing plants. Her father had just died, a victim of a broken heart and dead end prospects after being mustered from the Army as part of a reduction in force. It was the end of his career. With so many pilots let go after the war, no one needed his many years of experience piloting helicopters, so with nowhere left to go he returned to his small hometown on the Great Plains to nurse his deepening depression with ever greater amounts of alcohol. Following his death, relations between her mother and her mother's in-laws—Trinh's grandparents on her father's side—went from bad to worse, with each blaming the other for his passing. Trinh's mother barely spoke English, moreover, and life in this part of the Great Plains had been tough enough when her husband was alive. Now it was completely foreign. Going back to Vietnam was out of the question, but she knew of a small community of Vietnamese immigrants working at the meat packing plants up north, across the border in Kansas, so she decided to start a new life with Trinh there.

The boys stopped their whooping at Archer and turned their attention to her again as she stood. "We don't like you here!" they shouted as they pushed her back into the brick wall. "You're not welcome here, go back to the reservation where you came from!" They pushed her again, causing her head to bump into the wall.

"*Ouch!*" she complained instinctively, rubbing the back of her head. She looked back up at the boy, now in her face, and she could look directly in his eyes. She realized she was as big as he was, and she wanted space. She pushed him back. Without realizing it, the wall at her back allowed her to brace herself, making the push more forceful. Not expecting the forceful push, the boy fell back into his buddy.

"Hey! What was that?" he yelled angrily, and he rushed her to push her back into the corner.

Archer saw an open field behind them. She suddenly yearned to be out there, free. She looked back at the boy charging her, and just as he tried to push her again, she pushed his arms away and charged him back. She pushed him into his buddy. The boy tripped and fell and hit his head. In a sudden rage, she began to slap his buddy in the face first with her right hand, then left, and then pushing him back again. She started screaming and crying, all at the same time.

"You stay away from *me*!" She yelled through an explosion of tears. "Leave *me* alone!" She flailed indiscriminately at the boys, one now cowering on the ground, another running away and the third protecting his head with his arms from the onslaught of Trinh's blows.

"Whoa whoa whoa, stop this now this instant!" A teacher ran into the crowd of kids and pulled Archer back. "What are you doing? Why are you hitting these boys?" she yelled in an exasperated voice.

"They were hitting *me*!" Trinh cried as she flailed with her feet.

"Come on, let's go to the principal's office," the teacher said, either not hearing Trinh Archer's cries, or not caring to hear…

Archer jerked awake. This time she was confined to a bed with each extremity handcuffed to the frame. She pulled her arms, hearing the *clang! clang!* of the metal handcuffs against the spare bed frame. She then pulled her legs in concert with her arms, writhing back and forth in a helpless attempt to find a break in the frame. She began to see shooting stars in her eyes, a colorful menagerie of blood vessels screaming for oxygen in her brain. She then noticed a low ringing in her ears grow in prominence. The sudden fit of movement after regaining consciousness was driving her system back toward an unconscious state, she realized. She stopped thrashing in the bed, and she commanded her diaphragm to open fitfully, gradually, after her semi-panicked state. She became more conscious of the pain in her shoulders, neck and head after the blows she received in the…where was she, again? It was a blur. She felt some pain in her knees, too, apparently also wounded from her fall after being belted in the back by that…cop? Was there a cop there?

"Time to take her to the rendezvous point," a man said from behind her. Had he been there the whole time? Had he just walked in? Trinh Archer did not know. When she looked back, she saw a man with him hold up a vial of clear liquid, stick a needle in it and slowly pull on the plunger, drawing the liquid into the syringe. "This time, she won't have any opportunity to run…" the mysterious man said.

The man with the syringe stepped forward as others held her arms down. She tried to push against them but she could barely muster any strength. He inserted the needle, and Archer's world grew dark again.

CHAPTER 37 - AT SEA

Colonel Bradley scanned the monitors and maps in the Kaga's Flag Information Center. He and his small team of technicians had finished installing the last of his TOC's communications gear, and they plotted the latest location of McCarty and Solberg. Bradley grew nervous as he watched several objects approach their position on the feed from the circling Gray Eagle UAV flying above them.

"*Marine One to Base, we're not going to make it to rendezvous point orange. Multiple contacts approaching from west and northwest,*" McCarty said over the encrypted communications channel.

"Roger that Marine One, we're monitoring your current position and heading," Bradley responded. "We're sending units your way." Bradley turned to Newland, who stood behind him. "Ok, Lt. Newland, you know what to do. Go get our guys."

"On our way now," he said, and he headed to the deck of the Kaga.

• • •

"All right, gentlemen," Lieutenant Newland declared as he approached the command Osprey on the deck of the Kaga. "It looks like our services are needed sooner than we expected. Let's prep for probable hot evac and get airborne as soon as possible. Our original checklists are out the door now." Already the team was loading their operational gear onto the CV-22, its blades gaining speed overhead as the lieutenant secured his gear and buckled up behind the pilots.

"Nice of you to join us," Newland said to Sergeant "Mac" Suzuki, a last-minute addition as the Japanese special ops team member being groomed for leadership duties in one of Japan's expanding special operations units. Newland glanced out of the rear of the Osprey and saw his counterpart, Lieutenant Watanabe, lead his team onto the two waiting UH-60s. Chiefs Sato and Taguchi and their copilots had their birds ready to depart, they just awaited final permission to lift off.

"It's windy out there, sir," Chief Kirby said over the intercom after Newland put on his headset. "It's gonna be a choppy ride to the objective."

"Roger that. We talking Goofy Barnstormer choppy, or Six Flags Superman choppy?" Lieutenant Newland asked, referring to his team's informal measures of "choppiness."

"I'd say at least Space Mountain choppy, sir, especially considering the weather," Chief Kirby responded. "The typhoon that cleared the Japanese islands is gaining strength again over the Sea of Japan, just southwest of us. We're alright for now, though. Clear for take-off."

"Hey, as long as it's not Splash Mountain, we're good!" added Sergeant James "Johny" Johnston, high-fiving his seat mate, Staff Sergeant Vance Nicholson.

"You know it!" yelled Nicholson. "I already took my weekly bath on Saturday, I'm not due for another one in days!"

"Is that what that smell is…?" Johny retorted, holding his nose in feigned disgust. "Damn, you gotta clean that stanky ass more often, yo!"

"Let's go get our boys, Chief Kirby," Newland said, anxious to get the operation airborne.

"Roger that, LT. Lifting off now." Chiefs Kirby and Mills lifted their Ospreys into the air, and as they transitioned their nascells to a horizontal configuration and leveled off over the water's surface, Chiefs Taguchi and Sato lifted off in their UH-60s. Taguchi and Sato quickly found themselves trailing the faster Ospreys, which had begun their operational flight to retrieve their teammates by the time they had cleared the deck of the Kaga. Had this been a training mission, they would have cruised to the objective together, but this operational mission required utmost speed to the contact point. Any training would be conducted once all the members had returned safely.

"We're gonna take this motha fucka to 11!" Kirby, a fan of all kitschy movies and TV shows from the '70s and '80s, could not help from declaring excitedly as he leveled his aircraft mere meters over the sea and pushed his Thrust Control Lever forward.

"What is '*ma za fa kah*'?" Mac asked. With his broken English, Mac did not understand "motha fucka," nor did he catch the allusion to the 1970s movie Spinal Tap. He nonetheless heard the excitement in Kirby's voice, and they all felt the sudden increase in speed.

"It's this baby, right here…" Johny said, patting the side of the Osprey. "This is the motha' fuckin' cavalry, is what it is…!"

"Hell yeah!" Nick declared, holding up a fist to Johny. They bumped fists then popped them open in mock explosion.

The occupants of the V-22s saw Colonel Bradley standing with Admiral Okada on the deck as they departed. They did not see the communications officer run to the commanding officers' position as the Ospreys headed toward the darkened horizon, however.

"Sir!" a voice shouted from behind Okada and Bradley. "We have a report of an attack on the MSDF Maizuru base, our home port!" Both men turned, and Okada went to read the report while Bradley returned to his tactical operations center to get an update through his channels.

• • •

"Those look like *Komar* missile patrol boats. They're small but fast, and gaining on us," Solberg reported to McCarty. "The evac team better get here pronto."

"They're on their way, Solberg," McCarty responded. He looked to the horizon.

"Uh-oh, trouble," Solberg said as he continued to watch the approaching vessels through his binoculars. "Muzzle flashes. They're firing on us."

McCarty looked in the same direction, and then back at the horizon in front of them. "C'mon cavalry..." McCarty said as he raised his binoculars to scan the horizon. It was now early daytime but all he could see were storm clouds and flashes of lightening in the distance.

• • •

Chiefs Kirby and Mills pushed their cruising speed close to 300 knots, beyond the recommended top speed of 275 knots. Their speed exceeded the max speed of the Japanese team at under 200 knots, but the chiefs had agreed with the team leader, Lieutenant Newland, that they would pick up the stragglers on the return flight and brief them on the mission afterward. They weren't going to babysit on this mission.

"Five minutes to rendezvous."

"Roger, do we have an open line to the team?" Newland asked. "Let's see how they're doing."

"Establishing coms now...Ok, go LT, we're patched in. Blade One to Marine One, come in Marine One."

"*Marine One here, we're under fire, repeat, taking fire...*"

Ever member of the team had one thought. *Fuck.* Not for their own safety, but because they could not get to the fight any faster.

"How many contacts?" Lt. Newland asked in a calm voice that belied his eagerness to help his guys.

"*Two, small surface craft, probably Komar-class missile boats...*" the team heard a burst of fire on the other end. "*They've fired their 25s and shoulder-fired weapons, but so far have missed given the sea conditions...*"

"Roger, cavalry's coming Marine One, hold on." The lieutenant turned to the Chief Kirby. "Any way we can go any faster?"

"Already at 110% sir, not sure how much more we can push her..."

The LT patted the Chief on the shoulder. "Just get there safe so we can join the fight."

"Roger that," the Chief replied as he urged his bird forward.

• • •

"Can we get these guys down into the hold of the Stingray?" Solberg asked again. He covered Mi Yong and the boy with his body as he reached over the edge of the boat.

"Now it's really too dangerous, we can't have them stand to move to the Stingray," repeated McCarty. "And in this weather, I'm not sure they can keep their footing even if we weren't being fired at. The weather's probably the only reason they haven't hit us yet."

Solberg looked toward the sky. "I feel raindrops, not just ocean spray now." There was a sudden splash ten meters aft of the boat as a rocket-propelled grenade exploded. The boy screamed in response.

"One way or another, we're going to get real wet real fast," McCarty responded. Timing his motion with the undulation of the boat, he reached up and fired a three-round burst, first at one vessel and then the other, with one of the tracer rounds flying over the bridge of the approaching vessel.

"*Marine One, this is Blade One, we have you in sight...*" they heard over the radio.

"Thank God," McCarty muttered under his breath as he looked to the skies. He grabbed the receiver. "Roger, you have our permission to sink those motherfuckers and get us out of here." McCarty turned back to the approaching boats to watch the action unfold.

The crew of the boats saw the fast-approaching Ospreys too. They raised their weapons and fired in unison into the sky. McCarty saw one of the crew members stand to aim a shoulder-fired surface-to-air missile upward as well. McCarty rose from his prone position and fired another three-round burst at him, watching the tracers fly around him, and then aimed another three-round burst at him, which hit the combatant twice. His arms flailed and the launcher fired almost vertically into the air as he fell overboard into the waters below.

"Fuck yeah, sarge!" exclaimed Solberg.

The two Osprey flew overhead and circled the small boats as the pilots adjusted the nacelles. As they did so, their belly-mounted Gatling guns fired simultaneously at the two boats. One bored holes into the side of the first approaching boat just above the waterline, and the second fired through the plate-glass windows of the bridge and burst open the head of the vessel's pilot like an exploding pumpkin. The Gatling then took out two more combatants running from the bridge to the rear of the boat. McCarty and Solberg were close enough to hear screams from the boat over the wash from the Ospreys above and see bodies fall into the sea. They saw no return fire. The first boat began to lean into the water as it continued to be hit by rounds, and then explode as the remaining crew jumped into the sea. The second boat, without its pilot, began to turn in a circle at sea.

"Fuuuuuck yeeeeahhhh!" screamed Solberg and McCarty, as they both sat on their knees. Han and Mi Yong looked over the side of the boat too, even as their son whimpered. "It's ok, we're safe now," Mi Yong told him as she embraced him. A tear rolled down her cheek.

"Ok, now we can get the fuck out of here. Solberg, prepare for evac. We may have to scuttle the Stingray."

"Already there, Sarge," he said as he lowered himself into the Stingray.

McCarty watched one of the birds maneuver to a hover over their position in preparation to descend."

"*Let's get you boys home,*" the lieutenant said over the radio.

"Ready when you are," responded Solberg. The ramp began to open as Blade One descended to retrieve them. The tethered crew chief held onto a handle as he prepared to take on the passengers.

McCarty looked up and then over at the other Osprey. He saw a flash on the horizon, and then a streak overhead. Another flash, and then another streak.

"Holy shit, we're under fire again!" he yelled over the radio as tracers and more streaks flew overhead. This was more substantial fire than the other boats mustered, he realized. Solberg looked in the direction of the fire. "Larger vessel this time, maybe a *Shershen-*class torpedo boat? I see more armaments on the deck. Still a ways away but closing fast...Wait, make that *two* boats, headed this way..."

Blade Two turned toward the fire, and then McCarty saw multiple tracers hit the port nacelle. Its rotors came to a complete stop and smoke erupted into the air. He heard a sudden high-pitched *whir* as the other rotor attempted to compensate. The Osprey began to spin as Chief Mills fought to regain control.

"*This is Blade Two, we're hit, lost use of the port nacelle...*"

"*Blade Two this is Blade One, return to base, repeat return to base...*"

"*Roger, returning to base. Hope we won't have to make a wet landing...*" Mills declared as he turned to depart.

"*Blade One, this is Blade Three,*" McCarty heard over the radio. The voice had a noticeable Japanese accent. He turned in surprise to see two barely visible UH-60s approaching on the horizon.

"*Great to see you, Blades Three and Four!*" Blade One responded as it rose up into the air. Another streak flashed through the sky, and tracers followed its ascent. "*Request assistance in evac of personnel from below, will provide cover...*"

The request was returned with silence.

"*Blade Three, come in,*" Blade One repeated as it fired several bursts from its belly-mounted gun. "*This is Blade One, will provide cover,*" he repeated.

"*Roger, we have received permission to assist in recovery,*" Blade Three responded. Chief Taguchi had radioed back to his superiors to get permission to take part in this part of this mission, McCarty realized. *He'll never get permission to fire,* McCarty thought as he watched the UH-60 approach his location, *if it comes to that...* McCarty looked toward the approaching vessels now clearly visible on the horizon, and clearly bigger than the ones the Ospreys took out.

•　•　•

"*Base, we've got more company,*" Bradley heard McCarty announce on the encrypted communications link. Bradley repositioned the video camera on the Gray Eagle, and he too saw two larger vessels approaching.

Admiral Okada, who had just returned to the FIC and was standing next to Bradley, saw them too. "We will get our F-35s airborne," he declared. "We should be just in range for a flight there and back without refueling."

"Much obliged, admiral, but you sure that's a wise thing to do?" Bradley asked. "It might attract more attention from the North Koreans."

"You have a lot of attention now," Okada said, pointing to the feed from the Gray Hawk. "And we should be just in range for a low-level flight there and back, avoiding their radar," Okada added. "But this is what the alliance is for, right? We are obligated and legally able to protect our American allies if they are under direct attack." He issued an order to one of his aides, who then left the FIC. Bradley guessed that Okada told him to launch the F-35s.

"We'd be much obliged for the air cover, of course," Bradley said, still torn between the added air cover to complete the mission and the possibility of exposing both the mission and the Kaga Task Force itself to greater danger from the North Koreans.

Bradley turned to his TOC commo gear. "We see them too, Marine One..." Bradley said on the secure link to McCarty.

• • •

"...*Blade raid, this is base, we have two F-35s inbound, repeat two F-35s inbound, ETA 15 minutes,*" Colonel Bradley announced to the group.

"Roger, base, none too soon," McCarty responded. He turned to Solberg. "F-35s can't get us out of the drink, so we better do this right when we can."

"I'm on it," Solberg replied.

Blade Three positioned itself in a hover over the boat as low as it could without washing out the occupants.

"Shit, what the hell is this, sarge?" Solberg asked as a lone rope fell onto the small deck of their boat. "There's no way…this'll take forever!"

They both ducked as an explosion lit up one of the vessels. Blade One had scored a direct hit on the approaching vessel, which now appeared dead in the water.

"Let's just get the job done with what we got. Mr. Han, I'll take you up first and then we'll return for the others." He had already secured Han to the rope before he finished his sentence. He secured himself and then signaled for the crew to raise them both up, which they did in a miraculously short amount of time. On the way up he saw Blade Four fly between Blade Three and the now-immobile vessel, which was firing scattered shots first at one then another of the three birds. McCarty returned his attention to the task at hand. Sergeant Inamoto pulled Han and McCarty into the fuselage. Inamoto and Lieutenant Watanabe unhitched Han, and then McCarty told them to lower him back down to the boat.

"What're you doing, sarge?" Solberg cried out as he returned. "I thought I was going to…"

"Your turn, Solberg. You get the boy up…" he said as he attached the safety gear to the child and then to Solberg. "He knows you better," McCarty added. The boy's languid face was beginning to turn into a quizzical grimace as the meds wore off. "Take him up, I'll stay with her," he said, motioning for the crew to raise them up.

Just then, he saw an explosion in the sky. *Shit, Blade One is hit…* McCarty saw one of the engines burst into flames. Miraculously, Chief Kirby was able to maintain control, but the burning engine lit up the sky. *There's no way they'll make it back in that condition*, he knew.

"Blade Three, this is Marine One. Return to base immediately when you have Sergeant Solberg and the boy secured. That's a… *request*," McCarty declared.

"Roger," came the matter-of-fact reply as the three were pulled into the UH-60 above. Blade Three immediately began to pull away from the scene as tracers trailed it. Mi Yong watched the helicopter pull into the sky, and she screamed. "Han…!" McCarty pulled her to himself, keeping her from falling into the sea. "We'll take the submersible back…!" McCarty tried to explain to her over her wailing. She did not want to listen, however, and continued to watch Blade Three turn to head toward the horizon.

There was a splash ten meters from the boat. McCarty forced Mi Yong to the deck and covered her with his body, expecting another explosion. He waited as she whimpered under him, but nothing happened. He then rose up to see a head surface from the water, and the figure began to swim toward the boat.

Solberg?

"What the *hell* are you doing here!" McCarty yelled as he reached over the boat to pull Solberg from the water. "You were told to return to base, sergeant!"

"I heard you over the intercom. You *requested* that we return to base, or at least Blade Three. I'm not going to leave you and the woman here alone to face them!" Solberg shouted, gesturing to the *Shershen* in the distance. "Leave no one behind, damn it!"

Boom! They ducked as a round exploded several meters from their location, drenching the inhabitants and causing the boat to rock wildly.

• • •

"...*Return to base immediately. That's a...request,*" Blade Four's Chief Sato heard over the radio as he maneuvered between Blade Three, which was pulling in another of the passengers from the boats below, and the one operable North Korean combatant firing at them. Sato saw members of the crew attempt to put out a fire on deck, while another appeared to raise a...

Chikushooo! Sato forced his UH-60 into a sharp dive as a rocket-propelled grenade flew over him. He circled low toward Marine One on the surface of the sea below, now completely exposed to the approaching vessel. Sato saw McCarty pull a person from the water...*was that Solberg? Did he fall from Blade Three...?* He looked over at Blade Three, now pulling away from the scene of the fight.

"*Blade Four, this is Blade Three, return to base...*" Taguchi ordered.

Eh? he wondered as he circled the exposed Marine One below. An explosion rocked their boat, almost capsizing it. He then saw Blade One crash-land at sea and begin to take on water.

Tracers lit the sky to his right and left. He looked over his shoulder as he took evasive action to avoid being hit. Sato saw in his peripheral vision the AGM 114 Hellfire missiles on either side of his UH-60. His trigger finger caressed the arming function on his cyclic stick. *I'm an armed warrior trained for battle,* he thought to himself. *'Tsune ni heiho no michi o hanarezu...Never stray from the Way of the Warrior...'* echoed in his mind.

"*Blade Four, this is Blade Three, return to base, that's an...*" Chief Sato flipped the switch of his receiver to the 'off' position. His co-pilot looked at him, and then back at the incoming combatants below.

This is about honor not orders, this about not leaving the battle, this is about protecting my teammates no matter the cost... Sato thought to himself. "Our colleagues cannot wait until the F-35s arrive," Sato declared. He banked his UH-60 and lined his sights directly onto the North Korean combatant, arming his Hellfire missiles. He fired one rocket, and then another. The two rockets followed their laser guidance systems directly to the target, striking the North Korean vessel dead-on. Two explosions rocked the forward section of the ship, causing it to list in the water.

He circled the ship, but saw that despite the main structure being engulfed in flames, the remaining crew went to the aft section to secure hand-held weapons, including another rocket launcher.

"Shimada, I'm coming around. Can you provide some cover fire?" he asked on the intercom.

Sergeant Daisuke Shimada understood Chief Sato's tone: Sato was requesting, not ordering, him to provide cover fire that would probably lead to the deaths of North Korean combatants. His Chief had taken an extraordinary measure to protect their comrades in arms...their friends...

"*Ryokai shimasu,*" Shimada replied. *With pleasure.* He steadied himself and his weapon at the side door of the Black Hawk and opened fire. The crew members on the combatant below sought cover and began to fire toward Blade Four. And then Shimada saw it. A partially uncovered tarp exposed a pile of munitions on the aft deck. He aimed for that. Shimada walked his tracers up the deck to the middle of the pile and then...contact! He concentrated his fire on the pile until a huge explosion followed seconds later. He almost fell back due to the force. Blade Four shuddered at the explosion.

"*Yatta!*" Sato yelled over the intercom. "Direct hit!"

Shimada pumped his arm in satisfaction at the first defensive shots fired in a live, joint combat operation in international waters.

• • •

Colonel Bradley watched the scene unfold via the video feed from the Gray Eagle on the main monitor in the FIC. "*Yes!*" he whispered under his breath upon seeing the large explosion on the North Korean vessel. Now the immediate danger to his team was gone, they just needed to recover their personnel and return to the Kaga.

Bradley turned to Okada, who leaned forward on his command chair while he too watched the scene unfold. "Admiral, I think you can call off your F-35s for now, to avoid attracting additional attention from the North..."

"*Yosh,* agreed." Okada nodded at his aide, who bowed and carried out the wordless order.

"If you'll excuse me, I'll head to the air operations center to ensure our men return safely."

"Certainly, Admiral. I'll continue to watch things from down here."

Okada left the FIC for the AOC, and Bradley turned back to the monitors.

•   •   •

"Shimada, do we have room for the crew of Blade One?" Sato asked as he turned his UH-60 toward the wreckage.

Shimada looked at the now-foundering V-22. "We have room, barely, but I don't know about time..." He remembered the seemingly pilotless North Korean boat doing circles below. "If we secured that boat, though," Shimada said as he pointed out the slowly moving boat to Sato, "we could get them more quickly."

"Right, get ready," Sato ordered.

Shimada and Shinamoto secured themselves to the fast ropes as Sato positioned Blade Four over the slowly moving boat.

"*Ike!*" Sato commanded, and the two fast-roped down to the deck below.

The two fell on either side of the deck, and then aimed their MP5s in either direction. Blade Four's crew chief secured the ropes above. "*Heading to Blade One,*" Sato said over the radio, and the UH-60 lifted away.

Shinamoto checked the aft portion of the boat, kicking two motionless bodies and then moving to the opposite side. Shimada went forward, first around the partially exposed pilot's bridge and then into the bridge itself, where he saw the headless body of the pilot lying on the deck in front of the controls. Shimada pushed the body to the side with his leg, holding himself steady with a handle on the console to keep from slipping in the man's blood covering the deck.

Shinamoto came through the other entrance of the bridge, looking down at the body and then stepping over it to enter. "All secure..."

"Let's get over to Blade One," Shimada said as he took the controls and turned the boat toward the floating figures in the distance. "Push that body overboard, will you?" he said, motioning to the dead pilot.

Shinamoto reached down to grab the body by its trousers. He dragged it out of the bridge to the outside deck, and then he pushed it overboard. He stood and peered over the side to watch the body sink into the surf, and turned to re-enter the bridge.

Pop pop pop! A succession of firing rang out.

"*Aaah!*" Shinamoto cried out. "I'm hit!" He fell into the side of the open hatch and then forced himself forward into the bridge for cover, clutching his right shoulder. He pointed backward while grimacing to indicate the direction of the fire.

Shimada secured his MP5 in one hand as he pulled Shinamoto fully into the bridge with the other. He then pulled a grenade from his protective vest and pulled the pin, letting the spoon fall. Timing was essential—if he threw it immediately after pulling the pin, it would likely fall off the deck and explode next to the waterline, potentially blowing a hole in the side and sinking the boat before they could rescue the crew of Blade One. But if he held it too long, it would explode in the bridge, killing them. After exactly one second, he tossed the grenade aft and covered Shinamoto as it exploded one second later. He immediately thrust himself out of the bridge onto the deck, firing several rounds through the smoke as cover fire. The smoke cleared, but no one was there.

Shimada moved low along the deck to the end of the low superstructure, his back against the long tubes that held the anti-ship missiles that the *Komar* was known for. At the end of the tube, Shimada kneeled and reached his MP5 around and fired again. He peered around the tube, noticing a trail of blood leading to the other side of the boat and around the corner. He followed it and was about to fire around the corner again, but a volley of bullets hit the edge of the port-side missile tube Shimada used as cover. He thrust his MP5 around the corner again and fired blindly, with fire hitting the missile tube again. Then he heard another volley of fire and a scream. Shimada peered around the corner in time to see a North Korean fall against the railing and then roll over into the waves below.

"Shimada!" came a voice from the bridge. Shimada rushed to the bridge, where he found Shinamoto lying on the deck in the pilot's pool of blood, his MP5 in his left hand. Shinamoto had fired the last shots at the North Korean crew member, saving Shimada. "Shimada, let's go get the crew..." he wheezed, and then passed out.

Shimada pulled him to the other side of the bridge and propped him against the back wall of the bridge. He then turned to the control panel, revved the engines and steered the North Korean vessel toward the crash site where Blade Four was already rescuing members of the downed flight.

CHAPTER 38 - INVESTIGATIONS

Nishi arrived at the Maizuru maritime base as the sun approached its zenith in the overcast sky. It was more than coincidence, he thought, that the regional headquarters for the maritime operations was the location that came under vicious chemical weapons attack.

"Three sailors have died, while 29 are injured, including ten with serious injuries and external and internal burns due to the mustard gas attack," one of the investigators reported in his briefing to Nishi. "And we found this," he added, displaying a series of doomsday cult paraphernalia. Most of it was charred beyond recognition, but a few photos and portions of pamphlets clearly showed senior members of the 1990s doomsday cult.

Nishi nodded, recognizing the material but unconvinced about its implication. "Have you identified the body yet?"

"The recovery team has not yet been able to retrieve the pilot's body from the mangled wreckage," the inspector said. "Initial reports suggest the body is in pretty bad shape. It'll take time to identify him. Or her, I suppose."

Another investigator hurriedly joined the briefing session. "We just found this lying near the body in what was the cockpit," he reported, displaying a number of pins. "They appear to be pins from North Korea, the DPRK flag, and the two previous leaders," he said, displaying the recovered items to the small group.

"*Saaa*," Nishi said aloud as he held up one of the pins. "What does *that* mean? Items from a doomsday cult *and* from North Korea?" The investigators looked at each other. "Are you suggesting they might be connected?"

"Why else would the perpetrator carry them all on the helicopter?" Nishi's colleague answered.

And so close to the recent attempted smuggling operation days ago... Nishi thought to himself. He retrieved his phone and dialed Trinh Archer's number.

"*Tadaima, rusubanchu...I'm away now, but please leave your name and...*" Archer's voicemail began.

Okashii naaa. Nishi looked at his phone. *I haven't been able to get through to Aachaa-san for a while now...Menda is in critical condition because of some bizarre illness the doctors are unable to treat, and now Archer is nowhere to be found...*

Nishi turned to his colleague again. "We better report our findings so far. Tokyo wants updates every half-hour."

"Yessir. I'll contact the Prime Minister Office's crisis center immediately."

Another analyst approached Nishi. "Sir, we have the latest map plotting suspect cell phone locations in the region for the last several days, including some new suspect traffic..."

"Hmmm? Ok, hand it over." He glanced at the dozens of plots though out the region on the map. "What can I do with this?" he demanded.

"Sir, as you can see here, there are a number of plots in this area. Maybe there is a connection of some sort..."

"*Maybe?*" Nishi retorted. "Looks to me like they're all over the map. Some here in this region, where we are, others over here in the Kanto area," Nishi said, pointing to areas of the map. "Still others up here, to the north, not to mention the couple down here in the Kobe area..." Nishi looked up at the analyst. "Find me some *actionable* intelligence, not '*maybes*', and don't take me from the task at hand!" Nishi half-crumpled the paper and threw it back at the analyst.

The analyst took the paper and scurried back to his make-shift work location in a tent near the edge of the field.

Go easy on them, Nishi, he thought to himself. *They're just trying to help...* He flicked his cigarette on the gravel and pulled another from the now half-empty pack of cigarettes in his jacket pocket, the one he had just opened when he arrived.

• • •

Bennett and Tucker arrived at a nondescript building behind the Prime Minister's Official Residence at mid-day. While journalists were arrayed outside the front of the stately mansion that housed the Prime Minister's office, they were not allowed to set up their cameras at the back of the building where the streets were narrow and more closely guarded by police. They missed the arrival of Bennett and Tucker, who slipped into the squat, white building across the street from the residence with little fanfare. Called simply the "Cabinet Office" building, it housed the various units that oversaw the work throughout the Japanese government, including Cabinet Intelligence.

After being greeted by several cabinet aides, they descended to the basement and walked several hundred meters along an underground tunnel that connected to the second floor of the Official Residence, which was partially underground. The main entrance at the front was one floor above, on the third floor, so none of the reporters milling about the entrance saw the two Americans enter the elevator to descend to the basement, where the Crisis Management Center was located.

One of the aides opened the door for them, revealing a conference room filled with a cacophony of voices, typing, televisions, and fax machines. Technicians were busy setting up additional screens on one side of the room for video teleconferencing capabilities with the local police and Coast Guard units for real-time updates in addition to feeds from the Defense Ministry and National Police Agency. Others worked on rows of laptops set up on tables in the middle of the room. Most of the attention centered on a briefing taking place on an array of projectors at the other side of the room, however.

"...as you know, our concern lies primarily with the range of rapidly developing missile systems North Korea has tested in the region that are capable of striking any area in the Japanese archipelago, including major metropolitan areas of Tokyo, Osaka, Kyoto, with any type of weapon of mass destruction such as a nuclear device or chemical weapon..." a cabinet intelligence officer said as he briefed the Deputy Chief Cabinet Secretary Tokuda. As the briefer paused, Tokuda looked at the new visitors and, recognizing Maddy Tucker, acknowledged her and Bennett with a nod as they entered. He turned back to the briefer, who continued his briefing. "...the nature of this morning's attack is almost unprecedented, being delivered as it was apparently by helicopter and not by a missile. This demonstrates the danger represented by various types of delivery devices, from the localized air- and maritime-platforms such as the helicopter or boat, or by ballistic missile system that might be able to penetrate our current missile defense systems..."

"What do you mean by that? Aren't our PAC-3s and Aegis systems enough to defend from a short- or intermediate-range missile?" the deputy chief asked. Tucker saw that Tokuda knew the answer to the question—she even saw a glint in his eyes as he asked the question—but that he wanted to press the young officer to see how he would respond.

"Well, apart from reliability issues...no system is 100% reliable against a given target, after all..." the briefer explained, "we've analyzed the trajectory of the missile tests and they appear to be conducted with current missile defense systems in mind. Take the newly operational Kasei-12 intermediate range missile system, which the

North Koreans call Hwasong-12 and..." the briefer then to turned to Tucker and Bennett, "the Americans call the KN-17, for example." The briefer then returned his steady gaze to the deputy chief. "Not only is this road-mobile missile capable of hitting as far as Guam and Hawaii, because of its range it can be launched at a high arc well out of range of our currently operational missile and air defense systems. It can then re-enter the atmosphere at almost a straight, downward trajectory, achieving a rate of speed and angle that our PAC-3s would never be able to defend against. Unless we can destroy it during the launch phase, or even before it launches, we are almost completely defenseless against a ballistic missile of this type."

"But the threat represented by the attack this morning did not involve a missile delivery vehicle," Tokuda asserted in an authoritative voice. "The attackers used a helicopter to maim and kill innocent sailors. Our west coast is especially vulnerable to these types of terrorist attacks as well, since the distances to travel are shorter..." he said as if to clarify the briefer's earlier statement.

"That is true, this merely shows how many options a potential enemy has to inflict mass casualties and mass destruction now. In this case, we surmise that the attackers were attempting to prevent patrols from launching from that maritime base as scheduled later in the day. But the enemy has many additional options..."

"So are you saying this might be a precursor to another, perhaps imminent attack?" the advisor interrupted, this time with a serious question. "I need to know for when the new Prime Minister and reporters all ask this very question of me."

Before he could answer, another aide placed a print-out in front of him. He examined it, and then nodded. The aide then reported its contents verbally to the group. "Sir, our investigators have discovered some items in the wreckage. Of particular interest are paraphernalia that appear to originate from North Korea." The briefer motioned to his aide, now sitting at a computer console, who projected photos of the pins onto a screen at the far side of the table.

On the screen, three pins showing long-deceased DPRK leadership smiling broadly with the national flag in the background. Another pin featured the hammer, sickle, and calligraphy brush burnished in gold. And a third featured a DPRK flag superimposed over the entire Korean Peninsula, symbolizing a unified country under Pyongyang leadership. The group let out an audible gasp as they looked at the projected image.

"*These* were found at the crash site?" the deputy advisor asked, sitting forward in his seat. He looked at his aide, and then to Tucker and Bennett. "*Saaaaa, wakannai na,*" the aide said as the gathered intelligence officers pondered the question, and its implications. "I don't know...Why would skilled operatives bring along readily identifiable markers such as these on a mission of this visibility?" the aide wondered aloud. "Surely they knew the pins would be discovered and tie the operation directly back to the original sponsor of the attack, even if it was a suicide mission..."

"The investigators also found these," the briefer added when the screen changed to show charred paraphernalia from the 1990s cult.

"These too were found?" Tokuda asked aloud. He sat back into his chair again and folded his arms. "One thing is certain," he continued, "they are fanatics, dedicated in body and in spirit, and we must be prepared for any additional attacks." Tokuda turned to yet another aide standing behind him. "Get me Defense Headquarters, we must order more patrols all along the northwestern portion of Japan along the Sea of Japan. And get me imagery on the status of the known ballistic missile launch sites."

"*This will require additional military contingency planning,*" both Bennett and Tucker saw Tokuda whisper to his aide.

This can get out of hand quickly, Bennett thought. "*We need to give them an off-ramp before things go too far too fast and jeopardize the recovery operation*," Bennett whispered in turn to Tucker. Without waiting for her reply, he interjected into the briefing. "If I may, allow me to introduce myself..."

"Allow me to introduce Mr. Wilson Bennett, who as the U.S. Executive Secretary for the National Security Council is your counterpart, Mr. Tokuda," Tucker said formally before Bennett could finish his self-introduction.

Tokuda rose, bowed slightly and then shook Bennett's hand.

"We at the U.S. Embassy had plans to introduce Mr. Bennett under more auspicious circumstances, but this will have to do," Tucker continued as they exchanged curt greetings.

"Certainly, Mr. Bennett, welcome to Tokyo. I wish we could have provided a more formal welcome to you."

"*Sassoku desu-ga, Tokuda-san*," Bennett began, "to get quickly to the point given the circumstances, we have an ongoing operation that you should know about as you plan your response options. We have not received a status update yet but we thought it best to brief you now, after the election and given recent events," Bennett explained. "This could yield significant information for your intelligence services as well as for ours."

"And related to Bennett's efforts, as you know we have a joint U.S.-Japan task force working to shut down money laundering and illicit funding operations originating or passing through Japan..." Tucker began to say.

"The task force's director is on-site now, leading aspects of the investigation together with the Coast Guard. You see for yourself what they've discovered so far." Tokuda pointed to the screen in interrupting. "If this is linked to North Korea, this is a direct attack on the Japanese homeland and an act of war!"

"We recognize the gravity of the attack and the U.S. Government stands squarely with Japan on investigating and responding as necessary," Tucker continued. "We offer any additional resources and assistance you may require. We would like to deepen our efforts in working with the task force to determine the possible links to the smuggling operation and to give our operators time to complete their mission."

"What is this mission that is taking place now? Our Maritime Chief of Staff mentioned providing support to a U.S. mission, which was to be called a 'search and rescue exercise' if any of it got out. But he did not provide specifics..."

Tucker and Bennett looked first at Tokuda, and then at the intelligence officers around him. Tokuda then turned to his aides and dismissed them with a nod.

"Please, sit," Tokuda said, motioning to chairs at a long table next to his seat in the center of the room. He leaned forward to listen.

"Thank you, Tokuda-san," Bennett began. "We have a well-placed source in the North Korean scientific community..." Bennett paused as he looked at Tucker, and then continued, "that is to say, we have a *potentially* well-placed source in the North Korean scientific community that we are attempting to extract currently..."

An aide approached the small group and leaned to whisper in Tokuda's ear.

"What?" Tokuda responded. "Do not disturb our conversation." He failed to control his annoyance at the aide's sudden approach.

"But sir," the flustered aide said in a now-audible voice, "the Kaga is reporting North Koreans are firing on American and Japanese forces flying from the ship, and that they are returning fire..."

"Get me the Defense Chief of Staff, now!" Tokuda ordered.

Tucker and Bennett looked at each other, and then at the aide as Tokuda went to the private line in his office. "Can we use these phones, please?" Tucker stated rather than asked. Both Bennett and Tucker picked up the receivers.

"Press 9 to dial out," said the aide.

•   •   •

Shimada pulled his commandeered North Korean boat alongside the remaining wreckage of Blade One. Most of the V-22 had sunk, but the survivors had clung to the floating pieces of wing and fuselage as the battle had raged around them.

Shimada saw that Blade Four, hovering over another collection of wreckage nearby, had just pulled in a crew member from the water's surface, but he could not tell if it was the second or third recovery. He had lost count due to the gun battle moments ago. He guided the vessel slowly, looking for additional crew members among the wreckage bobbing up and down in the undulating surf. Wind gusts had increased and caused the rain to fall at almost a 45-degree angle. The rain and the dark clouds caused visibility to be reduced to meters.

"*Oi, oi!*" Shimada heard faintly in the distance over the pater-pater of the rain and the downwash from Blade Four hovering close by. Shimada found a spotlight and shone it in the general direction of the cries. The beam spotlighted first a wheel attached to some landing gear, then a blade from the proprotors, and finally a long section of wing on which he saw two bodies clinging to the edge of the far section. Shimada noticed the reflection of the light off of crew member's retinas, until man blinked and turned away at the sudden bright light aimed at him. *That must be Suzuki*, Shimada thought to himself, *and it looks like he's holding on to another crew member.*

"I'm coming!" Shimada shouted. He flashed the beam of light along his planed approach to ensure he could safely avoid other wreckage and other potential survivors. Once he was sure the way was safe, he returned to the bridge and piloted the boat toward Suzuki and the other crew member.

Once there, he saw that Suzuki was holding onto an unconscious Lieutenant Newland. They were weighed down by gear, and Suzuki had grown greatly fatigued in holding him to the wing while trying to remain afloat himself.

"Blade Four, this is Marine Two"—Shimada decided to give his vessel a new name during the operation for better operational security—"we have a crew member who is unconscious, are you able to retrieve, over?"

"Negative, Marine Two, negative, running low on fuel and will have to return to base. Can you retrieve, over?"

Shimada searched for a flotation device of some kind, any kind, but it did not look like this boat was equipped with one. He found a simple rope on the deck, and threw it over to Suzuki. "Blade Four, understood, Marine Two will retrieve and then return to base, over."

"Roger, good luck, over and out..." Shimada saw the outline of the UH-60 pull away from the wreckage site and head into the low-lying clouds above.

Shimada returned his attention to Suzuki, and it was clear he could not hold on to both the wreckage and Newland while also trying to tie a rope around him. Shimada took the other end of the rope and secured it to a handle bar, stripped off his boots and outer protective gear and then jumped into the water. He swam to Suzuki and Newland. "Hold on," he said. "I'll take care of this."

It was only then that Shimada saw the burns and cuts on Newland's head and face. Some of his uniform had been cut as well, but Shimada had no time to dwell on that. He pulled the rope around Newland's torso and secured it as much as possible. "Ok,

I'll go back to the boat and pull him and you onto the deck," he explained. He swam away without waiting for an acknowledgement.

Shimada climbed back onto the boat using the same rope he used to secure Newland but ensuring he did not pull any of the slack that remained in the water. While Suzuki held onto the rope, Shimada pulled the two alongside the boat. He then tried to pull Newland onto the deck.

"*Hrrrrmmmmmm,*" he grunted audibly as he tried to pull him up. "*Hrrrrmmmmpp,*" he grunted again, but he could not pull the man in full gear onto the boat. He then looked up and down the boat itself. In the back, he could see that there was a wench probably used for recovering small mines. He looked back down to Suzuki, who grimaced because of the rain falling into his face as he looked up at Shimada. "One minute! I will pull the boat forward and use the wench...!" He motioned to the aft portion of the vessel, but Suzuki was only dimly aware of what Shimada was trying to convey.

Shimada disappeared into the bridge again and slowly pulled the boat forward several meters. He then rushed to the rear of the boat, peered down at them to ensure they were in the right general area, and then positioned the wench over them. He then played with the levers to see which would lower it and which would raise it. Once he figured out how to operate it, he lowered the hook down to Suzuki, who was able to secure the hook onto Newland's protective vest. Shimada then slowly raised the unconscious Newland and pulled him onto the deck of the Marine Two. He then unhooked Newland and repeated the operation with Suzuki. Once on board, Suzuki kneeled against the superstructure to catch his breath.

"*Daijobu ka?*" Shimada asked after a moment. "*Yoku dekita zo,* you did good," he said without waiting for a reply, patting him on the back.

Mac nodded once in reply, collected his strength and then uttered "*yooosh...*" as he stood. "Ok, let's go get the rest of Marine One and get out of here." They then worked to secure Newland with Shinamoto in the bridge before they turned toward Marine One's location.

"Nice of you to come back for us!" McCarty declared as the missile boat pulled alongside. "Get her aboard first," he said, not wasting any time in lifting Mi Yong toward Shimada's outstretched arms.

"Solberg, let's you and I place some charges on the StingRay to scuttle it before we depart. And the sailboat too."

"Parties always save the best fireworks for the end, can't miss those!" Solberg replied as he jumped into the StingRay to retrieve the explosives. He felt lighter on his feet now that they were about to depart. He tossed several charges to McCarty from below as he set several more inside the StingRay.

Once set, they both jumped up to the Komar, which pulled away to a safe distance. Almost simultaneous explosions seconds later caused both of the small vessels to sink into the Sea of Japan, and Marine Two turned toward the Kaga.

• • •

Blade Four's Chief Sato and its passengers saw smoke billowing into the sky on their approach to the Kaga. They peered down at the surface of the undulating sea below and saw a large oil slick ablaze. Metal parts were strewn over dozens of meters around the oil slick.

That's Blade Two, the crew and passengers realized, but no one dared uttered those words. *They didn't make it to the Kaga...*

Chief Sato reached the Kaga minutes later and landed his craft aft of Blade Three. As soon as his bird was secure, he powered down the engine and the passengers and crew disembarked through the side doors. Sato himself opened his cockpit door and as he stepped down from his seat, he saw Chief Warrant Officer Hisamu Taguchi running toward him. Sato took off his helmet, laid it on his seat, and stepped forward to report to his commanding officer.

"*What the hell were you doing out there!?*" Taguchi shouted over the whir of various aircraft on the flight deck of the Kaga. "*Your orders were to return to the* Kaga *immediately!*"

"Sir, I..." Sato began as he saluted Chief Taguchi. Then Sato saw Taguchi raise his right fist as he continued to charge at him.

Smack! Taguchi landed his right fist on the side of Sato's face. The strike did not hurt so much as surprise Sato, who flailed backward and lost his balance.

Taguchi threw another punch at Sato, which landed on the top of his head as Sato fell to the flight deck. Taguchi knelt down over him and began to land more blows on him.

Their copilots saw the incident unfold and rushed to separate the two warrant officers, while deck crew jumped from the cat walks along the edge of the deck to join the fray. Taguchi tried to jerk himself from their grasp as others picked up Sato and pulled him away.

"You have been borderline insubordinate since you came under my command!" Taguchi yelled as he pointed at Sato, "but this is a truly unforgivable act! You disobeyed my *direct* order during a live operation, and you *will* face disciplinary action for your disobedience!"

"Discipline how you want, I will never leave my *teammates* on the battlefield! That is cowardice!" Sato yelled as he was pulled up from the deck, holding the side of his cheek but ready to return the fight if necessary.

Taguchi tried to charge him again but was held back by his copilot and other crew. Sato also tried to charge at Taguchi, but he too was held back.

"What is the meaning of this!" a commanding voice yelled from behind the crowd. Everyone turned to see Admiral Tetsuya Okada emerge from around the helicopter. He had just come onto the flight deck to see the crew of Blade Two and Four when the commotion began. Everyone stood at attention when they saw him, including Taguchi and Sato.

"Do you not realize that we are executing a live recovery operation now? This is unacceptable behavior!" Okada shouted first in front of Taguchi and then in front of Sato. He turned to the crew gathered around them. "Now get back to your posts. Dismissed!"

The crew then scurried away while Taguchi and Sato remained at attention.

He turned back to Taguchi and Sato. "You two just conducted one of the most important operations in the modern history of the Self-Defense Forces. You successfully rescued a North Korean family adrift at sea in horrible, stormy conditions, during a search and rescue exercise being conducted with our American allies. Do you understand what I'm saying?"

"Yessir," Taguchi replied as Okada stared at him.

"And you?" Okada asked as he approached Sato.

"Yessir."

"You had better understand! Because we are in potentially a wartime situation now!" Okada shouted at the two pilots, who returned Okada's steady, steely gaze with utter surprise. "The Japanese homeland was attacked by chemical weapons! *Maizuru base* was attacked, MSDF personnel are injured, dead even. We have received Maritime and Air Policing Orders to be on guard for additional attacks. North Korea is about to launch a missile, probably over the Japanese islands. I will *not* tolerate your petty bickering!"

"Yessir," the two pilots responded, still aghast at the development.

"Good. Whether these North Korean defectors are involved or not, I do not know, but as far as you are concerned, they were rescued during standard search-and-rescue training with our American allies. End of story. Now get back to your posts. We have work to do!" Okada turned to see an MSDF SH-60 Black Hawk land at its helipad, a crew of medical personnel arrayed on the deck with stretchers to treat the wounded. Okada ran to join them.

The two pilots strained to see at least three men on stretchers carried from the helicopters to the medical facilities below-deck.

Distracted by the scene, they did not see the watch officer run up to Admiral Okada. "Sir, North Korean vessel, probable missile boat, on a direct course for the Kaga!" Okada and the officer turned to run back to the bridge.

CHAPTER 39 - NEW BEGINNINGS

"Trinh, you can't keep letting them get under your skin," her gym teacher, Mr. Thomas, said immediately after class. He was new to the school too, and while Archer didn't know much about him or his background, she liked him. He spoke to her in a friendly manner, not plaintively or in the lecturing tones of the other teachers. "I know you've been through a lot, it's tough for you and your mother, I can see that," he continued as she looked down at her lap. "But if you keep getting sent to the principal's office, they'll expel you. You've already been in detention several times."

"Look, I'm going to start teaching classes at the local YMCA," he continued. "It's taken me a while to get settled, but when I start classes I want you to be one of our first students."

She looked up at him. "Student? Of what?"

"It's called *Aikido*, it's a martial art I learned while stationed in Asia..."

"You were in Asia?" she asked, intrigued by this new shared experience.

"Yes, I was stationed there while in the Air Force. That's where I started to learn Aikido."

"What is it?" she asked. She knew about Karate, famous now because of the recent film *Karate Kid*. And she had heard about Kung fu, because of the Bruce Lee movies some of the boys were into. But she had never heard of Aikido.

"It's using your foe's energy against him, turning a punch or kick into a throw or lock. It's less violent than some forms, but sometimes more effective."

Archer did not know what he was talking about then, but she later told her mother that she was going to the YMCA for an evening class, without telling her what that class was. Archer fell in love with the martial art the first time she was able to subdue her instructor during the first week of class.

When her mother learned about the course, she attempted to dissuade Trinh from taking it, partly because of its association with fighting but mainly, Trinh thought, because it was not of Vietnamese origin. Her mother relented if only because it was part of an after-school program, which meant more structured time in the afternoons while her mother worked two full-time jobs to make ends meet.

Archer's attention in school improved dramatically, and while she did not win many close friends because of her new passion, she gained quickly in proficiency in training with the mainly older and bigger students and was able to fend off the relentless bullying in her first year of school through more subtle approaches. That satisfied her and led to a quiet confidence that increased as she too matured. Her passion helped her to focus throughout her school years, and led her to study the history, culture and languages of East Asia, and ultimately to her current choice in career…

• • •

Trinh Archer did not know why she awoke when she did. She was at first groggy and disoriented. She heard voices, but did not know where they were coming from. She did not understand what was being said through the dark fog.

Only days later would she realize that whoever dosed the amount of whatever it was they gave her, probably measured an amount for an average-sized woman. An average-sized *Asian* woman, no doubt. Trinh Archer was no average woman, and her athletic and muscular build, together with her healthy and robust metabolism, meant that her body disposed of the drug, whatever it was, much more quickly than the thugs had likely anticipated.

"Just get the equipment, time is short," she overheard voices say. "Is the girl ready to be moved?"

I know those voices, she thought to herself. *I've heard them before.*

"Yeah, she's right here." Archer heard a tap, and she consciously realized she was in a wooden box. "She's been out since we left."

"Good. Transfer the cargo, and then we'll hand her over during the last exchange." *Hmmph*, she overheard him grunt.

She heard footsteps walk away, and more voices in the background. And then silence.

Archer was in a half-fetal position on her side. She pushed down with her legs, but the crate she was in was not long enough to accommodate her lengthy frame. She pushed downward harder in an attempt to break the side, but it was too strong to crack open. She was able to reposition her upper body facing upward, and she pushed on the top of the crate, but it too would not budge. She noticed a low light shine through the narrow seams of the wooden planks and through a few makeshift air holes in the box. She tried to look through one of the openings, but she could only make out shadows. It was nighttime, and she was apparently outside because she could hear the soft rustling of the wind in the trees and the flow of air through the seams of the crate on her exposed skin. And was that the sound of the surf in the distance?

She thought a moment. Everything was coming back to her. She remembered running to the *koban*, meeting with the cop, putting on the police officer's dark-blue jumpsuit that she was still wearing...trying to escape from those thugs and then being hit from behind…by the cop himself! *So he was in on it too, just as I thought…* She moved her head and neck around slowly, gingerly. They were less sore than before. Perhaps her body had time to recover a bit while she was out. She had enough room to move her arm, and she massaged her neck further.

Archer turned her attention to her surroundings. The voices had come from next to the box, and they walked away immediately after they stopped talking. That means they were standing. Kensuke, who she recognized by voice now, had tapped the box with his hand. That means the box was about waist-high. It also meant the box holding her was on the edge of something, since he was standing next to it. Perhaps a flatbed truck, she thought. And she could make out shadows in the distance as she looked into the darkness, toward the surf, so nothing was obstructing her view out into the distance.

She looked back toward the light. It was hung above the crate, from the top of a pole or perhaps the cab of the front of the truck, she could not tell. She could barely make out the contours of what seemed to be another crate next to hers, similar to the one she was in. It reminded her of something, of another time...

Her strength was returning. She tried to push on the lid of the box a little harder now, first with just her hands and then with the side of her leg as much as possible. She heard some creaking in the wooden planks and she felt a little movement, but it did not give way. She then tried pushing with her hands on one end of the box and her feet on the other, and again there was some creaking but no real movement.

She then tried to push outward on either side, but nothing. She tried to roll onto her belly to push up with her back and down with both her arms and legs. She paid little attention at first to the movement of the box as she did so, focused as she was on positioning herself to push against the sides. She strained and grunted softly, but nothing.

Ouch! She almost cried out. *A splinter.* She felt around the inside of the box, now conscious of how coarse and splintered the wood was. She picked the small piece of wood out of her palm, and rolled back onto her side. She started to feel a panicked desperation creep into her chest and she suddenly could not breathe. She hit on the sides of the box harder and harder out of fear. She began to sob silently, tapping again lightly on the side of the crate and then harder and harder.

She forced herself to stop, realizing she was close to uncontrolled panic. Archer closed her eyes and began to take deeper breaths. She allowed herself to feel the heaviness of her body where it lay. First she felt her feet, lying still, and then her legs. Then she felt her hips and her midsection, and then her chest. She felt her shoulder lying in still repose, and then her arm stretched out in front of her body as she began to concentrate on the heaviness of her head lying there.

As she lay there collecting her emotions, Archer had a sudden flash of memory. She remembered opening a crate very similar to this one, several years ago, and finding...a weapons cache. Her team had interdicted a weapons transfer in Afghanistan to the Taliban from...*North Korea?* Yes, small arms, AKs mainly, rocket-fired grenades, and...ground-to-air missiles... Yes, they were in exactly the same kind of container as this one.

She felt a sudden surge in energy again, a need to get out of the container not just because of her sense of claustrophobia or to escape from this gang of organized criminals, but because she knew now where she was being transported to. And then she remembered: The box had moved slightly when she rolled. It was not secured to whatever it was lying on, and moreover, she was at the edge of it. Perhaps there was a low wall or barrier between her and the ground, but perhaps not. If she could shimmy the crate to the edge and then cause it it to fall down to the ground, the force might loosen the planks enough so that she could break open the box. The movement might attract attention, but it seemed like no one was around now so she had a small window of opportunity.

She forced her body into the side of the box, rolling into the side and then back again with the portions that could roll. Again, back gently, and then forcefully into the other side. The box moved a little bit each time. Again and again, the box inched forward with each roll. She began to sense that she was at the edge, and that perhaps the box was starting to creep over the edge now... Again and again...*almost...there...*

"Ok, get the final boxes now...!" She heard in the distance. She tried once again, but then noticed some movement in the shadows approaching her position.

They must not have noticed the movement of the crate in the darkness, because they began to pick it up as if nothing had happened.

One picked up the section with her feet, and then the other began to pick up the section with her head. *Huunnnph,* he groaned. "*Omoi,*" he said under his breath. "Heavy. Hey, take it slow down the rocky steps, will ya?" the guy asked his partner.

"I've been taking it easy on you all night," the other murmured. "You getting a little old for this work, huh?"

"Shut up, it's slippery out here..." the other man responded, the strain now audible in his voice as he held onto the crate.

Archer didn't recognize these voices, but it didn't matter. She could hear the surf more clearly now. She only had a few moments before she was transitioned to...the boat she heard the men talking about before? She had to act now...

She could try rocking back and forth to make them lose their grip, but that wasn't likely... She looked upward toward the man carrying her, and then looked down along the corners where she could see his hands holding the crate through the seams. Maybe if...

She felt along the boards, and then felt a piece. No, this one was too short. But how about this one? She pulled a long, slender piece of wood from the craggily plank, and then another one. *Yes, these might do…*

She rolled over.

"Hey, watch it, keep a grip on it now…"

"You too, you're swinging this thing too much…" responded the other.

She positioned herself so she could see both corners of the crate. She held the long, slender pieces of wood along the seams at each side. She then poked one through the seam, gouging the man deep in his wrist.

"Oooowwwww!" cried the man holding up the portion of the box holding her head and torso. He instinctively let go but then caught the falling portion of the box with his knee. He shook his hand. "What the hell…?"

"Hey, why'd you stop…?" the other man said.

Before he could respond, Archer stuck the other piece of wood through the seam next to his other hand, again deep in his wrist.

"Aaaahhhh!" he cried this time, not just letting go with his other hand but jumping back half in fear of whatever it was that was pricking him. "Snake!

Archer rolled inside the crate to cause the man to lose his last grip on it, and then she braced herself for the fall. She hit the ground and heard a *crack* in the wood, and then another as the bottom half of the crate fell to the rocky ground below too. The other man could not hold up his end when his partner jumped back and she rolled suddenly.

Now was her chance. She pushed with her arms over her head as she pushed with her legs downward. The ends separated. She then pushed herself up on her arms and legs, causing the top to crack and groan. She pushed harder and harder until, at last, *snap!* The top gave way, and she stood up, first on her knees to look around, and then onto her feet.

"What the…?" said the man in front of her. He was rubbing his wrists, so she knew that he was the one she poked. He looked like he was seeing a body rise from the dead.

"Hey! You! Get back here!" His partner stammered, although he clearly did not want to chase down this newly emerged *oni* devil in front of them.

She whipped around to look at him, and then she looked up the hill they had come part-way down. There was one of several trucks, and then open space beyond. She began to run.

"Hey!" he yelled again as she ran off, and finally he set off after her. She dared not turn around, because she did not want the motion to slow her down. "*Hey, that's her! Damn it, get her!*" she heard from the pier.

She cleared the top of the hill and saw an open field ahead of her. A line of trees was visible in the distance. There were no houses or buildings around. They were somewhere in the country along the shore. She continued running to the trees, where she could perhaps disappear.

"*Fuck her, launch the boat without her, we have a schedule to keep…*" she heard in the background behind her. "*I'll take care of her myself!*"

Within seconds, she heard it. What sounded like firecrackers popping behind her followed closely by cracks in the air and ground around her. Single blades of tall grass shuddered as bullets passed through them next to Archer. *Shit, they're firing at me now!*

Archer made it to the tree line and ducked for cover behind a slim tree. More cracks as several bullets rustled through the bamboo next to her. One bamboo cracked when struck by a bullet, another snapped and fell over. She saw several men running in her direction. She turned and began running up the steep incline. That slowed her escape considerably, however, so she began to run at an angle to the incline, moving almost perpendicular to it. Her lungs burned from the sudden anaerobic need for oxygen. Her legs ached.

"*Ahhh!*" she cried as a bullet nicked her right shoulder. She felt the area as she continued to run. She felt a piece of skin dangle from an indentation, and a warm oozy substance trickled from the area. *Just a flesh wound, I hope...*she thought to herself as she continued to run through the wooded area.

She passed a thick clump of bushes and then headed directly up the steep incline. She used her left hand to steady herself as she climbed and avoided using her right arm in order to protect the shoulder wound from any further aggravation.

Archer cleared the ridge and stepped over a mass of tall weeds at the edge of the woods onto an unpaved road. She placed her hands on her knees to catch her breath, and a bead of sweat trickled from her temple. Her long, dark hair hung around her down-turned face in several matted clumps. She looked first one way along the narrow road, then the other. It was framed on one side by the woods she just cleared, and by another wooded cliff on the other, this one steeper than the one behind her. After summoning more strength following one last, deep breath, she began to run along the side of the road at a brisk pace, barely able to see.

The forest surrounding the road had grown quiet. Archer heard the pounding of her feet on the gravelly road, and nothing else. After rounding a sharp bend several hundred meters down the road, she entered another clearing and saw the outline of a dilapidated, two-story building in the distance. There were no lights on and no cars in its small and weed-infested parking lot, but she ran toward it hoping to find help of some kind.

She reached it at last. Although it still appeared somewhat modern and serviceable, it had clearly been abandoned years ago. It looked like a small warehouse of some sort. She pushed on the door, but it was locked. She pushed on another door, and it too was locked. She looked through the window and then tried to push it open, but it did not budge. She turned to look down the road, but saw nothing. She looked down on the ground, a saw a collection of rocks at the edge of what was once a parking area. She picked one up and threw it into the window. The sudden *crack* pierced the prevailing silence, propelled by a soft wind through the surrounding forest. She picked up another one to clear the remaining shards of glass from the window frame, and she climbed through the window.

She saw a chair at the other side of the small office and sat for a moment, panting. Her arms hung loosely along the sides of the chair as she flopped back in the seat. She cleared her matted hair from her forehead and eyes with her left hand, and then rested for another moment as she watched the window. She heard and saw nothing. She leaned forward to open up her diaphragm to take deeper breaths, and she looked around the room. There were two desks, one with an old-style rotary phone on it. She went to it and lifted up the receiver, but there was no dial tone. She dropped the receiver onto the desk, and began to rummage through the drawers. Some loose paper was all that she found. She turned to the door at the other end of the office, and tried to turn the knob. It was locked, but from this side. She turned the latch, and then walked through.

The room was almost completely dark, but she could tell it was larger than the other. She let her eyes adjust to the deeper darkness than the star-lit evening outside, and she felt she could make out shadows but that was all. The air was still and almost unnaturally cool. She began to feel her way through the room along the wall.

Then she heard something. The unmistakable sound of a vehicle's tires rolling slowly on the gravel. Almost imperceptible at first, the sound drew closer. She looked toward the door, but she did not see any indication of a headlight shining through the windows or doors of the building, or of any other lights.

They had arrived.

She stepped back to close the door, taking care not to create any noise, and she then felt her way forward more frantically now. She moved farther than she had before, with her left hand on the wall and her right feeling for any obstructions in front of her. There was nothing. But then she felt something on the wall with her left had. A light switch? No. Some sort of switch to open a garage door? No. She felt its outline. It was a metal case protruding less than an inch from the wall. It was slightly larger than a regular light switch. There was some sort of covering over it. She felt along the front of the case, and then she realized. It was a fire alarm. She lifted the cover from the bottom, and felt a lever in the middle. If she pulled it, the fire alarm would surely scare off Kano's thugs, and the fire department would discover her there. They surely would not be on Kano's payroll, why would they be?

She pulled it, but nothing happened. No alarm sounded. She returned the lever to its original position and pulled again, this time harder. Nothing. She fell back into the wall in disappointment, wondering what to do next.

As she sat, the light from a flashlight swept the office space she had just left. Light washed from under the door connecting the space with the larger warehouse, and it also highlighted shadows on a tinted window next to the door that she had not noticed until now. It cast just enough light into the room she was in so she could make out her surroundings. Archer sat along the far wall facing several tall shelves, beyond which was an open space with two long tables running the length of the room. The corrugated ceiling was two stories above, and a metal I-beam hung from metal scaffolding above that ran the length of the room from the closed garage door at one end to the far wall where Archer sat. It would have been used to hoist heavy objects from any waiting vehicle just outside the back of the warehouse to the worktables, but now it was rusting from disuse.

Archer saw a number of large hooks on the shelves in front of her. She surmised that the space had once been used to process freshly caught fish, with the large hooks used to pull and lift nets full of fish and squid, or large fish themselves. The hooks and other tools were covered with dust and cobwebs and portions of the metal had rusted. Archer grabbed the closest large hook by the handle that formed a "T" at the end, perpendicular to the hook that jutted out from the bottom. She held it up to examine the tip, which was sharp despite its rusting condition.

She crouched low to move to the other end of the room. Without thinking, she steadied herself with her free right hand, but she felt a sudden pain in her right shoulder. She switched to her left hand to steady herself and waddled to the far side of the room as it grew dark again, around the shelving units to the end of the workbench, where she continued to crouch.

The men had turned off their flashlights before trying the door to the warehouse. Archer heard the door open slowly, and after a few shallow footsteps, one of the men turned on the flashlight again. Archer looked away from the piercing light to keep her night vision intact, while trying to follow the movement with her peripheral vision. A figure had entered the room, she could tell from the corner of her eyes, and another followed. She could not tell if there was a third.

The figures crept slowly through the room, casting about with their flashlight. So far the angle of the workbench had concealed her figure, but she was not sure how much longer she could remain in place and unnoticed. She slowly moved at the far end of the workbench, still crouching low, as the figures moved along the far wall where she had sat just seconds ago.

Archer looked down at a cardboard box on the lower shelf of the workbench. A wooden handle stuck out, and she grabbed it. It was a hammer, even more rusted that the tools on the other end of the room. She stuck the hook through the belt loop in the back of her pants, and held the hammer in her left hand. She continued to come around the bench to the middle of the room as the figures reached the far corner. They stopped, shone their flashlight back to the middle of the room over the table above her, and then they began to move again.

"Wait, what's that?" one whispered to the other, pointing to the floor. The beam from the flashlight then repositioned downward. "Dark spots, almost like…"

Archer saw one of the men kneel down to the floor to inspect the spot. *Shit, my blood,* she realized suddenly. *I have to get out of here…*

"Blood," said the other man. "She's here," he declared as he stood up and rushed along the trail to the end of the room.

No time to run, she realized, *especially if they have guns.* As he reached the end of the long workbench and was about to turn the corner toward her, she stood abruptly and charged at him with the hammer. "*Aaaaaaiiiiii!*" she screamed as she swung the hammer at him. She saw that he held the flashlight in his left hand and… *that's my Karambit!* Archer saw as he turned toward her and drew back the Karambit with his other. "*Mother fucker!*" she screamed. She slammed the hammer down onto his right shoulder, causing him to drop the Karambit and collapse in pain. "Aaaahhhhh!" he screamed. She caught a glimpse of the other man in the room as the one in front of her dropped his flashlight to grab his injured shoulder. *Was that Kensuke?* she wondered.

She then looked down at the man as he crumpled in front of her to find the weapon he had stolen from her, but the tumbling flashlight's narrow and piercing beam flashed Archer in the eyes when it hit the ground. A large white light was now burned on her retinas, obscuring most of her vision. She kicked in front of her to make sure he stayed down, and she made direct contact with the thug's face despite her now half-blind state.

Archer knew another person had been directly behind him, and she thrashed in that direction but she could not see where he might have retreated to. She shook her head in a futile attempt to lessen the intensity of the white spot seared in her eyes, but it remained. She looked first at one corner of the room, then at the other, to give her peripheral vision a chance to catch any movement.

Archer tried to shut out the injured man's angry cries that filled the room. He was upset and trying to pull himself up to attack her again, but as long as he kept shouting epithets at her she knew where he was. The other one was silent, however. She glanced back and forth to catch any movement of the other man. Nothing.

Then an arm came crashing down on her from her left, hitting her on her forearm and causing her to drop the hammer. Despite the sudden pain she lowered herself instinctively, as another blow was sure to follow. It did, but it glanced off the top of her head as she spun around and backed away. Protecting her right arm, she flung her left fist around as she spun again, making contact with the man's upper chest. She now knew exactly where he was, and she threw a right roundhouse kick into his thigh, low enough to be sure to make contact. She then pulled her leg in to her body and snapped it back at him again with a sidekick, making contact with his shoulder as he fell. She only heard a muffled "ummph" as he fell back into the side of the bench, hitting the side of his head on his way down.

She had then realized the screams from the other thug on the ground behind her had stopped when a punch landed on her right shoulder where her wound was exposed. Her shoulder seared in pain and she grabbed it and winced. She tried not to scream this time, but as she attempted to collect herself the man grabbed her neck with both hands. He pushed her back into the corrugated metal garage door behind her, and he began to choke her.

"*Ucckkkhhhh*" was all she could muster as his grip tightened. She saw stars dance around the white blob that remained burned on her retina and prevented her from seeing her attacker directly. She tried in vain to push him away. She felt a sudden stab at her back as he pushed on her, and she remembered through the encroaching fog that she had the large hook at her back. She reached for it with her left hand, pulled at it, but it would not come loose. She pulled again, jutting her hips forward both to give herself some space and in a vain attempt to push her attacker away, but nothing. He then pushed his body into hers as he tried to finish her. Archer's arm was thrust back so that her hand slid from the handle of the hook to the shaft. But with the new grip, she was able to slide it out of her belt loop. She dropped her hand from behind her, using the weight of the hook as momentum to swing it down and around the back of the man chocking her. She pulled the hook into his kidney and jerked sideways to his spine.

"*Waaahhhh!*" he yelled as he grabbed his side.

Archer fell from his grip, and began to half-cough, half-gag as she took her first breaths. She fell to her knees and her left forearm, her right arm still stinging from the blow. Her back arced upward as she coughed several times and drool trickled from her mouth.

She sensed movement, and she looked over to the other man just in time to see him standing over her and pulling his leg back. She barely had time to roll out of the way of his oncoming kick. She rolled again as he tried to stomp on her with the same leg. She lunged for the hook, lying in the darkness by the door by her other assailant who was lying in a writhing heap on the ground. She grabbed it and swung along the floor, making contact with his ankle. He lost his balance and yelped as he fell to the ground.

Archer rose to her knees and then stood as best she could, and saw that he was rolling over to stand up again. She almost fell into his body, plunging the hook downward into his lower hip.

"Aaaahhhh!" they both yelled in unison, he from pain and she to summon the last energy from her depleted body.

Just as he pushed himself away from her, she stumbled backwards into the wall and slid down to the floor. The room started to grow darker again. She saw stars dance in her eyes, first at the edges and then they encroached on the white blob in her eyes, which by now had started to dissipate. She started to hear a high-pitched ring in her ears, and she could not tell if the room was growing darker, or lighter...

CHAPTER 40 – CONTACT APPROACHING

Admiral Okada entered the Combat Information Center on the Kaga and immediately began to examine the course of the missile boat. Instead of returning to his Flag Information Center below, Okada wanted to be in the CIC or the adjacent bridge to be closer to the action and to engage with his senior officers directly, his preferred method of leadership.

"Perhaps Colonel Bradley was right," Okada muttered to himself upon looking through the latest updates. "Maybe our F-35s attracted more attention to the Kaga." He turned to his flight operations officer, the Kaga's "air boss." "Let's get a helo-drone up to see what it is," Admiral Okada ordered. "It's a single combatant, reconnaissance perhaps, but probably armed with anti-ship missiles. More are sure to follow. We can't take a chance on this one."

"Yessir," the air boss replied. Within moments of the order being passed to crew on the deck below, a Japanese helo-drone was rolled to the far end of the deck of the Kaga, and it lifted off into the stormy weather toward the target. Its infra-red and multi-spectrum video and other signals-gathering sensors immediately began to relay information back to the Kaga via a secure communications link.

"What's the status of our F-35s?" Okada asked the air boss.

"The F-35 flight is returning as you ordered and on their final approach now," the Kaga's air boss said. "The second flight is refueled and standing by."

"Once the first flight has landed, secure them and launch the second patrol flight of F-35s. Make sure they are armed with joint direct attack munitions. I want them available in case that missile boat continues its approach. If necessary, we can laze the missile boat from the helo-drone for targeting with the F-35s' JDAMs."

"Yessir."

"Let's update Defense HQ about the missile boat, too," Okada said, turning to the comms officer. "Let them know we've secured most of the crew, but some members of Blades One and Four remain unaccounted for. Inform them that we're monitoring an approaching North Korean vessel as well."

"Yessir," the comms officers replied. Then he turned back to the admiral. "Sir, we just received orders to return to Maizuru base, immediately."

Admiral Okada looked onto the deck of the Kaga as rain began to fall. The first F-35 had just landed. He nodded at the comms officer once, without looking at him. "Send the update on the approaching missile boat, and the status of Blades One and Four," Okada repeated, without responding directly to the order.

"Yessir," the officer replied.

"Plot a course back to Maizuru base," Okada replied, looking into the rain clouds outside the bridge. "But stay on station for now."

●　●　●

On the other side of the Korean peninsula, a Japanese E-767 AWACS flew in international airspace over the East China Sea due north of the Ryukyu island chain that stretched from Japan's Kyushu island to Taiwan. The AWACS was over 400 miles from the Kaga, engaged in a separate but equally important mission. A bright red circle adorned both sides of its fuselage. Operators onboard were patched into the newly upgraded FPS-7 Fixed Air Defense Radar system, with one site on the remote Yonaguni island due south of their location that peered deep into North Korean territory. An E-2C flew ahead of the AWACS, watching and listening for other signals of the scheduled launch from the Saeho Space Launch Facility in northwest North Korea.

"Launch sequence has commenced," the Air Self Defense officer declared over the secure communications network, drawing from the multiple sensors. "Hawk One, prepare ascent. Three, two, one. Launch ascent," he ordered.

"Roger," the pilot replied. "Beginning ascent."

Hawk One increased altitude from 10,000 to 15,000 meters, and Hawk Two followed three seconds behind. They leveled off, turned due north, and increased speed. The F-15Js reached Mach 4, and then pulled up at a sharp 45-degree angle, their afterburners now fully engaged.

Each F-15J carried two modified missiles under their wings. They closely resembled the SM-3s carried on Aegis destroyers, but these had only two stages instead of the three- or four-stage missiles carried by their maritime cousins. With the F-15J as the transport vehicle, the missiles did not need a booster stage, and they were thus lighter and shorter, and launchable from an air-based platform. In theory at least. Japan had yet to conduct a live-fire test of the modified system until now.

Hawk One and Hawk Two continued to climb at a high rate of speed, a function of both their afterburners as well as the momentum they had achieved in their rate of speed flying at a level altitude prior to ascent. The North Korean rocket, however, would surpass this altitude in mere seconds once launched, so it was imperative the much slower F-15s achieved the necessary altitude and trajectory to match that of the expected launch trajectory of the rocket to destroy it.

"Final countdown to lift-off," the officer intoned. "Three, two, one...Space launch vehicle has successfully achieved lift-off. Prepare to engage."

"Roger," Atsuko Kajiwara, the lead pilot, said. She breathed deeply from her diaphragm as she fought against the increased g-force. "Approaching 24,000 meters now," she reported.

"Successful first stage separation. Rocket continues to climb," the operator said from the AWACS. "Free to engage in five, four, three, two, one. Engage."

Kajiwara's Hawk One fired the first of its two modified SM-3s, and then the second. Kajiwara then veered left and began to descend in the pre-coordinated move. Hawk Two trailed Hawk One by a matter of seconds.

"Hawk Two, free to engage in five, four, three, two, one. Engage."

Hawk Two launched its first and then the second of its two SM-3s. It then began its rapid descent, behind Hawk One.

Hawk One's first missile flew right of the rocket. The proximity fuse in the second fired behind the rocket, doing no damage. The AWACS operator continued to watch.

Seconds later, the third made contact but did not explode, causing the rocket to wobble out of control. Just as it plateaued, the fourth made a direct hit.

"Target destroyed, target destroyed," the operator said, his even voice hiding his glee at the success of the mission.

The Hawk One and Hawk Two pilots breathed easier now as as they descended, no longer fighting the g-forces of their climb and following the successful maiden engagement of the target. Kajiwara looked at her comrade flying Hawk Two, and raised her thumb in congratulations. *Good job*, she indicated as they began their return to base in Naha, Okinawa.

•   •   •

Chiefs Sato and Taguchi descended to the sixth deck of the Kaga, one deck below the hangar, and entered the main medical ward to check on their injured comrades. They wanted to ensure all their crew and members of the combat units, both the Japanese and the

Americans, were accounted for. The ship was already at general quarters, and with the arrival of multiple wounded personnel, there was significant commotion in the med ward. They stopped a passing nurse for any information on their comrades.

"Over there," she pointed and then rushed for additional medical supplies.

They looked in the direction she pointed, and saw a closed portal that was labeled "intensive care." They approached to look in through the small round window, and they saw Lieutenant Watanabe talking to a doctor on the other side. As if sensing that he was being looked at, Watanabe turned his steady gaze from the doctor toward them through the window. He motioned to the doctor that he needed to talk to them. The doctor nodded and then began examining a chart one of the nurses handed him.

"Sir, what is the status of the team members?" Taguchi asked after Watanabe stepped through the door.

"Two of the crew, including the pilot from Blade Two, are in surgery now," Watanabe said somberly, "and two others are being treated for light injuries. What of Blade One? What's the status of that crew?"

"Sir, we were able to successfully rescue several crew members from Blade One, who are being treated for injuries," Sato reported, pointing to several doctors and nurses surrounding sergeants Johnston and Nicholson lying on adjacent examination tables. "Several broken bones, ribs, contusions. It was challenging getting them into the UH-60, but we were able to stabilize them once on board."

They heard the sudden cries of a child from another corner of the room. They looked over and saw a boy crumpled on an examination table. He uttered something through his tears, but they could not understand what. He writhed on the table and shrieked, less from pain and more from fear of the new environment and the strangers all around him. They saw Colonel Bradley and what seemed to be the boy's father standing next to him trying to soothe him. The father looked at the two nurses around him, asked a question and then repeated in broken English, "Where is my wife?"

"That is the North Korean defector and his son," Taguchi told Sato. "The father kept asking about his wife, and his son cried all the way here. It was terrible."

"Calm down, Mr. Han, they are on their way," they heard Colonel Bradley say to Han. "They are just in another helicopter..." Bradley was so focused on the Korean and his boy that he did not see Watanabe, Taguchi or Sato.

As the scene unfolded, Watanabe turned to Taguchi and Sato. "What of the others, Shimada, Suzuki, the Americans?" Lieutenant Watanabe asked. "They had the wife, right? Where are they now?"

Chiefs Sato and Taguchi looked at each other. "Did you tell Admiral Okada that they're returning on the commandeered missile boat?" Taguchi asked Sato.

"No, I came directly here from the deck with you, to check on the team..." Sato said in reply. He did not mention, nor did he need to mention, the fight that took place on the deck.

"We better get up to the bridge, to inform the admiral that the rest of the team is coming on a North Korean missile boat!"

"*Eehhh...?*" Watanabe said in surprise. "What? On a *North Korean* missile boat?"

"*Shitsurei shimasu,*" Taguchi and Sato said perfunctorily in unison to excuse themselves, and they rushed out of the medical ward. Watanabe hurried after them.

●　　●　　●

"We've established visual contact," the helo-drone pilot said from his station in the Kaga's CIC. "It's difficult to hold the drone steady in this weather, though. It keeps getting blown around with sudden gusts of wind."

"Understood. Trying to laser-designate the missile boat now," the copilot said. "The rain is dispersing the beam from this distance. Try to get closer, will you?"

"I'll see what I can do..." The image of the boat increased in size on several monitors. "Ok, try again now," the drone pilot said.

"Got it," the co-pilot said, pointing at the designator visible in one of the monitors, "but unless you can hold the drone steady the laser will drift off-target."

"Understood, doing my best," the pilot said, fighting the controls.

The air boss stood behind them. He motioned to his comms officer. "Contact the F-35 pilots, tell them to target it and take it out."

"Roger," the officer replied. He relayed the orders to the pilots.

The helo-drone pilot fought the controls to hold the drone steady despite the wind and rain. The laser could be seen ranging wildly along the Komar missile boat in the monitor, first appearing on its bow, then on its engine, and back again. "Hold it steady, hold it steady!" the air boss ordered the pilots. The co-pilot wiped a bead of sweat from his upper lip. A sudden gust of wind jostled the drone, causing the laser designator to slip several meters from the boat.

"The lead F-35 pilot released his first JDAM," the comms officer announced behind the helo-drone pilot station.

•　•　•

"So, you're sure that the Kaga will know it's us coming toward them?" Solberg asked again, incredulous. "I mean, we're on a North Korean missile boat that's locked and loaded to sink ships like the Kaga. I don't think they'd take kindly to us showing up unannounced..."

"Chief Sato will surely have informed the Kaga that we took the Komar-class missile boat in order to rescue the remaining crew of Blade One and Marine One," Mac replied, keeping his gaze steady on the angry waters in front of him. He wiped away the rain from his face.

"Even so, as we get closer we should ensure that we aren't seen as a hostile boat," McCarty interjected. "We're on a North Korean ship, after all, and even if the Kaga knows it's us, other ships in the task force might not. Maybe we should slow down a bit so they don't think we're on an attack run."

"Understood," Mac nodded once and began to throttle back the komar.

McCarty looked up into the black and rainy sky. "I hope Colonel Bradley has that Gray Eagle watching out for us, too..."

"And even if they do know it is us, how do we make contact with the Kaga? The communications console is completely destroyed," Shimada wondered aloud, pointing to the hole blasted in the area where the radio would normally be.

"We can only hope they make contact with us first, fly a helo to us, or maybe a boat to help us transfer the injured to get medical treatment," Solberg said.

Boom! An explosion half-a-dozen meters from the port bow rocked the boat.

Shimada and Suzuki immediately recognized the explosion as a JDAM joint direct attack munition. They had practiced amphibious landings while their ASDF brethren practiced mock JDAM attacks on a near-by airfield many times. "They're firing on us! They don't know it's us!" Shimada yelled as a wave of water from the explosion rained down on them.

"Full reverse! You two get out on the deck to wave them down," McCarty yelled at Solberg and Shimada, "and Mac, turn this thing around to show we're not on an attack course."

Shimada and Solberg stepped onto the open deck and started waving in the rain, looking into the darkness of the stormy sky above. They did not know where to look or wave, so they turned slowly while trying to keep his footing as the boat came to a halt and turned in the water.

Boom! Another JDAM landed in the boat's path, where they would have been had they not taken evasive action.

McCarty joined Shimada on the deck, waving furiously to anyone who might see them. "There is probably an aircraft or drone of some sort observing us, that's standard procedure in targeting an enemy vessel like this..." he said hopefully. The rain continued to pour down on the Japanese and American soldiers.

"There, what's that!" Shimada shouted. He pointed at what he thought might be a small drone in the sky peering down at them. "Wave to that!"

• • •

"The crew has suddenly come out on deck, it looks like," the helo-drone operator said. "They seem to have come to a complete stop, too."

"What are they doing?" the co-pilot asked in turn. "Several crew members are waving into the sky. What's that mean?"

"Do they want to surrender? Are they defecting too?" the air boss asked as he leaned forward to peer at the monitors. "We'll have to get guidance from Ichigaya if that's the case," the air boss added, referring to the location of the Ministry of Defense Headquarters in Tokyo. "This is getting crazy..." The air boss stood up straight again and cocked his head slightly, sucking in air as he did so.

"Whatever it is, should we inform the admiral?" asked the comms officer, who had lingered nearby to watch the action.

"Yes, go inform the admiral," the air boss responded.

The comms officer went to the main bridge where Admiral Okada stood looking over navigation charts. "Sir, the missile boat has come to a complete stop..."

"Haven't our F-35s engaged it already?" Okada asked testily. He wanted to neutralize any remaining, dangerous units between his flotilla and the crash site to send one last search crew before returning to Maizuru base as ordered.

"No, sir, the first two JDAMs just missed the target."

"Just missed?" Okada responded, looking now directly at the officer. "What is the problem, why isn't it destroyed yet?" he demanded.

"The F-35s are coming around for another run, but sir, several members of the missile boat crew are on the deck, waving," he added.

"Waving? What does that mean?"

"We're unsure, sir, but the..."

"Sir, sir!" Chiefs Sato and Taguchi yelled in unison as they tried to force their way onto the bridge. The ship was in general quarters, so their presence on the bridge was technically forbidden.

"Let them on!" the Admiral bellowed, recognizing the officers. "What is it!" he yelled at them before they could approach.

"Sir," they said, saluting the Admiral, "some of our team members commandeered a North Korean missile boat to help rescue crew members who had crashed into the ocean near the original contact point. They're on their way here now!"

"Those are our boys?!" the Admiral yelled. "Why didn't you tell me on the deck!" The admiral pounded on the table and glared at them. He did not wait for an answer. "Tell our F-35s to stand down, immediately!" he shouted at the comms officer.

The comms officer, gasping in surprise, turned to run to the CIC to inform the air boss and the drone pilots.

•   •   •

"Target in range," the pilot said, his finger about to release the third JDAM. *We won't miss the North Korean adversary this time,* he declared to himself resolutely.

"*This is the Kaga, stand down, repeat, stand down!*"

What? "Kaga, say again?" the lead pilot demanded, his finger itching to release the JDAM.

"*Repeat, stand down! Those are Japanese and U.S. forces on that boat! Stand down!*"

The pilot banked to the left to look down at the boat, the weather clearing around it. The rain had eased, and he could see that the boat was now adrift at sea.

"*Ryokai,*" the pilot said. "Understood. Will stay on station until you can send a recovery team." He placed his weapons on safe and began a combat air patrol over the Komar-class boat.

•   •   •

"Well, what are you waiting for?" Okada asked Sato and Taguchi. "Go get your men!"

"Hai!" both pilots said while standing at attention. They bowed, turned in unison, and then ran to the exit to prep their helicopters, which had already been refueled and prepped for additional action.

CHAPTER 41 – THE LAST STAND

Archer jerked forward suddenly and shook her head several times. Did she pass out? Was she out for a while, or just a few minutes? The man on the ground to her side had stopped squirming, but she did not know where the other one was. She could not remember exactly where he went down.

She crawled over to the man on the ground, and tapped his pockets, first his right then his left. Archer did not know if he was dead, or merely passed out. She did not care. She felt what she was looking for, and then retrieved it. His cell phone.

She flicked it open, and then dialed the number from memory.

Bzzzt. Bzzzt. Bzzzt. It rang five times, and then came a business-like response. "*Hai.* Who is this?"

"Nishi, it's me, Trinh, Trinh Archer."

"Aa-chaa-San? Where have you been? I've been worried about you!"

"I...I was taken, in a car chase near...Kawasaki, I think, but I'm somewhere else now...not sure..."

"You do not know where you are? Can you describe anything? Signs, landmarks, anything?" Nishi asked in a rushed tone.

"No, it's in the countryside, along the coast, just a forested area..." Archer said slowly, attempting to remember anything that stood out in her surroundings.

"Ok, hold on, do not hang up, I'm going to have this call traced to the nearest cell tower..."

Archer heard some muffled voices as Nishi covered the receiver to order one of his underlings to trace the call.

"Ok, Archer, are you there?" Nishi asked, returning to the receiver. "We're working on tracing the signal now. Keep this line open for another minute, then you hang up and call local police, ok? 119..."

"Yes, certainly, Nishi," Archer said languidly. She was still dazed from the fight, but she was now letting herself relax a little now that she had made contact with someone she knew and trusted. She waited a few more seconds, and then hung up.

She looked at the phone. *I need to call Maddy, too,* she thought to herself. She thought back through the events of the evening so she could more clearly describe the situation... *Back of a truck, in a crate, men loading boxes and crates at a small dock, boxes, crates...*

Shit, crates! she suddenly realized. *There were more crates than just the one I was in...were there more women in those? More weapons? More shoulder-fired missiles? Where were they being shipped to...?* Trinh sat forward. *I have to stop that shipment, now...!*

She lunged forward and reached to the man on the ground again. She felt keys in his pocket and took them. She looked over to the other side of the workbench, and saw her Karambit. Kensuke must have dropped it, but he was nowhere to be seen. *No time to think of him now,* she realized. She retrieved the knife and rushed from the building to the small truck parked in front.

● ● ●

"Inspector Nishi, here are the results of that trace you requested."

Nishi examined the report, and the map. "Wait, are you sure this is correct?" he asked.

"Yessir, we double-checked."

"This is just up the coast from here, and it's..." Nishi looked up and then over at another assistant. "Oi, get me that report on the suspicious cell phone locations!" he yelled.

The assistant looked back at Nishi, annoyed to be called over so soon after being berated. He slowly retrieved the map from one of several folders he held. "Here you are," he said laconically and went back to his other work without sticking around to hear why Nishi needed the map again.

Nishi compared the two maps. "*They're at the same location, at the same time*," he mumbled to himself. "Oi! Get me the number for the local police in this town...here," he ordered a third assistant. "I think this is where the suspects might be..."

•   •   •

Archer parked the Suzuki mini-truck at the corner in the road several hundred meters from the entrance to the pier facilities. She got out and cut through the tree line and hugged a series of large bushes on her approach to the coast, out of sight of the pier. Once there, she cut along the coast toward the pier to avoid any guards.

She saw two young men standing at the end of the pier. They were smoking and talking in a relaxed but guarded manner with each other, apparently waiting for the boat to return from the ex-change. They turned to look to the end of the pier, but then turned back to each other to continue their conversation.

Archer too looked down to the end of the pier, and she saw what she needed: A five-meter speedboat that featured two outboard en-gines, not unlike the one that rammed and killed the unsuspecting Michiharu and his daughter Ayako days ago. It's probably a spare for the smuggling operation, she thought.

Instead of walking along the coast to the pier to get to it, she took off her slippers and entered the water. It was cold, but not dangerously so. She swam to the other boat lashed at the end of the pier. She swam on her left side and reached forward with her left arm for most of the swim, which slowed her down.

While Kano's henchmen seemed preoccupied with their conversation, Archer pulled herself up and into the boat. Crouching low, she untied the rope that secured the boat to the pier, and it began to float freely. She looked over the controls to familiarize herself with them, then she looked ahead into the distance to determine the best route. The steering wheel was a shiny metallic silver with a knob on the lower half. She crouched in front of it, grabbed the knob with one hand and started the outboard engines. She began to steer away from the pier by slight turns of the wheel's knob, still crouching low.

"Hey, what're you doing! Get back here!" she heard the two yell in the distance behind her as she pulled away. They began to run down the wooden pier as the boat first drifted, then accelerated from them. They had no way to chase her, because hers was the last boat docked there.

Which way, which way? she wondered as she pushed the throttle forward to gain distance from the shore. A kilometer out, Archer killed the engine, and she let the five-meter boat drift. She looked out to the darkened sea. The clouds overhead, remnants of the typhoon that had passed, lingered over the still-angry sea and obscured the starry sky above. The lapping of waves hitting the bow of her boat and the constant blowing of a breeze from the north were the only sounds she could hear in the stillness. She scanned the horizon for any sign of movement or any sounds of engines.

There, what's that? she wondered to herself as she caught a glimpse of a flicker in her peripheral vision to her left. It was small, just a pin-prick of light, and it came and went. She turned that way, focusing her intense gaze in the direction of the possible sign of activity in the distance. Was it the remnants of the stars she saw in her eyes back in the warehouse? Or were her eyes playing tricks on her as she stared intently into the blackness? Her grip on the throttle tightened, and she reached for the key to start the boat again if she saw another sign.

There, that's it again... She saw the sudden burning of red embers in the distance. *Someone is smoking there in the distance,* she realized. Whoever it was, they had their lights off, and they did not want to be discovered. Archer started the outboard engines and eased into the throttle, turning the boat toward the smoker. She could not tell how far he or they were from her location, or what they were up to. Could they be kids out for a joy-ride? Or another fisherman who had neglected to turn on his lights? She had no way to know, but she wanted to maintain the element of surprise so attempted to approach carefully and quietly.

A break in the thick, low-hanging clouds appeared suddenly, allowing a half-formed moon to peek through near the horizon in the distance. The moon reflected in the cold sea like a mirror. The reflection revealed the outline of a larger boat several hundred meters in front of her, next to a...was that submarine sail? The clouds closed again and the boats almost disappeared again into the darkness, but now she knew what she was looking at and could see the outlines of the vessels as she drew nearer. A couple of men seemed to be loading large items from the surface vessel, which was larger than Archer's and had a cabin, to the submarine, where another couple of men lowered them down into the hull.

The clouds parted again and she saw the men in the boat began to gather what appeared to be rope, winding it up, putting it down onto the deck as some distance emerged between the two vessels... The scene went dark again when the clouds above merged.

They're done with the transfer, Archer realized. *They're about to pull away...* Archer thought back to those crates. Whether human cargo or weapons, she seethed in anger at the implications: Forced prostitution or dead U.S. airmen. Neither was acceptable. *They will not get away this time!* she declared to herself.

She thrust the throttle forward just as the other boat began to speed back to the coast at an oblique angle away from both the submarine and her approach. They were no longer her target, however. She lined up the pointed bow of her boat with the highest point of the mini-submarine, its sail, ahead. The last hatch on the sub's sail slammed shut, she saw. All the crew were below now, and the submarine was set to dive for its stealth return to its base in North Korea.

*Faster, faster...*she thought as she could see waves crest over the hull of the mini-sub as she drew still nearer. Was it diving yet, or was that the wake of the other boat speeding away? She could not tell.

The sail grew steadily larger in size, even as it appeared to lurch forward and start to descend downward into the water. She adjusted her approach, angling the bow forward of the sail. She leaned into the steering wheel, forcing all of her weight forward as if to push the boat ahead. She had only one choice now.

Still wearing the belt from the police uniform she was given at the police *koban*, she pulled it off with one hand and then connected one end to the steering wheel and the other to the throttle stick next to console. Her course now set, she placed a foot on the side of the boat and watched the final approach of the sail dead ahead. She jumped from the side of the boat mere seconds before impact.

The bow of the boat hit the top edge of the sail head-on as the mini-sub was about to submerge completely below the water line. The bow of the boat careened over the sail, crashing head-on into the still partially extended ESM and radar masts on one side and the periscope on the other. The boat's bow lodged under the bulbous ESM equipment at the top of the mast and caused it to snap off. The ESM mast itself bent to the side from the sheer force of the impact. A secondary whip antenna also snapped off the sail. The periscope on the forward portion of the mast, meanwhile, caused the boat to tilt to its side at first as the boat's momentum carried it further over the sail, but then the periscope pierced the side of the boat. The collision bent the periscope, now lodged in the body of the five-meter boat as it came to a stop on the sail. The forward half of the boat had made it over the sail and had landed in the sea on the other side, its body caught by the periscope on one side and the bent ESM mast on the other, causing significant drag as the submarine attempted to gain forward speed. The five-meter boat's outboard engines continued to run at full-throttle, the blades of the screws whirring in the air.

The mini-sub halted its dive with the boat lodged on top, and then partially re-surfaced into a broached position, with only its sail visible above the waterline. The boat's bow sank further into the water, but its back end remained stuck on the periscope. The sub's hatch on the sail opened, and a member of the crew poked his head through the portal to look at the wreckage. While she could not see his face, Archer saw his head and hands gesticulate first at the stuck boat then to someone below in a very agitated way. The crew member pounded the side of the sub angrily, then he disappeared below again but left the hatch open.

Archer swam to the sail, which was less than a dozen meters away. The man re-appeared and climbed out just as she reached the side of the sail, the top of which was a half-meter above the waterline. She could tell that he was cursing under his breath, but he was otherwise completely occupied with the task at hand: He needed to get the five-meter boat off the periscope and sail so they could get underway.

He crouched on the sail and started to pry the boat off the periscope with a long crowbar. As he did so, she slithered halfway onto the edge of the sail forward of the hatch. The waves lapping against the mast concealed any noise she made. She grabbed her Karambit, and slashed at his back as he crouched. He stood suddenly, so that her Karambit sliced into his Achilles' tendon. His ankle-high leather shoes prevented the knife from penetrating deeply, but he yelped in pain at the cut nonetheless. He spun to see his attacker, Archer, lunge at him again with another slash of the blade. She made contact again, this time slashing his shoulder. She felt the Karambit slice more deeply this time, and she sliced again. He reached his arm up to protect himself from the sudden onslaught of slashes, and the blade sliced into his forearm. He yelped again, slipped on the edge of the sail, and fell into the water.

Archer grabbed the crowbar still under the boat and lodged it at the hinge of the hatch, propping it open. A gunshot rang out from below, and she threw herself into the water but remained next to the sail, watching. *I must delay them as long as possible,* she thought to herself.

A hand reached up to push the crowbar away, and she slashed at it with one hand and steadied the crowbar with the other while still in the water. She heard an angry voice shout from below. She did not need to understand his words to know that he was angry.

Shots rang out again, and Archer ducked along the sail instinctively to avoid being hit. She saw the end of a muzzle reach over the side of the sail and fire into the water in a straight line. They were firing blindly.

She jumped up again and slashed upward, also blindly. But her sudden appearance surprised the man above, leaning through the hatch, and caused him to fall back and fire again in the air. She slashed again on her way down, hit the weapon but otherwise leaving the man unharmed.

He now knew where she was, so she had to move around the sail fast. She went underwater and swam around the back of the sail and then under the bow of the capsized five-meter boat still stuck on top of the sail. She caught her breath under the boat, and then swam underwater to the front of the sail where the hatch was located. She heard a splash on the other side as the crowbar landed in the water. She jumped up to catch the man grabbing the hatch to close it again, and she slashed at him one more time. She made contact with his arm, and he too shouted in pain, but he was able to close the hatch on his way down into the mini-sub. She heard the clang of the hatch and the turn of the lock. They were going to depart regardless of the boat stuck to the submarine, she realized, and she backed away from it as the sub began to descend into the water.

She swam backwards and watched as the sail of the submarine turned toward the open sea. It continued to descend slowly into the water, and the boat, still appearing to be stuck on the periscope, continued to travel in the same direction. The boat too sank steadily back into the water until the waves began to crest over one side. Then it capsized, seemingly breaking free from the submarine below, and it came to a slow halt. It too began to sink into the sea from the multiple punctures.

Archer floated alone in the water, and sensing the obvious, that the mini-sub had gotten away, she slammed her left arm, still holding the Karambit, into the water out of anger and screamed into the darkness in front of her, now unable to prevent the escape of either group. She looked back toward the coast, the few lights barely visible at over a kilometer away. She took a deep breath, placed the Karambit in one of the pockets, and she began to swim.

Within minutes, Trinh Archer felt her muscles ache with exhaustion. The adrenaline she had run on for the past hour had run out. Her right shoulder now seared in pain, both from the open wound and from the saltwater coming into contact with it. She dared not look toward the coast, because each time she did it seemed ever farther from where she swam in the Sea of Japan. Each motion of her arm felt like lifting an iron bar over her head.

Something flashed. At first she did not notice, her mind now as tired and injured as her body. She found a small bit of comfort in the rote motion of her strokes. But the flashing seemed to continue. She looked up at the shore. Those were flashing lights, definitely. Despite the distance, the new sign of life directly ahead gave her encouragement. She swam faster now, with a sense of purpose. She dared not admit to herself that, if she swam too slowly, the ones driving the vehicles with the flashing lights, whoever they were, might leave the location.

She saw a spotlight ahead of her, illuminating first one area of the water, then the other. She swam toward the boat. Then there was another, then a third. The waves around her opened fleeting paths to the boat, then closed them off suddenly.

She stopped in the water. "Hey! Heeeeyyy!" she screamed, flailing her left arm above her head and the waves around her. She tried to remain afloat with her right arm and her legs kicking furiously underneath her to keep her buoyant. They seemed not to hear, and her new shot of adrenaline ebbed quickly. She stopped waving and put her head down to continue her slow swim toward them.

The sound of an engine became audible over the waves around her. And she looked up again. She didn't have the strength to wipe away the mangled hair falling around her face, but she could see through the strands that the spotlight had grown larger, and then disappeared again behind a wave. Another light seemed to illuminate the wave that separated them. She waved again, trying to reach over it and shout. Just as she opened her mouth, the wave of water crested into her face, filling her mouth and lungs with salt water. She tried to kick herself up enough to cough it out, but she could not force her face out of the water in time clear her lungs. She waved her arm above the waterline, but she felt her hand fall into the water, her legs now motionless...

CHAPTER 42 – A NEW MORNING

Archer awoke in a room seemingly filled with white cotton. She felt a warm heaviness holding her down on a soft and solid bed. She tried to lift her arms, but they could move only only a few centimeters. She felt a distant pain in one shoulder, and in her elbow on her other arm. She felt lethargic, groggy...

A voice began to pierce the cottony fog. "Archer? Trinh Archer? Can you hear me...?"

She tried to respond, but she only felt her vocal cords flutter softly as a weak breath emanating from her diaphragm. She moved her lips, but little sound formed.

"What is that, Trinh? What are your trying to say?" she heard a voice utter from the whiteness above her.

"Nnnn...nnnn." She tried to coax some sort of response to the voice near her. She blinked several times to clear the bright and milky fog from her eyes. Figures came into view, with large and thick halos around them.

"Yeeaaa...yeaaah?" she responded.

"Trinh, it is good to see you awake and with us again..."

Archer focused on the woman smiling at her. "Ma...Maddy?" she asked, perplexed at seeing her boss as Archer herself lay on her back under several layers of thick blankets. "Wha...?" she began to ask, looking at the other figures in the room.

"Give yourself time, Trinh. You've been through a lot," Maddy said, placing her hand on Archer's uninjured left shoulder.

Images and sounds of the past days began to flood into consciousness, and she tried to reach for her head with both arms and grimaced at the dull pain. Both arms were constrained, however, by IV lines, a blood oxygen monitor, and a blood pressure cuff. She felt the needle from one of her IV lines dig deeper into her arm as she tried to bend it to get some blood flowing into her arms.

"Take your time, take your time," Tucker said in a comforting tone. A nurse injected an additional fluid into Archer's IV behind her, which eased her into a more restful but awakened state.

"How did I get here? Wait, where am I?" she asked. "The last I remember I was swimming..." her voice trailed off as she tried to recall exactly how she had ended up almost drowning in the dark, cold water.

"We found you at sea, almost half a kilometer from shore," a male voice said. "Luckily the local police had some search crews looking for any additional smugglers, and they came across you just as you were going under. You must've been exhausted swimming that far from shore."

"Nishi-San!" Archer said as she tried to sit up to greet him.

"Easy, easy now," the nurse said from behind her. She eased Archer back into her reclining position on the hospital bed.

While she noticed the pain in her shoulder the most, Archer now felt aches and pains from various blows on her torso, back and shoulders as well. She knew they were dull now only because of the pain medication they must be administering to her.

"You are in Maizuru, at the hospital on base," Nishi said, pointed out the window. Archer saw the Kaga slowly pulling into the port on the clear October afternoon. "It was easiest to medevac you from the scene, to give you medical attention here even as we conduct a more thorough investigation." Nishi then leaned in to whisper to Archer. "With your help, we have collected many 'crimson leaves' over the past days," he said, smiling. "We continue to collect more leaves now, too."

Crimson leaves? Archer wondered. Then she realized what he was referring to, and smiled in return. "I'm glad I could help, but I don't know how...

"Your analysis was right, Trinh," Tucker added. "In addition to a large amount of fentanyl that we recovered in the immediate aftermath of the smuggling operation you uncovered, we were able to take down a nascent network of pharmaceutical front companies based in Japan to send fentanyl to North America. You kept saying distribution would transition to Japan and other neighboring countries once networks from China were cut off, and you were right. North Korea began to ship significant amounts to Japan, to skirt the newly regulated trade. Companies in Japan seemed more legitimate to U.S. authorities than those in China, but now we have better information to separate the front companies from the legitimate ones."

"But, didn't the bad guys escape? Can't they just set up new operations?"

"We made a number of arrests over the last 24 hours," Nishi explained. "We were able to trace your call to within a few kilometers of your location. But in addition, we were following a number of suspicious cell phones throughout the region. We weren't able to identify the cell phones or the users, nor were we able to decrypt the suspicious calls themselves. I had just reviewed the latest information on the whereabouts of those cell phones when you called, and once we had geo-coorded your location, I cross-checked it with the information on suspect cell phone activity and found one in the exact same location."

"Kano?"

"That's right, or at least one of his henchmen. Kano didn't have the phone with him when we apprehended him. But based on your collocation with one of the suspect phones, I was able to mobilize an NPA quick-response team in addition to informing local police. Which was fortunate, since there was a major firefight that ensued."

"But how did you get there so fast? They were on their way back when I chased them out to sea..." Archer asked.

"Which was a very foolish thing for you to have done, Trinh!" Maddy said as she smiled at Archer, clearly happy with the end results despite the danger.

"From what we could surmise when we finally arrived, you had ended up in an old fish processing facility, near a dilapidated and small port facility that hadn't been used in years. At least not for fishing. That's probably where you called me from, right?"

Archer tried to think to that moment. It was hazy. "Yeah...I believe so..." she said more as a question then as an answer. "It was dark."

"You pulled a fire alarm there, which caused the local fire department to respond first, not knowing what was going on. In fact, most locals had pretty much forgotten the processing facility was there," Nishi explained.

"But when I pulled the alarm nothing happened," Archer explained, remembering the incident through a fog. "How..."

"The alarm itself was an old manual bell that had rusted in place due to the salty conditions so close to the sea. Physically, it could not ring. But the signal to the firehouse was still operational, so the firefighters were dispatched to your location. It took them some time to get there, it was in a rural area and much of the road was overgrown with weeds, but when they did they found Kano's gang loading their final cargo," Nishi explained. "And I had called the local office of the NPA as I departed for your location, so the police were not far behind. Which was good, because Kano and his men started shooting at the firefighters when they arrived to try to get away."

"It was because of you that Nishi's local NPA office and the police were ultimately able to apprehend Kano and his men, and shut down their operation," Tucker added. "You were in quite a state when the police pulled you from the water," Tucker continued. "We'll get a fuller debrief of you later, but you must've been in quite a fight since Kano's men kidnapped you..." Tucker's pride shone in her eyes as she spoke to Archer.

"I tried to get away when I could, like we're trained..." was all Archer could muster in response to Tucker. "But what about the mini-sub?"

"Ah yes, the mini-sub. We were able to extract enough information from one of Kano's low-level men that there was indeed a sub involved in the transfer, but we couldn't start tracking it immediately. We deployed counter-submarine units from the returning 3rd Escort Flotilla and from Maizuru. The ones that could deploy at least, to the area. And the Kaga was deploying urgently to Maizuru because of the attack, so several of her escort vessels joined in the search. Ultimately we located the mini-sub just outside Japanese territorial waters, lying on the bottom of the sea. We've conducted some preliminary searches, but have found no bodies or cargo."

"No bodies? What about the crew? What about the crewman who fell overboard?"

"Crewman who fell overboard?" Nishi looked quizzically at Tucker, and then back at Archer.

"I cut him up pretty bad while he was trying to get the boat I rammed the sub with off of the periscope and sail. He fell into the sea, but I'm positive he was still alive."

Nishi squinted, retrieved a small notepad, and wrote a note to himself.

"You don't know where he is, do you," Archer asserted rather than asked.

"All we know for now is that the crew of the sub must've escaped, somehow. With their cargo, whatever it was. We have not found any bodies, or any suspicious persons, either on the sub itself or in the area."

"And the men who chased me into the warehouse?"

"The men?" Nishi asked. "The one we found at the warehouse will be without a kidney and probably some other organs, but he's lucky to have his spinal cord intact…" Nishi said with a glimmer in his eyes.

"What about the other one? There were two there. One named 'Kensuke,' and I didn't recognize the other."

"Kensuke? Hmmm," Nishi groaned again. He flipped through several pages in his notepad. "The one we discovered there said his name is Yoshioka, Hideo Yoshioka. We believe he is a member of a motorcycle gang." Nishi flipped the pages to a fresh one. "Kensuke, you said?"

Archer nodded once. "That's right. And you better find him before I do," Archer added.

Nishi jotted down his name and then looked up from his notepad, his nubbly pencil at the ready. "We'll need to get a full debriefing from you in the coming days, there are many loose ends, it seems." He was eager to learn more from Archer, but he could see from Tucker's glare at him from across the bed that he should wait to ask any more questions.

Archer thought back to the crates. "Were there any crates in the sunken sub, like the one I was kept in?"

"Crates? No, nothing. No cargo at all. The mini-sub was entirely empty," Nishi replied.

Beep…beep…beep. beep. beepbeepbeep… Archer's heart monitor started to speed up as she clenched her teeth and tightened her fists.

"Calm down, calm down," the nurse ordered, placing her hand again on Archer's shoulder. Another nurse injected a drug into Archer's IV behind her. The heart monitor gradually returned to normal, and Archer's body started to go limp again.

"There were other crates on the truck at the dock, others like to the one I was kept in," she said in a slow and methodical tone. "They had drugged me and were going to send me along with the shipment. There might have been other women in those other crates like me, or children even..."

"We'll look closely for them, Trinh," Tucker interjected. "But there were no indications of any crates, or women or children, on the sunken submarine. So you do not have to worry about that right now. Concentrate on getting better," Tucker ordered gently. "We need you back at work. There's a lot we have yet to do."

"How did it sink?" Archer asked, unsure whether to be relieved or upset that they did not discover anything, or any bodies, in the sunken submarine.

"We'll do a more thorough examination once we raise it, but several of the masts in the sail were damaged, bent," Nishi explained. "Now that we know you're the one who intentionally rammed it, we have a plausible reason why it sank so close to Japan. We found the damaged five-meter speedboat in the bay, but we could only guess then that it was involved. You must have caused leaks in the sail, probably slow enough that they could continue submerged for a while, perhaps wait for another submarine to rescue them..." Nishi explained.

"At any rate, the media does not know about the mini-sub yet, just the capture of the Japanese smugglers themselves. They're busy reporting on the chemical weapons attack here at Maizuru base..."

"I'm sorry, what did you say?" Archer interrupted, astonished at the news. "Someone attacked the base with chemical weapons?"

"That's right, you of course wouldn't have heard," Nishi began to explain. "One morning a few days ago, an individual flew a helicopter over a training field at Maizuru base, spraying mustard gas from nozzles. He caused several deaths, injured many, but he ended up crashing into the Echigo..."

"Wow," Archer whispered, remembering the Echigo from the original counter-drug smuggling operation almost two weeks prior.

"Given the location of the base so close to the site of the smuggling operation, and some leads we're following now after the initial arrests, we believe Kano's group sponsored the attack to delay any response from the Japan maritime units and the Coast Guard during their smuggling operation later that evening."

"And the mission, Bennett and Colonel Bradley and his men?"

Tucker looked at Nishi and the nurse, and then back at Archer. "We'll just say it was an initial success, but we have much more work to do..."

Archer nodded. She saw from the twinkle in Tucker's eye that the mission must've been quite successful indeed.

As if on cue, several men walked into the hospital room.

"There she is, the hero of the day," a tired-looking Colonel Bradley said as he entered the hospital room. Sergeants Solberg and McCarty followed closely behind, and Chief Warrant Officer Isamu Sato rounded up the group.

"Where did you all come from?" Archer said, surprised by the added visitors.

"We were just in the neighborhood, thought we would take in the sights," McCarty quipped. He turned to Archer in the bed. "I haven't met you yet, but I've already heard a lot about you. McCarty's the name," he said in greeting Archer.

"I'd shake your hand, but I'm a bit immobilized now," Archer replied, holding up her arms slightly above the bed to show him the multiple IVs and monitors attached to them. She looked at Colonel Bradley. "I hope to hear more about your op as well. From what little I've heard so far, it must've been one for the books..."

"In time, in good time," Tucker said, reminding her and everyone present that they could only talk about so much in this environment.

"I'm just stopping by to say my *sayonaras* to everyone, and to thank you for the hospitality," Bradley said. He turned to Tucker. "We just moved Lieutenant Newland to the transport back to the states, he'll need to have another surgery but he should be back to duty after a couple months of recuperation and physical therapy," he reported.

"Thank goodness for that," Tucker responded. "It's good he's out of intensive care now."

"Now that the last of our injured soldiers have been transported back stateside, I'm wheels-up in two hours," he added with a tired smile.

"I'm probably on the same flight, back to Tokyo at least," Tucker said.

"Back to Hawaii for some R&R?" Archer asked Bradley.

"Nope, direct flight to D.C. from Tokyo. Mr. Bennett already returned with the family and we have to brief on the..." Bradley then caught himself, looking at the two nurses in the room and the doctor passing in the hallway. "That is, I have some meetings to go to, then it's back to Hawaii."

"Ah, gotcha," Archer said knowingly.

"At any rate, I'm off now, I'm sure we'll catch up in the coming weeks. We'll trade stories on Tandberg, how about that?"

Archer chuckled. "You got it."

Maddy Tucker turned to Chief Sato Before she joined Bradley. "And thank you again for all that you did on this mission," she said, shaking his hand. "The ambassador has already talked to Defense HQ, he would like to present to you and your team with special recognition for your critical services on this mission. Without you, this would have turned out differently. You are a real credit to Japan!" She continued to shake his hand as she smiled.

"Thank you, ma'am!" Sato replied, letting go of her grip and bowing.

"I should get my things and head to the flight too," Tucker announced to the group. "Colonel Bradley, mind if I tag along?"

"I'd like nothing better!" he said, more energetically now. He held up his elbow as a chivalrous gesture. "Ma'am?"

"Why thank you, sir. And who said chivalry is dead?" Tucker placed her arm into his. "See you in a few days, Trinh," she said as they exited the room, "and get some rest!"

"Yes, and for my part, it was a pleasure to meet you too," Chief Sato said to Archer. "When you are better, perhaps we can see some sights sometime when we are both in Tokyo, hm?" Sato declared rather than asked Archer. "*Sore dewa, o-daiji ni,*" he said, before she could respond. He bowed and exited the room.

One of Archer's three doctors entered the room. "It's time for the patient to get some rest now," he ordered to the remaining occupants of the room.

"Very well then, I too shall leave. I have much paperwork to attend to!" Nishi nodded to Archer with a smile, and headed out.

"And we have some R&R to catch up on!" McCarty said. "Look forward to trading stories too, if you ever get out to Washington state...!"

"And seriously, let's work out sometime," Solberg added. "Maybe we could recruit you to our team! The country could really use your services in the field, rather than sitting at a desk all day long..."

Still not so bright, she thought to herself. "Certainly, I'll look you up..." He followed McCarty, and Archer turned to look out the window as the doctors entered to begin their next, thorough check-up of their American patient.

CHAPTER 43 – THE LADY AND THE LORD

Trinh Archer raised the head of her hospital bed and grabbed the remote control to the television. She switched it to the news channel, which carried the opening of the National Diet. Ayumi Seitoh, the first woman elected as Prime Minister of Japan, stepped to the podium to address her colleagues. After the opening pleasantries she humbly accepted the responsibilities of her new role. Then she reached what Archer knew would be a significant statement for a Japanese leader.

"The time for protests is past. The time for active defensive measures is upon us. It is the policy of the Government of Japan that we will be oriented by an 'offensive defense' strategy. We will actively defend Japan's territorial and national security on our land, in our seas, and in the air. We will actively defend ourselves from missile threats with an expanded missile defense capability that can defend against multiple points of the launch cycle, from pre-launch to re-entry. We will actively deny any maritime units from encroaching on our waters. And we reserve the right to take pre-emotive action against aggressors who demonstrate an immediate threat to our homeland. We will work closely in concert with our allies, but we will maintain the capability and determination to act independently if necessary."

She scanned crowd of her fellow parliamentarians and assembled journalists for effect, and then added: "And in this way, the family of Ayako and Michiharu Toda, and all Japanese families like them, will sleep more soundly at night knowing that we are doing our utmost to protect the citizens of Japan." The prime minister then stepped back from the podium, said "thank you," and bowed to the crowd.

The parliamentarians erupted into a cacophony of shouts and elevated voices, many in support, some in opposition…

I need to get back to Tokyo, Archer thought to herself. She stood in front of the window and began to stretch, as she saw provisions being loaded onto the Kaga for another patrol in the Sea of Japan.

•   •   •

"Representative Seikichi Tadaishi. I am NPA Senior Inspector Ryutaro Nishi. I am here to inform you that you are under arrest, for your connection to the illegal, criminal activities conducted by Mr. Takada Kano."

Nishi cuffed Tadaishi, and together with a uniformed officer, led him to a police van for the ride to be processed at the Tokyo Detention Facility.

From one of the many large kitchens in the TDC, the grandmotherly Michiko Fukuno silently watched the arrest unfold on the television on the far wall, and waited.

•   •   •

Tucker turned to the monitor-sized screen on her desk, and after punching a few numbers into the keypad, Bennett appeared. The words "TS-secured video conference call" appeared at the bottom of the Tandberg. "Congratulations, Mr. Bennett. I've heard that the preliminary debriefings have shown that our list of workers weren't janitors after all, but additional scientists and engineers associated with Pyongyang's nuclear and missile development."

"That wasn't supposed to get out yet, Maddy! You do have your sources, don't you? But yes, the information windfall has continued to amaze, to be sure."

"Remember, Wilson, I'm due to brief the Japanese on this 'windfall,' so don't leave me hanging. I gave my word..."

"Certainly, Maddy. It's a promise!"

"And the whole QZSS thing?"

"We dodged a bullet on that, Maddy. Not only do we have preliminary information on how Han planned to incorporate signals from Japan's quasi-zenith satellite system for ultra-precise targeting across the western Pacific, but also additional information on what Pyongyang intended. The danger to U.S. aircraft carriers in the western Pacific was incalculable..."

"Not to mention, the danger to Japanese in Japan itself," Tucker reminded him.

"Yes, certainly, and to our forces stationed there. But now that we know he inserted the wrong calculations into the algorithm..." Bennett stopped himself. "Wait, you got me talking again, Maddy!"

"I have your promise, right?" Tucker repeated Bennett's words.

"Certainly..." Bennett said again, but with less conviction this time.

Tucker didn't know if she could trust Wilson's promises. He had already shown himself to be a very forward-leaning, entrepreneurial NSC senior, and Maddy could not see that streak changing any time soon. "Let's make an agreement, Wilson," Tucker said. "Let's agree to work together on cases like these, hm? We can do so much better when we don't fight each other and concentrate on the real enemy."

"I like that proposal, Maddy," Bennett replied. "I need good allies like you, capable ones, who are able to cut through the bullshit in this town..."

"Well I'm not back in D.C. yet, but we have processes in place precisely because we fucked up in the past, either individually or as an organization. I know time was of the essence for this operation, and I really think this could've worked out had you...had we pushed this through the right channels and given just a little more time for the system to come to the right conclusion. The end result would've been smoother, I think."

"We got the Japanese to take historic action in direct support of what became a kinetic operation..."

"That caused some not-insignificant casualties among the service members involved in the operation from both countries. Three are still in the hospital, including a Japanese soldier still in intensive care. Let's not forget the costs here, Bennett."

"Well, Maddy, I hope for all of our sakes that your faith in the system in well-placed."

"It is, in the end. We're all here to fight the good fight. We just need to make sure we don't make the same mistakes we have made in the past."

"Mistakes cut both ways, Maddy. Sometimes we've been too aggressive, and other times not aggressive enough, or early enough," Bennett replied. "But in the end, I think together we can fight a very good fight, if we are allies."

"Thank you, Wilson. And I *am* your ally, whether it is here in the field or in D.C., so long as we play by the rules."

"The threat continues, Maddy, in many other places as well."

Tucker stiffened at the implication behind Bennett's comment, but she would not press her point further. *We'll have to watch this one closely*, Tucker thought to herself. *He's overconfident.*

"At least we know their exact capabilities on this, where they're at now, and can plan accordingly," Bennett continued. "We can also calibrate our and our allies' missile defenses to respond to their capabilities as they stand now...we have more clarity on where the Japanese are at in that realm too..." Bennett then leaned into the monitor, as if to whisper despite the secured nature of the VTC. "And as you caught me saying just now, he has indicated that he has left a significant Trojan horse in the main systems program just before he departed. Missiles may launch, but the warheads won't reach their destination. We got 'em, Maddy!" Bennett sat back in his high-backed, black leather seat and smiled.

"For now, perhaps," Tucker added. *How will they adapt?* Tucker wondered. *Their abilities may have been impacted for now, but the intent remains.* But Bennett appeared not to hear her, and he was already on to his next point.

"Han's son is receiving the treatment he needs," Bennett continued. "Indications are that he has the milder Becker MD, but more tests need to be run. And I'm going to put in for a medal for Han, and I want to put in for Archer too. Without her, we wouldn't have shut down the smuggling operation that funded and supplied Pyongyang's missile operations."

"Shut *this one* down, yes, but there are others," Tucker added. "Yes, we have found additional vulnerabilities that we'll be able to exploit, but what else will they pursue…" Tucker said, her voice trailing off. "But I'll hand it to you, Wilson, you pushed your position even when some of us, many of us, were skeptical. That takes courage in this business." The operational side of her was indeed impressed.

"We make a good team, Maddy, I look forward to working with you in the future."

"And I with you, Wilson." Madeleine Tucker ended the secure call, turned to her computer terminal, and began to type what would be her first of many official memos to her colleagues in the Cabinet Intelligence Office and at Defense Intelligence HQ outlining the newly obtained intelligence.

Made in the USA
Middletown, DE
27 February 2018